LOGAN'S ACADIAN WOLVES

Immortals of New Orleans, Book 4

Kym Grosso

MT Carvin Publishing
West Chester, Pennsylvania

Editing: Julie Roberts
Formatting: Polgarus Studio
Cover Design: Alivia Anders / White Rabbit Book Design
Photographer: Golden Czermak / FuriousFotog
Cover Model: Caylan Hughes

NOTICE
This is an adult erotic paranormal romance book with love scenes and mature situations. It is only intended for adult readers over the age of 18.

ACKNOWLEDGMENTS

I am very thankful to everyone who helped me create this book:

~My husband, for being my biggest supporter. I love talking with you about the hot love scenes I write. You give me great feedback and ideas. You are my inspiration.

~My children, for being so patient with me, while I spend time working on the book. You are the best kids ever!

~Julie Roberts, editor, who spent hours reading, editing and proofreading Logan's Acadian Wolves. I really could not have done this without you!

~My beta readers, Cat, Denise, Elizabeth, Gayle, Julia, Julie, Leah, Liz, Nadine, Sharon, Stephanie, Sunny, for volunteering to beta read the novel and provide me with valuable feedback. You are incredible!

~My street team, for all your kind words and for helping spread the word about the Immortals of New Orleans series.

Chapter One

Logan clamped his canines deep into the gritty fur until his opponent whimpered in defeat. The iron-tinged blood only served to further spur his anger. For months, he'd fought challenges to his claim as Alpha. Like the increasing winds of a hurricane, his power grew with every battle. Yet he'd been merciful, never killing another wolf. But tonight, he'd had enough. It was time to put an end to the challenges and force acceptance. As the sanguine droplets coated his tongue, Logan growled. The cowering brown wolf held still, cognizant that a struggle would surely bring his demise.

Sufficiently satisfied with the submission, the Alpha seamlessly transformed. His naked muscular body stood statuesque, rippled in unadulterated strength. Dripping in sweat and blood, Logan's dark eyes narrowed on the shaking form at his feet then rose to scan the sea of eyes watching him, waiting for his next word.

"This ends tonight," he growled, addressing the pack. "The next challenge set forth to me will end in death. There'll be no mercy. I am Alpha. Who here challenges me next?"

Power surged through his veins. Logan sent a small threatening tendril toward his wolves, both a warning and an ultimatum. A faint murmur from the crowd ended as quickly as it started. The tension was palpable, yet the hum of acquiescence danced in the silence of the night. A binding calm blanketed the pack as one by one each wolf crouched down in submission, tails wagging, acknowledging their new leader.

Logan felt it as sure as he knew he was wolf; *he was Alpha*. He closed his eyes, allowing the energy to flow through him, amplifying throughout every molecule in his body. Every wolf accepting, loving, giving all of themselves over to his reign. The seed of dominance had finally germinated into a fully grown tree of command, providing the protection and guidance the pack needed for survival. Thrumming in control, Logan's muscles tensed as he threw back his head, sucking in the chilled evening breeze. A victorious howl emanated from deep within his chest as he claimed his pack, his rule, his dominion. Rising to the call of their Alpha, the wolves joined in his song, celebrating their leader.

Logan stopped his call for only a second to nod in affirmation at his chosen beta, Dimitri. The confident but subservient brown wolf padded toward Logan, eyes darting to his pack mates in recognition of his status.

"Tonight, we celebrate," Logan ordered, shifting back into his large silky gray wolf. He gazed upon his wolves, raising his snout in a cool display of affection.

As they ran through the night, Logan contemplated how he'd gotten to this point. Long ago, he'd been born a pup in the Acadian wolf pack, chasing to keep up with Marcel and his friend, Tristan. It had been mere months since he'd helped Tristan save his mate, taking out the destructive Wallace pack in South Carolina. Then, he'd come to New Orleans to help relocate the abused women and pups they'd found. That fateful night when he'd gone to Marcel, he'd found him shot and dying. Given no choice, Logan had killed the perpetrator, who'd been Marcel's beta. Crying out into the darkness was of no use to stop the inevitable. As Marcel lay dying in his arms, bleeding out onto the floor, Logan had agreed to become Alpha of Acadian Wolves. Marcel was like a brother; he'd do whatever he asked. And Tristan, Marcel's true brother, was Logan's Alpha and best friend in Pennsylvania. But no more. He'd wanted to deny Marcel his dying wish. At first, he'd refused to say it. But as the life faded from Marcel's eyes, Logan accepted his fate, speaking the words that would forever change his life; "I am Alpha".

If it was only that easy. After one hundred and forty-two years of being wolf, he knew full well that his pack wouldn't simply accept the situation, relinquishing the role of Alpha to him, especially since he hadn't been home for so long. Rather than reneging on his promise, he'd fought week after week, sealing his commitment to Marcel. And tonight, threatening death to all who opposed him had been the final chapter in his ascension.

Logan had not truly believed he was Alpha until tonight. He'd been a second away from killing the wolf beneath him. Feral. Savage. Unyielding. This was who he was, who he was meant to be. He ran hard through the bayou refuge, leading the others. Acadian Wolves, his new pack, was his to rule.

As the hot spray sluiced over Logan's tanned corded muscles, a million thoughts raced through his mind. Jacked up from the fight and final acceptance from his pack, he willed the adrenaline rush to subside. But even the high of the night hadn't diminished the pain of losing Marcel. Nor did it ease the sense of loss that remained over being separated from Tristan. When Logan had agreed to take over Acadian Wolves, Tristan had encouraged him to take his rightful place, unwilling to hear any arguments to the contrary. At first, he felt betrayed that his friend would so easily capitulate to losing his beta. But as he'd heard Tristan say many a time, Alphas needed to make difficult decisions, put their own feelings aside for the greater good of the pack.

So in this vein, he'd made a conscious decision to do the same. Regardless of how he felt, his position and responsibility for each and every wolf superseded his own needs. He silently conceded that perhaps he hadn't fully understood what that meant until tonight. Bloodied and bruised, he stood firm, claiming his earned position.

Logan reflected on his former life as Tristan's beta. Nearly a half century ago, he'd followed him to Philadelphia. As the years passed, he remained close to Marcel and their sister, Katrina, who also relocated. His years with Tristan had been prosperous and for the most part, peaceful. He'd been happy. Content. Life was good. No, life was great. Then a single bullet had turned his entire world upside down.

As Logan floated into a quiet contemplation, the blinding, recurring vision launched uncontrollably into his thoughts. Instead of fighting the inevitable, he allowed the colors and movement to appear clearly, hoping he'd see her again. He'd been dreaming of her for weeks, yet with every vision, all he could see was her face. Angelic, sad hazel eyes begged him to help. Paralyzed, he could only watch her, wondering who she was and why she was in danger. Her full, pink lips called into the night, but he couldn't hear her plea.

The panoramic scene continued to materialize before him, but he was unable to direct the movie. The loss of control didn't deter him from watching, however. Goddess, she was beautiful. Her long curly blonde hair whipped across her heart-shaped face. Shaking the locks aside, she screamed uncontrollably until her words turned into rolling sobs. Immobilized, he watched as the monster's clawed hand reached around her neck.

In an instant, the jagged talon transformed her cries into soft gurgling. A bubbling line of blood spewed from her pink skin as he sliced open her throat. Logan's heart pounded against his chest; he thrashed against invisible bindings. A mixture of shock and acceptance flashed across her eyes right before she sagged to the ground. Gasping, Logan struggled, trying to reach her. But nothing came. No movement. No sound. The familiar black tunnel closed inward, ending the terrifying nightmare.

Logan's eyes flew open, and he realized he was still in the shower. He shuddered, wondering when the scene would play out in reality. The visions had plagued him his entire life, but he'd normally taken them in stride, knowing they didn't personally affect his own future. Even though he couldn't identify the alluring woman, he couldn't shake the feeling that her life intertwined with his. Was she a wolf who'd join his pack? An enemy? The emotion that had been deeply woven into the vision told him that he knew her. He cared for her. She was dying and he'd been restrained, unable to save her life.

Logan sighed in disgust. Dismissing the ominous premonition didn't seem feasible. The lingering apprehension wrapped around him like a lead vest. Goddammit. Who was she? And why the hell couldn't he save her? He didn't need this shit right now. No, it wasn't exactly the optimal time in his life to solve a disturbing, enigmatic vision. But like every other damning event that had slapped him lately, he'd compartmentalize the issue and deal with it.

The jarring of the door handle and a rush of cool air cued him to the fact that he was no longer alone. *Fuck, he hated this house.* Even though he'd moved into Marcel's country home out of necessity, it still felt uncomfortable. To his dismay, too many people lived with him. Granted, he'd brought it on himself by inviting them. Dimitri, his beta and longtime friend, had moved in at his request. And then there was Luci, Marcel's girlfriend, who also shared their home. Both Logan and Luci had witnessed Marcel's last dying breath. She'd collapsed into his arms immediately afterward, and since that moment in time, he'd felt responsible for her. So when he moved into Marcel's bayou mansion, he'd allowed her to stay.

But it was Katrina who shared his bed. She wasn't his mate but he'd felt oddly comforted by her warm body on cool winter nights. Out of grief, they'd clung to each other like a life raft in a storm. As if a kindred spirit, she'd been both sexually adventurous and giving, sharing herself with both Dimitri and him. He'd always been abundantly clear, however, that they couldn't continue on forever. Even if it had felt right at the time, she wasn't his mate. And it no longer was comfortable.

"Logan," Katrina called into the shower.

"In here," Logan responded.

He'd have to tell her tonight that it was over. It wouldn't be easy, but she needed to go back to her life in Philadelphia, and he needed to pay attention to business. It was time to go back to the city.

As warm silky skin slid against his own wetness, he fought the arousal that loomed to distract him from his task. Allowing her to wrap her body around his, he kissed her damp hair.

"Hey, Kat. We need to talk."

"Hmm...talk, huh?" She reached around to caress his ass with both hands, slithering against his semi-erect cock.

Logan pulled away slightly, not disconnecting his touch but enough to cup her face. Taking a deep breath, he narrowed his eyes on hers.

"You know I love you. But it's time for you to go home. We can't keep doing this."

"Doing what? This?" She smiled, reaching down between his legs to wrap her fingers around his shaft.

In a flash, he grabbed her wrists, bringing them against his chest.

"Yeah, that. Seriously, it's time. Now that I've established dominance, it's time for me to go into the city. I've got work to do. And you, my lovely vixen, have a business to run."

She sighed, leaning her forehead against him. It wasn't as if she didn't know what he was saying to be true. Reality was a bitch. A hard sigh escaped her lips at the realization that he was sending her home.

"Kat, we both miss Marcel. It's been hard on both of us. But you've got to go spend time with Tristan. Tend to your shop. And when things settle down, if you still want to come back here, you know you're always welcome. But for now, we're just using each other. It's not healthy…for either of us."

She shook her head in denial. "It's not like I don't know you're right. It's just…I miss him so damn much."

"I do too, baby, but this isn't the answer." Logan pressed his lips to her wet cheek. "It'll be okay. Go home. Comfort Tris. He needs you as much as you need him."

"When are you leaving for the city?" She lifted her head as he gently released her arms.

"Tonight. Dimitri and I are leaving in a few hours," he

told her with a small smile.

"I'll miss you. And Dimitri," she contemplated, accepting that her time in New Orleans was coming to an end.

The past months since her brother's death had been awful. The only thing that had made anything slightly tolerable was the hot nights she'd spent with Logan and his beta. Instead of openly grieving, she'd buried her feelings deeply. As sister to the slain Alpha, she chose to be strong for the pack, for Logan.

"I'll miss you too, but it's time. I didn't choose this, but it's my path. I've got to move on for the sake of my wolves," he explained. "And you need to let go of him. Marcel's gone. You need to be able to grieve. As long as you are here, you'll never move on."

The steel band that wrapped her heart in grief tightened. Wolves didn't die, especially not her strong Alpha brother. It was as if Logan's words made it real. She knew he was dead, saw them lower his body into the grave, smelled his scent in the earth every time she went for a run. He was truly gone.

Sensing her retreat within her own mind, Logan pulled her into his arms, cradling her head to his breast. "It's okay to let go," he whispered.

A gasp of devastation gushed from her chest before she had a chance to swallow it. The wave of depression washed over the walls of sanity she'd tried so hard to build. Digging her fingers into his shoulders, she sobbed, the anguish of losing her sibling no longer held at bay. Goddess, she missed her big brother. She knew in that moment that as much as she loved Logan, it was Tristan she needed. He was the only one who'd comprehend the heartache that tore her apart.

Logan held tight to his longtime friend, comforting her as best he could. He'd call Tristan tonight and have her home by morning. They both needed closure, and getting her to face her loss was the only way to commence healing.

"That's it, Kat. It's all right. Let it out."

Realizing how she'd lost it, she tried to pull away from him, but he held her tighter still. "Don't hide."

"But I can't…" she cried, desperately wanting to curl into a ball.

"You don't need to be the strong Alpha's sister. It's just me. And I'm the Alpha who comforts you now. Tomorrow, you'll be with Tris, and it'll all be okay. I promise." Purposefully, he let his power flow; calming waves emanated from his body to hers, wrapping her in a loving cocoon of peace. Refusing to let her retreat, he embraced her until she finally quieted. As her last tears fell, she looked up at him with awe, with the understanding that her friend was no longer her brother's beta. No, he was their equal.

Logan wore the veil of responsibility as if he'd led the pack his entire life. He'd fought over a dozen wolves to earn the title, and it had been respectfully earned. A double-edged sword, loving or lethal, depending on the situation, there was no doubt about the male who held her in his arms. Capable of ameliorating pain or inciting it, he'd provide guidance and discipline to the wolves. As if she'd woken from a long sleep, Katrina looked into Logan's deep blue eyes, shivering with the realization that he'd changed. Altogether deliberate and dominant, a new wolf had been born. He was Alpha.

Chapter Two

Logan sat on the cracked leather barstool watching his wolves celebrate. As he drank his beer, he smiled to himself, amused at the curveball life had thrown him. He felt exhilarated to be back in the French Quarter. After Marcel had died, he'd sold the Alpha's Garden District pack house, per Tristan's request. He was thrilled to be rid of the monstrosity, considering the death he'd caused and witnessed that disastrous night. There was no way he'd step one foot back into that house, let alone hold any pack activities there.

In contrast, his new home soothed his soul, reminding him of his Creole roots. Newly reconditioned, it mirrored his life. Long before Marcel's demise, he'd started restoring the early nineteenth century three-story corner mansion. But his newfound position had accelerated the renovations, so he'd be able to live in the city. As much as he loved running wolf, the urbane food and culture were every bit a part of who he was. He'd made sure that his wolves were close by in adjoining townhouses on his street.

The only wolf he allowed to live with him was Dimitri. The quaint guest cottage on the property gave them both the closeness and privacy they needed. While he'd grown up with Dimitri, the connection between him and his beta had grown stronger over the past month. Their relationship had deepened in both respect and trust. And while Logan had initially felt awkward about his need for a beta, he soon embraced the bond. They'd shared more than a house. Pack challenges. Business. Women. Their intimacy had grown exponentially each day, but Logan no longer questioned why. Instinctively, he knew it was as natural as the sun rising.

After returning to the city and pulling into the carport, Logan insisted that he and Dimitri go to Courettes for drinks and celebration. He felt the wave of contentment that had washed through the pack. They had needed a leader, one determined to withstand multiple challenges, and he'd shown he was worthy. And in return, he needed to be with them and around them.

Courettes was an open-air, casual French Quarter establishment. What made the bar unique was that, thanks to a witch's spell, only paranormals could see into the bar or enter. To humans, it simply looked like a quiet home with closed wooden shutters. Because tonight was an Acadian wolf celebration, few vampires and witches attended. As the zydeco band played, wolves danced sensually to the indigenous beats.

Sitting at the bar, Dimitri shot Logan a questioning look, realizing his mind was far from the party that was going on around him.

"Alpha, what's up?"

"Nothin'. Just feels good to be back home in the city. Life is good," Logan responded, gazing intently at the many she-wolves who'd begun to peel off some of their clothing as the atmosphere became more heated.

"You were amazing tonight." Dimitri clapped his hand on Logan's shoulder. "The pack, they're calm. It's finally over."

"Yeah. And I meant it too. I'm done. Next challenge ends in death," he stated coldly. Logan was so finished with this shit. Acadian Wolves were his and the next wolf who started a fight was as good as dead.

"Oh, I know. You made that perfectly clear. It was awesome, though, bro," Dimitri laughed. "When's Kat leaving?"

"Tomorrow." Logan pinched the bridge of his nose and plowed his hand through his hair. "She's still broken up about Marcel. Then again, it's not every day you lose your brother. Tristan is the only one who can really help her heal. It's not easy letting her go, but it's time for us all to move on. And today, my friend, is that day." He took a swig of his beer.

"Speaking of moving on…" Dimitri nodded nonchalantly over to a gorgeous redhead whose eyes flirtatiously flashed over to his and then back to the band. Her fiery curly hair fell to the middle of her back, accentuating her slim waist and full hips.

"Ah, yes, Fiona. She's been after me for the past two months," Logan confessed.

"No surprise there, I guess." The women had been circling around his new Alpha ever since the first challenge. But after tonight's edict, Dimitri expected them to become more aggressive, actively vying for Logan's attention. "Honestly, between Luci and Kat, you've had your hands full. I cannot begin to tell you how happy I am that we moved back here and out of that mansion."

"Yeah well, soon that mansion is going to be a clubhouse. It's Marcel's, not mine. And since he's not here, it belongs to the pack. Thank Goddess we're back in the city, though, 'cause I need my space. No offense, man." Logan laughed.

"None taken," Dimitri concurred and held up his glass. "I'll be good to go in the cottage house. Close enough but not on top of you."

Logan turned to him, smiling and nodding. They clinked glasses in cheers and drank.

"Alpha." Logan turned his attention toward the submissive voice that sang his name.

"Fiona, how are you? You look beautiful tonight." Logan acknowledged as he and Dimitri stood to greet the alluring wolf.

"Thank you, sir. Hello, Dimitri." She smiled and nodded at him.

"I must agree with our Alpha, cher. You look lovely."

She blushed in response, but didn't move away. "It's because of the challenge. Everyone can feel it. It's been so long since we've felt any peace...with Marcel gone and all."

"How about a dance to celebrate?" Dimitri suggested, glancing over to Logan.

"With you both?" She questioned seductively, batting her eyelashes.

Logan smiled in response, quickly weighing his answer. He supposed one dance with the attractive little she-wolf couldn't hurt. Gently taking her hand in his, he led her out to the dance floor, Dimitri following.

Fiona laughed quietly as Logan swept her into his arms. The music slowed, and Dimitri came up behind her, wrapping his arms around her waist. The threesome began to move as one on the dance floor and a palpable sexual energy snapped in the air. Sandwiched between the tall, sexy men, Fiona rejoiced at her successful seduction. She had wanted these men for such a long time, yet it had been the first time she'd touched them intimately. She immediately bared her throat, offering both the Alpha and his beta everything she was.

Logan, surprised by Fiona's gesture, tried to ignore her invitation. But as she rubbed her pelvis against his, it became difficult not to respond. He wasn't interested in bringing her home with him, but neither did he want to insult her. His beta, on the other hand, clearly felt differently. Logan watched as Dimitri bent his knees, brushing his hard arousal against her bottom.

"Hmm," she cooed, simply swaying back and forth, letting the men dictate the pace and direction of their hot encounter.

"Fi, look what you are doing to my beta," Logan whispered in her ear.

"Alpha," she moaned, digging her nails into his shoulders.

"I do think she's enjoying our dance," Dimitri commented, sliding his hands up her waist, his fingertips nearly touching the swell of her breasts. "Perhaps we could take this somewhere more private?"

"Yes," she gasped.

Logan's eyes met Dimitri's in an effort to silently communicate that he was about to bow out, when he realized something was happening outside the bar. He wasn't sure if it was the smell of her blood or the flash of her long blonde hair that first caught his attention. A bloodied woman tore down the street, vampires following her in pursuit. The woman from his vision. *What the fuck?*

"What is it?" Dimitri tensed, snapping his head around to the street.

"Sorry, Fi. Gonna have to do this another time." Logan kissed her forehead and took off toward the exit. "D. Outside. Now. Something's going down."

Wynter's lungs burned. She bent over trying to catch her breath as she hid behind the rotted wooden door. Her heart beat like a hummingbird as she considered her next move. It had been exactly two months and thirteen days, since she'd been taken hostage. Escaping had been no small feat. With nothing but time, she'd planned for days and had finally done it. Wearing only a dirty white lab coat over her bra and panties, she sprinted down the street. Disoriented, she was uncertain where they'd moved the operation. A quick glance up to the wrought iron balconies lined with cascading ferns told her she was in New Orleans. She shook her head in disbelief. *Fucking assholes.* Wynter had lost track of how many times they relocated her. When she'd first started working for them, she'd been in New York City. But after they'd discovered her intentions, she'd been treated like cargo; blindfolded, handcuffed and gagged as they traveled from state to state.

Endless days in the lab led into nightly bleedings by the vampires. They soon learned, however, that their virologist couldn't think straight if her brain lacked blood. But even after they stopped draining her, their threat remained clear and present. Screw up or argue too much, and they'd drag her to the floor, sinking their fangs into her flesh as punishment. As much as she'd kept her nose buried in the work, managing to mentally catalog their protocols, she'd lost chunks of time. She'd nearly given up hope of living, fearing no one would come for her.

Desperate, her plan had been flimsy at best but she'd rather die trying to escape than be imprisoned. Staking the vampire had been the easy part. Finding her way through the locked corridors had been quite another story. But she'd done it. She was nothing if not resourceful. As the fresh air hit her face, her heart raced, knowing they'd be hot on her heels. She stole a glance over her shoulder; the dark figure was quickly approaching. Her breath quickened in fright as she thought through what she'd do next. If she could disappear through one of the myriad courtyard entranceways along the street, she might have a chance. She could open a gate and lock it behind her, she thought. Or perhaps if she ran further, she could find safety within a shop or bar that catered to humans.

Heaving for breath, she wrapped her bloody fingers around the iron bars that led down a dark alley and shook them. Locked? No, she just needed to open the rusted latch. She fumbled with it as she heard the footsteps growing closer. Her eyes darted down the street and she caught a glimpse of an approaching vampire. Swiftly, she turned her attention back to the door. She grunted, pushing at the bar with her thumb. *Open, dammit, open.* Finally, the latch slid aside. It was at that very second she realized she'd run out of time. A bloodcurdling scream tore from her lips as familiar claws dug into her neck, spinning her around.

"Where do you think you're going?" The vampire sneered, holding her by the throat against the wall.

She choked for air, but didn't waste time answering him. In one hand, she held onto the stake and with the other, she continued to flick open the latch.

"I've got her," he called over to the second thug whose fangs openly wept with saliva.

Wynter's eyes teared. This couldn't be the end. Even though she started to feel the tunnel of unconsciousness closing in, she kicked and gasped in defiance. *Never give up.* They could take her but not without a fight.

"No," she croaked softly. He slammed her wrist against the plastered wall. The stake she'd been carrying slipped from her fingers.

Logan sprinted out of the club after the two vampires

just in time to see the larger one holding the human against the wall by her neck. *Why the hell are vampires attacking a human? In the wide open where anyone could see? Where the hell is Kade?* Kade Issacson, the head of the vampires in New Orleans, would kill these idiots for merely chasing after a human, let alone harming one. With no time to call him, Logan came up behind the vampire, reached around his neck and snapped his spine. He took in the sight of the wide-eyed girl, dressed in a lab coat, who coughed for air. Protectively, he pulled her into his arms, while glancing over to Dimitri, who'd slit open the throat of the other vamp.

"It's okay, you're safe," Logan assured her.

Wynter began to struggle, kicking and beating the stranger with her fists. Lost in panic, she didn't hear his words. Fear surged as she immediately sensed he was wolf. *Trust no one.*

"No, let me go! Please don't hurt me…I can't…" she began. She didn't feel good, her mind and body were beginning to shut down. If she lost consciousness, they'd take her again.

"Easy, sweetheart. Now listen," Logan said softly, refusing to release her. "I'm not goin' to hurt you." *What the hell was it with humans? Didn't she get he was helping her?*

Now that Logan had the woman from his vision in his arms, he wasn't going to let her simply walk away. He couldn't believe that she was actually here in New Orleans. Curiosity got the best of him as he let his eyes wander over her. She wore a dirty white coat that was missing buttons. Shoeless, her bare feet were blackened and bloodied. *What had happened to her?* Logan could feel the heat rising from her skin. She felt warm, too warm for a human. Notwithstanding her panicked state, she appeared physically ill.

"Please, just let me go. I swear I won't tell anyone. Please," she cried, fighting back the sobs that threatened to overwhelm her.

Wynter looked up at the attractive wolf who offered her help. Over six-four, with shoulder length dark brown hair, he towered over her small stature. Dressed in worn jeans and a black t-shirt, his well-defined biceps gave her an idea of the incredible body that was under his clothes. A distinctive power rolled off of him as he gently ran a finger down her cheek. *Alpha.*

She thought she'd hyperventilate at the thought. Oh my God, she needed to get away from him. She couldn't be certain if he was an enemy of hers or not. And if he was, she knew he'd kill her. Wynter knew that packs had rules. And some packs killed intruders and asked questions later. Seeing no other way to escape, perhaps she could convince him she was simply a wayward tourist being chased by vampires.

"I'm a tourist," she stammered. "I just got lost. If you let me go, I'll just get back to the hotel."

A tourist? Is she crazy? Logan could smell her lie and her fear. *Perhaps she's not crazy but frightened out of her right mind,* he thought.

"Okay, well, let's try this again, because I don't see many tourists on the run from vamps, dressed like you are.

Seriously, you're safe with me. You need to calm down, though," he suggested, with a low, reassuring voice. "Things will be fine. We'll get you cleaned up and then we're going to have a little chat."

He didn't want to stress her further but if she thought she was going to up and leave without telling him what was going on, she had another think coming. He glanced over to the ashes of the two vampires they'd killed. He was going to have to have a serious conversation with Kade.

"Please, sir," she continued to beg.

Logan grew irritated. Why was he trying to talk sense into the human in the middle of a dirty alley? It would be much easier if he could just command her like he could do with the wolves. He let a small bit of his power flow out toward her until she stilled in acknowledgement. He cocked an eyebrow at her in surprise that it appeared to work. Not all humans could sense the supernatural force he wielded. *Intriguing.*

"Listen to me, Miss. I'm going to say it one last time; you are safe. I'm sorry but you do realize that I can't just let you go? I've got some questions about what the hell just happened here, and you're in shock. We're going to go home now. Let's get out of this alley."

"No, no, no. Please just let me go. I'll go home. I'll..." She was about to tell him she'd go to the police, when she saw the vampires coming for her. Her heart caught in her throat. It wasn't just any vampire stalking toward them. It was him. The one who had repeatedly fed on her; he'd enjoyed it. Endorphins flooded her weakened system.

Logan shook his head. Much to his chagrin, she obviously didn't understand that she had no choice in the matter.

"More…more vampires," she whispered, unable to look away. Pointing down the street, she grabbed the wall in an effort to remain upright.

"Stay here," Logan commanded.

Wynter silently nodded, fully intending to run.

"Hey D, looks like a few more partygoers want to dance." Logan spun on his heels, taking off down the street to head off their attackers.

"What can I say, Alpha? You're a good-lookin' guy. Real popular tonight," Dimitri joked as he followed.

Logan grabbed the vampire, smashing him up against the wooden shutters of a townhome. Splinters flew as the wood cracked into several pieces. Tearing a shard off the structure, Logan staked him in his back. "Sorry, pal. Dance card's full."

As the second vampire attempted to bite Dimitri, he flipped him onto his back, driving the wood straight through the bloodsucker until he hit the pavement. He shoved up onto his feet and brushed the debris from his jeans.

"Fuck me. What the hell is happening tonight?" Dimitri huffed. "This is some kind of crazy shit."

"Goddamn vampires." Logan stood, scanning the street and was met with silence. "They're out of control."

"Kade must be going soft if he's letting his skeeters buzz the humans. Not good for tourism, ya know." Dimitri laughed.

"Yeah, I get the feeling that our girl's not a random human either. Shit. Where is she?" Logan asked, realizing she must've taken off down into one of the courtyards. Logan sniffed into the air. Humans were so naïve. It was just a matter of time before he found her. "Did you see which direction she ran?"

"No. But I'm guessing from her little tantrum that she doesn't want our help," Dimitri surmised.

"Well, she doesn't have a choice. I want to know exactly what went down before we saved her pretty little ass. Something's not right, and I'm going to find out what it is." Logan continued, deep in thought. "And she's not getting away from me either. Listen, I'm goin' wolf."

"You need me to go with?"

"No, go back to the party. Fi's waiting." Now that Logan had held the woman from his visions in his arms, he needed to know who she was more than ever. What was she doing in New Orleans? Why did the vampires want her?

"You sure?"

"Yeah, I'm sure. But do me a favor, will ya? Put a call into Kade's office and report our little scuffle. They can call me tomorrow. I've got a bad feeling this isn't over."

"You got it."

"Uh...one more thing...my clothes?" Logan grinned.

"Yeah, okay. You sure you want to do this, man?"

Logan laughed without answering. He ducked into an alleyway, away from prying eyes and threw his clothes and boots over to Dimitri. Not that he had a problem with nudity. Quite the contrary; he enjoyed being naked whenever he got the chance. But it was unusual for Logan to go wolf in the city, preferring to run wild in the country. Tonight, however, the woman gave him little choice.

Remembering her lack of clothing and shoes, he reasoned she couldn't have gone far. Where would a human run to in the middle of the night in the French Quarter? Bourbon Street would be the logical place for her to go. Since they were on the other side of the French Quarter, nearly at the river, she'd have quite a ways to walk in order to get there. At two in the morning, most shops would be closed. Even though she didn't seem to be of a criminal nature, she could try to break into a business or home. But that didn't seem likely given her frightened state, not to mention that she'd soon crash from exhaustion. Against the gate, she'd struggled to remain on her own feet. She'd shown signs of illness, trauma and malnutrition. She wouldn't get far.

Letting go of his human thoughts, Logan let the beast take over and do what it did best: hunt. The sweet smell of her remained strong in his memory. Running hard, he zipped down streets and walkways. As her scent grew stronger, the wolf grew excited. Having the capacity to run for miles if necessary, he was unyielding in his search. Soon, the prey would be his.

Chapter Three

Wynter sank into the shadows, contemplating her next move. Exhaustion racked her body. The lack of food and sleep combined with ongoing stress had taken its toll. She wished she could convince herself otherwise, but her mind was unclear; confusion blanketed her thoughts.

A creaking gate alerted her to a maid leaving one of the homes via a courtyard alley. She watched as the older woman looked around, as if to make sure no one was watching, then typed a code into a security pad. As the worker walked down the street, she swiveled her head, still checking for strangers, while the gate slowly closed behind her. Wynter's heart pounded. *A human? Help?* She closed her eyes for what seemed only a second, but by the time she looked again, the woman had strangely disappeared. The gate, however, was slightly ajar as if it was broken. The motorized hinges roared in protest, finally puttering into silence. Wynter leapt at the opportunity to get off the streets, within the safety of a gated house. Decision made, she stealthily slipped through the iron bars.

Wynter pressed her back against the arched stone wall, praying no one had seen her enter. Panting for breath, she reflected on what had happened near the bar and cursed her indecisiveness. For a minute, she'd actually considered giving herself over to the warm, strong Alpha who'd held her. With her cheek at his chest, she'd allowed herself the small indulgence of smelling his clean, spicy scented cologne. As his strong arms and low voice enveloped her, she wanted nothing more than to give herself to him. He was a stranger, yet the familiar strength of an Alpha reminded her of home.

But there was nothing about him that was like her Alpha. No, something about his presence incited an awareness that she'd thought was long gone; perhaps something she was not capable of experiencing. Raised by an Alpha, dates weren't exactly breaking down her door. Her guardian had seen to that. In high school, no one had had the guts to even ask her out, let alone try to kiss her. It wasn't until college that she'd dated humans, had sex. But once she graduated, she was too focused on work to make men a priority. An occasional fling was all she allowed herself, given the high stakes of her research.

In truth, she'd never been intimate with a wolf. She knew all too well that mating with one didn't always turn out well; her guardian had warned her off that idea. But the Alpha who'd just saved her jolted something within her libido; that brief encounter left her wondering if she'd made the right decision by running. His warmth, coupled with his caring words, aroused her. Maybe if she got out alive and her guardian approved, she could contact him later, she thought.

Wynter blew out a breath, realizing how ridiculous it was that she was even thinking of the stranger. Given her dire situation, she'd be lucky if she made it out of the city alive. *Focus, Wynter.* Silently, she inched her body into the archway until she reached a large courtyard. She stilled, listening for signs of people. Moments passed and she heard nothing but the trickling water bubbling out of the three-layered fountain that had greeted her arrival. Intrepidly, she padded out onto the red herringboned brick patio. Dim ground lighting illuminated a large rectangular swimming pool. Despite the old woman's temporary presence, no lights were on in the adjoining mansion or its rear cottage.

Wynter wondered if anyone even lived there. Obviously if the owners kept on late night help, the house was being used by someone. Or perhaps the property was a vacation home? Either way, she had to try to get help. But after knocking on both the main home and cottage's door, she quickly came to the conclusion that it was vacant. She sighed in disappointment, deciding to wait until daylight to keep searching for help. Even if no one was home, she was grateful to be off the street, inside the safety of a quiet yard. In the morning, she could search around the exterior for a hidden key or see if she could get in the garage. If not, she'd try another house. She could more easily travel during the day as it was a much safer time for humans. All she needed was a phone, so she could make contact. Then she'd be home within hours.

Another wave of fatigue rolled through her body. So tired, she thought if she could catch a few hours of sleep, she'd be well enough to keep going. Spotting a few chaise lounges, she tore off the padding. She would have loved to have simply fallen into the chair, but there was no way she could risk being seen out in the open. Dragging the cushions, she squeezed into a secluded nook in between the fountain and a few large potted ferns. She pushed the foam onto the concrete and prayed that she'd be lucky enough to avoid bugs, knowing full well that was wishful thinking.

Curling onto her side, she released a small sob. *How did I ever get into this mess?* The night was dry at least, but she could feel the temperature dropping. She knew she should look for better shelter, but she felt drained, achy. Physically, she just couldn't go on. The wave of lethargy weighed down her limbs, and she realized that she really didn't feel well. As her adrenaline levels dropped, the burn from within grew, alerting her to the fever. *Oh God no. This can't happen now.*

A spike of panic rose as a flash of possibilities ran through her mind. She knew that there'd been one too many occasions where she'd resisted. And in response they'd held her down; fed until she lost consciousness. She tried hard to remember what had happened during her blackouts. At first she'd been worried about sexual assault but that wasn't their thing. No, they clearly preferred pure pain and intimidation. The vampires they'd entrusted to guard her had only been interested in one thing, her blood.

But why was she feeling so weak? She prayed it was merely the stress, a cold. She'd take a simple rhinopharyngitis any day over the lethal viruses she'd handled in the labs. No upper respiratory symptoms presented. Perhaps she'd caught a cytomegalovirus. Even though the virus she worked on targeted shifters, she'd suspected for months that the others were working on other viruses and genetic modifications targeted at vampires, humans and other supernaturals that she wasn't even sure existed.

Another tear ran down her face. Wynter wished she'd never left New York. She felt indebted to her guardian, determined to help his race survive. He'd saved her all those years ago when her parents died. She'd been so alone. He'd been her loving caretaker, the one who brought her back from the devastation she'd felt when her home had been torn apart. She'd done the one thing she could do to help him, to help the pack. But now that she'd escaped, she wondered if she'd done the right thing. Shivering, feeling like a failure, she softly cried herself to sleep.

Glistening with sweat, Logan stared down in disbelief at where his wolf had led him. Like a baby lamb, his lovely dream girl was curled into a deep slumber. After taking note of the busted gate, he knew how she got into his courtyard. Questions swirled in his head. Did she know who he was? Is that why she came to his home? But if she knew him, why run? And why would she lay on the ground like a common dog, sleeping in the shadows? None of what had happened tonight was making any sense.

Black patches of dried blood mottled her face. The tattered coat did little to cover her bare legs. Goosebumps covered her pale skin as the temperature had dropped into the fifties. Seeing little choice, Logan shoved the plants aside, and bent down to her. Reaching for her face, he cupped her cheek. Damn, she was hot; not just warm, but burning up. He'd been right in the alley; she was sick.

"Aw, sweetheart, you're on fire. Now, why did you run? And more importantly, who are you?" he asked himself out loud.

Her unconscious response was to cuddle further into her makeshift mattress. Swiftly but gently, he slid his hands under her tiny body, lifting her into his arms. Logan cursed silently, angry that he'd let her slip away earlier. Even in the heat of the moment, the aroma of her intoxicating scent had caught him off guard. He stilled, taking a minute to lean into her neck; she smelled so good. Despite the sweat and blood, her underlying essence connected with his wolf.

Shocked and aroused by his reaction, he shook his head. What was he doing? His damn wolf needed to get his act together. The woman was sick for fuck's sake. Now wasn't exactly the greatest time to get a hard on. He huffed and took off toward his back door. It was turning out to be one hell of a day.

With one hand, he typed in the security code and awkwardly leaned into the retina scan, careful not to press her against the exterior wall. As the lock clicked open, he pushed the door inward and entered his home. He raced up the steps and headed toward his bedroom. It felt foreign, bringing a strange woman into his inner sanctuary, but there was something about her that told him she wasn't a threat. His visions. She needed him, but her origin and motives remained a mystery.

Logan strode over to his bed and sat on the edge, still cradling the girl. He'd hoped that with his inadvertent jostling she might wake up and answer his questions. But true to his luck that evening, she remained unconscious. Picking up his phone, he called Dimitri.

"Hey," he addressed his beta. "Listen up, I've got our runner. I need you to get Dana down here." Logan looked to her innocent face, wondering what kind of mess this human was wrapped up in.

"Dana? What's wrong with her?" Dimitri asked. If Logan needed Dana, he knew the woman had been injured. Dana was Fiona's half-sister, a doctor. Since she was hybrid, she'd decided on a career of human medicine.

"Yeah, Dana. The girl's sick. And tell them to get here as soon as possible. Listen, I've gotta go. Just get here, 'K?" Logan told him tersely, hanging up the phone. His patience was stretched thin. It had been one goddamned long day. And at this point, things looked to be getting worse, not better.

Unsure of how to proceed, Logan decided a cool bath would help bring down her fever. He knew she'd panic if she woke up with a strange, nude man in the shower, but he didn't have many options. Unbuttoning the few buttons on her coat, he tugged it off of her arms. His stomach tightened in anger as bite marks on her otherwise beautiful skin were revealed. Shit, he hated vampires. Tristan may have been best friends with a couple of them, but not him.

They could be animals. Bloodsucking, vicious monsters who'd turn on you just to get their next drink. He trailed his fingertips over the half dozen bite marks that littered her body, all in various stages of healing. Whoever had done this hadn't done it while lovemaking, ensuring the holes were sealed clean. Rather, it looked as if they'd bitten and retreated, as if they'd been inflicted to purposefully cause pain, debilitation.

He knew that feeding clubs existed. Some humans and shifters got off on pain. Others enjoyed the intoxicating rush of a vampire-induced orgasm. But even in those kinds of places, there were rules about sealing up wounds and they most certainly kept strict dress codes. No, something about this whole situation was off. Logan wasn't sure what the hell was going on but he planned on meeting with Kade as soon as possible. This shit needed to stop but now. If there were more like her out there, they'd all be fucked.

Logan laid Wynter on the bed so he could prepare the bath. He needed to get her cleaned up and most importantly bring her fever down. It didn't seem right that she wasn't waking up with all the commotion he was making. Even though it had been a while since he'd tended to a sick human, he knew that her lack of consciousness could be a serious issue. But his acute hearing told him that her breathing and heartbeat were both normal. For a brief second, he thought that he should throw her in the car and take her to the ER. Under normal circumstances he may have given it further merit, but this situation reeked of supernatural. She had the answers to his questions, and he was determined to get them. As soon as Dana got there, he'd seek her advice about taking her to a hospital.

He glanced over to her threadbare underwear and bra and considered the best way to go about giving a frightened human woman a bath. He laughed in irritation. *What could possibly go wrong?* As much as Logan loved being naked, and with a woman even more so, he decided that he'd better don a pair of boxer briefs. The last thing he needed was her freaking out, waking up slippery and barely dressed with a naked man she'd only just met. He planned to get her in the tub with him and hold her up so she didn't slip under the water. He figured ten minutes would be enough time to bring down her fever, at least until Dana got there. He'd let her decide what to do next. Being wolf, he didn't keep even an Advil in his house.

Logan picked her up and moved into the bathroom. He stepped into the lukewarm water and lowered them both in so that she laid on him. Her back against his chest, he took the bar of soap in his hands and twisted it into a washcloth.

"Okay, baby. Here we go." He spoke softly to her as if she heard him. She shuddered but never woke, so he kept going. "Just goin' to clean you up a bit. Look at what they did to you. Don't worry; you'll be healed in a few days. What I'd like to know is how you got mixed up with vampires?"

Logan found that he was unable to stop talking to her as he carefully cleaned her arms and face. Even if she didn't hear him, it was possible she'd wake at any second. He wanted her to know that someone cared, that she was safe with him. Logan gently washed her, avoiding touching her breasts. But he couldn't resist slipping his hands around her waist, feeling the smoothness of her belly. Fully submerged, he threw the washcloth aside and simply held her. Pressing his cheek to hers, he could feel her body temperature was lowering.

"That's a girl. You're going to feel better soon. Then, we're going to get to know each other," he whispered.

In the quiet of the night, he focused on listening to her heartbeat. His own heart squeezed in response, hoping that the woman he held would heal soon. He thought about the fucking vision. It was possible that he'd averted her death. He'd saved her from a clawed vampire. Maybe that was the end of it. But a nagging suspicion lingered; something told him that this was just the beginning of trouble.

Logan pushed out of the tub, reaching for a towel and gently dried the woman. Her skin puckered in response to the cool air, yet she still made no show of awaking. As Logan rounded toward his bed, Dimitri, Fiona and Dana ran into his room. He caught the smirk on Dimitri's face as his eyes dropped to his Alpha's dripping briefs.

"What?" Logan asked.

"And they say chivalry is dead? Nice briefs, sexy beast," Dimitri teased with a raised eyebrow.

"Fuck you, D," Logan shot over at Dimitri. Without missing a beat, he addressed Dana. "Hey, can you come check her out? I had her in a cool bath but she's still not conscious."

Dana came around the bed and set her medical bag on the night stand. "A human, huh? How long has she been like this?"

"Yeah. I can't be sure but I'd say she's been out for at least forty-five minutes. A few hours ago she seemed fine. Well, awake anyway. When I touched her earlier, I could tell she was sick, warm." Logan stripped and proceeded to towel off in front of everyone. Comfortable with nudity, the others barely noticed.

Dana continued the brief exam and checked her vitals. "This isn't good," she commented, fingering over the feeding holes riddling Wynter's body. "Who did this?"

"Don't know. But when I find out I'm going to kill them…if I didn't already. Dimitri told you 'bout the vamps at the bar?"

"Seems viral. Fever. Sleep deprivation. Stress." Dana pointed to the dark circles under Wynter's eyes and her short bitten nails. She lifted a hand to her nose and sniffed. A look of confusion washed over her. "You said she was human?"

"Yeah, why?"

"Well, this is very unusual. Tell me Alpha, what do you smell?"

Logan strode across the room and held his nose to the soft inner wrist presented to him. "She smells…smells." He stopped and shook his head. His mouth gaped open as he tried to process what was happening. "No. No, that's not possible. I'm telling you Dana, it's not fucking possible."

Unable to stop himself, he ran the tip of his tongue along her skin.

"No." Logan still refused to believe it.

"Yes, Alpha. She's wolf."

"But I'm telling you that when I saw her in the alley earlier there was no possible way she was wolf. I think I know a human when I smell one. And even if by some miniscule chance the scent of the vampire blood masked her true nature, why didn't she shift? I mean, look at all those bite marks. Some are at least a few days old. She could have shifted to heal them. And here's the biggest problem I see with her being supposedly wolf; wolves don't get sick. This woman is very sick. She's got a fever, for Christ's sake; the kind of thing you only see in humans. That just doesn't happen to wolves. What the hell is going on here, Dana?" Logan had switched over to his low, dominant Alpha voice. All the wolves lowered their eyes.

Dana took a deep breath and carefully chose her words. "Alpha, I don't know what's going on here. You're right on all counts. I mean, she scents wolf. But she's sick and that never happens. Look here, at these marks on her neck." She pointed to a series of marks the size of pinpricks that had scabbed over; under her hairline, they were barely visible.

"I don't know what this is. It almost looks like a taser. Or maybe…no," she stopped herself before saying something ludicrous.

"What, Dana?"

"It's just that it kind of looks like an old polio scar. You know, from the seventies. Or maybe it could be caused by some kind of a multi-needle injection device," she guessed with a shrug. "Whatever made it could be causing this fever.

But then if that's true, I've never seen anything like it. Wolves don't get sick."

Logan grew quiet with concern. He'd remembered the Canine Lupis Inhibitor drug that Tristan's mate, Kalli had created. Until he'd heard of that, he would have never believed someone could take a pill to disguise their wolf. And while this was completely different, a wolf getting ill was unheard of unless there was some kind of magic affecting her that could explain the illness.

"Could this be some kind of a spell? A hex?" Logan asked.

"Maybe. It's hard to tell. But you said her fever was really high when you found her, right? I just took her temp again and it isn't going up, so that's good news. Whatever is affecting her could be wearing off. If it's a spell or herbs, it seems short-lived. Tell you what. I'm goin' to take a few blood samples. I'll take them to the lab and personally run them, okay?"

Fiona approached Wynter and brushed a long strand of blonde hair from her face. Logan's jaw tightened in response to having yet another wolf touch his human. Noticing the subtle sign, she backed away from the bed and turned to him.

"Logan, if this is magic, I haven't seen it before either. That's not to say the witches aren't always trying to cook up things to thwart shifters and vamps," she said coyly. "I mean, you know there're always a few bad apples in the bunch. I'll ask around. I can also bring some healing herbs for her…if she still feels sick when she wakes up."

"Thanks, Fi." Logan paced, working through his plan of action. "Dimitri, call Jake and Zeke. I want them to set up a perimeter guard on my place. Have them fix the damn gate. No one gets in or out. I don't know how long she's going to be down, but my guess is this little bird is going to try to fly the coop when she realizes where she is."

"You got it." Dimitri nodded.

"Dana, I hate to ask the obvious question but is whatever's going on with her a threat to others?"

"Do you mean is what she has contagious? I'd go with no. I can't be sure but if it was brought on quickly and she's already rebounding, it could even be a poison of some kind. I didn't think of it until now, but considering the marks on her neck, it's obvious she was exposed to something. Sorry I can't tell you more," Dana said in defeat. She finished drawing blood, snapped the test tubes neatly into a carrying case and arranged everything back into her medical bag.

"Listen up everyone," Logan snapped. All eyes landed on his hard glare. "No one else in the pack is to know what's going on here with mystery girl, got it? I don't know who this woman is…this wolf is. But something's not right here. And until we figure out what's happening, I want to keep it under wraps. This is a direct order. Do not speak of this to anyone. The story for now is that she's a victim of a vampire attack and she's under my protection, nothing more."

The group nodded in agreement and began filing out the door. Logan stopped Dana, privately asking her if she could change Wynter into one of his t-shirts and boxers. As good as she'd felt in his arms, it felt wrong for him to touch her any further. It was obvious she'd been violated by vampires; he wasn't about to add himself to the list.

Logan had doubts about having the girl sleep in his bed, but his protective instincts told him to keep her close. She was vulnerable, and for at least the night, his responsibility. He wasn't sure whether it was his wolf or his heart driving his actions, but he felt compelled to watch over her, to protect her. In the morning, there'd be plenty of time for questions and rational approaches to solving perplexing conundrums. For now it was just him and her, resting, healing.

Clothed, Logan laid next to Wynter. He pushed over to his side and propped his head with the heel of his hand. He studied her face as if memorizing every curve of her chin, the swell of her lips. Something about her drew his interest. He'd like to have blamed it on his vision, but his visceral reaction to her scent concerned him. Alone and happily content for so many years, he couldn't fathom such an instantaneous and intense attraction toward a woman. Regardless, she smelled incredibly delectable to his wolf. Logan sighed. It would wait until tomorrow. He looked forward to her awakening, to forthcoming answers and mostly to getting to know the little wolf in his bed.

Chapter Four

"Hey sweetheart, can you hear me?" Logan awoke to a cry. Even though her eyelids fluttered, she didn't appear to be moving.

As if an elephant sat on her chest, Wynter felt immobilized, both tired and heavy. The soft bedding was her first clue that she was no longer outside. *Where am I? Please God, don't let them have captured me.* She took a deep breath, forcing her mind to focus. Her hazy vision presented the blurry image of a man. *No, no, no.*

"I've gotta go," she coughed, attempting to push upward. Feeling as if she weighed a million pounds, she got an inch off the mattress before falling backward. She licked her dry lips; tears brimmed in her eyes.

"Hold on there now. You're safe. How do you feel?" Logan asked, brushing the back of his hand across her cheek. She felt much cooler; her fever had subsided.

Wynter heard the sound of his familiar low voice wrapping around her like a warm blanket. The man from the alleyway. Thoughts spilled like droplets of rain as she remembered their brief encounter. He'd protected her. Sexy, dominant and altogether male. But, no, he wasn't a man. He was a wolf. *Alpha.*

"I'm Wyn. Wynter Ryan. I think I'm…" She closed her eyes, trying to piece together what had happened. She hadn't felt well.

"Sick. You gave us a good scare, but your fever's down." Logan finished her sentence. "Here, let me get you some water. You've been out of it for a few hours."

He reached over and grabbed a bottle of water that he'd kept near his bedside. Unscrewing the cap, he slid an arm underneath her neck so he could support her head. Bringing the rim to her lips, he watched as she swallowed a few sips. Almost feeling as if he was feeding an infant, he was careful not to choke her with too much liquid.

"Thank you," she whispered, aware that he was holding her. She gazed into his mesmerizing blue eyes. The handsome planes of his face were only outdone by the small smile he gave her. She'd been scared he'd hurt her. Jax had warned her about male wolves. But instead of being aggressive, her savior spoke to her gently, tending to her like an injured child.

"Do you need anything else? You really should get some sleep," he suggested, even though he wanted to ask her a million questions. Reluctantly, he laid her back onto her pillow and backed away.

Immediately, Wynter felt the loss of his warmth as he removed his arm from the crook of her neck. She barely knew him, so why did the brief embrace feel so good? She diverted her gaze, embarrassed by her situation.

"I'm sorry. I shouldn't have run," she began. "I need to tell you..."

"Shhh...you need to rest now. Tomorrow, Wynter. Tomorrow, we'll talk, okay?" Logan assured her. He could hear her heartbeat race; he assumed from anxiety. He sought to soothe her worries. "Just lay back and close your eyes, little wolf."

"But I'm not," Wynter protested.

"Hey now, no more words, okay? You need to get well." Logan moved away from Wynter. Logical thoughts pressed forward; he should let her sleep alone, go work in his office. He eased off the bed and turned off the lights. "You'll be safe here. Just rest."

As the room fell into darkness, Wynter grabbed the sheet out of fear. She hated the dark. Two long months of no sun had done that to her. The claustrophobia threatened to smother her. In the pitch black of the night, she let out a small sob.

"Please, please not the dark. Don't leave," she cried.

Logan flicked one of the soft hallway lights back on and returned to her side. Goddess, he knew he'd regret this in the morning. This was exactly how he'd ended up with a menagerie of animals as a kid. As if he'd found a stray puppy, he was already becoming attached. But he knew there was something special about this woman, something that would keep him from simply letting her go in the morning. He'd learned long ago that one could not fight nature. He sighed, aware of what he was about to do.

Against his better judgment, he slid into the bed next to her.

"Come here, Wynter," he ordered, wrapping an arm around her shoulders.

Goddess almighty, her small body fit his perfectly, and he was pissed at himself. Not only had he let Wynter into his home, his bed, he now had her conveniently and warmly against his chest. The dreams hadn't prepared him for the intense arousal and possessiveness that appeared to be rearing its ugly head. No, he couldn't let this happen. Establishing his dominance within the pack and securing his position as Alpha had been his number one priority. And now that that was accomplished, he needed to focus on continuing to nurture his already successful real estate venture, not become emotionally involved with a stranger.

As he allowed himself the indulgence of pressing his nose to her hair, he mentally shook his head. He didn't know anything about this woman. She seemed human, but now he distinctively scented wolf. And if she was wolf that meant she came from a pack. She belonged somewhere else, possibly to someone else. He cringed slightly at the thought she could be mated. No, that couldn't be possible. She felt so right in his arms. So terribly, wonderfully perfect. And it was all wrong.

Wynter had never been needy or scared. But in that moment, her vulnerability overtook her sense of reason. A small voice in her head told her that it wasn't right to let a stranger hold her, comfort her. Yet the attraction was too hard to resist. Certain that he was Alpha, she wasn't sure if it was his powers she felt humming through her veins or her own arousal, but his protective embrace spoke to her soul, calmed her mind. Acquiescing to his wishes, she cuddled her head on his shoulder and her hand on his chest. *Safe.*

The last thought that ran through her mind was that she needed to call home. God, she missed him. Surely, he'd be ripe with panic. Tomorrow, she thought. Tomorrow, I'll call him.

"Jax," she murmured right before she was lost to sleep.

Logan sucked a breath. *What the fuck did she just say?* He glanced downward. She was completely asleep, but there was no mistaking what she just said. No, it could not be possible. Jax. Jax fucking Chandler; the Alpha of New York City. He'd met him a handful of times. When it came to business, the man was fair, albeit having a flair for the dramatic.

The last time he'd seen the guy in Jersey, he'd presented Tristan with a 'present' of sorts. Of course the 'gift' turned out to be a wolf who'd been involved in killing one of Tristan's wolves. *It's the thought that counts.* In reality, Tristan couldn't have been happier with the present. During the event, Logan had observed Jax, who seemed to take perverse pleasure in watching Tristan attack and kill the wolf. He distinctively remembered Jax comforting Tristan after he'd taken a life, assuring him that he'd done the right thing as Alpha.

At the time he couldn't quite understand the interaction. But now that he was Alpha, he could easily relate to what transpired that day. Jax was merely supporting Tristan, giving him a peace offering after he'd aggressively pursued

Tristan's sister. Like leaders of countries, Alphas chose other Alphas as allies, all the while protecting their own packs. Logan had never thought it would be possible to have more respect for Tristan or Jax, but now that he was Alpha, their relationship was even more important.

Did Wynter belong to Jax? Was she his mate? He blew out a breath, knowing that it shouldn't matter. All that really mattered was finding out what the hell happened with the vampires in the alleyway and how a wolf could get sick. Both spelled serious trouble for not just wolves but all supernaturals in the area. The shit was about to hit the fan.

Chapter Five

Wynter woke refreshed, although alone. The bright sun streamed into her room, causing her to yawn. Months of sleeping on the floor, and she was finally home in her warm bed; it felt incredible. She pressed her eyes shut, willing her dream to continue. A sexy mysterious stranger beckoned to her in the distance. She could make out the definition of his abs, but couldn't quite see his face. She strained to listen, to run to him, so she could see who he was.

"Hey sunshine," a male voice called to her.

Startled, she jolted upward, eyes wide open. Scanning the room, she instantly realized her erotic dream of being held in a strong Alpha's arms must have been just that: a dream. *Where am I?* Panic set in once again as an imposing man with tattoos on his forearms approached her. Not the man from her dreams.

"Don't come any closer," she warned him. "I don't know how I got here but I'm leaving." She jumped out of bed, then quickly realized she was naked underneath a man's t-shirt and boxer shorts. *Oh God.*

"Listen, cher. No one here's goin' to hurt you. Just settle down," he suggested and gestured toward a bureau. Yogurt, granola, fruit and juice sat on a tray. "Now that you're feelin' better, maybe you can eat some breakfast."

She wanted to deny it, but her stomach ached in hunger. How long had it been since she'd eaten like a normal human being? Months? But how could she trust this stranger looming across the room? She glanced up at him. Definitely wolf. She could tell by his piercing green eyes. But who was he? Alpha? No, he wasn't Alpha. She'd been with pack long enough to tell this wasn't him. But the man from last night…was he real? She grasped the collar of her shirt, drew it up to her nose and took a deep breath. Clean, male with a touch of cologne. She nearly fell back into the bed taking in his scent. She sighed, closing her eyes. The male from last night. It was him. And it smelled so…good. Memories of their conversation played in her mind. She'd asked him to stay with her. And he did. He'd held her. The arousal she'd felt. Oh God. That couldn't be right. She was in so much trouble. No, no, no. Jax was going to freak out when he finally found her.

Dimitri smiled. *Yep, that's right, baby. Smell your shirt.* Little did she know that Logan was waiting for Dimitri to bring her to him downtown. Whatever had transpired last night between the two of them seemed to have rattled his Alpha. He'd watched as Logan tore out of the mansion at the crack of dawn. Even though he'd mumbled something about meeting preparations, Dimitri knew damn well that his Alpha rarely needed time to prepare for anything. He was the sharpest tool in the shed, both mentally and physically. On the way out, he'd ordered Dimitri to watch over the little wolf, see if he could get her to eat and bring her to the office.

Aside from the entertainment factor, Dimitri liked the idea of his Alpha concentrating on something other than challenges. And this lovely little lady was turning out to be a damn fine distraction, at least for the short term. But they still didn't really know who she was, and that was a wrench in the cog. If she belonged to another wolf or pack, they'd soon claim her. And as it was looking, she was a runner by nature and didn't plan to stick around very long. And then there was her mystery illness, unheard of among wolves. Maybe that's why Logan was all about business? He probably thought a passing attraction to the little wolf would be futile by nature.

Dimitri glanced at Wynter and decided they'd better get moving; he coughed to get her attention. He needed her to accept what was about to happen. He contemplated the best approach for getting her to comply. Deciding on going soft, rather than using force, he crouched down so he could speak to her on eye level, trying to seem less intimidating than he knew he was.

"It's okay, Wynter."

"You know who I am?" she asked timidly.

"Yes, you talked to my Alpha last night. You're remembering, right? His scent?"

"I..." She sniffed the ambrosial-scented fabric once again. What the hell was wrong with her? "I...I guess...yes. But I was sick, right?"

"Sure were. How're you feelin'?" He was genuinely concerned.

"I feel fine," she lied. Physically, she felt fine. But mentally, she was broken. Wynter stared out toward the window, helplessly shaking her head. Tears brimmed in her eyes, and she looked away.

Dimitri sat on the bed at her side and put a comforting hand on her shoulder. Surprisingly, she didn't shrug him off; she just let the tears run down her cheeks.

"I may be old-fashioned but the girls I know who actually feel fine don't cry, cher."

"I'll be fine. I'm just overwhelmed."

This was not going so well, Dimitri thought. He stood up and walked over to the dresser and poured her a glass of orange juice.

"Have something to drink," he told her.

With no energy to argue, she complied, reaching for the glass. The sweet acidy pulp tasted so good. She hadn't had juice for so long, and it made her feel as if she was doing something wonderfully normal. She wiped her tears away with the back of her hand and gave him a small smile.

"That's a girl. Are you sure you don't want to lie down? I was supposed to take you to see the Alpha, but he won't want you to go if you're not well."

"No, really, I'm okay." *I'd be better if I were home.* She looked up at Dimitri in silent defeat, wishing she could just get on the next flight out of New Orleans. But she knew better than to try to outrun a wolf. Well, she used to know better. She figured that last night didn't count; she hadn't exactly been thinking clearly. And now that she was in another pack's home, possibly the Alpha's, there was no way she'd get out on her own. She had to call Jax.

"I need to call someone. Can I use your phone?" she asked quietly.

"Sorry, but you've got to talk with the Alpha first. I don't want to point out the obvious, but we need to know why you were being chased by those vamps last night. And your fever. Alpha's got a lot of questions."

"But I have to call Jax," she protested. "I have to get out of here."

Dimitri stopped dead in his tracks, almost dropping the glass. *Jax.* There was only one Jax that he knew: Jax Chandler. Holy fuck. No wonder Logan was pissed this morning. Seems like the rules of the game just changed. Attempting to hide his reaction, he continued and handed her a yogurt.

"I'm sure my Alpha will be in touch with yours." He could only assume she belonged to the New York pack. And she'd slept with his Alpha. Yeah, this was going to be fun.

"He's not my Alpha. Well, yes he is but…" her words trailed off when she realized she was going to be interrogated ad nauseum about what had happened by the New Orleans' Alpha. Even if he'd acted caring last night, he'd want details about why she was in that alley. But she needed to talk to Jax first. Her eyes darted defiantly up at Dimitri and she said nothing more.

"Okay, little wolf, whatever you say."

"I'm not a wolf," she stated firmly, confused as to why

he'd call her that. Any supernatural worth their salt could tell she was very much human.

Dimitri laughed. "Well, that fever must have affected you a little more than I thought." He shook his head, irritated that she'd lie to him. The whole situation was turning into one shitload of crazy that he was ready to dump somewhere else. If that was how she was going to play it, he was ready to take a stricter approach with her.

"Wynter, this's what's goin' happen. You need to eat something and then we're going to see my Alpha. I called over to one of the shops this morning, and they delivered some clothes that should fit you." He pointed to several shopping bags lying near the closet door. "You're welcome to take a shower before we leave but I'd like to leave in an hour. Am I clear?"

"Crystal," she grumbled, conceding she wasn't going to get to call Jax. She knew that condescending, 'do what I say' tone all too well. When decisions needed to be made in a pack, it wasn't exactly the epitome of democracy. Pretty much the exact opposite. And given that she was neither a pack member nor a wolf, she had exactly zero say about her future at the moment.

Logan knew the second she'd entered his building. Occupying the top five floors of a renovated skyscraper on Poydras Street in the Central Business District, he ran pack operations as well as his own personal business. State of the art security had been installed throughout the building and a private, high speed elevator exited directly onto his floor. Logan watched on his plasma security screen as Wynter crammed herself into the corner of the lift, attempting to get away from Dimitri. Logan frowned, wondering what caused her to cower in such a fashion. He'd asked Dimitri to offer her breakfast and bring her to him if she was well. But clearly the morning had not gone how he'd planned.

Even though he'd told Dimitri not to touch her in any way or intimidate her, Logan was aware that his beta's presence didn't exactly put people at ease. A mere look from him would have most males shaking in their boots. Given Dimitri's massive presence, he could understand how the little wolf would be wary. The man looked like a badass enforcer, but in truth, Dimitri was quite the peacemaker within the pack. Sure, he was almost as deadly as Logan given the right circumstances, but in general, he approached life with calm and humor.

Logan swore, remembering the way he'd left her. Oh, he'd wanted to stay all right. But encouraging the uncanny attraction wouldn't help either of them. Holding her, smelling her, it had been too great a temptation. So instead of prolonging the torture, he'd made a judicious decision; he'd left the bedroom before he did something he regretted. Hearing Jax's name should have been enough to douse the flame that heated his burgeoning erection. But as her soft breasts pressed against his chest and her hand wandered up to the ridges of his bare abs, he'd nearly lost it. Erotic thoughts painted over any worries he'd had about the New

York Alpha. As she'd unconsciously draped her leg over his in her sleep, brushing her thigh over his hard shaft, he truly imagined he'd come in his boxers. So after three hours of barely sleeping, her intoxicating scent fully ensconced in his consciousness, he'd bailed.

He'd almost thought better of washing her scent away but doing so admittedly cleared his head. Not only did the she-wolf come with major baggage, she didn't belong to him and had called for another man. What was he thinking? He knew the best thing for all of them would be to have a nice sit down in his office where he could wear his professional veneer like a mask. He'd treat their interaction like he should, all business. He'd find out who she was, what pack she belonged to, why the vampires were after her and how the hell she'd gotten sick. The most logical solution was magic, he'd decided. As for the rest, she probably got in a fight with her boyfriend and decided a little fun in the Big Easy was in order. Somehow she got mixed up with some rough vamps who decided they'd take it a little too far. By the time he'd arrived at the office, he'd had the most logical possibility wrapped up with a tidy bow. And his sexual attraction to her was sealed up nice and tight into that same package…until now.

Glued to the screen, he observed her aversion posturing; her eyes darted to Dimitri and then back down to the floor. He could practically smell her fear through the fiber optics. Perhaps she should be nervous, but fear was not an emotion he planned on eliciting…yet. Logan wasn't into pain, but as Alpha, he'd do what he needed to do to protect the pack.

As Tristan had pointed out to him on many occasions, an Alpha's decisions weren't based on popularity; rather, they needed to be calculated and implemented in the best interest of the pack. No matter how much his dick longed for her, the small, but real, possibility of her being a threat existed. Even a pocket knife could kill a large man if used correctly. He needed to get his shit together and focus on getting answers instead of getting laid.

He'd already called Jax, letting him know that one of his wolves had gone astray in New Orleans. The brief but necessary conversation caused his gut to twist. *She does not belong to you.* He just needed to keep telling himself those words. It should be easy to remember, considering it was true. Oddly, Jax didn't claim her outright, but instead indicated he or one of his associates would be on a plane as soon as possible to assess the situation. Logan found that interesting in itself. What was there to assess? An Alpha knows all his wolves. But then again, after meeting Jax a few times, his penchant for drama tended to weave itself into everything he did.

The ding of the elevator caused him to suck a breath. This was it; time for answers. *Showtime.* Like clockwork, Jeanette, his secretary, buzzed his speaker, alerting him to their arrival. Jeanette, a human, had been working for Marcel for over forty years. She'd been crushed by his passing but agreed to Logan's offer to stay on, working for him. She was the consummate professional, and he suspected her loyalties ran nearly as deep as those of the wolves in his pack.

Dimitri knocked once on the door and strode into Logan's office, shutting it behind him.

"What did you do to her?" Logan accused, giving him a sardonic stare.

"Nothin', she's perfectly fine. You saw her. She's fed and dressed; just like you asked." Dimitri smiled and dropped into one of the tan leather seats facing Logan's desk.

"Really? Then tell me why she looks like she's scared shitless?" His mouth tightened into a fine line.

Dimitri diverted his gaze looking out the window and back to his Alpha. "It was nothing."

"What was nothing?"

"I swear I was gentle with her," Dimitri assured him. "She wanted to call Jax. I said no. I can't help that she's a little wisp of a thing. And well, I'm...I'm me." He gave Logan a lopsided grin.

"You think this is funny?"

"Well, boss, I must admit it's a little funny. I mean, come on. When was the last time a little she-wolf had the Alpha tearing out of his own home at the crack of dawn? And at the risk of pointing out the obvious, you still seem a little on edge."

Logan rolled his eyes, swiveled in his chair and glanced out the window to look over the cityscape. He took a breath and blew it out, frustrated. "Fuck, yeah, I'm on edge. You try sleeping with a girl like her for a few hours while she calls out Jax Chandler's name. Hearing his name should've been enough to make me treat her like a nun, but man, I was so not saying my prayers. It's so wrong."

Dimitri laughed out loud. "Well, she is fine, but she's not ours. And she very well may be going home tonight. You get ahold of Jax?"

"Yeah, I called him. Cagey bastard's playing his damn games. Says he's coming here to 'assess' the situation. Didn't claim her outright but didn't deny it either. As for little Miss Wynter out there…there's part of me that would like to keep her." Logan smiled over at him like he'd discovered treasure.

"She's not a lost dog, Alpha. You can't just 'keep her'."

"You'd be surprised at what I can do when I put my mind to things," he pondered. *Was he really considering keeping her?* Yes, yes he was. And why not? Jax didn't exactly claim her. Then again, aside from a few hours of cuddling like a horny, blue-balled teen, he didn't even know her. For all he knew, she had the personality of a honey badger.

"That you do. But as your beta, my advice is to go easy." Dimitri shook his head and laughed. Damn if his Alpha wasn't considering the unthinkable.

"I don't do easy," Logan remarked. "I do what I need to do. And right now, I plan to get the truth." He stood, walked over to the bar and pulled a bottle of water out of the mini-fridge. "Speaking of which, we have a meeting with Kade later tonight at Mordez."

"Mordez, huh? Love me a vamp club," Dimitri said sarcastically.

"Yeah, you and me both. You know the vamps. They can't meet in offices like normal people." He shrugged. "Bring Zeke and Jake in case there's trouble. Have them keep eyes on us...discreetly. You know the drill."

Logan detested meeting at a blood club as much as the next wolf, but he'd do it to meet Kade. If there was one vampire he remotely trusted, it was him. Logan would mete out justice when necessary, but it was Kade's job to get his people in line, not his.

"Done," Dimitri responded, making his way over to the door.

"Let's get this show on the road, shall we?" Logan said with a wry smile.

Within seconds of Dimitri's exit, Logan's blonde angel stood in the archway.

Heart racing, Wynter passed through the doorway and looked up at the magnificent stranger who'd saved her. As his eyes locked on hers, her breath caught in her lungs. *Alpha.* The word resounded through her mind like an echo in a valley as she looked over to Logan, who sat carefully watching her every move from behind his desk. Memories of his arms around her body in the heart of the night swirled in her mind. Her face flushed at the confounding arousal she'd felt. Although she tried so hard not to stare, it became impossible to stop. The Alpha was both incredibly sexy and handsome yet he looked dangerous as his lips formed a knowing smile. Dressed in a dark blue suit, his confident posture exuded power. And sex. She tensed as her desire flared again. No, no, no. How could she be attracted to an

Alpha? That could not happen. Jax would not be pleased, not one damn bit.

What was wrong with her? She'd been gone from society for months, and she was ready to throw herself at the first man to cross her path? Wynter reasoned that perhaps it was the drugs they gave her. Yes, that had to be it. Maybe she was still feeling the effects of her illness? But as she gazed into his eyes, she couldn't deny the lure of his powerful presence. She tried to shake it off; her brain told her to be cautious. She knew better than to assume a handsome man equated to nice. In her experience, she'd learned that Alphas were charming, often good-looking and exceedingly deadly.

She took a deep breath, trying to tamp down her reaction. *Do not think about how it felt to lie against him in bed. You don't even know him.* No matter how much her libido just got thrown into overdrive, she needed to get it the hell together. Concentrate, she told herself. She needed to call Jax, transfer the intelligence to him and initiate a new plan of action. Pulling over a façade of indifference, she exhaled.

With her misplaced emotions tucked away, she opened her eyes. The Alpha gave her a broad smile as if he knew exactly what she'd been thinking....every dirty, lustful thought. *This cannot be happening.* His voice jarred her back into reality.

"Have a seat." Logan gestured to one of the seats across from his desk.

It was not lost on him how Wynter averted her gaze submissively at his words. *Definitely wolf.* How could he have been so wrong when he first met her in the alley, thinking she'd been human? Sensing both fear and arousal from Wynter, he struggled to remain objective. His wolf sought to pounce on the prey that tempted him so. Logan reminded himself that he really didn't know this woman, no matter how delicious she looked.

He cursed silently as his eyes roamed over her jeans and the pale pink oxford shirt that was unbuttoned just low enough for him to see a hint of cleavage. He imagined that Dimitri had Melinda, one of his wolves who owned several shops, deliver her clothing. Even conservatively dressed, Wynter looked delightfully edible. Free from makeup, she was a natural beauty. While her skin looked pallid, as if she'd been out of the sun, her complexion was bright and clear.

Her long blonde hair was pulled into a tight ponytail. The spiraling curls sprang in all directions, and for a brief second, Logan wished he could snip the rubber band binding her hair, freeing it like the wind. How he'd love to wrap his hand around it while taking her from behind. Yes, indeed, that would be a sinful pleasure. Ah, but it was time for business. Perhaps if he convinced her to stay, he could play with her. But for now, he needed answers; answers that only she could give him.

"You're safe, Wynter." Logan watched her with interest as she sat, nervously playing with her fingers.

Startled to hear her name roll off his lips, she jerked in her chair. Apprehensively, she looked around his large office, checking out the space for an escape route.

"I…I'm sorry, Alpha," she stated, finally raising her eyes to his.

"Do you know who I am?"

She shook her head. "No. I mean, yes, I remember last night. Thank you for taking care of me," she managed.

"Yet you know what I am. You address me as Alpha. You can sense it, no?"

"Yes," she quietly agreed.

"My name is Logan Reynaud, and I'm Alpha of Acadian Wolves here in New Orleans," he informed her. Keeping his voice calm and low, he continued. "Listen Wynter, I'm not going to hurt you. But I need answers about what happened last night, okay? Let's start with what you were doing down in the alley. Why were the vamps after you?" He leaned far back into his chair, resting his hands on the armrests. He cocked his head, waiting for an answer.

"I…they…I was being held." Wynter forced her hands onto her thighs, attempting to relax. "I was working for someone. I had a disagreement with my employer. The vampires. They didn't want me leaving." Okay, that was the truth. Maybe not the whole truth but he couldn't possibly know that.

"So you were working in the middle of the night, tried to leave and they chased you?" The lilt at the end of his sentence indicated that he clearly didn't believe her.

"Well, yes. Please sir, it's complicated."

Sir, huh? While the mere mention of the word shot a rush of blood to his cock, he knew she was trying to conceal information. Sly little she-wolf, she was.

"So tell me, what kind of work do you do?"

She could tell he wasn't buying her story. Oh God, she wished Jax was here to help her. Wynter knew that telling lies to an Alpha generally ended in disaster. She needed to be very careful. Do not lie, but don't tell the whole truth.

"I'm a researcher. I've been working for a long time on some very important projects," she sighed. "I knew things. They didn't want me to leave. I escaped." There, she said it. Again, all truth…but not everything. The memories of being held against her will elicited a fresh sense of fear. As if she was still in the lab, her blood pulsed in panic, and she struggled to remain composed. Pushing down her sleeves, she attempted to hide the scars of her internment that remained on her arms.

"You were working for a company that kept its workers nearly naked and locked up? Is this correct?" Infuriated at her admission, he attempted to stay calm. What kind of monster would keep her imprisoned? And what were they doing in his city?

"Yes," she whispered. A small sob lodged in her throat. Why did she ever think she could work for that company? Although she'd done it to help the pack, it had been so foolish. Her lips tensed together, and she pretended to admire the New Orleans vista through the glass. *Do not cry in front of an Alpha.*

"And tortured? The bites. I saw them," he pushed.

Instead of answering him, she simply nodded, refusing to look at him. Wynter's face whitened at the mention of the bite marks that littered her body. Embarrassment washed over her even though she didn't deserve it. She tugged at her sleeves once again in an attempt to hide. Anger surged. It was none of his business what happened to her. Where the hell was Jax?

"Little wolf, don't be ashamed. These vampires…I know them. They can be vicious," he told her.

Her eyes flashed in confusion. Wolf? Why was he calling her that? Tears threatened to spill from her already reddened eyes. She just needed to go home. Jax would help fix things, including the mess that her life had become.

Logan hated that they'd done this to her. He could tell she was on the edge of losing it, but he had to know what happened. Fighting the urge to wrap his arms around her and offer comfort, he purposefully grounded himself behind his desk.

"Okay, why don't you tell me about the magic? Were you hexed? Do you remember what happened?"

"What magic?" she countered, perplexed by his questions. What was he talking about?

"You were sick last night. Wolves don't get sick," he reminded her.

"Yes, I know," she agreed, meeting his gaze. In truth, she wasn't sure what happened to her. "Wolves don't get sick. But humans do. I must have had the flu." Feeling claustrophobic, Wynter suddenly got up and walked over to the edge of the floor-to-ceiling window. At one time, she'd marveled at the view of New York City from this height. But this wasn't New York. At that moment, she simply wished to escape, as if hoping she could parachute out of the building.

"This is true, Wynter. But you're not human, are you? Last night you were burning up. Something happened. You need to tell me what you remember. Were you around witches? Tell me, little wolf," he asked tersely, growing impatient with her avoidance.

"Stop calling me that!" she snapped. This was it. She truly was losing it. Yelling at an Alpha was not her smartest move but she felt out of control. Why not go for broke? She turned around to face Logan, her back against the cool glass. "I was not around witches. I told you that vampires were holding me. I don't know why I was sick. End of story. Now, I need to call Jax. And I am not a wolf! Can't you see I'm human? You're an Alpha, for God's sake."

Wynter barely saw him coming. Logan leapt across the room, and as his body touched hers, she gasped. His hands pressed hard against the glass on either side of her head. The masculine scent of him wafted into her nose and she fought the instinct to rub her face against his chest. *Oh God, what had she done? How could she be so stupid as to challenge an Alpha? She really must be sick.* Unable to speak, she held still. Initially charged with fear, she realized very quickly that he wasn't hurting her. The tension between them escalated with every minute of silence that passed. And then she felt him, his nose grazing along the side of her neck. A small moan escaped her lips.

At the challenge, Logan strode across the room, pinning her against the wall. *He had to smell her, taste her. Why would she deny her wolf? Why play games?* Logan didn't want to hurt her. Oh no. If anything, he'd like to give her pleasure like she'd never known. But she kept insisting she was human. If she wanted to play, play he would. She was wolf, and he'd prove it to her. But as her sweet scent engulfed his senses, he began to lose control. His wolf clawed at his psyche, begging to take the woman. Like freshly cut roses, the heavenly aroma was familiar yet altogether unique and desirable, although her wolf lingered on the edge; she was there, he could scent her.

In an effort to prevent himself from ravishing her right there in his office, Logan plastered his hands so hard against the window, he thought it'd crack. At the sound of her moan, he darted his tongue out against her silky skin. He had to taste her. Just once. Ah fuck, no; his wolf wanted more. Eyes feral, he locked them with hers, taking her arm. He placed a small kiss to her palm before dragging his tongue along her wrist all the way to the crook of her elbow, releasing a growl of satisfaction.

Wynter's heart pounded as he gently took her arm into his hands. She shivered as he pushed up her sleeve and brought her delicate wrist to his lips. Wet with arousal, she couldn't break their connection as she stared deep into his mesmerizing eyes. *Oh my God. Wolf. Human. I'll be whatever you want me to be…just please, just take me.* Wynter thought her knees would give out, except he had her pressed up against the window. Lost in his spell, she responded by nudging her own hips against his hard arousal as he tasted her skin.

Logan groaned as the territorial need to take her consumed him. He needed to get things under control. *Jax.*

Fucking, goddamned Jax. His name alone should have killed his raging hard on, but it wasn't helping one damn bit. No, he needed to separate himself from her before he tore her clothes off. He closed his eyes and blew out a breath, but didn't release her.

"Wolf," he breathed into her hair.

"What?"

"Wolf, sweetheart. You're very much a wolf," he confirmed.

"No, I know I was sick but that just can't be." Wynter tried to move, but he wrapped his arms around her protectively. "I need to see a doctor. Please, Alpha."

Confused, Logan pulled away enough so he could look at her. He wasn't sure why she was denying her wolf. Considering her illness, he tried to be gentle, to calm her. "Wynter," he said softly, noticing that she'd rested her forehead against his chest. "Look at me."

Wynter complied, slowly raising her head. She was overwhelmed. One minute she'd felt a healthy dose of fear, then instantly she was overcome with lust for the Alpha before her. She didn't know him, but something deep down told her that she could trust him. He had nothing to gain from telling her she was a wolf. She suspected she'd been compromised somehow by ViroSun. How, she didn't know.

"Hey, I don't know what's goin' on with you, but we'll deal with this. And given that we've technically slept together, I think you can call me Logan." He winked in an effort to put her at ease. "Last night when you were unconscious, I had my doctor examine you. And before you ask, she's a hybrid so she knows about wolves and humans. But I need you to be honest with me. Why do you keep denying your wolf?"

She sighed, resigned to the fact that she needed his help. While it was true she had to talk to Jax, the man before her was offering her a lifeline and she desperately needed to grab onto it if she had a shot in hell of keeping her sanity. She had to explain to him, tell him more about what happened to her.

"I deny my wolf as you put it, because I'm not a wolf. I'm human," she explained, placing her palms against his chest. "Please listen to me. I swear I'm human. I've never in my life shifted. And I don't know why I scent like wolf to you. But you have to understand, the place I worked; they…they could do things. I was forced to help them do these things."

"Things? What kinds of things?" Logan didn't like where this was headed, but he tried to sound encouraging and not angry. He didn't want to scare her any more than she'd already been.

"I was working on many different things….mostly viruses. When I'd refuse or give them a hard time…let's just say there are parts of my employment that I don't remember. These people…they're evil. And capable of horrible things…things I never knew could be possible," she croaked.

Logan pulled her into an embrace and stroked her hair. "Whatever happened we'll figure it out," he assured her. He couldn't understand how a human could smell like a wolf, but a few months ago he'd been around wolves, who through pharmaceutical means, could hide their wolf, scenting as humans. Perhaps she'd been injected with something similar? "I need to know what exactly you were working on. Sounds pretty important if these vampires were willing to risk going after you out in the open like they did."

Wynter wrenched herself out of his arms and wrapped her arms around herself. She knew he wouldn't like what she was about to tell him. As much as she wanted to tell him everything, her loyalty was to Jax. Her Alpha had first rights to access the intelligence she'd gleaned in her captivity.

"I want to tell you. But…I can't," she said softly. "Jax. I have to talk to him first."

Logan's stomach clenched at the mention of the New York Alpha. He had to know. "Do you belong to him?"

Wynter slowly turned around and gave him a sorrowful frown. "Yes."

As the word left her lips, she wished in that moment it wasn't true. There was something about Logan. She wanted so badly to tell him everything. Her attraction to the gentle wolf couldn't be denied. But she owed Jax her life and her allegiance. Maybe after she talked to Jax, she could explore the budding feelings she had for the New Orleans' Alpha. But now was not the time. No, out of respect for Jax, she needed to speak with him first.

Logan blew out a breath. Needing to put distance between them, he returned to his desk and sat down. He leaned back and stared up at the ceiling, trying to concentrate. If she thought she could tell him that there was something nefarious going on in his city and simply walk away from him, she was surely delusional. The next question he was about to ask was critical to how he'd proceed with regards to her and his investigation.

"Are you his mate?" He held his breath, awaiting her response.

She froze. Jax's mate? She lived with Jax, wore his scent even. But she'd never revealed the true nature of her relationship with Jax to anyone. She and Jax agreed that it would be best if she lived with him, kept others in the dark. He assured her that that would be the only way she'd be protected under his care. Despite the fact that they'd agreed upon it in the past, she couldn't lie to Logan.

"I'm not his mate," she responded, not quite meeting his eyes. *Please, no more questions.* "Logan, I know you don't know me, but I'm begging you. You know how this works. He's my Alpha. What I worked on…it was with Jax's knowledge and approval. I knew what I was getting into or at least I thought I did," she huffed. *Yeah, I knew exactly what I was doing right up until I couldn't leave the compound and became dinner for the guards.* "I need to talk with Jax first. That's how it has to be. You know protocol."

Fuck protocol. He wanted the goddamned truth. But he knew she was right. If she'd been one of his wolves, working for him, she wouldn't be allowed to discuss business with another Alpha. That being said, New Orleans was his city and if Jax wanted answers, wanted her, he had to go through him.

Steepling his fingers, he pinned her with a hard stare. He suspected by the way she carefully responded that she was concealing the true nature of their relationship. Now why was that? If she was his girlfriend, why not just tell him? Maybe because he could have easily fucked her on his desk two minutes ago and she wasn't at all resisting. The scent of her arousal was overwhelming. But if she wasn't his mate, her attraction to another male shouldn't have mattered to her or Jax. No, it actually would have been expected. All wolves played the field, quite unfaithfully, until they found their mate.

So why all the secrecy? Deliberately, he'd let her think she'd won this round of questioning. Logan was determined to influence her into spilling every last secret including her darkest fantasies. But first, he needed to lay down some ground rules. Ah yes, rules were great fun especially when you got to make them.

"Sit down, Wynter," he ordered. She obeyed without question. It was evident to him she'd been around wolves long enough to understand it was in her best interest to listen to an Alpha. "Until Jax gets here, you are under my protection. And I assure you, you will be safe with me. But I've got a few rules."

Wynter should have known this was coming; Alphas and their rules. It was as if she was home. Oddly, she felt relief knowing that for at least now, she'd be safe from ViroSun. She was certain that they'd be looking for her. They'd want their research finished.

As she looked up to Logan, she was surprised to see him

smiling. She couldn't help but give him a small smile in return. What was he thinking? The rules, of course.

"What? Is something funny?" she asked.

"The rules," he continued, ignoring her question. If she was going to stay with him, he might as well have fun with her until she submitted to him fully. As soon as Jax landed, he planned to have a very long conversation with him about his lovely little wolf. "I don't have many, but these two you must follow without question. First, you will not leave my home or office alone. Ever. If for some reason I'm not available, my beta, Dimitri will be. In spite of whatever happened with you two this morning, he'll protect you with his life."

"Yes, don't leave alone…got it," she repeated, uneasy with how happy the thought of spending more time with Logan made her. This first rule would not be hard to follow, because she was scared to death that they'd come after her again.

"Whoever was keeping you captive may decide to kidnap you back. And I'm going to need your help finding the place where they kept you last. I'm guessing they've already made themselves scarce, but after we talk to Kade, we'll check it out."

She nodded in agreement.

"Second rule. I expect honesty. By taking you into my home, I'm assuming responsibility for your safety based upon the little information I have. But I will not put my pack at risk, you understand?"

"But I already told you there are some things I can't tell you," she interrupted.

"Yes. Protocol. I'm well aware about why you prefer to talk to your Alpha first. But other than that, no lies. I'm not playing games."

Wynter bristled at his tone. "I'm hardly playing games. You do realize that it was me who just spent two months imprisoned?"

"Sweetheart, I get it, but remember you're the one withholding info, not me. But I'm not worried. Very soon, I'm confident you'll trust me with all your clandestine secrets and desires," Logan predicted, giving her a sexy smile.

"Um, we'll see," she commented, returning his smile.

Wynter flushed, embarrassed by his insinuation. *Desires.* It had been forever since she'd had sex. Until last night, she'd nearly forgotten she was a woman. Being around Logan was like going from drought to flood. She stared at his lips, remembering the soft way he kissed her wrist and squeezed her legs together. A familiar ache between her thighs overwhelmed her. Taking a deep breath, she shifted in her seat and crossed her legs, attempting unsuccessfully to relieve her arousal.

Those sensual lips of his...on her skin. What would he taste like? As soon as the thought popped into her head, she tensed. If she didn't get it together, she'd be in his lap in two seconds, taking her fill of him. No, she needed to concentrate on something else. *Virus.* Ah yes, that thought dulled her desire. *They'd come for her...slice into her skin, stealing her blood.* That single thought was like having a bucket of ice cold water dumped over her head.

Logan sat quietly watching a wide range of emotions play across her face. His little wolf was terribly aroused but then within seconds he could tell she was thinking of something else, something scary perhaps. Best keep her on her toes. Perhaps he'd learn the entire truth before Jax got here. If he could get her to trust him, she'd break. It wouldn't take much, he reasoned.

"Well, now that that is settled, here. Call him." He took the phone on his desk and turned it toward her. It would matter little if she spoke to Jax. She had to know that with his exceptional hearing, he'd be able to hear what she was telling him.

"I can call Jax?" she asked, surprised he was allowing her to call home.

"Be quick though because I'm hungry," he instructed. He swiveled his chair, focusing his attention to his laptop screen.

"Hungry?"

"Yes. Time for lunch. And while I'd be quite satisfied eating in…just you and me, alone here in my office, I suspect things would be safer if we went out for lunch, if you know what I mean," he quipped.

"Uh, yeah. Lunch. Out would be best." She gave him a small smile, understanding his meaning. She shook her head, trying to ignore his comment and began to dial. *Eat in…or eat her?* Had he pushed further, she suspected she'd let him eat wherever or whatever he wanted. It frightened and excited her. She was finding it hard to think clearly around him as the thought of her spread out on his desk,

Logan feasting on her, popped into her mind. Before she could fantasize any further, Jax answered. The voice of her Alpha startled and calmed her all at once. Her eyes darted over to Logan as she made contact.

As suspected, Wynter had revealed few clues during her brief phone call with Jax. Logan suspected the New York Alpha knew he was listening and had kept the call short on purpose. From the brief conversation, Logan had failed to learn the extent of her relationship with him. He'd heard Jax call her the term of endearment 'princess'. *Close friends perhaps? Lovers?* It bothered him that he cared so much about even knowing the status. It shouldn't matter...yet it did.

Logan had been single for well over a hundred years, and he wasn't about to jeopardize his pack over a woman. It wasn't as if he didn't plan on making love to her; no, it was quite the opposite. As long as she wasn't Jax's mate, she was available. But considering her secretive nature, he wasn't about to start a sexual relationship without her full submission and disclosure.

Regardless of the lack of information exchanged during the call, Logan noticed that Wynter was visibly more relaxed as she hung up the receiver. He supposed the voice of her Alpha had assuaged any apprehensions she'd had about him coming for her. It was a shame that she'd leave him so soon, possibly even tomorrow if Jax managed a flight. Deciding to make the most of the afternoon, Logan stood and silently ushered her out of his office. Nodding to his secretary and Dimitri, he smiled as the elevator doors opened.

As they descended, Logan glanced at Wynter, wondering if whatever little nugget she was keeping to herself had the potential to destroy the peaceful coexistence they'd cultivated between vampires and wolves. His gut told him there was far more complexity to the situation than met the eye. With or without her help, he intended to scratch the surface, carving it wide open, exposing the organization that had held her captive. He was deeply troubled that even a few vampires were caught torturing, running down a human or wolf. Like with roaches, when you found just a few, you could be certain that you had an infestation. And Logan planned on carrying out a thorough extermination.

Chapter Six

The Directeur watched the Alpha lead his beloved *feminine scientifique* into the crowd. As he suspected, the beta followed as did a few other wolves. What little they knew. Try as they might, they couldn't keep her from him forever. No, she was his to command as he wished. The little fool thought she could escape him by running? Perhaps she was able to weasel her way out of the physical structure, but the city itself had walls. She'd go nowhere without him.

The Directeur was amused that they thought they could avoid his touch. The dimwitted wolves would never see his great Stratégie coming. And the vampires were far too arrogant to see their weaknesses, let alone acknowledge them. He considered the witches. Surely they thought they were above it all with their potions and spells. But they, too, would have their due. There needed to be limits. Discipline. Too long he'd waited on the sidelines.

When the Mistress had approached him, he'd sworn his allegiance. Beautiful, brilliant and deadly, she was far superior a being than anyone he'd ever met. And now he served at her side, creating the Stratégie. He had to admit she was correct about choosing his historic city as the premier location for the attack. There were far more supernaturals centrally located in New Orleans than any other city on the East Coast.

In truth, the Directeur thoroughly enjoyed creating. He fancied himself an artiste. For too long, Kade, Marcel and Ilsbeth, the witch, had enjoyed their shared ownership of his city. His patience wore thin as he cultivated a picture of an avant-garde New Orleans. Under his direction, he'd transform the city into the vanguard of supernatural supremacy. Soon he'd drag his wide brush of destruction across the city, until whitewash covered every surface. Then he'd paint his masterpiece.

His dick grew hard as he imagined his coronation. Sucking a breath, he ducked into an alley to adjust himself. He wished there was time to relieve the pressure, but he needed to focus on the task at hand. The little bitch. Yes, that is why he was here. To keep watch. Soon, he'd seize the opportunity to take her.

Noticing how they surrounded her, it became obvious to him that the Alpha was aware of the precious nature of his commodity. Indeed, they thought they could protect her, even in the open streets? Interesting, he thought. Why, indeed, would the Alpha take such a liking to the scientifique? Perhaps she'd told him what she'd been working on? And by now, her illness would have set in, taking root in her DNA. A wolf claiming to be a human? Unheard of; he'd think she was insane. And the stories of viruses? Well, she could have been working for anyone in the country. They'd never find the lab, and she knew it. Of course, it'd been moved. She knew their methods and processes. Any breach in security warranted relocation. They frequently moved locations, never staying in one home or city for very long. They couldn't risk discovery.

She laughed at something the Alpha said, and he seethed. She knew her blood was his. Her pleasure and pain were his as well. Breathing deeply, he smiled at the old man playing the trumpet and tossed a twenty into his plastic jar. He stood a mere fifty feet from the Alpha and as usual, went unsuspected. So perfect was his place within New Orleans society, they'd never suspect him. Delightfully ignored, he sat at the French Market bar and flirted shamelessly with the lovely barkeep. He stole a glance as the scientifique blushed. How dare the little slut wantonly bat her eyelashes at the Alpha?

The Directeur laughed out loud, watching as his feminine scientifique stood to leave with the Alpha. Silently, he vowed to inflict the harshest of punishments on her. The betrayal stung his cold dark heart. Not only had she lied when she began her employment, now she appeared to be taken with Reynaud, throwing herself at him. Perhaps he'd whip her mercilessly, drain and fuck her before setting her pretty feet back in the lab where she belonged. Ah, he wished he could do all that and more, but the Mistress would never allow it. No, the Mistress was so much more disciplined than anyone he'd ever known. Work came first over earthly desires without a doubt.

No bother, he'd wait. Soon, she'd finish her project, perfectly as expected. Then he'd have her all to himself as the reward he deserved. The Mistress would allow it then. As long as he didn't kill his scientifique, the Mistress would let him play with his toy. With the Alpha finally out of sight, the Directeur made the decision to remain in the quaint café. Invigorated by his reconnaissance, he slipped through the back entrance to the kitchen in search of his barmaid. As usual, the meek human never sensed his approach. With his hand over her mouth, no one heard the stifled scream as his fangs stabbed into her neck.

Chapter Seven

"She's lying," Logan commented, watching Wynter through the sliding glass door. Her lithe smooth legs bounced in the azure pool water. He wished he could see more of her but she insisted on wearing that damn cover-up. The sheer pink fabric strained tightly against her breasts; her erect nipples pressed through the small black triangles of her bikini top.

"Yep." Dimitri popped a potato chip into his mouth, admiring the new womanly fauna that had recently been added to their courtyard.

"She won't tell me everything I need to know."

"No surprise there." He bit another chip, unable to look away.

"I should send her to stay with Fiona."

"Most definitely."

"But look at those legs," Logan growled.

"Yes, indeed."

"And her breasts. Just so, so...perfect."

"Hell yeah," Dimitri concurred, watching her sun herself.

Logan shot him a glare. "My breasts."

"Whatever you say, Alpha." He smiled and raised an eyebrow. He didn't want to burst Logan's bubble, but they both knew she belonged to Jax. "So why are you in here and she's out there?"

"D, don't get me wrong. I know I shouldn't want her. But there's just something about her. I can't put my finger on it." Logan ignored the question and took a drink of his sweet tea. He really wished that she didn't fascinate him so much; things would be much easier. He sighed. "She's just. Well, I don't know. I just want her."

"And the problem is?"

"Technically, she belongs to Jax," he explained, adjusting his growing arousal. He watched with great anticipation as she slowly pushed up the sheer fabric, revealing her belly button. She was killing him.

"Mated?"

"No."

"Again…the problem is?" Damn, his Alpha was in big trouble if this creature had him tied up so badly. Amused with the situation, he grinned.

"It's complicated…ugh, will you look at her? Just take that pink thing off already," Logan groaned as she fingered the edges.

"Can't stop lookin' at her. And what's complicated? She's, um, a wolf; I think. Anyway it doesn't matter, bro. She's definitely *all* female."

"I told you. Jax didn't claim her but she told me that she belongs to him. She's loyal to him," he bit out.

"In what way does she belong to him exactly? You know that doesn't really matter…except for the protocol. If they're not mates, then it's lady's choice when it comes to sex," Dimitri reminded him. "What else?"

"Secrets. I don't like it."

"But you like her?"

"I said it was complicated." Logan shrugged.

"Nothin' complicated about those legs," Dimitri laughed. "Nothin' at all. I bet they're quite flexible even."

Logan growled in response.

"Just sayin'."

"Being Alpha isn't always easy, you know. It can be very hard as a matter of fact," Logan commented.

"Sometimes when things are hard, it can feel really good." He wagged his eyebrows at Logan.

"Nice mouth, D." The frustrated Alpha began to undress in front of him. "I've gotta check on her."

"And you're in here with me because?" He left his question open ended waiting on Logan's response.

"Because my beta, we're letting her relax. Building trust," he explained. "And then, my friend, after that, it's time to ease the truth out of our new guest."

"I see. And how do you plan to do that?" Dimitri glanced out once again to admire the lovely she-wolf lounging on their patio.

"Watch and learn," Logan told him, tossing his shirt and pants onto the sofa.

"Yeah, okay, Alpha," Dimitri laughed. He surmised that if anyone could get control of the situation, it would be

Logan, even if that entailed getting up close and personal.

Dimitri admired how his Alpha wielded his confidence and charm like a sword. Even during the tensest of interactions, the wolf never lost his cool. Damn if his Alpha didn't have some moves, and he reckoned he probably could learn a few tricks from the master. Dimitri laughed as he watched Logan stroll out the door buck naked. Whether this went well or not, it would be entertaining.

Wynter nervously tugged at the suit she'd borrowed from the pool house. What man kept a stock of women's bikinis in his pool house anyhow? A playboy. A hotter than hell, sexy Alpha playboy. One with the bluest eyes she'd ever seen and an easygoing personality that made her want to cuddle into his lap like a purring kitten. She sighed, supposing she shouldn't let herself go there. This was only temporary. As soon as Jax arrived, she knew she'd be whisked back to New York City and reality would commence. She loved the urban scene of the Big Apple but she couldn't help but notice how the quaint French Quarter seemed to speak to her soul. When they'd returned from lunch, she was surprised to see how lovely the courtyard was in the daylight. Complete with ferns, flowers, fountain, pool and hot tub, the entire back yard screamed relaxation.

Captivity had made her both claustrophobic and pale, so the sunshine bred a sense of vitality back into her heart. Logan must have sensed her craving as he suggested she go for a swim. She wished she was stronger to refuse the gift but she just wasn't. Nearly jumping with excitement, she happily took him up on his offer and was even more delighted when he offered her a suit. She supposed that he skinny-dipped, being the wolf that he was. But being the very human she was, or at least thought she was, a suit was a welcome addition.

Wynter swore she could literally feel the cells in her body healing as she basked in the afternoon sun. The cool pool water splashing her feet offered the perfect complement to the stones beneath her towel which emanated heat onto her back. Maybe not heaven but it was damn close to it, she thought. As she soaked up the sun, her thoughts wandered to the conversation she'd had with Logan at lunch. Admittedly, she'd been scared being out in the open where they could find her, but Logan had assured her she was safe with him. Every time she nervously looked around, he'd placed a calming hand to her shoulder, reminding her that she was no longer alone, protected. Not once did he ever raise his voice or make her feel like she'd done something wrong. Even though he knew she hadn't told him everything, he didn't press. Rather, he'd kept the conversation light, asking her where she went to school, her favorite colors, foods and movies. Breakfast at Tiffany's, she told him. And he didn't laugh but instead asked if maybe she'd like to watch it with him sometime after the drama was over.

If she hadn't known any better, she'd have thought she was on a first date. She laughed to herself, realizing how crazy it seemed. But she couldn't deny her gravitation toward the wolf. Logan was undoubtedly the most charismatic man she'd ever met. Both witty and assured, he appeared to approach life with a cool confidence. Yet he wasn't arrogant or demanding. She was finding it difficult to shake off her body's reaction to how he'd tasted her in his office. She'd wanted him to go further but he hadn't. He kept her on the edge of sexual tension all afternoon, and she found herself hoping he'd touch her again, kiss her.

Wynter groaned at the thought. Jax would kill her. While she'd on occasion found a wolf attractive, Jax would have gone ballistic if she'd asked to date within his pack. If he only knew the lustful thoughts that bantered about in her mind, he'd have a fit. She loved him so much, but as Logan pointedly asked, she was not his mate. Jax had to know she couldn't go on forever living with him. Yet she owed him her loyalty and respect. She'd given him her commitment to see her mission through to the end. And while she was no longer working in the lab, she also wasn't finished.

Her thoughts wandered back to Logan and she smiled. He'd been incredibly dominant and sexy in his business suit earlier. And the night before when he'd held her so tenderly, she'd wondered what it would feel like for him to run his hands all over her skin. The possibility that she could maybe have a relationship with him thrilled her; even if it was just a fantasy. Maybe after the mess with ViroSun was cleared up, she could come back down to New Orleans. She admonished herself for even getting her hopes up; the chances were slim that Jax would simply accept her desire to see Logan again.

With her being human, Jax wouldn't hear of it. She'd have to convince him somehow that she could make this decision on her own, but she knew it wouldn't be easy.

Logan quietly padded out of the house. While he prided himself on knowing how to move stealthily in the most dangerous of situations, he hoped she'd scent him right away. Yet Wynter seemed oblivious to his movement. It seemed strange that she didn't even notice him. Most wolves would have immediately reacted. He slowly waded into the water, never taking his eyes off of her. He could hear from her heartbeat that she wasn't quite sleeping; day dreaming perhaps? Time to wake his little wolf.

Wynter startled at the sound of a splash. She quickly pushed up onto her elbows and scanned the area but didn't see anyone. Just as she was about to recline, she caught sight of the most glorious vision she'd ever seen. *Oh. My. God. Logan.* Before her eyes, his six foot five, tanned, muscular body rose from the water like a dripping hot Greek God. Stunned and captivated, she watched as the beads of water rolled off his smooth skin. Unable to control the impulse, her eyes roamed over his wet body from his broad muscular shoulders to the hard ridges of his abdomen. The very smallest dusting of hair trailed down into the water, where she was quite certain she'd find him naked.

Logan laughed out loud at her reaction, snapping her attention back to his face. He shook his shaggy hair and water sprayed all over her legs. She flinched slightly but didn't look away. He was simply the most magnificent male she'd ever seen. Immediately, she pulled her legs together, as desire rushed to her belly. She didn't need an expert to tell her the shark in the water was hungry. She knew he was dangerous, ravenous for his next meal. And oh how she wanted to be bitten. At a loss for words, she returned his smile, waiting for him to speak.

Logan watched her take in the sight of him and tried so very hard to ignore the signs of her arousal. He found it amusing the way she tightened her thighs together in an effort to remain composed. *Ah yes, little wolf, the Alpha knows what you want, but will you give it to me? Let's see where this takes us.* Smiling, he approached slowly and smoothly, making her wonder what he'd do next.

He enjoyed keeping her on her toes. And now that she'd had time to relax, to be lulled into a false sense of security, he intended to take advantage. As his cock jerked, he wondered, though, who was going to take advantage of who. The closer he got to her, the harder he had to deliberately keep himself from ripping off her clothes and sinking into her sweet heat. Needing to touch her, he placed his hands on her knees. She did nothing to stop him. He could almost feel the electricity sizzle as his cold hands touched her hot skin.

"Ah," she moaned, not exactly protesting.

"Enjoying the sun?" Logan asked softly. His hands held tight to her knees, not moving.

"Yes. It feels so good. The sun…I needed this."

"I see you found the suits Fi brought you," he acknowledged. He'd arranged for clothing to be sent while they'd been at lunch.

"Thank you. I really appreciate everything you've done. I don't know how I can repay you for helping me." *Ah, so that's where all the new suits came from.* Wynter knew it was silly but she felt relieved to know that he'd brought bikinis to his pool house just for her.

"Just showing you a little southern hospitality is all. I've got lots of things to show you as a matter of fact," he laughed.

"I just bet you do," she flirted. "And something tells me that I'd like to see them."

"Well, I'm sure that can be arranged after we're done with our business."

"Yes, that." The reference to business dulled the ache between her legs considerably. How could she forget?

"I got a text from Jax," he mentioned nonchalantly. "He can't get down here tonight. Looks like he'll be here tomorrow at the earliest."

"Why not?" she asked, concerned he wasn't going to come for her. She was about to get up but Logan held her still, placing his palms on the tops of her thighs.

"Snow. Airport's closed. No flights in, no flights out," he explained in a calm voice. "But don't worry; I told him that I'll take good care of you."

"I'm sure you will," Wynter replied sarcastically. And wouldn't she just love it, she thought.

He smiled broadly. Truth was that he wasn't a damn bit upset that Jax was delayed. It gave him more time to get to know Wynter and hopefully, find out what secrets she held.

"In the meantime, we're meeting with some vamps tonight."

Her face went white with fear. Too soon. They'd take her. As much as she wanted to trust Logan, there was no way she could be around another vampire.

"Hey there. It's okay," he coaxed, caressing her skin. "Come on, look at me, Wynter."

She complied, meeting his eyes. Once again tears threatened to fall. "You don't know…what they did. I can't go back."

"I told you that you're safe with me. No one will get to you while you are in my protection. Do you understand?" he asked calmly. *What did they do to her?* He'd seen the bite marks, but hadn't delved any deeper. A serious expression washed over his face. "I would never put you in danger. Ever."

A tear ran down her face as she struggled to maintain contact with the powerful Alpha. She wanted to trust him, but it was so very difficult after everything that had happened.

"Listen sweetheart, I don't know what happened to you…what they did to you, but I promise to stop whatever's happening. Do you remember?" He had to ask. In a low, soft voice he proceeded, trying to be as nonthreatening as possible. "You can tell me…what they did to you. The bite marks…I saw them. They're mostly on your arms, but there were a few on your legs…your thighs."

Wynter closed her eyes and then opened them slowly. She'd thought long and hard about her periods of unconsciousness. "I wasn't raped," she stated definitively. "That is something I'd know. But everything else…"

She'd been violated. Bled. Infected. She looked away from him, embarrassed that she even had to discuss it.

Logan waited for her to finish. He wanted to hold and hide her so that no one could ever hurt her again, but he needed her to open up to him.

"There were times in the beginning...the guards...they fed on me. I was conscious. But then they stopped because the blood loss made it hard for me to work...I couldn't think straight. They eventually figured out it was slowing my progress," she recalled with disgust. "So they stopped...for the most part. If I refused to work, they'd attack me...shove me against my cot...their fangs." She rubbed her arms, reliving the pain.

Logan deliberately calmed himself. He detested the bloodsucking demons he'd met over the years. Yes, most vampires were mainly well integrated within society. But some vampires skated the edge of morality, often justifying the torture they inflicted on their victims. He refocused on Wynter, absorbing every detail she shared.

"The bottom line is that there are missing time periods. I don't remember. Did they bleed me? Yes. Did they infect me with something...change me? I was human. Now look at me," she pleaded. "I don't know what they did...I don't know what I am...I don't know..." Her words trailed off as she shook her head in frustration.

"I'm sorry," Logan told her sincerely. "I don't know what they did to you either, but I promise you that we'll find out."

"I don't know, Logan. This was my responsibility. It's so

messed up," she confessed.

"Right now, you're safe. And we're going to work things out. Now, of course, it would be a whole lot easier if you'd tell me everything, but I get that you need time with Jax. I may be new to this Alpha gig, but I assure you that I've been a wolf a very long time. I know protocol. Been livin' and breathin' it for over a hundred years. The last thing I want to do is get you in trouble with your Alpha. In the meantime, we're meeting with Kade Issacson tonight. Yes, he's a vampire. And as hard as it is to believe, he is one of the good guys. I hate to have to drag you there with me, but I can't leave you alone, and this can't wait."

Wynter pursed her lips, unsure that any vampires could be anything less than vicious. But she wanted to trust him. "You're sure? You're sure the vampires won't attack me?"

Logan laughed, "Questioning the Alpha, huh? Seems we're going to have to work on those pack skills of yours."

Wynter gave him a small smile in return. "Ha, ha. Funny wolf."

"And you, too, are a wolf."

"So you say."

"And that is what counts. Hey, I want to tell you a story."

"A story, huh?"

"Yes. A story," he confirmed. "A few months ago in Philadelphia, my Alpha met his mate, Kalli. The interesting thing about Kalli is that she's a lovely little hybrid, but at one time, she denied her wolf. And in the process, she just happened to invent this nasty little drug that essentially masked her scent and stopped her from shifting."

"So if she took the drug you would think she was a human?"

"Exactly." Logan let his hands wander down to her calves as he spoke. Goddess, she felt so good.

"And do you think that is happening to me? Maybe they drugged me?"

"Well, if you were human and now you are wolf, they did something. A drug? Maybe. The drug she created? No. But my point is that there're always things in this world that we don't understand. People will always push the frontier of what we think is possible. Biology. Nature. It's always changing. Slowly but changing. And like what Kalli did, supernaturals and humans are finding ways to accelerate the process regardless of whether it's the right thing to do."

If you only knew, she thought guiltily.

"I'm Alpha for a reason, Wynter. Like Jax, I've been around a long time. I'm not going to sugarcoat what I sense, what I know. You may have been human when you started but I can tell you with certainty that you're wolf now. I don't know how they did it or why they did it, but it's who you are."

Wynter stared off, refusing to verbally acknowledge what he was saying. Deep inside, she knew he was right. Her recovery, even since this morning, had been accelerated, deviating far from what would be considered normal for a human. She was feeling good. No, not just good but excellent. As a scientist, she knew there was no logical reason to explain it. After being bitten and chased, it should take her days to recuperate.

"Look at your skin," he urged, rubbing his hands up her shins until he reached her thighs. Gently placing his hands on her knees, he parted her legs and moved toward her until the insides of her thighs straddled his sides. His fingertips teased the small strings that barely held her bikini bottoms together. *Ah, finally got her attention,* he thought with amusement.

Wynter had barely been listening to his words when she felt him open her legs. At his intrusion, she snapped her focus back on his eyes, not moving but simply watching him as he grazed his palms up over the tops of her thighs until he reached her hips. She didn't try to stop him; she wanted his hands on her skin. Her eyes locked on his as his big strong hands skimmed over her body, flaring her arousal. *What was he saying? Something about her skin?*

"That's it," she heard him say. "Look at your skin. It's healed."

The bite marks were healed. Small pink spots were the only evidence that anything had happened to her.

"I know. I feel it," she admitted.

"Yes, I'm sure you do. I know you're scared. But it's going to be okay. Tell me, what do you know about being wolf?" His hands roamed upward. Goddess, her legs were smooth and silky, begging to be touched. He kept going, pushing the pink fabric upward.

Lifting her arms, Wynter let him remove the sheer barrier that covered her skin. Part of her wanted this, him. Moreover, she yearned to reveal her body and soul to this man, hating to keep secrets from the Alpha who sought to help her. He tossed the fabric aside, and she gasped as he tugged her into the water against him. Her smooth belly met his rock hard abs, and she really thought she might pass out from the rush.

"I…I grew up around a pack," she confessed.

Logan brushed his lips to her hair, resisting the urge to kiss her. Gently, he cradled her in his arms, letting her float along the surface. She held his gaze, never looking anywhere but to him.

"Let go, Wynter. Trust me?" he smiled down on her.

She was helpless to resist. Having no idea what he was doing, she gave in to her desires. "Yes."

"Relax. Let yourself go. I promise to keep you safe."

Wynter willed herself to go limp within his incredibly strong arms. And even though she knew better than to let a wolf touch her, she reveled in the experience of trusting him. As she closed her eyes and the cool water washed over her, every nerve lit on fire with need. In spite of the heat, she opened her hands, her thighs, until she was completely relaxed. And all the while, he never let her go. He adjusted his hold, carefully supporting her upper back and bottom with his hands.

"That's it. You're so beautiful. So calm and at peace," he crooned softly. "Like this, we'll talk about wolves. Tell me about your pack, what do you know?"

"I grew up around wolves. My parents worked with the pack…for Jax. I…I wasn't allowed around the pack that much when I got older. They were afraid I'd get hurt but I knew it'd never happen. My friend, Mika. She's a wolf," she said proudly.

"Okay, so our behavior. Our habits. You must have seen something." Logan watched her soft pink lips break out in a broad smile at his words.

"Ah yes. Wolves. Well, you like to run on a full moon. I never got to see them but I knew."

"That is true. What else?"

"Wolves are competitive. Mika's an alpha. Hates when she loses to me at tennis." She laughed, remembering their last match. "She breaks quite a few racquets. It's actually kind of funny. Good thing she makes a lot of money working at that law firm."

Logan shook his head at the thought. "Sounds delightful."

"She's okay, just a little short tempered is all. Never with me, though. She gets mad at herself. Which brings me to my next observation," she continued. "Loyal. Wolves are very loyal to their friends, their pack."

"That's correct. See, this wolf thing is going to be easy for you." He noticed she frowned at his comment. He kept pushing to distract her from her thoughts. "What else?"

Wynter tried to keep her face impassive as the next idea popped into her head. Considering an incredibly hot wolf was holding her against his bare skin, she reasoned it should have been the first thing she told him.

"Come on then. It can't be that bad," Logan commented as she hesitated to answer him.

"Naked." Her eyes flew open and met his. She giggled. "They love being naked."

"Yes we do. Clothes are very restrictive. Highly overrated."

"I can see that you practice what you preach."

"And how do you feel about that? Does it embarrass you?" He queried as his fingers wandered to the knotted strings tightened against her back.

"I'm not sure how I feel. I mean, it's not like I was allowed to run around naked. I just knew they did. Jax wouldn't be crazy about me doing it though. Not fair really. A double standard I suppose. Believe me; I think the whole pack would freak out if I decided to join them."

"I understand how you are worried about what your pack would think but how do you feel?" He pulled on the strings, releasing the knot. The cords floated freely in the water, no longer tied.

Wynter felt his fingers move along her back. It was if she could actually feel the coolness wash over the skin that had been covered by the small strap. With the tension loosened, her top drifted easily across her breasts but didn't fall away.

"I think…I think it'd be freeing," she whispered, aware of the message she was conveying. Oh God, she wanted him.

"Are you sure?" he asked, seeking her approval. His fingers traveled up to her neck, pinching the remaining knot that held tight around her neck.

"Yes," she breathed. "Yes, I'm sure. Please." She released a small gasp as he tugged the cord free and the flimsy material floated away. Her nipples hardened at the thought of Logan seeing her this way.

Logan didn't think his cock could get any harder but he was wrong. The sight of her gorgeous, perfect breasts nearly made him drop her. He ran his fingers through her wet hair then slowly trailed them across her throat. Skimming his fingertips down the valley of her chest, he stopped to rest his palm upon her belly.

"You're incredible. So, so beautiful, Wynter." He couldn't take his eyes off her face. She was struggling with her own arousal. And selfishly, he considered whether he should make love to her right there in the pool. But she needed to learn from him, not just pleasure but what it would mean for her to be wolf.

"Logan, please," she moaned, closing her eyes.

"Breathe, baby. You're doing so well. Relaxing. Almost naked," he joked.

"Almost," she agreed. She opened her eyes and gave him a sensual smile.

"You sure? Once you go wolf, you never go back."

"Yes, stop teasing me," she cried. She wanted his fingers on her, in her. What was he doing?

With great restraint, Logan slipped his fingers into the side of her bikini bottoms, ever so gently gliding his fingers across her hip. Effortlessly, he tugged the strings on one side then the other. As the panties floated away, no barrier existed between them. *Goddess almighty, she was exquisite.* He wanted so badly to take her. From her reaction, he knew it'd be easy. He watched her chest heave up and down in anticipation of his touch. But in the moment, he was certain he'd never be satisfied with having just part of her. He needed the truth. Craved it.

Overwhelmed with arousal, Wynter moaned loudly in

protest when he removed his hands. Why wasn't he touching her? Didn't he find her desirable? *Oh God, she was naked in a pool with the New Orleans Alpha. Jax was going to freak out if he found out.* Her heart began to race with worry.

"Little wolf, you need to stop thinking so much. Lay back and relax into the water. I've got you, now. Just listen to my voice," Logan told her. His patience was of far greater strength than his libido. He wanted to fuck her, but it would be on his terms not hers. "That's it, just breathe....in and out. Hear the sounds around you. Smell the scents in the air. Soon, little wolf, you'll be born into your new life."

Obeying him came naturally as she forced herself to listen to his calm voice. Despite her water-filled ears, the sounds became louder. The more she concentrated, the more she heard. Music played in the distance. A car horn honked. Footsteps echoed on the pavement, coming closer and closer. Wynter's eyes flashed open to Logan's and then she rapidly turned her head, seeking the source. Dimitri. Her cheeks heated in embarrassment.

"Please," she croaked, trying to sit up and cover herself. Logan brushed a calming hand over her hair and her eyes caught his.

"It's okay. I'm here with you, baby. Holding you. Protecting you. It's just Dimitri. He's wolf. And by the way he's looking at you, I'd say that he agrees that you're every bit as amazing as I think you are."

"But I…I…don't know," she protested.

Logan nodded to Dimitri who continued walking and eventually entered his home.

"Whatever you feel, it's natural. Even arousal, it's what we are."

Wynter didn't want to talk about what she felt; it was wrong, dirty. She was so horny; that had to be why she'd felt so aroused when Dimitri looked upon her bareness. She wasn't really attracted to him, yet she'd reacted. And Logan, he simply drove her mad with need. Skin to skin, her proximity to him overloaded her senses. Her pussy ached for him, yet he made no attempt to kiss or touch her. She struggled to find the words to tell him how she felt.

"Please Logan," she groaned. "This is…I'm so…I feel…"

Logan knew exactly how she felt, and he felt the same. He reached across her body and caressed her slippery breast, finally giving in to the temptation. His cock throbbed, begging to be inside her as he watched her wriggle within his grasp. She moaned in response, and he slid his hand up her chest, settling it on her cheek. Running his thumb along the seam of her lips, her mouth parted at his touch, allowing his thumb to enter. She wrapped her lips around his finger as if she was sucking his cock. *Fuck, she was pushing him to the brink.* Logan sucked a breath at the feel of her simulating oral sex on his hand. He pulled his thumb out and spread the moisture on her lower lip. .

"What do you need, Wynter?" He knew he shouldn't touch her but Goddess; she was so responsive.

Wynter's eyes opened, meeting his. "I need you," she whispered.

Barely audible to human ears, her soft words were all he

needed to act. Sliding his hand to cradle the nape of her neck, he brought her to him and kissed her. Water sluiced downward as he pulled her tightly against him, hungrily taking his lips to hers.

Jolted upward, Wynter readily met Logan's lips, wrapping her legs around his waist. As his tongue pushed into hers, she thought she would melt away. Like a tight coil that had just been sprung, all her energy released into their embrace. Her hands raked into his damp hair. Clutching at him, she never wanted him to let her go. She writhed her slick mound against his abdomen, unable to reach the friction she sought. But the taste of him would have to sate her for now, because he didn't touch her there yet. So she simply let herself go, accepting whatever he'd give her.

At the first taste of her, Logan pressed Wynter up against the side of the pool. She tasted like the sweetest peach, so entirely ripe for him. She'd met his kiss with hunger, not fear, taking and giving. He couldn't remember the last time he'd felt an instinctive connection with a woman. It was as if her energy was pouring into his veins, heightening all his senses. Logan deepened the kiss, barely able to restrain himself from grabbing his shaft and thrusting it deep into her. He could feel her swollen folds below wriggling against the small nest of hair above his rigid flesh. It would be so easy to slip into her heat. But he swore that he wouldn't take her like this in the pool. No, when he took her for the first time, there'd be no secrets between them. She'd have to be as emotionally bare as she was physically.

A buzzer sounded faintly as he felt her wrap her small

fingers around his cock. "Fuck," he grunted at the feel of her touch. She was a fast little wolf, he thought. It felt so good, but this wasn't happening now. He grabbed her wrist, bringing it quickly to his chest and placed her palm flat against him.

The rush of desire flowed throughout Wynter's body. She was done waiting. Her whole life she'd been waiting for something, for someone to make her feel this way. It was as if she was coming alive for the very first time in her life. Animalistic. Wanton. Free. She couldn't get enough of Logan. As he kissed her, she gave into her instinct to take; reaching down between her own legs, she found his hard arousal. It felt enormous in her fingers. Desperately wanting to bring him pleasure, she stroked it up and down until he breathed a groan into her mouth. She felt his firm grip manacle around her own, denying her. *Why? Why was he stopping?* No, this couldn't be happening.

And as his lips pulled away from hers, she slumped forward, desperately trying to catch her breath, her sanity. Oh God, she'd done something wrong, she just knew it. But she didn't even care. She just wanted, yearned. Logan made her feel and she didn't want to go back to who she was.

Their foreheads pressed together, hearts beating frantically from their encounter. Slowly, they both opened their eyes, panting. Sensing his visitors, Logan retreated.

"Wynter," he breathed. How he'd managed to have enough control to remove her hand from his dick was beyond him. He seriously thought he'd have to go stick his cock in an ice bucket after this tryst. Painful as it was, this wasn't the time or place for their first time. But after that one kiss, he was quite certain that without a doubt, he planned on making love to her long and hard as soon as she revealed what she'd been really doing in New Orleans.

"Logan, I…I'm sorry…I shouldn't have." *I'm sorry? No I'm not.*

"No, don't lie, baby. Remember the rules," he reminded her with a brief kiss.

She laughed, still clutched onto him, their eyes mere inches from one another. "Okay, not sorry," she admitted.

Before she knew what was happening, Logan's hands were on her waist, hoisting her onto the edge of the pool into a sitting position. His eyes never leaving hers, he pulled a sun-warmed towel from behind her and covered her with it.

"Thank you," Wynter responded softly, somewhat shaken by their kiss.

"You're very welcome." Logan smiled then looked over his shoulder. *Company.*

Female voices jarred her connection with Logan, drawing her attention to two women who'd obviously been watching their interaction. Dimitri took the redheaded woman into his arms, kissing her on the lips. Obviously, they were more than friends. The other woman, dressed in a tight black pencil skirt and red bustier, with long black hair and bangs, stared at Wynter. Very Goth, Wynter noted, wondering if the women were also wolves. A hand to her knee brought her focus back to Logan.

"Why don't you go upstairs and relax for a while?

Fiona," Logan gestured over to the redhead, who appeared as a love child with her peasant skirt and wild curly hair. "She's going to help you get settled in."

Wynter's brow wrinkled at his suggestion.

"Hey, trust me, Fi's okay. She was here last night. She won't hurt you. You'll see. It'll all work out....now go. I'll see you in a few hours," he promised, and swam over to greet his guests.

Jealousy flared in her stomach as she watched Logan emerge from the water, exiting the pool, his sheer masculinity on display for all to see. To her dismay, both women turned their attention to his amazing body, letting their eyes roam all over him. *Who wouldn't look?* The man was utterly confident, good-looking and oh so very Alpha. Of course, he'd have women chasing him left and right.

That very second, reality came crashing down upon her. She wasn't in some fairytale where the girl got the prince. She was in serious fucking trouble with a major corporation who planned on dragging her sorry ass back to the lab to finish the abomination she'd started. And the gorgeous Alpha she'd been throwing herself at five minutes ago only wanted the information she held so he could protect his pack, not to mention that he probably had a different bitch warming his bed every night.

As she stood, she caught a glimpse of him wrapping a towel around his waist. The fabric tented, barely holding in place. Like a crushing blow to her gut, she watched as he took the Goth Chick into his arms and hugged her. The erection she gave him was touching another woman, and it sickened her to the core. Turning her head, she gathered her cover-up, and stood. Her bathing suit appeared to have sunk to the very bottom of the pool, and she had no intention of going in after it. Inaudibly to others, she swore that she heard something growl. *Was it her?*

This wolf thing was starting to get on her nerves. *Did she really have an animal inside of her?* Instead of letting fear rule her, she took a deep breath, closed her eyes and tried to picture a wolf, her wolf. *Where are you?* Wynter saw nothing and huffed in frustration. If she was a wolf, it was only a matter of time before she shifted. She knew from her friend how it worked. Somewhere inside her lurked the beast that would claw to the surface, and there wasn't a damn thing she'd be able to do about it. The wolf was part of the human and vice versa.

Either way, she was disgusted with herself and Logan. Disoriented and confused, she didn't understand what had just happened. Wynter could have sworn she'd felt something emotional between them in the pool, something other than just lust. But now? Now, he seemed quite content to rub the evidence of his arousal against a strange woman right in front of her. She steeled her nerves, feigning indifference, and casually walked toward the group. *Let the fun begin.*

Pulling the towel tightly around her, every muscle in her body tensed as she approached. Determined not to shatter, she tried to ignore her feelings. Her eyes darted over to Logan once again. No longer hugging, Goth Chick cupped his face, running her blood red fingernails down his cheek.

They seemed to be having an intense conversation, and she wondered if they were lovers.

"Hi there. Feeling better?" Wynter heard the redhead ask.

Tearing her eyes away from the sight of Logan and the other woman, she gave Red a tight smile. "Yes, much better. Fiona?"

"Yes," Fiona grabbed one of Wynter's hands, giving it a quick squeeze. She was holding a few large shopping bags. "Nice to see you looking better. We were worried about you last night. You were so sick but now I can see everything's just fine."

Fine? Really? So not fine. Not even close, Wynter thought.

Before Wynter had a chance to respond to Fiona, she glanced up to Dimitri who gave her a warm but knowing smile. "Looks like you got some sun. Enjoy your swim?"

She tried very hard not to roll her eyes at his smart assed question and settled on giving him a cool smile.

"Swim. Yeah. It was a great *swim. Swimming* is awesome," she said, shaking her head. Is that what wolves called it now? Did swimming equate to writhing naked against the hottest Alpha male she'd ever seen? These wolves seemed to know their way around euphemisms.

Dimitri laughed heartily at the feisty little wolf's response. She certainly looked to be getting hot and heavy with his Alpha. And now, her behavior was bordering on aggressive. Almost as if she was territorial. Interesting.

"Leave her alone, Dimitri," Fiona told him with a light swat to his shoulder. "Come on now, I'm sure your swim was quite lovely before we arrived. Are you ready to go get settled in your room?"

"Certainly," Wynter responded in an almost professional tone. As if she was compelled, she could not keep her eyes off Logan as Goth Chick proceeded to trail her talons down his bare shoulder, settling her palm on his chest. A hot anger surged from within and before she knew what she was doing, Wynter found herself walking. Easily squeezing her small but strong body between Logan and Goth Chick, she wrapped her arms around his waist and kissed him.

Logan had been arguing with Luci yet again. He'd meant to introduce the women but the disagreement became a priority as she insisted she had rights to stay with an Alpha, to stay with him in his French Quarter home. He'd explained that there was no way she was living with him. She had to stay in one of the pack apartments. Yet he'd cordially hugged her as always, aware that Wynter had been watching. Sure, he felt strongly about Wynter and planned to explore their relationship further. But he still didn't trust her, and it was best that he conduct business as usual. And Luci was business.

A split second passed before he registered what was happening. One minute Wynter was talking with Fiona and Dimitri and the next, she stalked toward him like a lioness on the prowl. As his eyes locked on hers, he soon found that in a role reversal, he was now prey. Wynter pushed Luci aside and pressed up against him, possessively taking his lips. He welcomed the warm feel of her tongue darting into his mouth. He'd almost forgotten they had an audience, putting on quite the show for his pack members. Never in his life had a female demonstrated this kind of alpha, dominant behavior toward him. And damn if it didn't turn him on even more. He knew he should break it off, tell her no, especially given that she'd done it in front of pack, but her sweet taste enthralled his senses. Vacillating between taking her to the bedroom and pushing her away, became unnecessary when without warning, she released him. She'd been the one to back away, yet still remained between him and Luci, looking directly into his eyes.

"Thanks for the *swim*, sweetheart," she purred, with a glare that conveyed both lust and anger. "See you tonight."

That would teach him, Wynter thought as she proceeded to walk around Logan. Remembering exactly the kind of determined woman she was, there was no man on this green Earth that was going to strip, feel and kiss her senseless and then rub himself onto another woman two minutes later. No damn way. For as long as she remained in this pack of his, she could either be a doormat or establish her role as an alpha female. She'd spent a lifetime of listening to what other people thought was best for her, and it was damn time she stood up for herself.

If Logan wanted Goth Chick, he could have her, but she'd be damned if she let him fawn all over her with her 'hard on'. No, that was her erection; she'd done that to him. She supposed she should be embarrassed, but as she opened the sliding glass door, she could have cared less. Let him think about that kiss, because it might be the last one he'd get from her if he thought he could use her like that. So not happening.

As Logan watched Fiona chase off after Wynter into the house, he looked over to his beta in disbelief over what had just happened. Dimitri gave him a big shit-eating grin, fully enjoying the performance. Luci, on the other hand, seethed, crossing her arms; clearly annoyed that another woman, not her, was living with the Alpha.

Logan shook his head. "D, get Luci settled, would ya? I've got some business to attend to."

"Yeah, I bet you do, Alpha," Dimitri laughed, pointing Luci toward the gate.

"Not funny."

"Good luck with that," he added, unable to resist teasing his Alpha. It was going to be fun to watch Logan handle the new female.

"Yeah, right." Logan turned his back to Dimitri and walked into the house. As he entered, he cocked his hand upward, giving him a wave. His beta was freakin' hilarious. And correct. Something in the back of his mind told him that he was going to need a hell of a lot more than luck to handle his little wolf. Oh yes, her territorial display had been very intriguing, indeed. Considering her behavior, he couldn't wait to see her wolf, and ultimately her submission would be the greatest prize he'd ever earned.

Chapter Eight

As Wynter flew into Logan's home like a bat out of hell, it occurred to her that she had no idea where she was going. She'd been so angry, jealous if she admitted it, she had to get away from Logan and his touchy feely woman. With his kiss still seared on her lips and adrenaline pumping, she finally came to a halt when she reached the foyer. She placed her fingers to her forehead and took a deep breath, trying to understand what had just happened. *Why did she feel that after one kiss with Logan she now wanted to rip the face off of that strange woman as if she were a rabid animal? Where was she even going?*

Glancing at her surroundings, she was stunned at the understated elegance of Logan's home. Wynter noted that someone had taken great care to restore the meticulously kept rooms. Ornate crown molding covered every facet of the ceilings. The cream-colored paint complemented the taupe walls and cherry hardwood floors. A round marble table held a large vase of Asiatic lilies mixed with large pussy willow branches. The enticing scent of the flowers permeated the air. As she caught a glimpse of the living room, she admired the intricately patterned oriental carpets and period piece antique seating. It was a far contrast to the contemporary great room into which she'd first entered the house.

Her eyes swept up the magnificent curved mahogany staircase, and it occurred to her that Logan's bedroom was upstairs. Even though she'd never forget the way Logan had held her that night, and of course the awkward exchange she'd had with Dimitri, she'd hardly taken the time to look at where she'd been. Unable to recollect the décor, she wondered if she'd ever see his room again. After her aggressive exhibition in the courtyard, she wasn't sure what he'd do next.

Wynter's face heated, recollecting their intimate tryst in the pool. She'd felt animalistic, unable to get enough of him. As he walked away and touched that strange woman, she was angry. But it had felt more than that. It felt as if she needed to stake her claim, let the others know he was hers. She'd never been the jealous type but then again, she'd never met a man like Logan. It was silly, she knew. In no universe was he hers nor did she belong to him. She reasoned it must be the changes to her body's chemistry. If the change to her cellular structure could intensify her senses, it was entirely reasonable that her emotions were heightened as well.

Fiona's voice pulled her from her deep contemplation, bringing her back to the fact that she'd been standing immobile, like a statue, in the vestibule.

"Wynter, hold on," Fiona told her, somewhat amused at

her behavior. She placed a comforting hand on Wynter's shoulder. "You okay?"

"Yes, I'm fine," she assured the young woman.

"Well, I've got to say that I've never seen anything so hot. I mean, damn, girl. Possessive much?" she laughed.

"I don't know what you mean. I just…I guess I'm not exactly myself yet," Wynter admitted sheepishly, embarrassed about her behavior in the courtyard.

"Well, Luci won't be crossing your path anytime soon, I can tell you that. Come on, now." Fiona started up the staircase. "Nice place, huh?"

Yes it was. She wondered how Fiona knew Logan's mansion so well. Another one of his women, she supposed. Resigned that she still needed Logan's protection, Wynter obediently followed Fiona.

"Yes, it's beautiful. I've never seen anything like it," Wynter replied. She could literally feel the history oozing from the walls and wondered who'd lived in the home over the years and how old it was.

"He's been renovating it for a long time. But since he became Alpha, he sped up the work."

Fiona opened a heavy wooden door. "Here we go. You're here in the 'Rose Room'. Logan's down the hall just in case you get lonely." She winked. "This is his favorite guest room, you know. I think it says, 'feminine but rich'."

Wynter marveled at the rose-colored walls trimmed in metallic gold crown molding. A day bed with curled gold framing topped with cream-colored pillows took center stage. A lovely cream coverlet adorned with pink and red roses brought life to the piece. A dainty crystal chandelier dangled above.

"It's something, isn't it?" Fiona asked, opening large closet doors. "So, here we go. While you guys were out, I stocked the dresser and closet here with a few clothes. Dimitri said the clothes this morning fit so I bought more things…shoes, all that good stuff."

"You shouldn't have gone to so much trouble. I won't be here long," Wynter insisted, fully anticipating that she'd be leaving soon.

"Logan wants you to be comfortable, and besides, you are going out tonight," she reminded her.

Wynter bit her lip, now mortified by what she'd said at the pool. Hoping she'd spend the remainder of her time alone, waiting for Jax, she'd forgotten that Logan said they were going to meet someone later.

"Yes, I suppose I am." Wynter turned toward Fiona who was getting ready to leave.

"Don't worry, it'll be fine," Fiona stated confidently.

"Hey, I just want to thank you for everything. I know I was really sick last night. You guys helped me, and I know you didn't have to. Thank you."

Wynter didn't even know these people and they were helping her. True, she'd been trying desperately to help their race, but they had no idea what she'd done or who she was. Still, they'd been treating her with respect and kindness despite the fact she'd been less than candid. But instead of throwing her back on the street, they'd fed her, clothed her, saw to her medical needs.

Fiona smiled. "Really, it's no problem. We all need help now and then." She turned to walk away and then hesitated. "By the way, not sure if Logan got a chance to tell you, but my sister Dana, the doc who saw you last night, she got stuck at the hospital today. I know she ran some tests, but before you ask, I don't know anything. She'll probably be over in the morning or call later tonight."

"Thanks, I really appreciate it. People…they just don't…they just don't do these things," she said as if she were deep in thought.

As Fiona waved goodbye, Wynter considered what Jax had done for her. Saved her from a life of foster care. He could have turned his back on her at any time, but never did. Maybe it was wolves and their undying loyalty? Her parents had been loyal to him, and he'd, in turn, been loyal to them by taking her in, protecting her.

She wanted so badly to tell Logan everything she knew, but it was Jax who deserved her allegiance. When she talked to him on the phone, Jax had barely made mention of her work. He only wanted to know if she'd been all right and that Logan was treating her well. If he'd asked about what had happened over the past two months, she'd have told him everything, despite the fact Logan was listening. She supposed doing so would have been fair game. But to tell Logan, to disclose everything she and Jax had worked for without his permission, she just couldn't bring herself to do it. Lust or not, Logan was most likely a temporary distraction in her otherwise boring life.

Despite all of her exceedingly rational thoughts, she

couldn't stop thinking about him. After watching the way he'd touched Goth Chick, hugging her, allowing her to continue to touch him, right after he'd been so incredibly intimate with her, it cut her in two. She couldn't make sense out of her feelings, because never in her life had she felt such an intense attraction to a man. Even if she were able to comprehend the biological ramifications of her changes, she couldn't deny a loss of control when it came to how she felt about the Alpha. It appeared as though the tendrils of their incipient connection were evolving in tandem, weaving and strengthening with each second they spent together. And for Wynter, the experience threw her solely into unchartered waters.

After a long shower, Wynter steadied her emotions, committed to getting through the evening with Logan without incident. But as she descended the staircase, butterflies began to dance in her belly, as she nervously anticipated Logan's reaction to her earlier behavior. Alphas could be unpredictable, and she wasn't certain how he'd address her interruption of his conversation with Goth Chick. It was bad enough that she'd been aggressive, obstructing his view of a pack member. But it was the kiss she'd planted on him that had her really worried. It had been a possessive, 'get your hands the fuck away from my man' kiss. She knew her intention wouldn't be lost on Logan and fully expected he'd call her out on what she'd done.

Her emerging wolf clawed at her mind, and she wasn't sure she wanted the message to be lost on him. No, clearly her wolf was staking some kind of a claim. Unfortunately, the human, and logical part of her, seemed to be taking a vacation. Torn between holding on to the threads of her humanity or letting go altogether, giving into her untamed cravings, she couldn't decide if what she'd done was wrong or just a natural part of who she was becoming.

So when Wynter reached the landing of the stairs, she deliberately kept her eyes low in submission. She stole a fleeting glance at Logan, who looked fabulously handsome and with his usual air of danger. His wet hair was neatly combed, and he smelled deliciously spicy and masculine. He was casually dressed in a crisp white dress shirt with rolled up sleeves, and dark dress slacks. She swore her panties grew wet within seconds of being in his presence. It was ridiculous, she knew. Like a teenage girl with a crush on the quarterback, she tried desperately to hide her arousal. But no matter how hard she attempted to shove the carnal thoughts into the deep recesses of her brain, she couldn't seem to control the visceral reaction to the man.

Logan watched intently as Wynter carefully but gracefully navigated the steps. Altogether stunning, Wynter wore a little black dress that tightly hugged her curves. Off-shoulder sleeves accentuated her newly tanned arms, and formed a perfect v into the valley between her breasts, revealing the swell of her cleavage. Resplendent and sexy, she blushed upon his gaze. Her pack experience became apparent as his submissive little wolf looked away. Logan smiled; she simply had no idea how beautiful she really was.

Logan had thought about Wynter's kiss all evening. Even though he intended to play it off, refusing to bring it up at dinner, he had so not forgotten. In a display of dominance, Wynter had shown her alpha tendencies. The way she'd pushed Luci out of the way, then given him that branding kiss; it had amazed him and frightened him all at once. On the one hand, he'd enjoyed the hell out of her choosing him, and he desired her intensely. On the other, he wasn't looking for a mate and didn't want to hurt her. But hell, the way she'd responded to his touch in the pool was positively remarkable.

During dinner, Logan soon found himself enchanted by Wynter's witty humor and intelligence. It was clear to him that she'd been well schooled even though she avoided talking about her career. He knew it was all directly connected to her secrets, the reason why she'd been in New Orleans. But the light conversation allowed him to get to know Wynter better, without her worrying about his expectations.

A look here and there, flirting and blushing, stirred his attraction to her. Although the sexual tension between them hung like a tight electrical wire in a storm just waiting to explode, he'd decided not to snap it during their meal. A glance every now and then to Dimitri told him that his beta was fully aware of their growing connection. The easy banter between him, her and Dimitri flowed naturally, feeling comfortable and easy. He wondered if he'd ever be able to share her like they'd done with other women, seriously doubting it.

Surprised by the easiness of their discussion and the non-mention of the incident by the pool, Wynter relaxed, getting to better know both Logan and Dimitri. Like Logan, his beta radiated a lethal sexiness that appeared to attract women like bees to honey. From the hostess to the waitress, women shamelessly flirted with both men. Controlling her jealousy wasn't as easy as she hoped but Wynter managed to keep it together. While "Kitty", the server, fawned over Logan, Wynter silently recited the periodic table. *Gotta love science.* It did help a little to take her mind off the very uncharacteristic need to throttle the waitress.

After the spectacular dinner with Logan and Dimitri, Wynter relaxed, forgetting where they were headed. However, upon their arrival at the vampire club, her heart raced as she exited the car. Even though both Logan and Dimitri reassured her that she'd be safe with them, seeds of doubt floated. What if one of her former guards frequented this place? What if Kade didn't believe her? What if it was a trap? *Trust me,* he'd told her. She wanted so badly to listen to the cocksure Alpha's words of assurance. Aware that she had no choice in the matter, Wynter wrapped her hand tightly around Logan's arm, holding her breath as the doors opened.

By the time they got to Mordez, Logan's cock was once again painfully hard. He silently cursed as he thought of a half dozen ways he'd like to pleasure the devilishly sweet woman whose bare legs brushed against his own the whole damn way from the restaurant to the club. As she reached for his arm and gave a nervous laugh, he reasoned she had no idea what she was even doing to him.

Collecting his thoughts, he focused on the task at hand. By the end of the evening, he hoped to have the situation with the vampires sewn up neatly, although he knew from experience, things rarely went that easy. Putting on his game face, he swung a protective arm around Wynter and nodded to Dimitri. Time to roll.

The door to Mordez swung open, and Logan guided Wynter into the dark haven. An older gentleman dressed in a tuxedo immediately rushed over to them.

"Mister Reynaud, please come in. We're so honored to have you visit us tonight," he gushed.

Logan acknowledged him with a curt nod, keeping Wynter safely tucked against his side. Dimitri rounded up to her other side so she was effectively surrounded by the two large wolves.

"Will you be taking a seat in the theater, this evening? Charlotte is just about to take the stage. Or if you'd rather, the Cleretti room has recently imported the most wonderful, very rare Italian Barolo. You must try it. As for the other rooms," he coughed and glanced to Wynter, sniffing the air. He gave Logan a knowing look before continuing, "Our private room. Their shows start much later. While I'd be happy to reserve your seating, considering your company, may I suggest that it may not be appropriate….for your guest."

Wynter shivered; a chill settled over her skin as the man spoke to Logan as if she weren't there. The way he looked at her, albeit for only a second, made her queasy. Vampires.

Wynter remembered all too well the hungry look in their eyes and the flare of their nostrils right before the pain came. She cringed. He looked as though he was sizing her up like a glass of the wine he'd just mentioned.

"The theater is fine for now. We are meeting Kade Issacson later this evening. We're a bit early, though," Logan explained with not so much as a blink of an eye. "Please ensure our privacy."

"Yes sir. Your needs are our utmost priority," he assured the Alpha. Stealing a glance at Wynter, he licked his lips but quickly turned away. "Please, this way."

Wynter noted the darkened lobby and thought that if they were looking to scare people from entering, keeping it exclusive, they certainly did a good job with that. The flare of candles provided little illumination onto the stone encased foyer. A soft lull of Dixieland jazz poured into the small space and she detected the faint smell of mold. She supposed the club owners were going for a quaint antique décor, congruent with the city's history. However, in her opinion, the vibe was nothing short of creepy. She looked to the older maître d' who'd been speaking to Logan, and caught a glimpse of his pointed canines. He winked at her right before he pushed a black curtain aside. Clutching at Logan a bit tighter, she bravely stood her ground.

Both Logan and Dimitri appeared taller to her, their attitude cold and deadly. Their lips were drawn tight in serious expressions that projected dominance. Far removed from her easygoing dinner date, a dangerous creature had replaced Logan. As a wolf, this was his true nature. Wynter took note of Logan's demeanor, promising never to forget exactly what and who he was.

Emerging from the claustrophobic passageway, Wynter was amazed at the luxurious room in which they'd arrived. Reminiscent of a nineteen-forties tiered dinner theater, the area looked capable of holding at least fifty patrons, all comfortably seated in rows of clam-shelled, semicircular booths classically upholstered in red crushed velvet. The light from the small votive candles on the tables reflected off the blackened plaster walls. The darkened stage eerily sat empty awaiting its starlet.

As Wynter slid onto the seat, she breathed in relief as Logan and Dimitri flanked her. They towered over her small frame, and she felt safe nestled between them. Utterly fascinated that a place like this existed, her eyes roamed overhead to the massive crystal chandelier that precariously hung from the oval ceiling. The booths were arranged on a curve so that every person had a good view of the stage. Wynter glanced over to the patrons seated nearest to them who were laughing and drinking. In their element, they looked almost human until she caught a glint of a fang.

Logan must have discerned her discomfort, because he placed his hand on her thigh and gently squeezed. She looked up to him, noticing that his face had softened. God, this man was killing her inside. Protective and deadly to loving in sixty seconds, every facet of him intrigued her, making her want him even more.

"You okay, Wynter?" Logan asked softly.

"Um, yeah, thanks," she uttered not realizing she'd been

holding her breath. As she spoke, her gaze traveled to a pair of lovers. While she couldn't see faces, she could clearly see the tracks of blood running down the woman's backless dress.

"You're shaking. Look at me," Logan instructed, watching how she naturally complied. "You're safe. You are not in a lab. I promise you, nothing will happen to you here that you don't want to happen."

"What's that supposed to mean?" she replied indignantly. Was he implying she wanted to be bitten?

"Look around you, sweetheart. This place is a dark playground where people live out their fantasies. This one just happens to be run by the vamps. But wolves have them too. We come to watch and be seen, to play and be played with. The vamps, they come for the blood. And the shifters, witches and humans all come for different reasons. Some want a walk on the wild side, some want to be bitten, some want sex. Places like this serve a need," Logan told her matter-of-factly. "In Philadelphia, Tristan runs an upscale club. Similar to this one. I'd say his is more urban in nature, but its function is nearly the same."

"You come to these places often?" *Please say no. Please say no.* She couldn't believe what he was telling her. Why would he purposely hang out with vampires?

"I used to help run one in Philadelphia, but here, this is too dark for my tastes." Logan briefly stopped talking when a waitress came to their table. Without saying a word, she efficiently poured glasses of champagne. Setting the bottle in an ice bucket, she quickly scampered away. Logan handed Wynter her glass and continued. "As I was saying, this club can be quite dangerous if you don't know what you are getting into. Of course like Tristan's club, I expect there's tight security. That being said, it doesn't mean that people don't get hurt."

Logan didn't want to scare his little wolf. He simply wished to provide her with knowledge of what existed in his world. Neither evil nor good, the city could be utilized for both, depending on one's intentions. The veil separating the planes of supernaturals and humans was extraordinarily thin in the Big Easy. It was easy to get in trouble if one didn't know what they were doing. Deciding to shift the focus, he changed topics. He knew of one subject that would definitely take her mind off vampires.

"So, Wynter, care to explain what happened at the pool today?" He glanced over to Dimitri who gave a small grin, and then back at her.

Wynter nearly choked on her champagne. What the hell? Where did that come from? Had he been waiting all night to take her off guard? Logan was entirely too confident. Two could play at that game, she thought. Forgetting the 'no game' rule he'd insisted on, she dived right into her answer, which answered his question with a question.

"Whatever do you mean, Alpha?" She batted her eyelashes at him then smiled at Dimitri.

"Come now, you seemed quite bothered with me, running hot and well, hotter. And that kiss…by the side of the pool…in front of everyone. Hmm?"

"Oh, do you mean the kiss you gave me in the pool? That one? I do believe everyone saw that one. Or was it the kiss you gave the other woman who came to the pool? You know, the one you gave her while still exhibiting the," she paused, pretending to give it great thought and then pinned him with a stare. "How should I say it? The one you gave her, wearing the tented towel that I gave you?"

More champagne please...now. Wynter swore her blood pressure rose twenty points just thinking of the incident. A few hours ago she'd told herself to play it cool, but her plan didn't seem to be working out the way she'd imagined it.

Dimitri laughed out loud at her response. His Alpha was going to have his hands full, all right.

Logan smiled. He supposed he should have thought better of kissing Luci with an erection the size of Mount Everest. But in truth, it'd just been a peck hello on the cheek.

"Is my little wolf jealous? You seemed quite, how should I say it? Angry with me," he mused, taking a sip of his drink.

"Nothing to be jealous of. This...this thing between us," she flushed with embarrassment, "it's just...it's just a chemical reaction brought on by whatever they gave me....what they've turned me into."

"A wolf. You can say it."

"Fine. Yes, it's that wolf thing. I'm sure it'll pass. Besides, I have no claims to you." She looked away and stared into her bubbling glass.

"Agreed. You don't have a claim on me. We've just met, after all. Besides, you haven't even shifted yet," he goaded in an effort to test her reaction to his agreement that he wasn't hers. A surge of delight touched his heart as her eyes flashed in anger. Perhaps she didn't believe her own words? She really didn't like it when he repeated them.

"And you have no claims to me either," she quipped, quickly recovering. "I don't belong to you."

Why that hurt, he couldn't say. It was the irrefutable truth. And that was the crux of his problem. Part of him wanted her, not just in bed, but wanted her to belong to him and with his pack.

"So you honestly believe everything that happened today at the pool was just a side effect of your transition to wolf? Hormones? Is that what you're saying?" he pressed.

"Who was she anyway?" Wynter completely ignored his question. She had to know if there was someone else in his life. "The girl at the pool? Is she your girlfriend?"

"Luci?"

"Yes. You know, the woman rubbing all over you, drooling like a St. Bernard in heat." Oh great, she'd just reduced herself to name calling. Whatever. She had one foot in; she might as well jump in all the way.

Logan laughed. Boy, she really was jealous. And why did he seem to enjoy that so much?

"Luci. She was Marcel's girlfriend," he explained, trying to choose his words carefully. He was pretty sure she wouldn't like the rest of the explanation. "I allowed her to live with me in Marcel's bayou mansion. You know, while I was busy establishing my role."

Wynter deliberately closed and opened her eyes, taking

time to process what he'd just said. *He did not just say what I think he said.*

"So you are living with her?" *Just perfect. I really am an idiot.*

"No, I said she *was* living with me...as in past tense. And it was only because she already lived in the mansion, and I didn't want to kick her to the curb."

"A humanitarian? Bet it was difficult," she drawled.

"Well with Kat there, I..."

"Who is Kat?" This just kept getting better.

"She's Tristan's sister. But it wasn't like..." He wanted to say that it wasn't anything close to what he'd felt for her, but bit his tongue. "It wasn't like you think, Wynter." Logan's eyes saddened and his voice wavered slightly as the emotions of Marcel's death unexpectedly rushed over him. It had only been a couple of months and it was still hard to comprehend that he was dead.

"Marcel. He was my friend, my mentor. And my Alpha at one time. A few months ago, he was killed. It was difficult for everyone, but Katrina and I...we were just trying to get by. I promised him."

"Promised him what?"

"I'd take over for him." Logan emptied what was left in his glass and set it down. This was not at all what he planned on discussing with Wynter tonight. This conversation was finished.

Wynter saw the sadness in Logan's eyes and recognized his pain all too well. The loss of someone you loved could never be erased or undone. True, the pain would lessen as time went on, but when you lost someone so close to you, a part of your heart and mind would never be the same. She gleaned that he hadn't been Alpha for very long and wondered how he was coping. As a human spending much of her time observing Jax, she would never have known that Logan had just taken over his pack. He seemed such a natural leader. Yet, whatever he'd been doing over the past couple of months must've taken a great emotional and physical toll on him.

Even though there was a part of her that hated that he'd slept with other women, the rational part of her brain finally won out the battle. She swore it was that damn wolf making her so jealous. Of course, he had other women and in the moment, she didn't care. She only wanted to take away his hurt, ease his suffering. Wynter reached to him, lovingly placing her hand on his cheek and looked deep into his eyes.

"I'm sorry," she whispered. "I'm sorry for your loss. I know...I know how it feels. I promise it'll get better someday."

With her words, she wanted to break down and cry, opening up to him about her own parents, everything that had happened with Jax. She'd been so scared and lonely, lost to the world. But she couldn't tell him. It would lead to other questions; ones she wasn't ready to answer.

Logan wrapped his hands around her wrist, holding her hand to his face. His eyes locked on hers in a heated stare. Whatever anger she'd held about Luci and Kat had melted away. This woman, a virtual stranger, genuinely cared that he was hurting over Marcel's death. Kindred souls, they both had experienced great loss at death's hand. His heart constricted. He wished they could forget this Kade business and just go home and be alone. Logan's eyes fell; he glanced at her soft, inviting lips. *Why did he want this woman so badly?*

Their connection was broken as a spotlight flooded the stage and a lilt of music filled the room. Wynter glanced up to the stage, and tried to pull her hand away, but he guided her palm onto his thigh. Logan didn't want what they'd just shared to end. As if she grounded him, the physical touch of her palm, however slight, stoked the fire within his heart.

Wynter considered how precariously close to danger she was. While she'd initially been worried about the vampires, Logan changed the subject and now all she could think about was him and her own feelings that were spiraling out of control. She prayed that it really was just chemistry. Deep down, though, she suspected her feelings were real, and it scared the living daylights out of her.

Wynter's thoughts were interrupted as the big band music boomed from surround sound speakers. A high-heeled burlesque dancer seductively pranced onto the stage. Quite beautiful, with voluptuous curves, the brunette slowly slipped one leg to the side then rolled her wrists; her graceful hands flowed like ribbons into the limelight. Flicking open her red ostrich feather fan, she concealed her body, with a wink. Sweeping it up and around, she continued to tease the audience by caressing the plumage up and over her body.

Playing and tantalizing, she flirted while skillfully

removing her gloves, one by one. A man whistled as she threw them to patrons in the front row. Turning her back to the audience, she deftly removed her bra, never revealing her breasts. She swung the garment round and round, then flung it across the room. Though the feathers artfully brushed over her creamy pale skin, revealing little, her erotic display captivated the crowd. The dancer bent over, shaking her behind, and encouraged the audience's catcalls.

Her mesmerizing hips rocked side to side, sexy and slow. As anticipation grew in expectation of the big reveal, Wynter glanced up to both Logan and Dimitri, who, astonishingly, weren't watching the show. Rather, both men were intently watching her, and she blushed. Giving them both a small smile, she drew her attention back to the stage just in time to see the woman raise the fan clear over her head. Striking a pose, she proudly displayed her red sparkling pasties and perfectly matching panties for everyone to admire. The audience clapped wildly in appreciation, while she curtsied.

Wynter had never seen a woman strip before but found the experience both arousing and erotic. The artistic dancing seemed to have the same effect on the crowd as she noticed several couples begin to intimately touch and kiss in response. As the dancer pranced off stage, Wynter felt a tug on her wrist.

"Did you enjoy the show?" Logan inquired with a grin. Judging by her heartbeat, he knew she did.

"Yes. I've never been to a burlesque show before. She was amazing." Wynter caught both Dimitri and Logan raising their eyebrows at each other. "What? Can't I admire art?"

"I just find it interesting that you spent all that time around a pack and weren't exposed to any nudity," Logan commented. He couldn't understand why Jax would keep her so secluded from his wolves.

"She didn't seem to have a problem with it this afternoon," Dimitri joked.

Wynter's cheeks heated and Logan laughed.

"No, my friend, she didn't. And I must say that I very much like her that way."

Wynter was about to protest and tell them both that it hadn't been her idea to strip in the pool, when the maître d' from earlier rushed over to Logan. He efficiently ushered their party out of the theater and into a different area of the club. Within minutes, they were seated. Their small circular table barely held enough room for their glasses but provided them with an excellent view of the room, including the bar and adjoining dance floor.

Scattered tables filled the lounge, leaving only a small area around the bar stools for standing room. Checkered stone floors and blackened walls adorned with gas lit lanterns reminded her yet again of the club's dark nature. A long copper bar ran the length of a wall where men and woman waited for drinks. Several glass tubes filled with a dark red substance ran from the ceiling down into taps. *Wine? Blood?* She couldn't tell without getting closer and there was no way in hell that was happening.

Sitting between Logan and Dimitri, she felt secure, but curious. "What's with the tubes?" she whispered. "Please tell me it's wine."

Logan lowered his voice. "Blood. They serve it many ways. Live donors are usually preferred by the vamps, but this room is more of a waiting room so to speak. When donors are ready, they can go to private rooms. The disco also has semi-private areas. Feeding occurs everywhere here…even in public."

Wynter's eyes widened and her mouth tightened in surprise, and Dimitri jumped in to explain further.

"The people who come to these clubs…they enjoy it," he told her.

"Enjoy being bitten? Here?" She'd heard it was true but had never really discussed it with anyone who could verify the rumors.

"It's not like I'm into it, but hey, I don't judge. Everybody's looking for something. Humans, wolves, witches, vampires, they're all here for a little kink. Public feeding. Public sex even. You've got voyeurs and exhibitionists and everyone in between," Logan added. "I'm surprised you didn't ever go to a club like this in New York. I mean, there's no doubt this place is a little heavier than most clubs, but that's only because the vampires run it."

"Yeah, they don't mind pushing the envelope of what's unacceptable, which isn't much. It's kind of a free-for-all," Dimitri pointed out. "I'm actually surprised Kade would come here. I didn't think he was into all this, but what do I know?"

"I guess I was sheltered. But Jax, he'd never go somewhere like this." Sure, she'd been sequestered from the nudity but never did she imagine that these clubs could be commonplace in Jax's life or anyone else in his pack for that matter.

"Trust me, Wyn. Even the almighty Jax Chandler has been in a club like this. He's the New York Alpha. He may not like to be bitten, but then again, you never know," Logan sniffed. "But the sex? To see and be seen. Oh, he goes. And if you think he doesn't...well then maybe you don't know him as well as you think you do."

Logan considered her reactions and comments about the club, and it occurred to him that even though she was an adult, she hadn't been exposed to the supernatural culture at all. A whisper of innocence laced her words, and he couldn't help but want to be the one to help her learn.

"Just because I live with Jax, that doesn't mean he tells me everything." Wynter played with her hands, reflecting on her ignorance. She knew she'd been kept in the dark. Her parents had insisted on it, and when they died, Jax continued the ruse. She felt like an idiot, living with an Alpha, yet inexperienced with the way of wolves. "He's a wolf. I'm just a human. We're both busy."

"What do you mean, just a human?" Logan asked. It was going to be interesting when his little wolf shifted. It would finally be real to her.

Wynter was about to attempt to come up with a witty comeback to his question, but noticed both Logan and Dimitri go on alert, both putting their hands possessively on her thighs. As much as she wanted to reflect on how she felt about having two men touch her at once, and oddly, she really did, she was more curious about the spectacle across the room that had captivated the men's interest. She squinted, attempting to see in the dimly lit room and wished whatever supernatural wolf powers she might be getting would apply to her eyes. It wasn't too long before she saw a sight that very much held her attention.

A woman with long flowing black hair writhed on top of a man's lap. His face was altogether buried in the woman's neck and as she moved up and down, it became apparent that they were having sex. Her long flowing skirt covered any evidence of their coupling, but the telltale movement of her hips on his provided little question as to what they were doing. Surprisingly aroused by the sight, Wynter watched intently as the man and woman grunted in ecstasy. Blood ran down the woman's neck, and the man slowly lifted his head. Wynter gasped as the vampire's eyes snapped open and locked on hers.

Chapter Nine

The vampire had licked his bloodied lips and then smiled at her. And that was the exact moment she'd recognized him. Monsieur Devereoux, from New York City. *One of the university's most influential benefactors was a vampire? What was he doing here in this club? Oh my God.*

Her mind raced, as she struggled to compose herself. How was she supposed to talk to Monsieur Devereoux right after she'd watched him have sex? Wynter had found it difficult to tear her eyes away. And oh dear Lord, he knew she'd been watching. Not only did he know, he liked it and smiled at her. Wynter's heart beat frantically as Léopold confidently strode across the room. She tried to look away and could hardly believe this was happening. Logan would know and she'd be forced to tell him everything.

Dressed in a stylish all black suit and tie, Léopold Devereoux looked as debonair as she'd remembered. His perfectly coiffed hair accentuated his model good looks and lithe muscular body. As if he'd stepped out of an issue of GQ, the man was exceptionally handsome. Yet tonight, there was something different about him, an otherworldly, dangerous edge to his presence. All heads turned to watch him as he made his way toward their table, and she'd almost forgotten where she was until he stood before them offering his hand to her. Wynter heard him address her and swallowed the lump that had lodged in her throat. As she did so, she gave a brief nod to both Logan and Dimitri who stood protectively at her sides. Clearly angry at this development, their faces were set into hardened frowns, staring at him.

"How lovely to see you again, Dr. Ryan." Léopold bowed his head slightly, never taking his eyes off hers. Wynter struggled to respond as the shock of hearing his familiar French accent brought forth the reality that he was who she'd thought he was. Time stopped as she gaped in disbelief. She'd just voyeuristically watched as he covertly yet openly, made love to that woman in his lap.

"Monsieur Devereoux. Why, hello. Very good to see you again," she managed with a cough. *What was she supposed to say? Thanks for letting me watch you have sex. And oh by the way, you're a vampire?* She dug deep to find appropriate diplomatic words that seemed to elude her. "I'm surprised to see you here. Are you wintering in New Orleans?"

Léopold took her hand gently into his before pressing his cool lips to her skin. Logan growled in response, and he quickly released her hand. He gave Wynter a puzzled look, sensing she'd changed. *Wolf? Now how did that happen when she'd clearly been human? And where was the ever possessive Jax, letting his little human out to play with strange wolves?*

Very interesting indeed. Amused, he smiled at the trio and addressed Wynter.

"I could say the same of you. New York winters can be cold, no? And I see you've taken up with a new Alpha. Hmm," Léopold observed and nodded to Logan. "Monsieur Reynaud. We meet again."

"Monsieur Devereoux," Logan acknowledged without emotion. "This is my beta, Dimitri. Please call me Logan." He reluctantly gestured for him to sit.

"Logan it is." Léopold grabbed a chair from a nearby table and sat. He crossed his legs and picked a piece of lint from his trouser.

From the minute Logan spotted Devereoux, he knew that this evening was fucked. The last time he'd seen the powerful vampire, he'd been in Philadelphia. And while Léopold had been helpful in locating his Alpha's mate, it was no secret the vampire was extraordinarily dangerous. Where the hell was Kade? Why had he sent his maker to meet them? And what exactly was Wynter's connection to the most lethal vampire on the east coast?

When Léopold had kissed her hand, he'd nearly lost it. Logan decided right then and there that he'd be having a sit down with Miss Ryan or Dr. Ryan or whoever the hell she was as soon as they got out of there, because he was sick of the damn lies. Protocol or not, he was done with all the secrets. If he had to call Jax himself tonight, he'd have the truth. In the meantime, he had to deal with Devereoux.

"Where's Kade?" Logan inquired but then was interrupted by Wynter.

"He's not my Alpha, Monsieur Devereoux," she corrected Léopold. "And please call me Wynter."

Logan gave her a stern look. *What the fuck was she doing? Did she have a death wish?* A she-wolf didn't go announcing in the middle of a vampire bar that she wasn't with her Alpha, especially in his city. A lone wolf was a vulnerable wolf. Every protective instinct in him told him to throw her over his shoulder and drag her back to his home.

"Please forgive her ignorance. Wynter is under my protection," Logan explained to Léopold and then turned a hard stare on Wynter. "So until Jax gets here, you're mine." *Mine.* He knew how he was using the term, and it wasn't as if she was a mate. But in the back of his head, the idea bounced around briefly, and it bothered him to think he'd even go there.

Dimitri shot him a look of surprise. Hearing his Alpha go all territorial and call a woman his was unusual, given the conversation they'd all just had in the theater. So far, this evening wasn't going how he expected. He readied himself for more surprises, sizing up the vampire at their table.

Wynter held her breath for a minute, stifling her anger. *Why was Logan saying that she was his?* Jax always made it known that she belonged to him, with his pack. No matter what feelings she was developing for Logan, it could be no other way.

"No, Logan," she argued. She needed to explain the situation to Léopold. She couldn't have him running off to Jax, spreading the misconception that she now belonged to Logan. No, that could not happen. Jax would be pissed, for sure. "While it is true that I'm under his protection, I don't belong to him."

"Ah, seems mademoiselle can't decide where she belongs, Alpha. Perhaps she needs to be schooled in wolf rules, no?" Léopold laughed, well aware of the implications of their conversation.

"Wynter, on this, Léopold is correct. Look around you. This club. Anything goes. By entering, your consent has been granted. If you didn't belong to me, you'd be free to be taken. This is my city, and at least for tonight, you're mine. No one will touch you without my permission. And that's not happening. Now tell me how you know each other," he ordered.

Wynter quieted at his words. Was that true? If he didn't claim her as his wolf, anyone in this place could go after her? God, she hated this club. Great, now Logan was angry at her, and it made her stomach twist. She hadn't intended to make him mad. In fact, she found herself wanting to please him. He'd been so kind to her, and this wasn't how she dreamed of repaying him. In truth, part of her wanted to belong to him. But after their conversation, he agreed that she had no claim to him. She sighed in defeat. Looking around, she realized he was right. What good would it do to declare she belonged to Jax or worse, pretend that she was a single female? It was too dangerous.

"Wynter. Explain. Now," she heard Logan say. Maybe this wasn't how she'd pictured telling Logan, but at this point, she had no choice but to tell him the truth…at least more of it anyway. Uncertain about what Léopold would tell him, she realized it would be best if he heard it from her.

"We…we met last year at a charity gala," she stuttered. "You see, I used to teach, well mostly did research. Virology. There was a fundraiser at the Guggenheim."

"Dr. Ryan, here, gave an excellent speech about the implications of trans-species viral infections. Quite interesting. And how is Jane Doe doing? Your case study?"

"Well, I haven't seen her in a few months," Wynter said sadly. Emma, her best friend Mika's sister. She was the entire reason she'd gone into virology and decided to work at ViroSun.

"Pity, no? You see, Alpha, Jane Doe was a hybrid. Although if I remember correctly, you didn't specify which type of shifter; only that she was a child."

"Well, yes. She's a teen now."

"Hybrids don't get sick. What's wrong with her?" Logan asked.

"Um, it's complicated. It's a long-term illness and it could be fatal, I'm afraid," Wynter commented, trying to avoid his questions. She neglected to specify that she knew Jane Doe and that she had a viral infection. "So anyhow, that's how we know each other. Monsieur Devereoux's made very generous donations to the school, helping to fund our research."

Emma's illness had been the catalyst for Wynter going into virology. Early on, Wynter had suspected leukemia. But unlike human leukemia, which could be treated, sometimes even pushed into remission, this leukemia was lupine in nature. And like feline leukemia, she suspected that it would eventually be fatal. The quagmire rested in the fact that shifters, even hybrids, were supposedly immune to viruses.

She hated lying to Logan. It was wrong and she knew it. But she'd promised Jax that she'd keep everything confidential. As far as she knew, only Jax and his beta knew about the virus. But Logan deserved to know as well. This was his city and he was putting himself out there, killing the vampires who'd attacked her. This was far from over and she knew it. They'd come for her. And she suspected his pack could be in danger because he'd taken her in and protected her. Her heart ached. She couldn't take the guilt. She decided then that if Jax wasn't in New Orleans by the morning, she'd call and ask for permission to tell Logan everything.

Logan tensed as he listened to Wynter explain how she knew Devereoux. The story of how they'd met seemed feasible, but he could tell she was still withholding the truth. When she finished speaking about the sick girl, he noticed she withdrew from the conversation entirely. She wore her sadness like a mask as she stared into her drink. It was as if she held the weight of the world on her shoulders. Whoever the hybrid was, Wynter must have known her. It wasn't just a case; no, it was personal. And like how Wynter had been sick when he'd first met her, it made no sense how a hybrid could contract an illness. Just what exactly had she been working on in New Orleans? He was about to probe further when Devereoux interrupted his train of thought.

"And to answer your other question, Kade is out of the

country. And Luca is with him. Business. I do apologize for the surprise. But I'd prefer not to have the whole city on alert that he's gone," Léopold elucidated with an air of arrogance.

Logan simply nodded, not sure about whether he believed his story. He didn't trust the vampire as far as he could throw him. Kade's damn secretary knew their meeting was important, and she'd lied. It seemed like lying was par for the course when it came to vamps, he thought.

Without warning, two large vampires came up behind Léopold. They flashed their exposed fangs at Wynter, and she wondered if they did it on purpose for intimidation. Or maybe they were getting ready to feed? She backed up as far as her chair would let her.

Unfazed by their presence, Léopold blithely introduced the two vampires. "Pardon my manners. These are two of Kade's men. Étienne and Xavier."

Étienne, a young blonde vampire, appeared to be in his mid-twenties, and he gave Wynter a cool smile that didn't reach his eyes. Not wanting to be impolite, she managed to return the smile. She glanced over to the older, exceptionally well-built vampire, Xavier. It appeared to Wynter that perhaps Logan knew the vampire, as he acknowledged him with a handshake.

"Go feed. I still have business here with the Alpha," Léopold ordered with a wave of his hand. The vampires were gone from sight within mere seconds. "Now, where was I? Oui, our meeting. So I understand there was a scuffle of sorts. Something about vampires? I admit, it doesn't sound unusual, but how can I be of service?"

"As much as I'd like to speak with Kade, if he's left you in charge, then I'm afraid I must bring this matter to your attention," Logan began, his low tone emanating anger. "Last night, we were in a local shifter bar off Decatur when four vampires attacked Wynter."

Léopold frowned. He liked the pretty doctor very much and wouldn't want anything to happen to her, not to mention that he and Jax were old friends.

"I'll get to the short of it. Wynter was held captive by her employer and told us that this organization's been using vamps as guards. They did a number on her. Bites, feedings. The usual," Logan told him with a tick in his jaw. His eyebrows furrowed in anger at the thought of what they'd done to her. "She escaped and on her way out, we fought and ended up staking a few of them. Now, I'm sure you know how this works. Under normal circumstances, we'd hold the offenders and turn them over to Kade. But last night, I had no choice."

"Oui, I understand," Léopold replied, skimming his finger over the rim of a glass that was sitting on the table. His voice held an edge of rage, yet his demeanor was controlled. "This is not acceptable…at all."

"So that brings me to you. First of all, it's likely this operation is still here in the city. But my immediate concern is Wynter's safety. She was doing work for them, and they'll probably be back for her. It'd be nice if we knew whether the vampires belong to Kade."

"I can assure you that all in Kade's line are well

accounted for. So either these vampires were from outside the city," Léopold paused as if in deep thought, "Or someone in Kade's line is making children without reporting it, which as you know would be a great offense. One that generally ends in death. Now that you've brought this to my attention, I'll certainly look into it."

"You should also be aware that Jax is coming to New Orleans. He was delayed due to the snow, but he'll be here soon. At that time, I expect we'll have more information," Logan hedged. He didn't wish to reveal that Wynter hadn't told him everything. And frankly, even if she had, he wasn't sure that he'd share it with Devereoux. Yes, he was grateful for his assistance but at the end of the day, he didn't trust him.

"I see. We're finished, no?" Léopold's dark mood seemed to transform back into a playful tone.

"We're finished," Logan confirmed, noticing that Wynter still appeared unresponsive. He wanted to take her home as soon as possible and force her to tell him exactly what she'd been doing in New Orleans. And he wanted every last detail, no more half-truths.

"A dance then, pet? Come, it's been too long," Léopold asked innocently, raising an eyebrow at Wynter. Sensing her hesitation, he glanced over to Logan, requesting permission. "Would you allow it, Alpha?"

Logan's gut churned at the thought of any other man putting his hands on Wynter. But was he going to refuse the bastard whose help he needed? He considered it. After all, Wynter knew Devereoux and didn't seem at all afraid of him. If anything, she was overly friendly with the guy; she hadn't outright said no to the dance. With an air of nonchalance, he glanced at Wynter who looked like a deer in the headlights. He wondered, was she attracted to Léopold? How well did they know each other? A flare of jealousy flamed, but he quickly reined in his feelings.

Fuck, she was driving him crazy. He'd specifically told her earlier that they didn't belong to each other and then when pressed by Léopold, he'd done a one eighty and publicly announced that she was his. Even though he'd said she belonged to him to protect her, his heart was starting to wish she really was. And his cock, well, his cock had already claimed her.

Putting his ego aside, Logan decided he'd allow one dance. One dance. That's all he could handle. And Léopold had better keep his damn hands to himself.

"Wynter, a dance?" Logan asked, stifling the jealousy that tightened in his chest.

Wynter gave Logan a surprised look. Dance with Léopold? A vampire? Her gut told her no, but her mind told her she was being silly. No matter what she'd just seen him do in the club, it had just been sex. He hadn't at all showed a proclivity for violence. Moreover, he was an acquaintance of Jax's.

"You'll be safe. Remember, you belong to me," he stated with confidence, his eyes pinned on Devereoux's.

"I…um…of course…yes," she accepted, not wanting to insult Léopold. Even though she was nervous, he'd been enormously supportive of her department at the university. But as she rose to take Léopold's hand, she wished it was Logan who'd asked her to dance.

Chapter Ten

As soon as she hit the dance floor, Wynter instantly regretted leaving Logan's side. The smell of blood, sweat and sex permeated the room. A sea of undulating bodies, in various states of dress, danced all around her. The separation felt unnatural and panic set in; she should never have accepted this dance.

Wynter gasped as Léopold pulled her tightly against him. She frantically swiveled her neck, in search of Logan. Léopold spun their bodies in a circle, and she caught a glimpse of Logan staring at her. She visibly relaxed at the sight of him. Léopold abruptly slowed his movement. With his lips inches from her ear, he spoke softly to her, all too intimate for Wynter's comfort.

"Quite a mess you've gotten yourself into, I see. Now tell me, my sweet doctor. Why did you lie to the Alpha? Ma chère, tis not wise," he advised.

"I haven't lied. You must understand, Monsieur, I've got to follow protocol. Jax is my Alpha," she explained breathlessly, surprised at herself for revealing that much to Léopold.

"Ah, but you have lied. You may have made your home with Jax at one time, but I can assure you that you now belong to Logan," he lectured, although satisfied with her candor. Léopold pressed his nose to her neck and sniffed. Wynter flinched. He laughed and spun her once again. "And your scent…it didn't seem possible, even to one as old as me, but you are indeed wolf. I must admit that I'm not sure whether to congratulate you or apologize for this unusual development."

"The Alpha, he's very much a bachelor. It may just be a passing fancy. It doesn't matter, though. I can't belong to him….he's just protecting me. As for being wolf, they did something to me. I'm not convinced that it's permanent. I haven't shifted," Wynter found herself confessing to the vampire despite the way he intruded on her sense of privacy.

There was something compelling about Léopold. The first time she'd met him, he'd seemed like a good-hearted man, such a generous donor. He'd taken great interest in her projects. But tonight, he kept her off kilter, she suspected on purpose, wondering what he'd do next. The way he'd smelled her skin and then laughed at her reaction was disturbing, yet he spoke to her as a man who cared about her future. It both intrigued and frightened her.

"Even on the clearest night, we sometimes cannot see the stars that shine most brightly. If you refuse to imagine the possibilities, the constellations will go unnoticed. Release yourself from these bindings. Your Alpha, he yearns for you, but does not know who you are to him," Léopold observed. How ironic it was that two hearts could meet and not know they were mates. He'd seen it many times and always found it tragic how cruel and wonderful fate could be.

"Yearning and loving are two different things. I'm not sure what I am to him. He feels responsibility because he rescued me," she speculated, engaged in the curious banter with Léopold. "Besides, the past few weeks I've lost sight of who I am, I'm afraid."

"Ah oui, nasty bunch, who captured you. Sounds dreadful. I cannot begin to tell you how sorry I am for what happened. But you are due for a rebirth, no? You will listen to me. Your destiny is with the Alpha. You must not fight this, pet. Some things are meant to be."

"You're a romantic?" she stated in surprise.

"Sometimes yes. Sometimes no. I prefer to think of myself as a realist. For as long as I've lived, there are some things that are even beyond my control."

Wynter said nothing as she caught sight of Logan shoving Dimitri's arm away, as if he'd been holding him back. Her breath caught as she saw him approaching with a feral look in his eyes. What the hell?

"Your Alpha comes for you, no? His possessive nature cannot accept another's hands on you as an unmarked wolf. You like experiments, do you not?" Léopold noted, jovially placing a kiss to her shoulder. He was enjoying this all too much, but he'd prove his point, nonetheless.

"Is this a test?" she snapped, trying to retreat. What was he doing kissing her like that? Her heart beat wildly at the sight of Logan coming straight at him.

"You feel it too, don't you? Your wolf. She craves him,"

he whispered into her ear, pulling her close against his body. He stopped dancing, holding her still, and continued. "And he cannot resist the demands of his beast."

Wynter recoiled at the intimacy Léopold forced upon her. His warm breath on her neck sent chills down her spine. As he turned his head down to look at her, she noticed his fangs had descended. *Vampire.* On the verge of hysteria, her stomach rolled. Shocked and disoriented, she stumbled backwards as he released her from his hold. The music spun in her mind. Léopold stood chuckling, then bowed toward her, bending one arm behind his back and extending his other hand toward her, as if he were some sort of medieval royalty. A scream bubbled in her throat yet she was unable to make a sound.

Before she knew what was happening, Logan embraced her. Wynter eagerly wrapped herself around her Alpha. The realization of what Léopold had been saying slammed into her consciousness. *Logan was her Alpha.* She wasn't sure how she'd known the creature existed, but in her mind's eye, her wolf released a tortured cry. Logan's scent enveloped her being, and both her human and animal psyche accepted the safety of his presence.

"Logan." Wynter reached for the words but they fell from her grasp. She needed to tell him everything about Emma, the contagion and God help her, how she felt about him. Relief and lust swept through her as he pressed her into his chest.

"Never again," he promised. Against his better judgment he'd let her dance with Léopold. But the second Léopold had touched her, his wolf maniacally clawed to emerge. The need to mark Wynter overwhelmed him. It wasn't prudent or logical, he knew. They'd only known each other a day. He hadn't even made love to her yet. None of it made any sense but his wolf needed this woman. Logan had to have her now. Publicly. To claim her.

"Don't let me go," she begged. Dancing with Léopold had driven whatever animal instincts she had to the surface. It felt wrong, terribly wrong. And now that she had Logan in her arms again, she wasn't going to waste another second of her life being afraid. Logan was her Alpha. She would tell him everything and beg for Jax's forgiveness later.

"I'm taking you now, Wynter. Please don't deny me," he growled.

"But we need to talk… I've got to tell you…" The music blared a pounding erotic beat, and she felt his hard length press against her belly. She tried to fight the desire, to be the sensible person she'd always been. The old Wynter would have left the club. Yet, no longer the person she once was, all she wanted was him, more than anyone she'd met in her life. She craved her lips on his skin, wrapped around his cock. Submitting to both her own cravings and his wishes, she'd give it all to him without question.

"Talk later. Let's go in there. Now," he instructed, pulling her toward a sofa that was somewhat concealed behind red, translucent ceiling-to-floor fringe.

Tugging her into the small alcove, Logan couldn't wait any longer. Driven by the flicker of excitement he saw within her eyes, he knew she wanted this every bit as much as he did. Raking his fingers into her hair, he kissed her. A hungry desperate kiss. He pushed his tongue into her warm mouth, sucking and tasting, incited by the wild intensity with which she returned his kiss.

Aroused beyond reason, Wynter greedily ran her hands all over Logan's body, grasping the front of his shirt and yanking it out of his pants. She moaned loudly, running her palms up his bared ripped abdomen. Her pussy ached with need; she wanted him in her now. As if he sensed her thought, Logan cupped her bottom, lifting her up so she could wrap her legs around him. Writhing her pelvis up against his rock hard erection, she gasped in pleasure as tendrils of her release built.

Standing, Logan continued to plunder her mouth while unzipping the back of her dress. Pulling down one sleeve, he exposed her breast which was every bit as spectacular as he'd remembered from the pool. *No bra? She was a little wild after all.* He tore his mouth from hers and captured a nipple with his lips. Like a starved man, he laved it into a firm little point, letting his teeth graze the tip. "Your breasts, oh Goddess, they're so delicious," he groaned.

"Take me," she breathed as he placed her onto her back on the sofa.

Logan fell to his knees before her, never breaking eye contact. Roughly, he pushed up her dress. She heard a rip and realized he'd taken her panties. Wynter felt him push her knees wide open, his lips on her inner thigh. With Logan's head between her legs, she briefly considered her surroundings. The tassels provided a false sense of privacy as she noticed Dimitri across the room. *Was he watching them?* Barely cognizant of where she was, her beast took over, uncaring of who saw them. The animal in her wanted them all to see, to know he was hers. For the first time in her life, she tossed all preconceived ideas about what was right and wrong when it came to sex. Any last doubts disappeared as Logan's tongue swept through the seam of her wet folds. The only thing that mattered was him. Rocking her hips upward, she sought out his mouth on her pussy. She plowed her fingers into his hair, pulling him into her.

Logan slid two fingers down between her labia, surrounding her clit. Squeezing them together gently, her tiny nub protruded, and he lightly flicked his tongue over and around it. Humming into her flesh, he laughed a little when she pushed up at him, tugging his hair. Oh yeah, his little wolf was lovin' this, and he couldn't get enough of her essence. He lifted his head slightly to watch her reaction and he licked over her lips.

"You taste so good, sweetheart."

"Please," she moaned, needing more contact.

"That's it. Tell me, Wyn." His fingers slid through her wetness and teased at her entrance.

"I need…I need. Fuck me. Please."

Logan laughed, slowly pressing two long fingers into her wet tight pussy. Pushing them in and out, gradually increasing the pressure and rhythm, he watched as she ground her hips in tandem.

Wynter opened her heavy-lidded eyes, focusing as he

pumped his fingers into her. He smiled at her right before he pulled them out all the way and slid a digit into his mouth, tasting her. Slowly he withdrew it from his lips and plunged his fingers back into her. Her body arched as she cried out in ecstasy. Never in her life had anyone driven her to such delightful insanity.

"That's it baby, fuck my hand," he encouraged. Needing more of her sweet pussy, he crushed his lips against her clit. He made love to her with his mouth, flicking his tongue over her swollen pearl. As he sucked hard, drawing it into his mouth, she began to shudder beneath him.

Between his fingers and his warm lips, Wynter's body was set on fire. Sensations of pleasure and pain rocked her into climax as Logan latched onto her sensitive flesh. She screamed his name over and over, thrashing her head from side to side. Every inch of her skin tingled. But he gave her no reprieve.

Within seconds, he'd withdrawn his mouth, rose up over her and took her mouth to his. Tasting herself on his wet lips drove her further into the erotic madness. His fingers continued to press in and out of her, hurling her into a second orgasm.

"Logan," she cried into his lips.

Pressing his forehead to hers, Logan pulled away. *Fuck, he'd really lost his shit.* Her honeyed cream still lingered on his lips, and he struggled to resist his true desire. He wanted to thrust his cock deep into her hot sheath, expecting it would be the best sex of his life. But goddammit, he had done this to her in the club. It was so not how he envisioned making love to her the first time. He needed to get her home now, in his bed.

The cell phone buzzed in his pocket, but he ignored it. Cupping her cheek, he gently pulled down her dress so that she was no longer exposed.

"Home...let's go home," he suggested in a restrained voice.

Wynter simply nodded, tugging at her dress. *What the fuck did she just do? Oh that's right, she'd just let the Alpha of New Orleans go down on her in a club, while others watched.* Okay, not the brightest idea she ever had but as she straightened her clothes, she realized she didn't care, not even one little bit. The only thing on her mind was getting back to his house as soon as possible so they could make love all night long.

Logan closed his eyes, and adjusted his rock hard dick. Damn, he hurt. But there was no amount of pain that would drive him to have sex with her in this place. He'd temporarily lost control, giving into the temptation. And she'd tasted damn sweet. But what surprised him most was how amazingly open and sensitive she'd been to his touch. He couldn't wait to get her home.

His cell buzzed a second time, and he glanced at the text. From Fiona, it read: *Alpha, need you at Dana's house ASAP. Hurry.* What the hell? His beta shot him a concerned look, and he knew it wasn't good.

Logan opened the curtain and yelled over the noise to Dimitri. "Fi needs us. Let's catch a cab."

They pushed through the crowd moving quickly

through the club. Keeping Wynter at his side, he protectively guided her until they were outside. Dimitri opened the door to the car. Wynter jumped in the back seat, confused by their sense of urgency. Logan followed and Dimitri took shotgun.

"What's wrong?" she asked. "Is everything okay?"

Logan held up his hand to silence her, holding his phone to his ear.

"Fi, what's going on?" Logan inquired with a dominant tone that told Wynter that whatever it was, it was deadly serious. His face darkened, and she knew instantly that something very, very bad had happened.

Chapter Eleven

The Directeur scowled as he left the club. Because he was hiding in plain sight, she never saw him. He'd lingered patiently in the shadows, waiting for the opportunity that hadn't come. '*Good things come to those who take*' was his motto. Just a tiny slip and she'd be back in his arms and her essence in his veins. The ruse had worked beautifully for two months. She'd never known that he'd been drinking her blood. He'd even hidden his guilty pleasure from the Mistress. No, she wouldn't be pleased.

As the evening wore on, the watch dogs never left her side. Irritated that he couldn't snatch her, he had been forced to play his role. He'd always told his mother that he should have been an actor. For when the mongrels touched his property, he remained in the distance, calmly stewing. Like magma bubbling and building inside the core of the Earth, his rage burned deep inside. Eventually, he'd let his anger flow like a river of lava, destroying everything in its path.

The Director spat on the sidewalk, forced to leave the

club. The urge to steal her was great, yet the Mistress called on his service. The Mistress must be obeyed. She'd reward him greatly, he knew. Still, he barely restrained his shaking hands from strangling the little bitch for touching the Alpha. Retribution was his only solace. Soon, he'd punish her for her indiscretions.

The volcano rumbled. The sides cracked, the seeping evil tunneled toward the surface. It was time to release the vehement steam of wrath on a victim who'd meet his deadly kiss. A willing sacrifice would sate his need to kill, for now.

Dana was dead. Fiona was crying hysterically, explaining how she and Luci had found her, sprawled on the bed. The word 'blood' was tossed around, and Logan expected a grim scene. After he'd finished talking to her, Logan had hung up and handed Dimitri back his phone.

"Maybe Wynter should stay out here," Dimitri suggested.

"No," he responded definitively. "She's going to be pack soon. And she's mine."

"Okay, then," Dimitri commented, getting out of the cab.

He found it interesting to watch Logan's reaction to Wynter. It always amazed him how mated males were usually the last to know. They often alternated between outright denial and beating on their chests like territorial gorillas, before finally accepting and succumbing to the fact they'd found their mate. In the meantime, he imagined it was going to make for some interesting conversations.

As they ran up the steps to Dana's Magazine Street apartment, Wynter glanced around, noticing that the area was well kept and populated. Chic clothing stores, antique shops and restaurants peppered the thoroughfare. Large columned Greek revival styled homes and colorful Victorian cottages were interspersed throughout the neighborhood. A bustling chic café across the street buzzed with late night patrons and served drinks at a sidewalk tiki bar. She wasn't sure what had happened to Dana but if she'd been murdered, her attacker must have blended into the area, and committed the crime silently.

As they entered the apartment, nothing appeared out of sorts. Tastefully decorated in an eclectic mix of antiques and modern pieces, it was neat and clean. As soon as Fiona saw them enter, she rushed over into Dimitri's arms. Luci sat as still as a statue, and scowled at Wynter with abhorrence.

"Where is she?" Logan inquired in an authoritative tone.

"In here," Fiona cried. "She's in the bedroom. I just don't know who would have done this. We were supposed to go clubbing tonight. But then we found her…like this. How could they do something so awful?"

Wynter quietly gasped as they arrived in the small bedroom afraid of what they were about to see. She grabbed onto Logan's arm as she took in the scene, and he briefly touched her hand with his. The white shabby chic décor was splattered with blood. Dana's body had been awkwardly positioned on the bed, so she appeared as a puppet. Wearing nothing more than a purple bra and matching panties, her grayish skin was mottled with bite marks. *Vampire.*

Wynter found herself walking toward the body, both drawn to and horrified by the bites. A wide open slit across Dana's thorax exposed her spine. As a researcher, it wasn't as if she hadn't seen a dead body, but never in her life had she seen one decimated to this extent. Her eyes roamed over the marred pale skin and letters that had been scrawled into the flesh. The monsters had left a message: *SCIENTIFIQUE.* Scientist. No one else called her that; it had to be him. He'd addressed her in that manner in every single message he'd sent during her captivity. She'd never seen his face but had known him only as Director Tartarus. A chill swept over her.

Why would they go after the doctor? Logan had told her that she'd taken blood samples. Was that why they'd gone after Dana? To get the blood? Or hide the results? But why not just take her? Then it occurred to Wynter that she'd been with Logan the entire time. Maybe they were afraid of the Alpha. Her mind whirled and she considered a possibility far worse than the ominous directive. If they'd somehow changed her DNA so that she was wolf, they could have caused Dana's death by giving her a virus. They had access to any number of highly contagious diseases. And while they hadn't yet perfected a virus for wolves, Emma, a hybrid, was ill. And like Emma, Dana was also a hybrid. Panicked, she attempted to get Logan's attention while he knelt next to the bed with Fiona, who was crying uncontrollably.

"Did anyone touch the body?" she asked, putting a hand on Logan's shoulder.

"She's not a body!" Luci screamed at Wynter. "She's our friend. And she's Fi's sister."

Logan turned his head, and growled a warning at Luci.

Despite Luci's attack, Wynter pressed the issue. "Did anyone touch the body?"

"No, no one touched the body. Okay?" Luci responded curtly. "Can someone tell me what in the hell she is doing here?"

"Logan, we need to get everyone out of the room," she told him quietly.

Logan glanced over his shoulder at Wynter, unsure as to why she was behaving so strangely. "Please, can you just give us a minute? Fi's just lost her sister," he pleaded.

"I know, and I'm so sorry, but Logan, this message. It's for me," she explained with a pleading look.

"Out, everyone out," he commanded. *What the fuck?*

"But Alpha, please," Fiona cried. "I need to stay with her."

Logan hugged Fiona to his chest. Wynter turned her head at the sight, admonishing the small misplaced pang of jealousy that fluttered in her chest.

"It's okay, Fi. I'll be right out. Luci, stay with her. Dimitri, stay. I want you here for this."

Luci shot Wynter a menacing grimace on the way out of the room. As soon as the door closed, Logan turned on her. "What in the hell are you doing, Wynter?"

"They know I'm with you. The people who took me,"

she said, carefully approaching the body.

"I'm sure whoever took you knows you're with me. It's not exactly like we've been trying to hide that. We've been all over the city today."

"It's the message." She gestured toward Dana's stomach. "Scientifique. It's me. No, I mean, that's what he called me."

"Who called you that?"

"Him. The person who kept me. I never saw him," Wynter recounted with fear in her eyes. Logan never took his eyes off of her as she continued. "Director Tartarus. I only communicated through email with him. And sometimes text messages before they locked me up. But once I was captured, the guard would bring me a flash drive with a single text file on it in the morning. There'd always be one with a letter of sorts…directions from him. At the end of the day, I was instructed to save my results back onto the drive and then I'd give it back to the guard. It was my only communication with him."

"Tartarus. Very funny," Dimitri huffed.

"What?" Wynter asked as she knelt next to the bed, looking carefully at Dana's skin.

"Tartarus. Greek mythology. A place where gods would be sent for punishment," Logan explained.

"A punishment to fit their crime," Dimitri added.

Logan watched Wynter remove the lamp shade from the bedside light, pick it up and shine the light into the soulless stare of Dana's eyes. "What are you doing?"

"Honestly," she sighed. "I just had to be sure that she

wasn't sick. I mean, Tartarus. He knows disease. The company I worked for...he'd have access to all kinds of viruses. And even though you told me she was wolf, she was hybrid..." *Like Emma.* "I needed to see for myself. From what I can tell, though, there's no indication of illness. No jaundice, lesions, weight loss. And if you saw her last night and she was healthy...then it's unlikely. But the bite marks. Whoever did this tortured her. She died from exsanguination when they slit her throat."

Just like he'd seen happen to Wynter in his dream, Logan thought. But he knew it wasn't Dana's face in his vision.

"She knew him. Maybe well or not. But she liked him," Logan said with his arms crossed.

"What makes you say that?"

"Make up. Hair's done. The bra and panties."

"I agree about the underwear, but she was going out with Fiona and Luci. Maybe she was hopeful," Wynter said, playing devil's advocate.

"Or maybe she planned on meeting him there? Look around the room. There's no sign of struggle. He targeted her to get to you. But the fact is that he may have known her." The thought that Dana could have known her attacker bothered him. He'd question the girls and see if they knew anything about who Dana had been dating. "Even if he didn't know her, vampires can be very persuasive."

"Logan. I'm not sure if you're planning on calling the police or taking care of this on your own, but in either case, this body..."

"What aren't you telling me, Wyn?"

Wynter shook her head. It was now or never. She'd tell him the truth.

"Emma."

"Huh?" Logan raised an eyebrow at her in confusion.

"Emma. The girl Léopold mentioned. Jane Doe. The one I spoke about at the charity event. She's not just a case study. She's part of Jax's pack. A hybrid. And she's really, really sick." The thought of Emma made Wynter want to crawl into a ball. The girl was going to die, and she still hadn't found a cure.

"Yeah, you said that at dinner, but what's that got to do with Dana?"

"Logan, Emma is going to die soon if I can't find a cure. And it's not just that she's sick, it's *what* made her sick. A virus. You can't tell anyone what I'm about to tell you," she pleaded. Brushing the hair from her eyes, she sucked a breath and blew it out, shaking her head. "You know my friend, Mika, I told you about; Emma's her sister. Her doctors all agreed that her condition was caused by a viral infection but they couldn't explain it. I mean, hybrids don't get sick let alone get terminal diseases. It made no sense. Jax was worried that if word got around about her condition, his wolves would panic. So, her parents brought her to his country home, where she now gets round the clock nursing. I had to do something; something to help her. So I changed my major and started studying virology instead. During my doctoral program, I finally narrowed down the virus, it looked familiar. I should have known." She began to pace.

"It wasn't a natural virus to wolves or humans, but it shared visible traits with other known viruses. But what it most looked like was the feline leukemia virus; and of course that retrovirus has a poor outcome. But it wasn't an exact match. And as we know, wolves are immune to both homosapian and canis lupus diseases as well as most other typical causes of mortality. And while it is true that viruses mutate and adapt to their environment to survive, it's a moot point. I've been investigating, trying to find out if maybe someone gave her this virus. Or created it somehow, manipulated it, perhaps utilizing shifter blood."

As Logan stood listening, it occurred to him that no matter how strong the attraction was that he felt for Wynter, he really didn't know her at all. The way she talked was formal and direct, like a doctor, but he detected the pain she tried to hide. Like he'd suspected, her case was personal. And she'd gotten herself into this mess for her friend's sister? Who does that? *Wolves did that.* They had loyalty that ran as deep as an abyss. But she'd been a human living with an Alpha wolf. Why would she risk her life to save a hybrid wolf? Why was she still living with the Alpha? Who was the woman he almost made love to an hour ago? So many questions and very few answers.

Logan pinched the bridge of his nose, attempting to shake off the distracting thoughts. He needed to focus. Growing impatient, he blew out a breath. An hour ago, he'd been ready to claim this woman in front of everyone. Sure, it may have been a jealous, lust-driven temporary insanity, but still, it didn't negate what happened. As she stood before him now, she was no longer the vulnerable woman he'd held in his arms. No, this person was someone he didn't know at all. A researcher who was up to her eyeballs in some serious shit. And one of his wolves was dead as a result.

"Get to the point, doctor," he warned coldly.

"When I was offered the fellowship at ViroSun, I should have suspected something was off. They're one of the top ten virology companies in the country, typically known for their advanced work with next generation antivirals and vaccines. I'd just earned my doctorate, so why did they pursue me? I thought it was because of my relationship with Jax, but it was Emma. They wanted my knowledge of her and the viruses. I made the mistake of bringing samples of her blood to my lab. I had to know if she was intentionally infected; they had all the latest equipment I needed to find a way to save her," she said quietly. Sadness laced her words and she tried not to cry. She should have never taken that job. She should have listened to her gut and refused the tempting carrot.

"Shortly after I started, they slowly began pumping me for information about Emma…my 'Jane Doe'. I'd done lectures, so they knew of the case. But I could tell they knew exactly who it was. One day someone actually used her name. Later that day, I tried grabbing all the data, to get it to Jax. I was going to leave. And that was the day they locked me in the lab. And I thought, 'how could this happen?' I was working in a large office building. I don't know how they did it. They just locked me in and the next day, they had me moved and on the road. I never knew where I even was. It was always just me in a makeshift lab with the vampires."

Wynter regretted her decision to take the data. She should have just walked out the door that day and gone to Jax. They must have been monitoring her through a camera, known what she was doing with the files. She rubbed her eyes, glanced up at the ceiling and then back to Logan.

"And I have to tell you, Logan; I was close to figuring out what caused it, how it works. But they still don't have what they need yet. It's not finished. The scary part is that I've suspected for some time that they want to make it portable, so it can be actively utilized…on hybrids at first, eventually wolves. You need to know that even though they don't have me, they have the data. I don't understand why they still want me. It doesn't make sense. I already told them most of what I knew about Emma. They could find another scientist to work on it, but this," Wynter gestured to the blood spatter and the words written on the body. "This tells me they aren't going to let me go. I don't know why. I'm so sorry they killed Dana. Sorry I haven't told you everything. I really wanted to tell you but…"

Logan had heard enough. "Yeah, I know protocol. What a bunch of shit, doctor. I take you into my home, and you don't think you owe me the decency to tell me that you've been working on a virus that could have the capability to kill wolves? Fuck," he grunted, shaking his head.

He didn't want to come down so hard on her but he was beyond frustrated. Seriously? A virus that attacks wolves? A corporation looking to exploit the virus? What she was saying didn't seem possible. What was it about the godlike Jax Chandler that drove her to keep this a secret?

"But they can't yet. I told you, that's why they wanted me. I'm sorry," she whispered.

There was nothing else she could say. It was ironic that the past five years she'd done nothing but devote her life to research, all in the name of protecting wolves, and she was no closer to helping Emma. To add to it all, she'd opened her heart and body to an incredible Alpha, one who was very much pissed at her at the moment. She was a fool to have even thought for one minute he'd understand. As her thoughts drifted to Jax, she almost felt relief. If he found out she'd been with Logan, he'd be angry with her too. Her heart broke, because there had been no doubt how she felt about him earlier. She'd been willing to give herself to him in every way, and it couldn't have felt more right. In his arms, she belonged to him. He was her Alpha.

But maybe it had been the wolf who'd claimed him as Alpha? The entirely human part of her now doubted her own feelings. Logan's disappointed expression left no room for misinterpretation. He didn't want her here with him or his wolves. Now that he knew the truth about what was going on with ViroSun and why she was imprisoned, he could align with Jax and deal with the issue on his own. As she watched him, she could see the wheels turning, the ever present leader calculating his next move in the war strategy.

A commotion in the next room jarred her back to focus, and she straightened her back when she heard Léopold's voice. What was he doing here? Was he somehow involved in Dana's death? She quickly sidled up behind Logan, close but not touching. As the door flew open, she held her breath.

Unbeknownst to her, Logan had texted the dark vampire in the car after Fiona had mentioned the state of the body. Logan couldn't be certain if vampires were in charge of this operation or not. True, vampires had tortured Wynter and had a hand in Dana's murder, but in his long life, he'd learned that things weren't always as they appeared. What he hadn't mentioned to Wynter was that it was possible more than one person had killed Dana.

"Thank you for coming," Logan told Devereoux and nodded over to Dana.

Léopold wasted no time, going directly to the body. Picking up the cold arm, he sniffed at the skin and darted his tongue over the small wounds. Unceremoniously, he stood and rubbed his nonexistent five o'clock shadow. Contemplating the situation, his menacing eyes met Logan's.

"Her neck was the fatal blow, no? There's a lot of blood. But someone did drink from her. These bites aren't just for show. No, they took much blood before killing her."

"But there's no signs of struggle," Logan indicated.

"Oui. Pleasure bites, perhaps. It would explain her relaxed positioning, the peaceful look in her eyes. I believe she knew him. Or her." Léopold gently slid his fingers over the woman's eyelids, closing them.

"That I hadn't considered. But your guards were all males, correct?" Logan asked Wynter.

"Yes."

"But still, there's nothing here to indicate the sex of the killer," Logan agreed. "It appears she hasn't been sexually assaulted although an autopsy would be needed to confirm. I don't smell sex."

"The scent is exactly what disturbs me," Léopold pointed out, fisting his finely manicured fingernails.

"We didn't smell anything," Dimitri told him.

"The she-wolves were the ones who found the body," Logan explained. "What do you smell?"

"Ah, it's so very faint, but vampire. And to my great dismay, it is from my line. Perhaps not a direct child," he reasoned. "No, it cannot be. They've all been accounted for. Isn't that interesting? Where did you say you found Wynter last night?"

"Down near Decatur. Courettes. I sent a couple of my guys down there last night afterwards, but they didn't find anything. But if you've got a scent, we should go together," Logan suggested. "Give me an hour and I'll meet you there. First, I've got to get Fiona and Luci home safely."

"They'll be gone," Wynter added softly.

"It's a longshot, but if it gives Devereoux more information about who he's looking for in his ranks, then we're going," Logan said tersely. "Dimitri, take Wynter home."

"I can go with you," she interrupted.

"No, you can't," Logan disagreed. No fucking way was she going anywhere near that place, putting herself in danger again. Logan needed to get away from her for a while anyway. She was clouding his judgment. He should have sent her to Jax the minute he found her. Because of his overactive libido, he'd allowed her to stay and worse, he played with her. The confusing emotions would endanger her and his pack.

"But I could help you find where they kept me," she continued, until Logan turned on her. Wynter's feet moved backward on their own until she'd backed up against a closet door. She'd never understood how the pack and an Alpha communicated, but she swore she could literally feel his anger emanating off of him, snapping across her skin like a whip.

"You. Will. Go. Home. Do not argue with your Alpha, Dr. Ryan. You will learn soon that there are consequences for disobedience within the pack. Do not test me," he growled at her.

"But Logan…" Wynter's eyes brimmed in tears as he admonished her in front of the others. She wanted to scream at him that she wasn't a wolf but thought better of it.

"Not another word. Now go." Logan's face hardened and his eyes fixed on hers before he turned his attention to Dimitri.

"Get her out of here. And keep her safe until I return."

"You got it."

"Hey D, one more thing. Did you call Zeke and Jake? I need them to deal with Dana's body."

"Yes, Alpha."

Dimitri moved over to Wynter and gently put his arm around her. "You okay?" he asked, aware that Logan was watching his every move with her.

Wynter nodded silently. She wanted to leave; she hated this place. She already sensed how Logan had distanced himself from her, well before he yelled at her. No, the embarrassment of being chastised was just the finality she needed to know she had to go home to New York. Confused and alone, she wanted nothing more than a hot shower and to crawl into a bed. She might have to wait to go home to the city, for Jax. But she was good at waiting. Being held captive had taught her that.

If she really was a wolf, she could continue to live with Jax, at least until he found a mate. He'd proved a million times over that he'd protect her, of that she was sure. Jax was everything she'd needed when there was nothing. And by some cruel fate, she once again had nothing. No job. She had a degree in a career that she didn't look forward to jumpstarting. Her health was questionable, infected with an unidentified agent. Her mind would be forever broken by the memories of the torture she'd endured. And the small place she'd begun to open in her heart for Logan was a figment of her imagination. Like a mirage in the desert, the oasis was transforming back into sand.

The last thing she saw when they left the apartment was Fiona curled into Logan's arms. Luci stood next to him, caressing the back of his head. Feeling nauseated at the sight of another touching him, Wynter tried to look away but not before Logan's eyes flashed to hers. His impassive facial expression gave no clues as to what he was thinking, but she recognized the flare in his eyes. *Passion.* Whether filled with hate or love, a storm brewed within him.

Chapter Twelve

The Mistress celebrated the death of the meddling doctor. It couldn't have gone more smoothly, except perhaps for that diabolical vampire. She hadn't counted on him being in New Orleans. Kade would have been much easier to deceive. But Devereoux, he was an entirely different creature. Much too clever for his own good. But now that she knew he was here, she'd be more careful.

She cursed the Directeur. He'd been sloppy, indulging the pretty hybrid in foreplay before killing her. He should have merely slit her throat, leaving no clues as to what kind of creature had taken her life. How unfortunate for him that the ancient one now suspected the Directeur's lineage. Idiocy and arrogance would be his downfall. From the minute they'd met, he'd aspired to a stature well beyond his capabilities. It served him right to be taken down a peg.

If they identified him, she'd eliminate him. Pity, but she couldn't have his mistakes thwart her plans for her Acadian Wolves.

The cab ride back to the mansion was a blur. Wynter didn't want Dimitri to see the tears streaming down her face. She'd looked in the other direction, staring aimlessly into the dark city streets. Long ago, she'd learned that emotions equated to weakness. She may be broken, but she'd never let them see it. A survivor, she'd get through this like every other dreadful experience. Ten years ago, she thought nothing would match the pain and devastation when her loving parents were brutally murdered in a carjacking. It had felt as if a shard of glass had cleaved open her heart. She mourned them for years until life had become tolerable. Up until six months ago, she'd begun to hope that she'd maybe create her own family someday, filling that void in her chest that had never quite mended.

Tonight, Logan might as well have torn her in half when he yelled at her. One minute she'd been ready to make love to him and the next it was over before it started. The final blow had been how he'd allowed Fiona and Luci into the comfort of his arms so quickly. Her cerebral, human self knew that he'd been attending to their grief as Alpha, but her soul felt crushed. Her wolf yelped wildly at the sight, not understanding what she was seeing. The beast was growing stronger. Angry and hurt, her emotions swirled like an out of control tornado uplifting and destroying anything in its path. None of the feelings meshed with her normally levelheaded approach to life.

The wolf within seethed, aware that her Alpha was in the

hands of other females. Wynter closed her eyes, trying to push the animal away, but it kept at her, unrelenting. The full moon was only days away, and she suspected there was a chance she would indeed shift. *Oh God. How could this be happening?* She'd been afraid to ask them where Dana had taken her blood or what the results were. She figured that she'd do her own analysis once she got back to New York. Other than the wolf, no physical discomfort or illness remained from her ordeal. No, all the pain she felt was in her own mind. Restless and heartbroken, Wynter didn't know how she was going to get through the night.

Before she knew where she was, she realized she was standing inside the guest room. Had Dimitri walked her all this way? She didn't even remember getting out of the cab. Exhausted, she sat on her bed and put her face into her hands.

Dimitri was worried about the little wolf. She hadn't spoken the entire way home. He couldn't even imagine what it would be like for a human to transform into a wolf. Even if she lived with wolves, it didn't make her one. Adapting to their lifestyle would not be easy. Listening to Logan reprimand her was difficult. But she'd needed to learn that she couldn't openly challenge the Alpha, especially after everything that had transpired; Dana's death, her own confession.

Observing her listless state, his suspicion that she was Logan's mate grew stronger. Her wolf needed her mate, and he'd been with another woman. That alone would have driven her wolf berserk. But it was more than that; Logan had withdrawn after the scene at the club. For a minute, he thought he might have to hold Logan back from tearing Léopold apart limb by limb. Jealousy didn't even begin to describe his Alpha's behavior. He'd watched his Alpha possessively sweep Wynter off her feet. And she, and her wolf, ravenously attacked him in return despite her otherwise modest human nature. It was the hottest thing he'd witnessed in a long time. After seeing her in the pool earlier, Logan wasn't the only one walking around today with an agonizing erection.

Dimitri wished she'd just come clean from the beginning. Protocol was one thing; endangering pack members was an entirely different story. But to be fair to her, he and Logan had taken her into their home knowing someone was still after her. She'd shared as much. The whole situation summed up to a clusterfuck of monstrous proportions. He sure as hell hoped that Logan and Léopold found some kind of clue soon before all-out war broke out in New Orleans, because if they didn't, he was certain his Alpha would tear up the city to find Dana's killer.

Dimitri watched Wynter slump onto her bed. He needed to do something to help her get through the night; something that did not include touching her too much. His Alpha may not have understood what the female meant to him yet, but Dimitri wasn't fool enough to test his theory. When Logan came home, he'd go in search of her. Similar to Wynter's current reaction from being separated from Logan, the pull to be with her would be too much to resist.

"Hey, Wyn. It's going to be okay," he reassured, sitting

down next to her on the bed. "Come here."

The bed depressed and Wynter felt a strong arm around her shoulder. And even though it wasn't the man she wanted, she was oddly calmed by his touch and welcomed his presence. He was warm, and like Logan, his scent was appealing, safe. A sob wrenched from her chest, and she clung to him, seeking comfort.

"That's it, cher." Dimitri wrapped her all the way into his embrace. While he found her attractive, especially after watching her with his Alpha, he only sought to give her peace. There was nothing sexual about the situation for him. Oh no, a cryin' woman was a libido killer, in his book. "It's not your fault."

"I should have told him sooner," she cried. "But it wouldn't have mattered. They want me. I may have to go back to them. They won't stop."

"No, don't think so. You're not going back. Do you think your Alpha would ever let that happen?"

"Jax or Logan. Who is my Alpha?" She pulled away; her eyes were swollen and red. "I don't know who I am, Dimitri. Where I belong. Hell, I don't even know what I am. How could they do this to me? Wasn't it enough to drain me? To chew on me like rodents? And now, I'm just a freak."

"You're wolf, cher. And it's going to be okay. It may not be easy but you'll get through it. As for your Alpha, only you can make that choice."

"I haven't slept with him," Wynter confessed.

"Logan?"

"Jax," she stated.

"Okay, then." Dimitri wasn't sure if he was ready for this conversation but he steadied himself for what came next.

"We live together, making people wonder, leaving it ambiguous to everyone…well, except for his beta."

"Now why would you do that?"

"My parents. They were murdered. I was fifteen," she whispered. She kept her head down. "My Dad worked for him. He was his accountant. They were pretty close friends. Jax trusted Daddy with everything. One day I was in my parents' loving home in Brooklyn and the next thing I knew I'd been moved into Jax's Manhattan penthouse. I had no other family when they died."

"I'm sorry," Dimitri offered, and wrapped his arm around her once again. "It must've been really difficult. You were so young."

"I hated Jax at first. He was overbearing. What else can you expect from an Alpha? But he cared about me….really cared about me. The first year, he never left my side. Seriously, pretty much wherever he went, he made sure I was with him," she reminisced. "He filled my days with school, friends, horseback riding…all kinds of things to keep me busy and growing up right. He loves me."

"Like a father?"

"Like an Alpha," she responded quickly. "No, Jax is quite aware that I'm a woman, but if he's ever wanted me that way, he never told me. We're friends, but he's Alpha. I know that, respect him."

"So why the pretense?"

"He insisted on it. I didn't mind. I mean, the wolves, he

kept me from his pack for the most part. I don't think he wanted me around the males. He kept telling me I'd grow up to find a human. It sounded reasonable. It didn't really bother me."

"But why not just tell Logan?" Dimitri persisted.

"I don't know. He asked me if I belonged to Jax, and I do. I did. Or at least that's how it felt before, but now everything is so confusing." She rubbed her face with the back of her hand, trying to dry the tears. "But when I went to dance with Léopold…he frightened me. I saw his fangs, and he kept talking to me about Logan. And I don't know…all I knew is that I wanted Logan and…"

"What?" Dimitri could hear the hesitation in her voice.

"I felt like he really was my Alpha," she said with a shake of her head. "How crazy is that? I mean, I've known the guy for what? A day? Maybe a very long intense day. So to have that thought in my head…him being my Alpha. It's insane, yet it felt so real."

"Sometimes things in life don't make sense, cher. Sometimes our feelings," he put his hand on her chest above her heart, "our gut; that's what you've got to trust. Now I know you're some kind of a scientist and you like data, facts and all that business. But you know since you've been around Jax that that's not how things work in the pack. Fate, she directs the life show. And you've got to trust your heart."

Wynter listened intently. Maybe he was right but she was still ripe with confusion.

"Now look, you've made me all sappy," Dimitri

laughed, trying to lighten the mood. "Don't tell Logan. I won't live it down."

"You've gone and spoiled that dangerous mystique of yours," she smiled. "I'll try to take your advice, and I promise I won't tell Logan."

"Oh cher, you don't need to worry about that danger part. Let's hope you don't ever need to see it. Now come on, go get a shower. I'll get you some tea and then you're goin' to bed."

As Wynter emerged from the bathroom, she stared at herself in the long mirror. Dressed in a pink camisole and underwear, she noticed her naturally curly hair had now gone completely haywire, but her skin was smooth and flawless. Too flawless. Unnaturally so. It was physically impossible for a human to heal at this accelerated rate, she knew. Part of her was relieved that she actually looked better than she had prior to taking the job. The other part of her shivered in trepidation. Her molecular structure had changed and was still in flux. Would she shift? Would it hurt? What would it feel like to be an animal?

A blanket of despondency shaded her otherwise optimistic spirit. It was then that she realized why she was so utterly miserable. She missed Logan. More than lust, she wanted to get to know him and talk about things that only lovers would share. Thoughts of what it would be like if they made love danced through her mind. But then that nasty bit of reality cropped up, slamming her back to what was really happening. The reason she was here alone, her lack of transparency.

A sigh drew her attention away from her spiraling misery. She startled at the sight of Dimitri watching her. His one hand was propped on the door jamb, and the other held a steaming cup. At first, she'd found him a little scary with his massive presence, tattoos and sharp goatee. But he'd shown himself to be gentle and caring, and she understood why Logan chose him as a beta.

"Hey, brought you tea." He offered her the warm beverage. "You look beautiful. I mean, tonight you looked great. But look at you; you're all healed."

"Yes. Not very humanlike." She gratefully took the mug, sat on the bed and took a sip.

"No, but it's natural…for a wolf," he countered.

"Can I ask you a question?" She knew she shouldn't ask but she just couldn't take not knowing.

"Ask away. My answer, that'll depend on the question."

"Fair enough. Is he with those women? I'm sorry, I shouldn't have asked." She buried her face into the cup, regretting her question. How embarrassing was it to be so insecure?

He smiled, thinking that they were going to drive each other crazy before admitting what was going on between them.

"Logan's single. As in not attached. That being said, my Alpha's all about business. I'm fairly sure that he's with Léopold right now and not out messin' with girls."

"I feel horrible," she cringed. "I shouldn't have asked. It's none of my business."

"Don't be so hard on yourself. Trust me; there are things at work here that you don't understand." *Like he's your mate.* "Logan'll be home later, cher. Ya'll will work it out. Until then, you need to listen to your beta. I know what'll make you feel better," he predicted, taking her by the hand.

Wynter nervously followed him, unsure of where they were going. But as soon as he opened the large door, she knew. Logan's scent engulfed her, and her wolf rejoiced.

"What are we doing in here?"

"You know where you are, don't you?"

"Yes," she managed. A flick of a light revealed Logan's bedroom. Immaculate, but sparsely decorated, a king sized cherry four-poster bed invited her. A simple white cotton down comforter covered the bed along with a topping of several white pillows. A matching dresser sat across the room in between rectangular windows, and night tables flanked the mattress. Several large potted tropical palm trees added an organic flair to the décor.

She stood frozen watching Dimitri, who walked over to the bed and pulled back the comforter. What was he doing? Wynter tried desperately to quell the nervous flutter in her stomach.

"Come, cher. In you go," he commanded.

She raised an eyebrow at him in confusion. There was no way in hell that she would get into Logan's bed with his beta. No freaking way. Wynter had made enough mistakes for one evening, thank you very much.

"Don't worry, I'm not getting in bed with you," he promised. "Not that I wouldn't want to, but Logan would kill me. Stop stallin' and get on over here."

Wynter smiled at Dimitri. "I don't know. I'm not sure Logan would want me in his bed," she hedged.

"I'm tellin' you. Logan doesn't know what he wants. But this'll be good for you and him. Now get in." He continued to hold the linens up, gesturing in a sweeping motion for her to get in the bed.

She knew she shouldn't do it, but the temptation was too great. The scent in the room was like walking into a chocolate factory and damn if she didn't love chocolate. Just one small bite, a taste, and then she'd leave and go to her guest room. As she pushed her feet into the bed, the smell of Logan grew stronger. Like a cat, she shamelessly rubbed her face into the pillowcase. It felt incredible. Desperately, she kneaded the mattress and pillow, letting the calm of Logan wash over her. She didn't understand why it was happening, and she didn't care. This man, this Alpha, she needed him; he was hers. Oh God, she prayed they'd reconcile. As she drifted off to sleep, all she saw was Logan's face.

Chapter Thirteen

Logan went to the cupboard, pulled out a bottle of scotch and poured himself a generous glass. God damned fucking vampires. Logan cursed them to hell, worried that it was just a matter of time before they attacked another one of his wolves. He and Léopold had gone over every square inch of the blocks surrounding Courettes, and they'd found nothing. Granted, the eccentric vampire had caught a scent off of Dana's body, but it wasn't enough. Despite the failure to find anything, Léopold had assured him that he'd find the lab's location. But Logan didn't trust him, and sure as hell couldn't wait around for Léopold. His pack was in danger, and he needed to take immediate action to protect them. In the morning, he'd planned to call Jax and have it out.

He'd been so angry with Wynter. Still, he felt like shit for yelling at her. But he was sick of the lies. Well, he knew they weren't exactly lies; more like an omission of facts. And even though she may have had her reasons, it still was a bitter pill to swallow. Coupled with her challenge, he'd torn into her, treating her like he'd treat any wolf. And therein lies the rub; she wasn't just any wolf.

The look on her face when she'd left the apartment had ripped his heart out of his chest. Yes, he sought to provide comfort to Fiona and Luci, but he should have never let the women touch him like that. Only an hour earlier, Wynter had opened herself, allowing him to touch her, taste her. He'd been so disrespectful. He wouldn't blame her if she didn't forgive him.

Footsteps alerted him to Dimitri's presence.

"Hey, how'd it go?" Dimitri asked, grabbing a glass, looking to join Logan in a drink.

"Not good," he replied, falling into an overstuffed chair. He propped his feet onto an ottoman.

"I take it you didn't find the lab, huh?"

"Nope. We didn't find a damn thing. Devereoux is certain whoever it is is from his line. But of course, he's as slippery as an eel."

"And Fi?" Dimitri asked all too innocently.

"Fi's Fi. She's upset, of course. But you know, she wasn't exceptionally close to Dana. The two fought like wildcats. Still, they're sisters…half-sisters. Whatever. Luci's staying with her. I didn't really have time. Had to meet Devereoux down at Courettes. How the pack loved seeing him," Logan said acrimoniously, throwing his head backwards into the cushion.

"Yeah, I bet," Dimitri concurred, taking a long swig. He coughed as the caustic liquid burned his throat. "So, uh, what about Wynter?"

"What about her?"

"She's upset."

"Yeah, so am I," he spat out.

"Well it wasn't that way at the club. Y'all seemed in tune then," Dimitri mentioned. "Pretty hot, man."

Logan let that sink in a minute before responding. Goddess, she was amazing. The sweetest he'd ever tasted.

"Yeah, it was," he began. "Didn't go so well after that."

"Yeah, not so much," Dimitri commented, looking into his drink.

"This thing with her…it has me distracted. I've fought hard to be Alpha. The pack needs me." Logan swiped his hand over his eyes, replaying what happened at Dana's. The scene at the apartment was jacked. Guilt dug at him, knowing how he'd treated Wynter. "Fuck, I'm an asshole. How is she doing?"

"I'll be honest. She wasn't lookin' so good earlier. She's torn up about what's happening. I think the whole wolf thing's freaking her out too. But don't worry; I took good care of your girl. She's doing fine now." Dimitri darted his eyes to the side and then finally looked over to Logan and smiled.

"What'd ya do, D?" He blew out a breath.

"Nothin' you wouldn't have done."

Logan stared over at him. "Seriously? Tell me you didn't…"

"Not that. Although, she's sweet, man. I mean, really sweet. Tonight she was wearing these tight little panties, and those breasts…Oh Goddess, save me," he said dramatically, putting his hand to his chest.

"Mine," Logan reminded him with a smile.

"Ah, but are they? You were a little harsh tonight, almighty Alpha," he taunted.

"Still mine, smartass."

"Well, great one, if you want to keep said breasts, you'd better make nice. Your little wolf is getting ready to high tail it back to New York tomorrow," he lied.

"She is?" Logan asked in a panicked voice. *What the hell was wrong with him?*

"Let's just say you shouldn't have let Fi and Luci rub all over you like cats in heat. You know, giving that kind of grief counseling isn't doing you any favors," Dimitri half-heartedly joked.

"Fuck." Letting his anger drive his actions wasn't the smartest thing he'd ever done. He knew full well how jealous Wynter had been when they'd talked earlier in the club. And he couldn't blame her after he'd gone all territorial on her after seeing her dance with the vampire. If he were truthful, he'd admit that he knew the sight of Luci touching him would hurt Wynter. He shouldn't have let it happen.

"Fuck is right. She didn't like it at all. On the upside," he laughed. "She didn't like it at all."

Logan rolled his eyes.

"Seriously, bro. How would you feel if she didn't care? Think about it. It's not really that bad, all considered." Dimitri shrugged.

"What exactly am I supposed to consider? That my life

has been upturned in the past twenty-four hours by a human female? Who's a wolf? That I'm losing it because I'm preoccupied by a woman? And now, one of my own wolves is dead. You and I both know I've got to focus all my priorities on running this pack, D."

"She could be your mate, Logan," he posed quietly. Dimitri's lip curled up on one side, as he waited for a reaction.

"You've got to be joking. No way. I know I've been distracted, but come on," Logan pleaded. "Where is she?"

"Okay, believe what you want, man, but I'm telling you that there's something about that woman...you and her. Today at the pool and then at the club. You've been with lots of females, of all species, but this is different. She's," he took a deep breath, shaking his head, "She's responsive. To you, hell, even to me."

Logan growled at his beta.

"As if I'd touch her without your permission," Dimitri assured him. "It's just that she calmed down with me, and I felt comfortable with her...like I've known her for a long time."

"So what happened?"

"Let's just say that I knew what to do," he said proudly. Dimitri stood up, walked over to the sink and put his empty glass in it.

"And that was?"

"She's in your bed."

"What?" *In his bed?* Even though he acted surprised, there was no place he'd rather have her.

"You heard me. And it worked, by the way. She fell right asleep."

"Have I told you what a great beta you are, D?"

"Yeah, and don't fuck it up." Those were Dimitri's last words as he walked out the door.

Logan laughed. As sure as he was sitting there, he knew without question that Wynter would challenge and reward him in ways he'd never known. But was she his mate? He'd honestly never given it a thought. Whether out of denial or ignorance, he hadn't considered why he'd been nearly obsessed with her since they'd met. She'd gotten under his skin; that was for sure. All he knew was that he had to go to her. Whether she forgave him or not, he needed to say his piece.

On his way up to his bedroom, Logan contemplated what it must be like for her. Her captivity, surviving being bitten and now, her illness or whatever they'd done to her; it was all too much for one wolf, let alone a human to take. Learning to live as a wolf wouldn't be easy, but he was determined to guide her during her transition. And that was the crux of it. He wanted to be the person who stood at her side, not Jax. In spite of everything, it was the fact she lived with another man that irritated him. The New York Alpha would arrive soon and she'd leave.

Cracking open his bedroom door, Wynter's delectable scent hit him, drawing him to her side. Like an angel, she slept peacefully, looking as if she belonged there. *In his bed. In his home.* The temptation to touch her was great, but he needed to shower before lying down. Not only did the stench of death cling to his clothing, he was reminded of how he'd let Fiona and Luci touch him.

After a quick shower, Logan toweled the moisture off his body, letting his thoughts wander. He considered what Dimitri had told him about Wynter. How could the Goddess send him a human as a mate? A human who may or may not be a wolf? Who belonged to another Alpha? Shit, it'd been a long night. But knowing the woman was ten feet away in his bed had him wide awake. They needed to have a real discussion before they made love. Unless she submitted to him, accepted him fully as her Alpha, they had no future.

Steam poured out of the bathroom as he opened the door. The anticipation of touching her again put his system on alert. Even though she was fully covered, he knew the taste of the lovely she-wolf who lay beneath. It would kill him to talk first, play later, but it was the right thing to do. Lifting a corner, he slipped in underneath, his naked skin grazing the sheets. Unable to resist, he slid forward until his chest was against her back and wrapped a hand around her waist. *Damn, she was dressed.* He supposed he didn't want Dimitri taking care of 'everything'. It'd be his pleasure to peel off the flimsy fabric that clung to her body. She stirred and her bottom brushed against his semi-erect shaft. *Sweet mother of nature.* Soon he'd take her like this, he thought; slamming his cock into her tight pussy from behind. He sucked a breath, willing his self -control to kick in. *Better talk quick before I come right here.*

"Wyn, baby." He kissed the back of her hair, inhaling

deeply. She smelled so good, like a breath of fresh air.

"Hmm," Wynter responded sleepily. Within seconds, she realized Logan's hard chest was against her. Something about his scent calmed her wolf. But then she remembered how angry he'd been. "Do you want me to leave?" *Please don't make me go.*

Logan gently rolled her toward him so she was facing him. "No, sweetheart. I want to talk about what happened. What's happening with us."

"I'm sorry," she whispered, slowly opening her eyes to meet his. On her side, she reached forward and placed her palms to his chest. She swore she could hear his heartbeat.

He laughed a little. "I'm the one who should be apologizing. I was an ass tonight. I shouldn't have treated you like that."

"I didn't tell you everything. I challenged you in front of everyone," she responded, looking down to his abdomen. Even though she was supposed to be apologetic, and she truly was, the man made her horny as hell. For the love of God, she could lick him all over and never eat another meal.

"The challenging business, well, it's true that's something we can talk about, but honestly, I was just trying to protect you. It could've been dangerous. But the most important thing from now on is that we can't have any more secrets. Seriously, Wynter. And that includes no more withholding the truth. If I don't have all the facts, I can't see the whole picture. It puts all of us at risk."

Wynter nodded.

"Still, I shouldn't have been so harsh…especially since

you haven't been wolf for very long," he continued. His eyes roamed over her body; the swell of her cleavage threatened to spill out of her top. "I know you haven't been around wolves, not in a pack anyway. You haven't even shifted yet. After everything that's happened to you…I should've gone easier."

"No more secrets. I promise. But Jax…"

"I know you're worried about Jax, but I'll talk to him and…" *I want you to be mine.*

"I'm not with Jax, not the way you think."

"What?"

"I haven't had sex with him," she interrupted. She lowered her eyes and spoke softly. "He's my guardian. A protector. A friend."

"Why didn't you tell me?" Logan felt as if a thousand pound weight had lifted with the news that she hadn't slept with Jax.

"When my parents died, I was only fifteen. Jax, he took me in that very day, and he's been in my life ever since. He only wants to protect me. That's why he wanted our relationship to remain kind of unclear…to others. He claims me as his, like you did. After all he's done for me…you need to understand. I owe him everything. I didn't want to be disloyal," she explained and then added, "Growing up, and even now as an adult, he doesn't want me around the wolves. Well, he's okay with Mika, but he'd never let me date wolves when I was younger. Believe me, he won't understand."

"I can't blame him. Wolves, we're passionate, but aren't always gentle." He smiled.

"Maybe I don't want gentle," she said seductively. "Maybe I just need the right wolf."

Logan pulled her into an embrace so that her head and body was flush with his. As she molded into him, he wrapped a leg around hers allowing his erection to press into her belly.

"Logan, there's something else. I'm so embarrassed, but I need to tell you. Tonight, when I saw you with Fiona and Luci...my wolf, she...she's so strong...I don't know how to control her...the way I feel..." She couldn't finish. The jealousy had nauseated her.

"Wyn," Logan began, gently raising her chin so she'd look into his eyes. "I'm really sorry. I should have never let Luci touch me after what we had just shared in the club. It was wrong. I shouldn't have let her near me...not like that, anyway. Let's just say that if someone had touched you like she'd done to me, I would have...well, you saw how I reacted to Devereoux earlier. Our wolves, they are an extension of ourselves, and sometimes, they feel and act like what they are, animals. As such, they have a tendency to fiercely protect what they perceive to be theirs."

Relief swept over Wynter. In response, she rubbed her body against his in a slow rhythm. She pressed her mound into the ridge of his hard shaft, seeking to alleviate the throbbing ache between her legs. She cursed that she was dressed when she felt his velvet tip brush against her inner thigh. Her fingertips dug into his back.

Logan's hand slipped from her waist around to her bottom, sliding into her panties. He cupped her ass and traced a finger up and down her cleft, massaging her flesh. His hips pushed into hers, slowly grinding, creating the pressure they both sought.

"I was so angry when I saw you with them. It's like I've lost control of my emotions. I've never been like this before. I can feel it. I'm changing," she admitted. "But it's more than that. I know we've just met, but I want you so much. I've never felt like this…not ever."

"I feel the same way. There's something about you. Us. You have no idea how much I want to make love to you," he breathed, kissing up the side of her neck until he reached her ear. His low sexy voice reverberated between them as he told her what he planned to do next. "Tonight, you're mine, Dr. Ryan. All. Night. Long."

"My Alpha, I'm yours," she whispered, baring her throat. Never in her life had she done this for a man, yet she knew what it meant to wolves. Open and vulnerable. Submitting to him, accepting all that he was. The man. The wolf. The Alpha. And before the night was through, she'd be his.

With a growl, Logan flipped Wynter onto her back. The sight of her submission threw his wolf into a frenzy. Grabbing the hem of her camisole, he ripped it off of her in one smooth motion, exposing her full creamy breasts. Roughly, his lips captured a hardened rosy peak. Taking the tip between his teeth, he tugged then laved it over with his tongue, groaning in male satisfaction.

Wynter gasped as he bit down on her nipple. Pain and pleasure rippled throughout her body, hurling her toward an orgasm. She raked her nails down his back, pushing her hips upward, seeking the pressure she needed. As she heard the sound of her cotton panties tearing away, she moaned.

"Fuck, Wynter. You're so beautiful," he panted as he continued to caress her. He couldn't wait to sink himself into her. "And you smell so good."

"Logan," she cried, in response to his touch.

"We'll make love slower next time," he promised, sitting up on his knees. He splayed her legs open and pulled her to him so that his cock was pressed at her wet entrance. "Look at you, so perfect."

She gazed up at Logan, allowing him access to both her body and mind. With her thighs spread wide, he swiped his thumb down her wet crease, brushing over her taut nub. She shivered in response, so close to coming.

"Your pussy is so, so wet and tight." He pressed two long thick fingers into her tight channel, and she moaned. With his other hand he continued to circle on her clit, increasing the pressure. "Ah yeah, does that feel good, baby?"

"Yes," she responded breathlessly.

As he pumped in and out of her with his hand, he took his rigid flesh and stroked himself. Without entering her, he slid his cock through her swollen lips, coating himself in her juices. Once, twice, three times, its plump head grazed her tender hood.

"Yes, Logan," she screamed. His silky hardness tantalized her clit, driving her over the edge. Exploding in an erotic release, she shuddered uncontrollably, digging her fingers into the sheets.

Logan loved how responsive she was to him. As she came, he drove his straining shaft into her pussy in one full thrust. *Fucking unbelievable,* he thought. The hot walls of her channel clenched around him like a fist, pulsating as she rode the wave of her orgasm. Logan hooked his arms underneath her knees, pulled out and slammed into her again. Like an animal, he took her over and over, encouraged by Wynter's words.

"Yes, harder. Logan. Oh God, yes!" Wynter licked her lips as she saw his thick cock disappear into her. His face was tense with restrained emotion as he pulled out and lost himself inside her once again. No other man had ever taken her so forcefully, possessing her with his passion. His power was altogether addictive and consuming. As Logan filled her completely, she was desperate for more.

Relentlessly he thrust in and out of her, increasing the pace. The harder he fucked her, the more he resisted the instinct to take her from behind. He knew that if he did, he couldn't control the need to mark her. His wolf howled in protest. She was his. But he hadn't discussed it with Wynter. Hell, he hadn't even thought about it himself. Up until now, he'd never had the urge to mark anyone in his life. Sweat beaded on his forehead, as he fought it, pushing his wolf to the side. No, if he marked her, it would be on his own terms, not the beast's. Logan cared too much about Wynter to do that to her without her permission.

Rolling them to their sides, he brought her torso to his and kissed her. A long loving kiss seared their connection. As he drove into her again and again, his fate became clear. Wynter was his. How did this happen? The question flashed and quelled. It didn't really matter. In the moment, she was everything.

Wynter kissed Logan back, feverishly clawing his ass with one hand while holding the back of his head with her other. Nothing in her life would ever be the same. The sinewy length of him stroked inside her, while the nest of his curls brushed against her clitoris. Her climax rose, and she frantically arched up against him, relishing his hard thrusts. She cried Logan's name into the darkness as her passion crested, the climax spilling over her like a waterfall.

Hearing his name on her lips, Logan plunged into her one last time. Her pussy contracted around him, massaging him into release. Groaning in ecstasy, he convulsed in orgasm. His hot seed spilled deep into her womb.

Together, they lay quietly rebounding from the soul-shattering experience they'd just shared. Logan held Wynter tightly, stroking her hair, hardly believing how incredible it had been. An unspoken intimacy bound them and neither wanted to break it.

Logan heard a small sigh against his chest. "Baby, you okay?" He kissed her hair.

"I just...Logan, you don't know," she whispered. "So close...I've never felt so close to someone. It's crazy."

"I know, sweetheart. It's okay. Trust me," he begged. He couldn't lose her now that he had her.

"I just...I can't go back." So relaxed and well loved, Wynter snuggled into his warmth.

"No, you're never leaving me. Not ever." Logan kissed her forehead as she fell asleep.

Everything had changed in his life. He thanked the Goddess he'd been able to restrain his urge to mark her. They'd have to talk tomorrow. He'd always known that someday this could happen to him, but he still wasn't prepared for it. Yet he knew there'd be no controlling destiny. For her will was too great, no matter the efforts of those who tried to resist her wishes. As he drifted off to blackness, there wasn't a cell in his being that wanted anything else than to be with his mate. *Wynter.*

Chapter Fourteen

Logan heard the thunder rumble, but it was the warmth of his mate at his feet that caught his attention. She'd woken him the best way known to a male; her soft lips wrapped around the hard length of him. *What had he ever done to deserve her?* Wynter perched over him, her legs straddling his. Ringlets of her mane scattered over his belly, obscuring his view. He pushed the offending strands aside in time to watch her take him all the way down her throat.

As she rose upward, her lips released his cock with a pop, and she lifted her eyes to meet his with a seductive smile. He hissed in response, but she didn't relent. No, she fisted him with her hand, stroking his wet shaft and lifting it so she could access all of him. Her tongue licked along the soft crinkled skin of his tightened balls right before she took one into her mouth.

Logan threw his head back into the pillow in ecstasy.

"Fuck, you are killin' me," he groaned and pumped his hips up toward her mouth. "Yes, that feels so good."

Wynter merely hummed happily as she continued her

assault. Waking to the storm had been the impetus for her pleasure. Wrapped in his arms, she'd let her hands wander all over his sleeping form, hardly believing they'd actually made love. Once her fingers had discovered his hardened dick, the craving to suck him overcame her. Now as she caressed his straining erection and laved his testicles, the juncture of her thighs flooded in excitement.

She glanced at Logan, who wore an expression of strained satisfaction and then shifted her attention back to his cock. Her tongue darted out to lick the drop of seed seeping from his tip, and then plunged him back into her moist mouth, sucking and stroking the base with her hands. She loved his taste and sought to feast on him, inch by delectable inch. She moaned in protest as strong fingers on her arms stilled her actions.

"Baby, stop. Ah shit, I want to come in you," Logan grunted, easily pulling her upward. "Let me see you. Do you know that you're the most beautiful creature I've ever seen?"

Wynter merely licked her lips and hovered her hips above his. She took his throbbing erection into her hands and swiped it over her clit, throwing her head back. Logan wrapped his hand around hers, guiding his pulsing cock to her entrance.

"Fuck me," he demanded with choked desire.

Obliging, Wynter smiled, lifted upward then swiftly impaled herself onto his body. A scream passed her lips as she writhed against his thighs. They both held still but a second, allowing the enormity of him to stretch the contracted walls of her tender flesh. With a breath, Wynter slowly moved against him, her eyes on his. She struggled, unsuccessfully, to hold back the ripples of climax that claimed her.

"That's it Wyn, come for me," he grunted. "You're so goddamn hot."

Logan loved watching her come. Everything about her was unexpected and sensual. As she spasmed above him, he lifted to reach her breast with his mouth and latched onto one of her rose-colored nipples. He moved one of his hands from her waist to caress her other pebbled tip. But it wasn't enough. The need to consume her drove him insane. Releasing her swollen tip, he pressed his mouth to hers. The kiss was wild and frantic. Her hands now caged his head, supporting her weight while she bent into him. Her hips surged down onto his cock, hurling him closer to his own orgasm.

Logan rocked himself up into her, guiding her to his rhythm. His hand wandered to her ass, slowing her movements. Her loud moan against his lips stirred his exploration of her bottom. His forefinger wandered down her ass, brushing over her rosebud. As he circled the puckered flesh, he noticed only a moment's hesitation on her part, and then she encouraged him to continue.

"Logan, ah yes," she cried into his kiss. "Don't stop."

"Oh yeah," was all he could manage before gently inserting his forefinger into her tight hole. Gliding it in and out, he could feel the taut ring of muscle begin to relax.

Logan couldn't believe his little wolf was so open to this experience. *Goddess, did she know what she was doing by giving him such an adventurous mate?* Oh, the things he would do to her. Just the thought of fucking her ass was enough to make him come. Not today, though. No, he'd prepare her, take it slowly. Wynter's ragged breath and increased writhing in response told him that she was enjoying the feel of his touch. He inserted his finger all the way into her, pressing it in and out in accord with his thrusts into her pussy.

Wynter hissed at the dark intrusion that only served to amp her arousal. The pressure filling her threatened to explode. Arching her back, she cried out Logan's name, letting the strong sensation roll through her entire body. As her orgasm crashed into her, her walls spasmed around his shaft and Logan lost it.

Mark her, raced through his mind. *Bite her now,* his wolf told him. His canines elongated in response to the lupine call. He bit his lip, drawing blood, in an attempt to fight the carnal urge. Fiercely thrusting upward, he fought for breath, as he exploded into her hot core. Shuddering from his white hot release, he turned his head and licked the crimson liquid from his lips.

Falling back onto the pillow, he grunted, roughly pulling Wynter into his arms. She easily slid off his sex, immediately shaping herself to his body, like she'd been made for him. Logan's heart slammed against his ribs as he stared up to the ceiling. He'd barely been able to restrain himself. *What if he had bitten her? Was he really ready to be mated?* The woman did amazing things to him in bed, but he hadn't known her for very long at all. Just because his wolf wanted to claim her, that did not mean he had to accept it.

He needed to get his head on straight. If and when he made love to her again, he needed to show her his true nature. Rough and hard, the wolf wouldn't go easy. Maybe he needed to avoid her altogether. The confusing emotions tightened in his chest. Logan silently admonished himself for almost giving in to the temptation to mark her. It was as if he'd temporarily forgotten the bloody battles he'd endured over the past two months. His hard-fought effort to fulfill Marcel's wishes had come to fruition. The distraction that was Wynter Ryan threatened his role as Alpha. *Protect and lead my pack.* That was his destiny.

Taking a mate so soon into his reign could put that into jeopardy if he didn't lead with clarity and objectivity. Loyalty between what he felt for the little wolf and his role as Alpha warred. Fate would not allow him to deny his mate for long; he'd go insane trying to do so. He needed to figure out how to have both. Before he marked her, he'd need to carefully contemplate the ramifications as opposed to allowing a momentary lust-filled roll in the hay to dictate his future.

Wynter's breath slowed and she glanced up to Logan who appeared deep in thought. Her heart constricted. She could fall for this man in a New York minute. Logan would devour her if she let him. Ironically, that was exactly what she wanted. *Her Alpha.* She couldn't remember the last time in her life she'd ever felt so at peace.

"I don't want to leave," she said softly against his chest.

"You're not going anywhere, sweetheart," he assured

her, glad she couldn't see the worry reflected in his eyes. Fuck almighty, he'd almost bitten her. He needed some distance before he did something he regretted.

Chapter Fifteen

Logan sat at the kitchen table, drinking his coffee and browsing through work emails. A solid dose of business was exactly what he needed to give him a brief respite from his otherwise chaotic life. The sound of the sliding glass door's security pad beeping alerted him that Dimitri had arrived. He looked up to see his friend, strolling into the family room.

"Hey, D. Coffee's on," he commented, not looking up from his iPad.

"Hey. Beignet?" Dimitri held up a small white bag. He walked into the kitchen, took a clean mug off the counter and poured himself a cup out of the carafe. "Where's Wynter?"

"No thanks. Wyn's upstairs. Showering."

Dimitri put a palm to his chest with a smile and closed his eyes, taking in the thought of her bathing. He lived to tease his Alpha. If Logan had found his mate, it could provide him with hours of material, at least until the novelty of having her around wore off.

"What are you doing?" Logan asked, now distracted by his beta's antics.

"Wait, oh yeah. Just picturing that in my head," he laughed. "You sure she doesn't need any help up there? I'm excellent with a loofah. Yeah, I'll volunteer for that duty any day of the week."

"You're a dick," Logan replied with a smile, shaking his head.

"Speaking of…"

"Don't say it. She could hear you, you know," Logan warned.

"So?" Dimitri sat down, leaned back in his chair and raised an eyebrow at Logan.

"So what?"

"So…how'd it go last night?"

"As if you couldn't hear?" Logan asked sarcastically, refusing to look up from his screen. Dimitri lived across the courtyard but with his preternatural hearing, he probably had heard every last moan.

Dimitri broke out in a hearty laugh. "Got me there," he conceded. He picked up a beignet and pointed it at Logan. "You know, I'm not a total asshole. And for the record, I don't exactly go listening in on your business on purpose. Believe it or not, I do have a life that doesn't include you all the time. And hey, I was very good last night. I do remember someone thanking me for being such a wonderful beta. So let's hear it. Last night she was pretty broken up. I just want to know how she is."

"Yeah, 'cause you're caring like that," Logan said, taking a long drink.

Dimitri took a bite of the pastry and waited patiently for at least thirty seconds before he added, "You know you want to tell me."

"Tell you what? That she's the single most fucking unbelievably passionate little wolf I've ever been with? I am still not over how she woke me up this morning." Dimitri was right. Not only did he want to tell him how he felt about Wynter, he wanted to tell everyone. He wanted to scream it from the rooftops. And that there, was exactly his problem.

"Let's see, D, what else should you know? How about this? She's totally distracting me from my Alpha responsibilities. Oh, you'll like this one; I almost marked her last night." Logan sighed heavily, raked his hand through his hair and clicked open another email.

Dimitri smiled quietly. His Alpha was so far gone. If he'd just give into this, things would go a lot more smoothly. It wasn't as if he didn't feel for him, he really did. It wasn't as if he was itching to be mated. But he'd watched enough wolves over the years go through the process to know that you just had to accept it. You could go easy or you could go hard. But one thing was certain; you were going…and your mate was going with you.

"What, no words? No smooth advice from my beta?" Logan lifted his head, giving him a small grin. He was so fucked.

"I could help you," Dimitri suggested slyly.

"Yeah and how's that?"

"This mating thing. I could give your wolf a little

competition. Make him jealous. Kick him into drive. All I'd need to do is hug her a bit, maybe give her a kiss? Call it my beta duty. I'll take one for the team," he teased.

"No." Dimitri was enjoying this a little too much, Logan thought. Just wait until it happened to him. Big man wouldn't think it was so funny then.

"Come on. Just a little kiss. Your wolf, he'd go nuts and overrule any of that logical sludge that's cloggin' your brain. It's better that way. Get it over with fast. Just like jumping into the pool on the first day of spring; sometimes it's best to dive right in. Sure it's cold, but man, does it feel good if you just go for it. Or like a band aid. You know it's better to rip it off quickly."

"No, D. Don't even. Do not touch her," he warned lightly. "No, I just need to ride this out. Concentrate on finding this lab. Dana's killer. When it's over, I can reassess what's going on, claim my little wolf properly. I'm not an animal."

"Yeah, you kind of are, bro. You know, last night she felt pretty good in my arms. I'm excellent at comforting women," he baited.

"Don't go there." Logan flashed his eyes from his tablet over to Dimitri.

"She smelled so good," Dimitri crooned. "So soft too."

"No."

"Just sayin'."

"Leave it be, D. I'll deal with this when the time is right. I know it'll be hard to resist the urge to mark her, but I've got this." *Not really, but I'll try.*

“Does she know?” Dimitri inquired, stroking his goatee.

“No. And honestly, how am I supposed to tell her? She hasn’t even shifted yet. I don’t even know if she knows about being marked or mated or any of that wolf stuff. In all seriousness, I can’t keep my hands off her. And as much control as I have, my friend, and I have shown great restraint, I’m not sure how long it’s goin’ to last…with or without your help. I fucking bit my lip so hard this morning that it bled.”

Dimitri laughed again picturing that scene. Priceless. After all, it was kind of comical. Well, as long as it wasn’t happening to him.

“Listen, I know I should tell her but there’s a lot of shit going down. Not to mention that I’ve known her all of two days,” he insisted. “And there’s Jax, which is a whole other issue.”

“I get it. Not sure what to tell you. But if your wolf wants her, you know as well as I do that it’s going to be damn near impossible to deny him. It’s just a matter of time.”

“With Dana dead and some psychopath running around with viruses, my love life should be the least of my problems. We’ve gotta focus, D.” Logan changed the subject. “I just got a text from Devereoux. Looks like he’s found the location of what he thinks is the lab. Cagey bastard didn’t give me the address. Told him to be here within the hour.”

“Sure you want the vamp here? What about the office?”

“No, too many humans around. We’ll meet in my conference room here at the house. Don’t worry,” Logan stated without emotion. “If he crosses me, he’ll be leavin’ in an urn.”

This was exactly why Logan was Alpha, Dimitri thought. The guy could joke around with him and show compassion for his wolves, but at the end of the day, he'd tear the throat out of the enemy without a second thought. A lethal weapon. After what happened to Dana, his Alpha would take swift revenge.

"Can you get the guys over here?" Logan asked. "I'm hoping the vamp is ready with building schematics and details. I'd like to take this place out as soon as possible."

"I'm on it. Anything else?"

Logan blew out a breath and shut the cover on his tablet. "Jax. Looks like the weather up north is clearin' up. He could be here tonight, tomorrow morning at the latest. I was going to call him about Wynter, but this conversation needs to happen in person."

"Is that goin' be a problem?"

"No, just wanted to give you a heads up. Our main focus is tonight, takin' out this lab. I don't know how this thing is going to go down with Devereoux. I don't trust him, but we don't have many options. Also, we're going to have to bury Dana soon; her mom's making the arrangements. The full moon's in a couple of nights too. So I want everyone out of the city right after the funeral."

"Done."

The men stopped as soon as they heard Wynter padding down the stairs. Logan looked over to Dimitri with a knowing look and mouthed, "Not a word."

Dimitri rolled his eyes and sighed. The female really was driving his Alpha mad.

"Hi there," Wynter greeted as she strolled over to Logan. She placed a kiss on his cheek and smiled at Dimitri.

Wynter felt the cloudy skies clear after talking to Logan. No more secrets. She wasn't sure where their relationship was going, but after making love, she hoped they were meant to be. She wasn't a fool, she'd heard about mates and how it worked between wolves. Wolves could mate with wolves and even humans every now and then. But was she destined to be Logan's mate? Of that she couldn't be sure. She wondered if it was something that would just smack her in the head. Maybe after she shifted she would know?

As she looked to Logan and his beta, a rush of happiness broke across her face. She blushed like a schoolgirl. It was so irrational yet she just couldn't help how good it felt to be free: physically, emotionally, and sexually. Logan knew all there was to know of her past. So did Dimitri. Not only that, she'd been made love to thoroughly during the past twelve hours. Being with Logan drove her to new sexual heights. In the past, she'd never been so adventurous. But his touch to her skin ignited her libido; she wanted him in every way and position she could get him.

In the shower, she spent the time fantasizing about Logan, the next time they'd have sex, and actually was hoping that he'd push her further. Not that she'd had a lot of sex with other men, but it'd always been strictly vanilla. With Logan, she imagined she'd let him do anything and everything with her....except for sharing him with another woman. The feel of his fingers in her ass thrilled her, and she couldn't wait to take it further. She laughed silently to herself. She really was changing and damn, if she wasn't enjoying it.

Logan, still seated, wrapped a hand around her waist, pulled her to him and kissed her hip. It felt so good, so natural to have her in his home.

"You want coffee? Something to eat?" he asked lovingly.

"I can get it, thanks," she said with a caress to his cheek. She poured herself some coffee and took a beignet out of the bag on the counter. "So what's up? You guys are awfully quiet all of a sudden."

The men exchanged a look. How much should they tell her? Dimitri averted his gaze, deferring to his Alpha. Logan decided to tell her about tonight. She had every right to know what was about to go down.

"Devereoux thinks he's got a location on the lab. We're goin' in tonight," Logan disclosed.

"We're having a meeting here in a little bit," Dimitri added.

Wynter, determined not to let it get to her, didn't miss a beat. "Okay, I'm in. So when is the meeting? Who's coming?"

Logan coughed. She seriously wasn't thinking of going back to the lab? "Devereoux. He'll probably bring a couple of his vamps."

"I want to go with you…to the lab," she stated, popping a pastry into her mouth.

"No," both men said at once.

She nearly choked. After a chew and a swallow, she propped a hand on her hip. "I could get the data, find the blood samples, help transfer any samples. I know what I'm doing. Listen, I'm not crazy about going back in there, but someone with knowledge of viral transports has to go. That is unless you happen to have another virologist available who's just dying to go into a dangerous situation with a high probability of injury or death." She raised an eyebrow at them.

Dimitri shook his head no. Logan, on the other hand, considered her argument. This was exactly why he should not be involved with Wynter. They needed her. His heart said 'no fucking way', but the objective leader in him told him she was right. He played the scenario through in his mind. They go in guns, teeth and fangs blazing, kick some ass, tear open a vial and end up infecting the neighborhood with some unknown contagion. No, there had to be a way to take her as part of the team and keep her safe.

"Okay, you go," he decided.

"Um, Logan, maybe we should talk about..." Dimitri started.

"She goes," Logan reiterated. "Wynter's right. We'll put someone on her. She stays in the car until we've got an all clear. Then, she'll come in to evaluate the lab."

"Okay, she goes then," he agreed reluctantly. As much as he didn't want her to go, he knew Logan was right. Who else could they bring who had knowledge about viruses?

"So, it's settled. Anything else I should know? God, these things are good," she moaned, closing her eyes. Powdered sugar covered her lips.

For a brief second, Logan considered licking the white powder off her lips, flipping her onto the table and thrusting into her right there. From now on, he was so keeping a supply of beignets in the house. Damn, she was hot. And completely unaware of what she was doing. His little wolf was going to be the death of him.

Logan looked over to Dimitri whose jaw was wide open. Even his beta was not immune to the way she slid her tongue over her pink lips and inserted a finger into her mouth, moaning in ecstasy.

"D?" He snapped his fingers, trying to break him out of her spell.

"Yeah," Dimitri said as if in a daze.

"D," Logan said louder with a smile.

"Sorry." *Yeah, not really sorry.* He grinned back at Logan. "So, what were we talking about?"

Logan laughed at how ridiculous they both were acting. There was no denying that she was captivating. Sensual without being overtly sexual. Maybe the most humorous part of the whole thing was that she was his mate. As she continued licking and sucking her sugary fingers, oblivious to her effect on the males around her, it occurred to him that if Dimitri noticed, so would others. His wolf would not stand for it one bit. Sure, he might eventually share her with his beta but it'd be on his terms. And it would only happen after he'd claimed her, marked her as his own.

Logan sat solemnly at the head of the table in the conference room. When he'd renovated, he'd ensured that his office had an adjoining meeting room. Unlike the other rooms in his home, this room was uber-sleek, modern and secure. Twelve high-backed leather chairs surrounded the boat-shaped mahogany conference table. Trimmed in a black inlay, the well-oiled wooden surface gave off a sheen. A large flat screen monitor hung on the wall behind the captain's chair. Overhead, a retractable projector extended from the ceiling.

Glancing over to Wynter, he almost regretted bringing her to the meeting. Concentrating on something other than how he wanted to tear off her clothes and get her back in bed was going to be a challenge. Beautiful as always, she'd pulled her wild hair back into a ponytail, exposing her sun-kissed neck and shoulders. The spaghetti-strapped royal blue sundress hugged her breasts and fell just above her knees. A hint of lip gloss shone on her soft lips; the same magic lips that'd been wrapped around his cock earlier this morning. She looked up to him with a small smile as she played nervously with the pen in her hands.

Logan quickly refocused his attention to Dimitri who ushered their fanged guests into the room. His face hardened as he nodded to Léopold who'd brought Étienne and Xavier with him. Zeke and Jake followed, cautiously eyeing the vampires. After everyone was seated, Dimitri sat next to Wynter so that she was safely nestled between him and Logan.

Wynter heart raced at the sight of the vampires. With his typical arrogance, Léopold gave her a broad smile as if he'd known she'd slept with Logan. Her face heated as he took his time undressing her with his eyes. A glance to Logan, whose eyes were flared in anger, told her the gesture was not unnoticed. When Léopold finally stopped looking at her breasts and caught her gaze, he nodded as if to say, 'nice rack'. She rolled her eyes in disgust. Léopold may have been gorgeous, but he was trouble, big trouble. After that dance, a cautious smile was all she could manage. *Shit, this was going to be a long meeting. Why was she here again? Yeah, that pesky virus business.*

After reviewing schematics of a small abandoned factory in the Warehouse District, the group agreed on the side entrance. Wynter had tried to tell them that even though she suspected there were other scientists on the premises, the operation was small. It had to be considering the frequent relocation. Regardless, there had to be at least one room for the guards and maybe one for whoever was running the show. But Wynter couldn't be sure because she'd never left the lab.

Every time they'd prepare for a move, it was on short notice. The guard would tell her to pack her equipment. From flasks to pipettes and test tubes to beakers, everything had its container. Similar to the portable labs being used by students in a university, they hadn't relied on a sedentary lab. She wasn't sure how they made quick work of relocating the larger, high priced ticket items like the microscope, incubators and centrifuges. But like clockwork, the next lab would be set up within a day.

After an hour's deliberation, the team decided to let Léopold go in first. He suspected that someone in his line had created children for the sole purpose of protecting their endeavor. Logan was more than happy to let him deal with his own, but when it came to finding the killer, he wanted first dibs on meting out justice. It was the least he could do for Dana and Wynter.

By the end of the meeting, Logan's wolf was strung out, not at all happy with the testosterone filled room. His lips formed a tight line, listening to Léopold pontificate about how he planned to kill his children. Digging his fingers into the chair arms, he observed how Étienne stared at Wynter a little too much. At no point did the vampire take notice that the Alpha watched him like a hawk. He wasn't sure if he sensed a sexual intention or blood lust from him, but he wanted the blonde vampire out of his house.

"Enough," Logan declared. He rose and placed his palms down onto the table's smooth surface. "Devereoux, as much as I appreciate you cooperating with Acadian Wolves, I think we've covered everything. We'll meet you there at nine."

Léopold stood, giving a slight nod to Étienne and Xavier. Dimitri followed suit, intending to accompany them out of the house. As he did, Léopold boldly strode across the room, directly approaching Wynter. Logan growled, pushing in front of her.

The dashing vampire merely chuckled. "Alpha, you've found your wolf, no? I won't harm her."

"It's okay, Logan," Wynter stated calmly, determined to show no fear. She slid around Logan to face Léopold directly. Logan wrapped his arm around her waist, keeping her close to him. "Monsieur Devereoux, I appreciate your help with this. They'll come for me otherwise."

"Brave fille. No matter what you think, I won't let them have you...whoever *they* may be." He reached for her hand, and Wynter found herself allowing him to take it. Logan visibly tensed as Léopold kissed the back of her wrist, letting it go as quickly as he'd taken it.

"This is important. We mustn't fail," she insisted. Wynter brought her palm to her chest, feigning courage.

"A lost battle is a battle one thinks one has lost," Léopold stated.

"Sorry?" Wynter asked.

"Sartre," the vampire quoted. "I'm optimistic, given that they haven't moved."

"We shall see tonight, won't we?" Logan commented.

"That we will...that we will," Léopold repeated, waving a hand in the air as he left the room.

By the time everyone was gone, Logan's confidence regarding the probability of finding the killer had risen.

"Odd vampire, isn't he?" Wynter noted.

"That he is. My gut tells me he abides by some code of honor, but don't ever mistake him for anything but what he is," Logan warned.

"A monster?"

Logan smiled. "Battle not with monsters, lest ye become a monster."

She laughed. "Another quote?"

"Friedrich Nietzsche," Logan confirmed. He took her hands in his. "We have a few hours before it's time to leave.

I know I should be encouraging you to go relax, take a nap or something sensible like that."

"Relax, huh? How 'bout a bubble bath? Or a massage?" She winked and dragged her finger down his chest.

"A bath sounds good to me as long as I'm in there with you." Logan pulled her flush to him, burying his head in her neck and growled. "You drive me crazy, do you know that? I can't keep my hands off you."

Wynter giggled, growing aroused, loving the feel of his warm lips on her skin. She looked over to the table and gave him a sexy smile. "My Alpha," she began seductively. "You know, I just noticed that this is a really nice table. Sturdy. Long. Hard."

My Alpha? Logan's cock thickened at her words. *The table isn't the only hard thing in this room, baby.* He glanced to its wooden top then back to her with a smile.

"African mahogany. A friend custom made it for me. You like?"

"Oh I like. I mean, it looks very functional. I bet we could get a lot of *work* done at this table," she mused with a wink. Meeting his eyes, she gave him a suggestive smile and cocked her eyebrow. She slid her hand down between his legs and cupped his hard arousal. "You know, I always wondered what it would be like to be a secretary. I've been looking around here, and it seems you're in need of some assistance."

Logan hissed, closing his eyes. Holy shit, that felt amazing.

"How about *I* fill in for your secretary today?" she asked. "I'm very good at dictation, sir."

Wynter had never in her life been so forward. But after making love to Logan, she craved him more than ever. As though she were addicted to a drug, she needed more. The warmth between her legs grew painful. Feeling flirtatious and horny, she didn't think it would take very long to entice him into her fantasy.

Logan eyed Wynter, hardly believing he could be so lucky. *His naughty little wolf wanted a romp in the office? Seriously?* His brain said 'no way', but his burgeoning erection said, 'hell yes'. He'd have to be careful not to get carried away. His wolf wanted this woman in the worst way, sought to claim her.

"Sweetheart, I don't think you know what you're askin'. My wolf, he's restless." He gently nipped at her collarbone, as if to give her fair warning. If he took her, it was going to be rough and hard.

"But I do…I know exactly what I'm agreeing to." Wynter leaned into Logan and placed a kiss to his chin then dragged her tongue along his bottom lip and kissed him.

"Do you now?" Logan grabbed a fistful of her hair, gently pulling her head backwards. Revealing her neck, he licked at the hollow until she gasped.

"I need it…need you…here…" Wynter breathed.

"Do you submit, little one?" He peppered her with soft kisses. "Is that what you crave?" He pushed up her dress, reached between her legs, sliding his fingers into her slick folds. She tried to move, and he stilled her, holding her by the back of her hair.

"Yes, oh God, yes," she cried.

He drove a thick finger up into her hot pussy, tracing small circles over her clit with his thumb. "Like this? Is this what you want? Oh, yes…yes you do. You're so wet."

Closing her eyes, she nodded and moaned. *Submit? Dominate? It was all good.* She'd do whatever he wanted as long as he made love with her now.

"Turn around," he commanded, pulling his hand out of her panties. "Hands on the table, Miss Ryan."

Wynter complied. No longer able to see, her breath grew rapid in anticipation of what he'd do next.

"That's a girl. Spread your legs," he growled. With his knee, he prodded them open. "Sorry, but these have got to go."

Pushing up her dress, he exposed her bottom. He extended a claw, easily tearing the strings of her thong. She moaned as the cool air hit her skin.

"Please," Wynter begged. Swollen with arousal, she needed him back inside her.

"Patience, baby." Logan bent forward, placing his hands on the front of her thighs and then slid them upward, taking the dress with him. "Arms up. Hands back on the table, now."

Wynter obeyed and caught a glimpse of the dress as it fell to the floor. Fully nude, she leaned over the table.

"Now that is a beautiful sight," he crooned. "I must say that I've never had a secretary like you in my entire life. I suppose you're correct. This table will do nicely. We can get a lot of work done here."

She giggled and went to turn around so she could see him.

"Don't. Move," he said tersely, trying to stifle the urge to slam into her. He was ready to come right there. But she wanted a fantasy. So he'd take his time.

"You still want to play?" he asked, confirming she really wanted this. There was no going back, once they got started.

Play? She was stark naked bent over a conference table with the door to the room open. Dimitri could walk in and see them at any time. A thrill ran through her. Was she really doing this? The old Wynter was conservative and reserved, but the new Wynter; it seemed her wolf wanted to explore and experience everything as long as it was with Logan.

"Yes, Alpha," she assured him, spreading her legs a little wider so he could see into her.

Logan bit his fist, watching her open for him. She was upping the ante, he knew. He'd see her and then some. Logan unbuckled his pants with one hand while running his other down her back. His fingers wandered over her anus until he reached the wetness between her legs. He felt her shiver under his touch.

"You've been a bad, bad secretary, Miss Ryan," he began with a wry smile.

"Yes, yes I have," she agreed. *Oh God, why wouldn't he just fuck her already?*

Logan removed his hand and slowly stood to her side. She looked up at him and smiled.

"You were flirting with my coworker, weren't you?" Her full breasts were heavy with arousal; their rosy tips hardened. Logan loved how turned on she was by their role play.

"Yes. I'm very sorry." She gave him a sexy nod and flashed her eyes at him.

"You need to learn that I do not tolerate that kind of behavior in the office. Perhaps you need a spanking?" he suggested with a raised eyebrow. Logan walked around the table leaving her all alone.

"No, no I don't. I promise I won't do it again."

"I think you might like it," he said playfully, wondering how far he should push her. This was a little kinky, even for him. Dimitri would have a field day if he came back into the house.

"Let's see, Miss Ryan. Should I punish you in private? Or," Logan reached for the doorknob but released it. As if he were deep in thought, he paused, raising an eyebrow. "Maybe you would like me to leave the door open."

She knew she should tell him to shut the damn door, but the words never came. No, she wanted the thrill of knowing anyone could come in and see them. What the hell was wrong with her? She dropped her head in embarrassment, laughing silently to herself.

"You want everyone in the office to see us? You do, don't you? You are a naughty little secretary aren't you?"

"No, I…" she protested.

"You want to do more than flirt with my clients? Two men at once? Is that what you fantasize about, little wolf?" Leaving the door open, Logan quickly rounded behind her.

"No," she lied. Throbbing with need, she began to breathe heavily. The sound of his zipper coming undone rang in her ears.

"Tell me the truth, Miss Ryan. I don't like it when my secretaries lie to me."

She shook her head in denial.

"You are a bad girl," Logan said as his slapped her ass. He could not believe he was doing this with her but at the same time, who was he to deny her fantasy?

She cried out as a sting hit her cheek. "Yes!" she yelled. *What did she just say?*

Logan gave a small laugh, wondering if she was saying yes to two men or to being spanked, and suspected it was both. The scent of her arousal made him hot with need; he knew he couldn't keep this up much longer. He caressed her reddened cheek and then slid two fingers into her hot core. Wynter pushed back on him with a pleasured hiss.

"I can't believe I hired such a naughty secretary. Goddess, this is so hot, Wyn." He broke character and kicked off his pants, letting his hard shaft press into the cleft of her bottom.

"Yes, please don't stop," she pleaded.

"Do you promise to be a good secretary? No more flirting?" He was finding it hard not to laugh. How the hell did this get started? Oh yeah, the conference table.

"Yes sir, I promise. Just keep on…ah," she moaned as he gave her what she needed. His fingers pressed in and out of her wet sheath.

"I'm going to fuck you, Wynter. Now," he growled against her neck.

The sexy whisper in her ear sent chills across her body. She panted in anticipation.

"Hard. And fast. Until you scream for more." Logan withdrew his fingers. Cupping her chin from behind, he slid the creamy digits into her mouth. As she sucked her own juice off his fingers, he placed the head of his cock between her legs.

"Logan, I can't wait. Oh my God," she sighed. Dirty talk had never been her thing, but damn if it didn't make her ache. She needed him now, filling her.

His wolf roared. Her submission and playfulness was more than he could have ever asked for in a mate. Unable to draw out their game, he slammed his cock into her from behind all the way to the hilt. He grunted, holding still for a second. He wanted rough but didn't want to hurt her.

Wynter cried his name as he filled her completely. His long thick flesh stretched her core, and she needed him to move. Gasping for air, she released a whimper, trying to get him to thrust.

"Fuck, Wyn. You make me so hot," he withdrew and plunged into her. "That's it, sweetheart. Take all of me."

"Yes!" she screamed, pressing back onto him. Letting her hands splay forward, she pressed her chest onto the cool table, allowing him to go deeper.

"Oh yeah." Logan slammed into her again and again, fisting her hair so her head lifted off the wood. He reached around, sliding his hand under her chest so that he could hold her breast.

"Fuck me. Harder," she encouraged. God, she loved making love with this man.

Logan's wolf went feral for his mate. Barely aware of his

canines extending, he moved his hand from her breast to her belly so he could pull her upright. Bending his knees, he continued to penetrate her with the hardness of his sex. The sound of flesh meeting flesh reverberated throughout the room, driving them into an animalistic fervor. Guiding her head using her ponytail, he sought her mouth, sweeping his tongue into her parted lips.

Wynter craned her neck backwards, kissing him passionately in return. Her body was on fire, the hot pool of her arousal stoked by his movement. As his fingers moved from her belly down to her wet folds, she cried out again. The pressure of her orgasm was so close. Within seconds, the searing climax rocked through her body, throwing her into spasms of pleasure.

Logan hadn't planned on losing control, but in that moment, Wynter was his life. His present and future. No longer would he live his life alone. He'd blame it on his wolf, but in truth, it was the heart of the man who wanted to claim this woman as his own. As she tumbled over into her release, Logan surrendered control to her and to his own nature. With a wild cry of blissful agony and pleasure, he flooded into her, pulsating in orgasm. The walls of sanity came crashing down around him as his fangs bit into her shoulder.

Chapter Sixteen

What did I do? Fuck. Fuck. Fuck. Logan was shocked at what he'd just done, but as he gently took Wynter into his arms, cradling her to his chest, he couldn't summon an ounce of remorse. Instead, his wolf, categorically satisfied, howled in victory, invigorated that he'd marked his mate. Logan knew that it shouldn't have happened like this. But if she'd been a wolf, he wouldn't have needed to explain it to her. It was a natural act after all. Hell, in a perfect world, Wynter would have already marked him back.

Logan carried her up the stairs, quickly finding his bedroom. Before he made it to the mattress, Wynter had curled into his body like a purring kitten and drifted off to sleep. Without disconnecting, he carefully laid on the bed, bringing her with him so her head rested on his chest. Gliding a finger along her shoulder, he smiled. His bite was already transforming into a unique design. Like Wynter, it was small, beautiful and understated. Two intertwining loops had appeared; Logan likened them to linked souls, independent but co-existing as one. It was a sentimental thought, he knew, but a sense of pride clutched at his chest nonetheless.

But what was Wynter going to think when she saw the mark? A nagging twinge of concern spiraled into unanswered questions. What if she rejected him? Denied him as her mate? She hadn't shifted, after all. The concept of claiming and mating was lupine, and she still clung to human expectations and cultural beliefs. Even though she lived with Jax, she'd told Logan that he'd kept her out of pack business, away from wolves. He didn't need to think too hard about how Jax was going to react. Not that he could blame him for being irate, but eventually even Jax would accept it. As Alpha, he'd understand that wolves couldn't deny what nature demanded.

Logan hugged Wynter tightly, placing a kiss on her forehead. He silently grinned at how crazed he'd become when she insisted on role playing. It wasn't as if he hadn't experimented sexually; he'd lived a long time. But he'd never in a million years expected his little scientist to play secretary. When they'd first met, she seemed reserved, afraid of her own nudity, even. Their interaction in the pool was meant to open her to the way of wolves. But he'd had no idea how creative she'd become. The memory of how she'd looked standing naked, bent over that table….Goddess, she was sexy.

She felt so soft and warm in his arms, his heart constricted. Not only was his wolf rolling over in adoration of his mate, Logan could fall for this female. Maybe he was in lust, he reasoned. That would make much more sense.

The harder he tried to comprehend the why and how of the situation, the more frustrated he became. This was exactly what he'd been telling Dimitri. No matter his wolf's desire for his new found mate, his inner conflict about it was distracting him from more pressing matters.

The last thought in his mind before he fell asleep was that he needed to get his shit together before they left to find the lab. Logan decided to talk to Wynter about the mark when they got back home. They didn't have time for heavy emotional discussions before going off on a dangerous mission. No, it would wait. Logan cleared his mind of Wynter and focused his thoughts on the killer, on what he'd done to Dana, how he'd tortured his mate. That was all it took to release a fresh river of anger, fueling the revenge he would mete out in just a few short hours.

Wynter dressed in black jeans and a t-shirt that Logan had left for her on the bed. It all seemed very James Bondish to her, but she trusted they knew what they were doing. As she pulled on her socks, she let her mind drift to Logan. When she woke, he was already freshly showered and dressed. With a quick peck to her cheek, he trotted downstairs without saying a word about what had happened in the conference room.

She breathed a sigh of relief, considering what they'd done. At the same time, she felt no regret. As if a magician had revealed the hidden dove, she'd bared her newborn sexuality. She could have blamed it on her wolf, but Wynter knew the truth. Like a caged tigress, she'd been waiting for the right man to unleash her from her prison, unlocking her true nature. Wynter laughed, thinking about how she'd encouraged him to bend her over that table. The way he'd made love to her had been phenomenal. Rough yet gentle, the passion and intimacy embraced both her body and soul. The electricity between them sizzled, threatening to burn down the room.

What surprised her the most was the way he'd tenderly scooped her up in his arms afterwards, petting and caressing her. There wasn't a moment when they'd lost physical contact. As they lay in bed, his soft lips to her forehead sent tendrils of warmth through her body. Wynter wasn't sure if he'd been aware that she'd felt every loving touch and feather-soft kiss. Emotion welled in her chest as she considered her feelings.

Wynter ran her hands through her curls and attempted to lasso her hair into a scrunchie. When she reached back to do so, she felt a small raised area near her neck. *Had he bitten her? Given her a 'love bite'?* Yes he did. And damn, that had been hot. She remembered how the slight pain had pushed her into another orgasm when he'd done it. Was that some kind of kinky wolf trick? Maybe next time, she'd bite him back? She smiled at the thought.

Wynter's focus drifted back to what they were about to do. *I'll be safe...I'll be safe.* She kept saying the mantra over and over. She knew that Logan wouldn't have agreed to let her go if he didn't think he could keep her out of harm's way. If she could just get her hands on the data, she might be able to cure Emma. As she stared at her face in the mirror, she promised to herself that she'd keep her eye on the prize.

"Brought sandwiches," Dimitri commented, taking a big bite out of his po'Boy.

"Thanks, been so busy, I haven't even thought to eat. Are Zeke and Jake ready?" Logan asked.

"Yeah, they're over at my place loading the cars. You ready?"

"Born ready." Logan sat down at the kitchen table, grabbed a muffuletta and started eating.

"Anything you want to get off your chest?" Dimitri noticed his Alpha had been avoiding eye contact with him since he'd come down, which was unusual. Yeah, Logan was definitely trying to dodge talking about something.

"Just eatin' my sandwich. These are good. Where'd you get them?"

"So how's that new table workin' for ya?" Dimitri thought he'd try another tactic. Oh, he'd heard, all right. It almost made him want to go try to find his own mate…almost.

"Fuck off, D."

Laughing, Dimitri almost choked on his food. Bingo. He'd hit the topic.

"You know that I'll never be able to concentrate in there again, don't you? Don't worry, I didn't stay for the show," he assured him, wagging his eyebrows.

"She's my mate," Logan stated nonchalantly, waiting for the ribbing that didn't come.

"Guessed as much. Does she know?"

"No way, man. She hasn't even shifted. I mean, you've talked to her. She hasn't spent a lot of time with wolves. What I mean is that even though she lives with Jax, it sounds like he keeps the pack activities on the down-low."

"Full moon's soon. She's goin' have to learn," Dimitri advised and took another bite.

"Yeah, there's something else." Logan casually placed his sandwich on his plate and proceeded to drop the bomb. "I marked her. And before you ask, she doesn't know."

"What?" Dimitri involuntarily spit his food out in surprise.

"And here's the thing, D, I know I should feel guilty or something rational like that." Logan leaned back and closed his eyes thoughtfully and then stared over to Dimitri. "But I don't. I feel fucking great. I guess I'm an asshole to feel that way. But I'm tellin' ya, it just feels good…really good. She's mine, and I want others to know it. And in that conference room, she was just so…I can't even tell you what it was like. She's beautiful. Playful. Spirited. My wolf…he just wanted her so much."

"Listen, you can't beat yourself up about this. You're a wolf. This is what we do. You know it. And I know it. It feels right because that's how it's meant to be. She'll understand when you tell her." Dimitri stood, slapped Logan on the shoulder and walked over to the sink. "So when are you going to tell her?"

"Tonight. But not until we get back. Right now, I've gotta focus on what we're about to do. Did you bring that item I asked for?"

"Yep, right there on the counter." Dimitri pointed to a holster and gun.

"Okay, thanks. Here she comes," Logan warned, hearing Wynter walking toward the kitchen. "Hey, sweetheart. D brought dinner."

Logan offered her the tray and hoped plying her with food would soften her for what he was about to suggest next.

Wynter joined them, took a sandwich off the plate and bit into it. "Oh. My. God. This is awesome. I could so live down here. Between the beignets and everything else I might weigh five thousand pounds, but who cares?" She laughed.

After a few minutes had passed, Logan stood, took his plate to the sink and then picked up the bag sitting on the counter.

"I've got something for you," he told her. He pulled the Lady Smith out of the holster and checked the safety.

"What the…?" she gaped.

"It's a gun, Wyn."

"Yes, I can see that," she stammered. "But do you really think this is necessary?"

"Yeah, I do. I'm not taking any chances. When we go in, you're staying locked in the car with Jake. But just in case…always need a plan B," he replied, continuing to check to make sure everything that he'd requested was there.

Logan took the magazine out of the gun, checked it and set it down.

The reality of what they were about to do made Wynter stop and take a breath. Even though she had to do it, it would be difficult to go back to the same place where she'd been held captive. No longer having an appetite, she wiped her mouth with a napkin and pushed the plate aside.

"Come over here," Logan told her. Wynter got up from the table and stood next to him, watching him work.

"Here you go…just lift your arms," Logan instructed, slipping her arms through the black leather shoulder holster. He adjusted the straps so it fit properly. "There you go. Have you ever used a gun?"

"Well, yes, but…" She straightened her back and moved her arms, trying to get used to the feel of it on her body.

"When was the last time you went shooting?" He looked her over, waiting on her response.

"Well, it's not like I'm a sharpshooter, but Jax insisted that I have one. You know, late night in the city and all that good stuff. Honestly though, I don't carry it with me most days."

"When was the last time you used it?"

"I don't know." She rubbed her hand over her forehead, trying to think. Geez, had it been that long? "Maybe a year ago?"

"Better than nothing. Take it out and let me see you load it."

She did as he asked, and then promptly put the gun back into its sheath.

"That's a girl. Now, let's review what we've got, okay?

Silver bullets. Eight in a clip. There's loaded magazines ready to go both here and here." He pointed to the ammunition pouches attached to her holster.

She nodded, but her expression didn't match her assent. Her brow knotted in worry.

"You're going to be safe, Wyn. If something happens, do whatever Jake tells you, okay? Also, there are stakes in the car. Lots of them. Take one with you when you get the go ahead to come into the lab. Just in case."

"Got it," she said with determination. Grabbing a bottle of water, she unscrewed the top and took a long drink, wishing it was whiskey. When she looked up, two large men walked into the kitchen.

"Jake, Zeke, meet Wynter. She's my…uh," he fumbled for the word. *Mate.* No, not the time. "Girlfriend."

Logan glanced over to catch her reaction. Her face flamed, and she failed to hide the smile evident in her eyes. Yep, girlfriend worked just fine.

"Nice to meet you, Wynter. I'm Jake," said the taller man. His blond hair was tightly cropped. He confidently strode around the table and joined them. If she hadn't known any better, she would have thought law enforcement. Maybe military?

The other wolf, standing at the door with his arms crossed, merely gave her a nod. His cool demeanor bristled Wynter. She wondered what his issue was, that he couldn't even offer up a simple 'hello', and determined that maybe her presence wasn't welcome. Wynter made eye contact with him and set her bottle on the counter.

"Don't worry 'bout Zeke over there, cher. He's just the muscle. Lucky for you, you've got the brains lookin' out for you tonight." Jake told her with a smile.

"When will we know if it's safe to go into the lab?" Wynter asked Logan.

"I'll send Dimitri out when it's okay for you to come in. But until he does, you stay in the car with Jake. We've got to be crystal clear on this. Don't move out of the car until he says you can. Now, the cars...they've been specially outfitted for occasions like this. They've been custom armored. Bulletproofed. Even so, we're going with redundancy in case we run into any problems. You, Jake and I will go in one car. Dimitri and Zeke in the other."

After a long pause, Dimitri rose from the table, as did Jake. Wynter waited until Logan indicated they were leaving and tugged on his sleeve. Without warning, she hugged him tightly. Wynter wanted to tell him how she felt, worried that something bad would happen to him.

"Logan, please be careful. I...I need you," she confessed. It was as much as she could manage.

Logan cupped her cheek and tilted her head up to his. "Nothin's goin' to happen to me, sweetheart. We'll be in and out before you know it. Then we can come home and maybe we'll play 'policeman' without the gun...just handcuffs," he teased, trying to make her smile.

"Well, as long as it involves a thorough strip search, I'm in," she joked lamely.

"Seriously Wyn, we'll all be safe. Now let's go get the bad guys."

"Okay," she reluctantly agreed.

Before she knew what was happening, Logan kissed her. It was a brief loving kiss, confirming what she felt in her heart. And it could not be more simple…or complicated.

Chapter Seventeen

The short drive from the French Quarter to their destination felt as if it took hours. By the time they'd reached their location, Wynter's mind raced, hoping the operation went smoothly. With her nerves working overtime, she played with a stake, envisioning having to use it. Vampires were fast. By the time she had it aimed, they'd be at her throat. Now the gun? That would work. Maybe she hadn't used one in a while, but she reasoned it was like riding a bike. And there was nothing more she'd enjoy than blowing a big hole in one of her former guards.

The Warehouse District had experienced a renaissance of sorts. Many of its abandoned factories had been converted into trendy clubs and condos. Wynter stared at the building where the lab supposedly had been moved. Unlike its chic counterparts, the dilapidated structure looked desolate. The scratched-up tan and black logo depicting leafy sugar cane stalks was plastered on its second story brick exterior. Since it had no yard and edged the sidewalk, she wondered how they'd set up a lab without being seen.

"It's a go," Logan stated and opened the car door. He looked to Wynter then Jake. "Wait here. Don't let anything happen to her."

"I'll protect her with my life," Jake replied. He looked over to the building and back to Logan. "Looks quiet."

"Yeah, a little too quiet. Okay, gotta go. Devereoux's here." Logan watched the dark vampire step out of a black limousine. He shook his head; only a vamp would ride a limo into battle. Both Xavier and Étienne soon exited the car and followed Léopold. With a wink to Wynter, Logan shut the car door. "See ya on the flip side."

As soon as Logan walked away, Wynter crawled over the center console from the back to the front passenger seat. She glanced to Jake who was performing reconnaissance through a pair of high-powered binoculars. They observed Logan approach Devereoux and gesture for him to go first. The men walked down a side alley until they reached a black steel door. All eyes were on Logan. He silently held up his fingers. Three. Two. One.

Wynter couldn't see exactly what was going on in the dark of night, but it seemed like they entered pretty quickly. Did they break down the door? What just happened? They'd entered within seconds. It seemed all too easy.

"Not good," Jake commented quietly.

"What's wrong?" Wynter whispered.

"Door's unlocked. Feels like a set up."

"Oh my God. Can you warn Logan?" she asked, trying to keep her voice low.

"No need. He'll know. We sit tight. Here's another pair

of nocs. You can help scope the area," Jake suggested, hoping the task would keep her mind off the fact that Logan was in the building.

The whole vibe felt off. Jake wished Logan would get the hell out of there. Wynter seemed to be holding up well, all things considered. He cracked the window a quarter inch, and concentrated on listening for sounds of a scuffle. The barren silence cloaked the night like an ominous premonition.

"How long will they be in there?" Wynter inquired as she struggled to focus the lenses.

"Something like this shouldn't take long at all. The building isn't that big to begin with and I haven't heard any fighting. It's dead out there."

"But that could be good, right? Maybe they just staked them really quickly," she said hopefully.

"Shhh. Did you hear that?" A tiny click was all he heard, and then silence.

"What?"

"Shhh," he whispered. "Put on your seatbelt. Something's not right."

Trying not to panic, Wynter silently pulled the strap into place.

"I can't hear anything…" she started to say but never finished the thought.

As the blast hit, the car rolled onto its side and Wynter screamed. Mercifully, blackness fell over her the second she jolted against the window.

Bodies. Six dead bodies to be precise. The stench of death hit as soon as the vampire opened the door. With decomposition well under way, flies swarmed around the maggot-covered bodies.

"Jesus Christ," Logan cursed. He held his sleeve to his face and swatted the insects away. "These are humans."

"I'm tellin' ya. This is some sick shit." Dimitri coughed for air. The smell was nearly unbearable.

Logan moved closer so he could get a better look at the corpses. "With the way they're bloating, I'm guessing they've been in here for a few days. They all look pretty young…in their twenties. What the hell is this, Devereoux?"

"Dinner," Léopold commented with disgust. He pulled out a neatly folded handkerchief and put it over his nose. "He's making new vampires. They've little control. Kill easily when feeding."

"Great. Okay, well I don't like this. The unlocked door. It's too quiet," Logan surmised. "We should get outta here."

"I believe you are correct, Alpha," Léopold agreed. No one in his line made vampires without registering them. And his tip about the lab's location was looking more and more like a trap. Never one to lose his cool, he tried to contain his rage, yet could not resist the urge to descend his fangs.

As Logan was getting ready to pull everyone out of the building, a single red flickering light drew his attention. Alerting the group, he raised his hand and pointed silently to an adjoining room. Stealthily he approached, taking care not to fall through the rotted floorboards. The wide open space was empty save for the carcasses of a few dead rats and a portable table. A black laptop sat atop; its power button pulsed a glowing beat in the darkness. As the others gathered round, Logan swiped his finger across the pad, waking it out of slumber. When the screen appeared, a single message in black and white froze on it: *'The scientifique is mine. Nowhere is safe.'* Logan's heart lodged in his throat. *Wynter.*

As fast as his feet would carry him, he ran toward the exit, screaming Wynter's name. By the time he'd reached the sidewalk, he caught a glimpse of her face through the car window as the fiery explosion detonated. Logan and the others were shoved to the ground as the shock waves hit. The roar of the blast sent rubber shrapnel flying into the air, raining down onto the street.

A split second later, Logan sprinted toward the wreckage of the SUV, which had been thrown onto its side. Through smoke and debris, he climbed up to the driver's seat door. The blackened windows obscured his view.

"Wynter!" he screamed into the car. A low moan emanated from inside it.

Logan grunted as he yanked open the door. Gas and dust from the airbag deployment wafted into the air, causing him to cough. He managed to elevate the door fully, exposing the deflated white side curtain bags.

"Hold it open," he ordered, noticing that Léopold had climbed up onto the hood to help. Léopold took hold of the door and effortlessly ripped it off its hinges, tossing it into the street.

Dimitri flipped open his switchblade and passed it forward to Logan, who knifed at the plastic. They tore off the curtain, revealing the inside of the compartment.

"Wyn! Can you hear me, baby? Say something," Logan called into the car. Silence greeted him. As the powder settled, he was finally able to see Jake, whose left arm and face were badly injured.

"Shit," Logan spat out upon seeing the damage inflicted on his friend. "Jake, hey man. Come on, wake up buddy."

With no response, Logan continued talking to him. "We're gonna get you out now. You're going to be all right after you shift."

"Cut 'em down. I'll hold him up so he doesn't crush Wynter," Dimitri suggested. Jake, secured in his seatbelt, hung downward like a marionette on its strings. Thankfully, since he was belted, he hadn't yet fallen onto Wynter.

"Ready, D?" Logan asked as he started slashing at the nylon belt. Dimitri held tightly to Jake. "That's it."

Together, they heaved their friend up and out of the car. Dimitri took Jake in his arms and laid him out on the street.

"Zeke, get him out of his clothes now. He's gotta shift," Dimitri ordered. "I'll be right back. I need to help Logan get Wynter."

Logan's breath caught as Wynter came into view. Still in her seatbelt, her head rested against the sagging airbag. Although she was unconscious, her heart still beat strongly. Logan leaned all the way into the car until most of his body was inside. When he reached the straps, he frantically cut at them.

"Wyn, sweetheart. I'm here. I'm so sorry." Logan pushed the hair out of Wynter's face and kissed her forehead.

Logan cursed; his heart tore in a million pieces seeing her like this. He'd said he'd keep her safe and he'd failed her. Guilt washed over him, and he prayed she'd be okay. He felt the emotion swell up in his chest. Seeing her hurt and vulnerable was more than he could bear. Her heartbeat was steady, but she remained unconscious. He kissed her again, this time on her cheek.

"Please, baby. Wake up now. I need you here with me. You're my..." he choked but couldn't finish.

She moaned and her eyes fluttered. "My Alpha," she whispered.

Thank the Goddess, she'd woken. He wished he could tell her right then about how she was his mate. But sanity won over and he focused on the task at hand; he needed to get her home. They could talk later.

"We're goin' get you out of here, okay? How do you feel? Are you in any pain?"

"Fucking vampires," she coughed. "Do you believe this shit?"

"Fucking vampires," he agreed with a small smile. She was a fighter. His fighter, filled with spirit. An Alpha for an Alpha.

"Hmm," she moaned. "What happened?"

"Someone set off an incendiary device. Not sure how they got it on the car, but it had to be a vampire to get it on without anyone seeing or hearing."

"Jake...he knew. He heard something."

"We'll talk about it later, baby. All right, my tough little wolf. Let's get you out of here." Logan hugged his arms under hers. "D, I'm comin' out."

Dimitri grabbed Logan's hips, helping to hoist him and Wynter out of the car. When they were finally extricated, Logan scooped her up, never letting her feet touch the ground. Logan glanced to Jake who had blacked out on the pavement. Naked, he still hadn't shifted. Second degree burns blistered along his cheek. He began to regain consciousness and groaned in pain.

"Come on, Jake. You gotta shift, man," Logan heard Dimitri say. Zeke was bent down on his knees at his side.

"D, I need you to take Wyn," Logan ordered. He couldn't believe what he was about to do.

Logan had always known that decisions weren't easy for an Alpha. Challenge after challenge, the brutal mauling between wolves had proved that fact early on in his reign. No, easy didn't equate with what was right. Even though he'd just gotten his mate back, he'd have to relinquish her. Trust his beta. Jake was his responsibility and damn if he'd let him die because he couldn't shift on his own.

Dimitri stood, sensing Logan's internal struggle. But as he expected, his Alpha put pack first, above his personal needs. Arms outstretched, he patiently waited to accept Wynter.

"Hey, sweetheart," Logan spoke softly to her. She slowly lifted her lids to look at him. "I need you to go with Dimitri for a minute."

"No," she protested with a small moan. Within the

warmth and safety of Logan's embrace, she didn't understand what Logan needed to do or why he'd leave her.

"Just a minute, baby." He kissed her cheek lightly. "Jake needs me. He's burned real bad and is having trouble shifting. I promise you'll be safe with D. This'll just take a few minutes. Then we'll go home. Trust me."

"Okay," she agreed quietly.

"Do not let her go. Not one second, D," Logan instructed, his tone of voice deadly serious. His eyes locked on Dimitri's as he gently placed Wynter's body into his arms.

Dimitri cradled her head into his chest, breathing a sigh of relief. Jake desperately needed his Alpha. At this point, he was too far gone to heal on his own.

"I'll be just a second," Logan promised, running his hand lovingly over Wynter's hair.

Sirens wailed in the distance. Naturally, someone had heard the explosion and had called the authorities. Logan wanted to get out of there before the police came asking questions. New Orleans had a supernatural police force, P-CAP: Paranormal City Alternative Police. But at the moment, Logan couldn't trust anyone, not even P-CAP, to find Dana's killer. He knew they'd come to him eventually when they found the charred car, but he'd deal with that later. It'd be easy enough to tell them it had been stolen. Besides, after they found the dead bodies riddled with bite marks, they'd be busy breathing down Kade's neck for a while.

The Alpha crouched down to the pavement so that his

head was level with Jake's, taking his hand. He bent over so that his mouth was inches from his friend's ear. Concentrating, Logan let his power flow, urging Jake to listen, to obey. No longer moaning, Jake could sense his Alpha. His eyes flew open, staring into space as if he was devoid of awareness. Jake's comatose expression didn't worry Logan; the mental connection to the injured wolf strengthened.

"Jake, now listen to me, buddy. It's me, Logan. You've got some pretty bad burns here. I know you're feelin' tired but you've gotta shift. You hear me?"

Jake's eyes closed and in that second, Logan's heart caught in his chest. This would go a whole lot easier if Jake was awake. Jake coughed, his eyes darted to Logan's in acknowledgement. The flesh on Jake's forearm and face had already formed boils, and Logan could feel the pain radiating off his wolf.

"That's it. Okay, we're gonna do this together." Logan began to strip, tearing off his own clothes as fast as he could until he was entirely nude. Calling on his Alpha demeanor, Logan brought forth his dominance. It was time to get his wolf to shift.

"Jake, this is your Alpha. You will shift, do you understand? No matter how tired you are, no matter how much pain you are in, your allegiance is to me and pack. On the count of three, you're going to call on your wolf. Are you ready?" In truth it was a command, not a question.

A tear ran down Jake's cheek as he gave a small jerk of his chin in acceptance. *No matter the pain.*

Logan stared into the young wolf's eyes, until Jake averted his gaze. "Concentrate, Jake. Here we go. One. Two. Three."

Effortlessly, Logan transformed into his wolf. Yet he was unable to supervise the ease of Jake's shift. But at this point, Logan didn't care whether or not his transformation went easily. The only thing that counted was that he shifted. Logan howled, his gray wolf scenting Jake's. A whine alerted Logan that, even though Jake had experienced considerable torment, the shift was complete and effectual. Logan licked Jake's snout affectionately, relieved at the outcome.

Barking at Dimitri, he signaled for the group to move out. Since the one SUV was destroyed, they'd take the other vehicle. Zeke opened the hatch and Dimitri moved to lay down with Wynter. Thinking better of it, he merely sat in the back, holding her, waiting for Logan. Jake, as wolf, jumped into the back seat.

Logan shifted back to his human form so he could address Léopold, who'd been sniffing around the wreckage.

"Vampire," Logan called out to Léopold.

Léopold approached cautiously, recognizing the Alpha was in a fierce state of protection. Between his mate getting injured and the near death of another wolf, Logan would snap if pushed. Léopold held up his palms, lowering his eyes in an attempt to get the human part of Logan to rise to the surface.

"This! This! This cannot happen again, you hear me? Unacceptable, Devereoux. Who'd you get the intel from?" he growled.

"'No worse fate can befall a man than to be surrounded by traitor souls,'" Léopold quoted cryptically. "William S. Burroughs."

"But who is the traitor? You said yourself that someone in your line was at Dana's apartment. I'm tellin' you right now, you'd better deal with this. He almost killed Jake and Wynter tonight," Logan yelled, angered by Devereoux's games. "We can't afford any more mistakes."

"He plays with us," Leo pondered. "But for what purpose?"

Logan raked his fingers through his hair and blew out a breath. As much as he hated to admit it, Léopold was right. Whoever had done this knew exactly what they were doing. They wanted to demonstrate power, drawing out the expectation of kidnapping Wynter. It was a show. And the show was meant to intimidate and instill fear.

"Perhaps, but assuming that's true, then our friend doesn't know me very well. Because now I'm just pissed. And from what I've seen of you, he'd have to be a damn idiot to take on his sire."

"Well, he wouldn't be the first to lose his head. And I mean that quite literally. This person is not a direct child, but in my line. Clearly he's a little power hungry, no? I assure you that this isn't the end. No, merely the beginning. If I have to stake every last one of my children, he'll be found."

Logan turned to leave and paused. "We need to get him before he goes for Wynter. We're moving out of the city tomorrow night. Be in touch, Devereoux."

"That I will, mon ami. That I will," Léopold assured the Alpha, fading into the darkness.

Logan walked to the SUV and sat next to Wynter. He gently took her into his arms and rolled onto his back so she lay atop his torso. With a nod, Dimitri closed the hatch, jumped in the car and they sped off toward his mansion.

Chapter Eighteen

For days, the Directeur had grown dismayed and impatient; it had proved more difficult to kidnap her than he'd originally planned. But all the negativity was now erased by a single blast, replaced by self-gratification. He puffed his chest, exceedingly proud of his plan. It had gone off brilliantly. The Alpha had been delightfully put in his place, unable to protect his scientifique. Like a fool, he'd left her alone with a guard dog. Not entirely alone, as he'd hoped. But this small display of his power would show them how weak and pathetic they all were. The arrogant ancient one would never find out it was he who led him down this path of destruction. He loved watching the vampire squirm, dreaming of the day he'd stake him into ashes.

He silently rejoiced as the Alpha was forced to relinquish his mate. As he predicted, the Alpha would save the burned wolf. The dogs would always choose their pack over her. He restrained himself from laughing at the irony. The mongrels would never accept her, because she'd never truly be wolf.

The ungrateful little bitch would learn soon that it was

his hand that had granted her the supernatural gift. The Directeur closed his eyes, reveling in his genius. His great experiment had been spectacularly successful. The full moon would rise soon. And his creation, like a caterpillar turning into a butterfly, would transform. The final test. Ideally he'd have her within her cage in time to witness her shift. They'd celebrate together, making love well into the night. She'd be eternally grateful, begging to live out her life as both his lover and colleague. With their extraordinary minds at work, they'd perfect the viruses in no time at all. His fangs descended, aroused by his musings. As he walked away, he smiled. Very soon, his scientifique would be in his arms, thanking him for his loving gift.

"You can put me down. Really, I swear I'm fine," Wynter insisted. Logan had carried her from the car all the way into his bedroom. She looked down at her arms, which had been scratched by the airbag. "It's amazing. I'm healing already."

"Indulge me." Logan entered the bathroom and sat her on a settee, one he had argued with the decorator to be unnecessary at the time. "See, we're already here and now we're going to take a nice hot bath. Then it's time for bed."

The walls and floor of the enormous bathroom were inlaid with black Spanish marble. It housed a blocked glass shower, modern bamboo vanity with double sinks and separate area for the toilet. An oversized, square-shaped Jacuzzi edged the rear wall of the room. Logan had thought, like the settee, that it had been an unneeded extravagance. Yet the tub he'd finally agreed upon was modern and masculine. Reaching over, he turned the spigot on and returned his attention to Wynter.

"Let's get you undressed first," he suggested, helping pull her shirt off over her head.

"You don't have to tell me twice. I feel so dirty from all the smoke," she told him and started to take off her clothes.

She unsnapped her bra, unzipped her pants and let Logan pull off her jeans and panties in one swift tug. She smiled, realizing that even though Logan had set her down, he'd never once lost physical contact with her.

"Okay, you first. Here we go. Is it too hot?" Logan lifted Wynter up and eased her into the steaming water.

"Feels so good," she breathed. Whatever soreness remained from the accident seemed to melt away.

Logan undressed quickly, taking time to throw their clothes into a laundry chute. Seeing that the tub was nearly filled, he turned off the spigot.

Wynter's eyes roamed over his incredibly well-toned body as he readied to join her. When he turned, she smiled, admiring his broad shoulders that tapered into the smooth muscles of his back and buttocks. His bronzed skin accentuated his exquisite musculature. Logan spun around to face her, and the vision of his washboard abs and hardened chest nearly took her breath away. Like the lithe and powerful animal he was, he advanced toward her. Spellbound, Wynter's eyes fell to his semi-erect cock and then back up to his eyes. Logan shot her a sexy smile, and she knew she'd been thoroughly caught ogling. But she didn't care. This was her man, her Alpha. All hers.

Logan loved that his little wolf enjoyed watching him, but he fought his own arousal. She'd just been in an accident, and he planned on pampering and caring for her, not jumping her bones. But he could tell she had other things on her mind besides bathing. And the way she looked, so beautifully naked and wet, it would be damn difficult to resist her.

He hissed as he stepped into the bath, and slid behind Wynter so that he could feel her in his arms. Spooned perfectly in place, he moved his hips slightly so that the length of him fit nicely against the cleft of her bottom. Logan couldn't seem to get enough of her, and he wondered if the urge would ease once they fully mated. When the car had exploded, he thought he'd die himself. It was then he realized the full extent of his feelings for his mate and the implications of losing her.

Without speaking, he softly rubbed her shoulders. Logan couldn't resist lifting her hair, revealing his beautiful mark. He knew he needed to talk to her about it and hoped she wouldn't be mad. Reaching for the small bottle of shampoo, he began washing her hair. He smiled when she released a small moan as he started to massage her scalp. Logan couldn't remember ever doing this for a woman, and it excited him to know that she appreciated the small gesture, an intimate yet simple task. He lovingly caressed her springy curls and rinsed them in turn.

"Logan," Wynter eventually spoke. "Thanks for getting me out of there tonight."

"You don't have to thank me. The minute we walked in there, we all knew something was off. I should have just left."

"Did you find anything?" she asked.

Corpses. Logan opted to tell her about the computer instead. "The place was empty except for a laptop. Dimitri grabbed it. It's probably wiped. But if they left anything at all, D will find the crumbs. Let's hope they got sloppy."

"Really, nothing else?"

"No, I'm afraid it was all just a ploy to get to you…to us. Devereoux's a pain in my ass, but he's right, they're trying to play with us. Intimidate."

Wynter didn't respond, thinking of how easily they'd gotten to her.

"Hey, let's not talk about this anymore tonight. We've got other things to talk about. Lots of things, actually," he disclosed. *My mark. The fact that you're my mate.*

"Okay."

Logan took the bar of soap and lathered his hands. "We should probably talk about tomorrow." He blew out a breath. "We've got Dana's funeral. It's here in the city. At twilight."

"Don't wolves usually have some kind of special thing they do? I mean when my parents died, I remember going to Jax's country house. Mom and Dad weren't wolves, but Jax, well, he did it his way," she explained. "Buried them on his property. They've got headstones but he told me that wolves don't."

"Well, yeah, that's true. We usually bury the body on

our land. 'From the earth we came and back into the earth we go' and all that stuff. We use scent and then later, memory, to know where someone's been buried," Logan described. "But Dana, she's a hybrid. She was pretty much raised by her human mother. Her father died in a challenge when she was younger."

"What happens during a challenge?" Wynter asked.

"Anyone can challenge an Alpha if they want to lead the pack. Honestly, though, it doesn't happen very often." *Except when you become Alpha like I did.* "You fight…as wolf."

"Do challenges always end in death?"

Logan paused, wondering how much he should tell her. Marcel had killed Dana's father during a particularly nasty battle for power. Everyone in the pack knew and accepted the fact without bitterness. It was pack law. He himself had threatened to kill the next wolf who challenged him, to quell dissension.

"Not usually but occasionally it happens. Not all with wolves is dark, nor is it light," he asserted. "The bottom line is that too many challenges to the Alpha disrupt the flow of nature. When it's going on, there's no peace. It's not good for anyone in the pack."

"Yeah, I can see how if people are always peckin' at the Alpha, they wouldn't ever feel like they could rest. I mean, how is the Alpha supposed to be leading if he's always in a sparring match?"

"So like I was sayin', Dana's mother raised her. And her family's plot is in St. Lafayette cemetery. She'll be interred there."

"But why at sundown? Don't the cemeteries close at night?"

"Yes and that's exactly why we prefer it at night. She may have human family, but she's got us too. Wolves may want to shift. We don't need spectators or tourists. No, this'll be private. It may not be what I would want for myself, but the least we can do is support Dana's wishes. Generations of her kin have been put in that plot."

"I'll come with you if you want," Wynter offered quietly.

"Of course you will, sweetheart. I'm not leavin' you alone for a second," Logan told her with a kiss to her shoulder. "After we leave the funeral, we're taking off. Goin' bayou. It'll make it harder for this psycho to find you. Plus the full moon is in two nights."

"It is?"

"Yes, it is. But you know that, don't you?" he chuckled.

"Yes. But that doesn't mean I want it to come. I mean, who knows what's going to happen to me? Could be anything. Or nothing."

"Or something in between. Either way, I'll be there for you, Wyn. No matter what, you can count on me," he said with conviction. "You can trust me."

"Logan," Wynter paused. The thought of shifting was terrifying. "I'm scared. I know I can't control what's happened. But I do…I trust you.'"

Logan's heart warmed at her words. She really did trust him and not just with the shift either. Yet he still hadn't told her that he'd gone and marked her. That wasn't the kind of man he was. To go any longer withholding the truth would not only be disingenuous but could forever fracture their relationship.

"Listen, Wynter, I've got to tell you something... something I should have told you earlier," Logan began.

"Hmm...yes.' Wynter reached out, seeking Logan's wrist. Once found, she wrapped her hands onto his forearms, and brought them around her waist.

"Today, in the conference room." How the hell was he supposed to tell her he'd lost control?

"Ooh, is this dirty story time? Because that one is my favorite," she joked, trying to lighten the mood. All the talk about the funeral and death weighed heavily on her mind. "Once upon a time there was a wolf and his secretary. I love this one."

Logan laughed. "Well yes, something like that." He cleared his throat and dramatically continued. "Once upon a time, there was a smart and sexy princess who was very brave. This princess, she'd been captured by terrible monsters; monsters who wanted to keep her in their tower. But the princess outwitted the monsters and escaped. The monsters were angry and roamed the kingdom looking for her. But a prince found the princess and rescued her. And he slayed the monsters."

"Ah, sounds like a very interesting premise. Seems as though I may have heard this one before," she teased.

"You see when the prince rescued the princess, he thought she was the most beautiful and courageous girl he'd ever met. The prince, he was quite taken with the princess. But it was complicated because there were many others who wanted her." Logan wasn't sure where he was really going with this story but thought he might as well keep at it.

"One day, the princess and the prince decided to make love...in a conference room," he laughed. *How corny could he get?*

Wynter also chuckled. "Here comes the dirty part."

"Don't laugh. The princess had been a naughty girl, and in the prince's defense, he can't stop thinking about her. He cares about her very much."

"Does he now?"

"Yes, you see, even though they like making love," Logan cringed at how he was going about telling her. *Almost there.* "The princess, she's in his heart. He's been alone a very long time. The princess, she makes him feel alive. He wants her, like no other woman. She is his. He just knows."

Wynter's breath caught. She knew full well she was the princess. And he was the prince...the prince who wanted no other. *What was he trying to say?* She prayed he wasn't going to break her fragile heart.

"So what did he do?" she asked innocently.

"Wyn, I've got something to tell you." Logan spun Wynter around until she straddled him. Face to face, he'd tell her what he'd done. "I know this seems a little fast, but my instinct never fails me. We've only been together a few days, but when you're a wolf...sometimes your wolf, it knows things." Goddess, he was fucking this up.

Wynter searched his anguished eyes. What was he trying to say?

"Earlier today...in the conference room. You need to

understand, the urge was so strong. I should have talked to you but it just happened."

"What happened?" Wynter asked in surprise.

"When we made love today…it was amazing. I'd been fighting it, but I just couldn't any longer. I know I should be sorry but I'm not. I care about you…a lot. I want you to stay here with me," he told her.

"What, Logan, what did you do?" she whispered, taking his face into her hands. As she leaned into him, her breasts brushed his chest. Her lips were mere inches from his.

Logan held her eyes, distracted by the caress of her soft nipples against his chest. *Concentrate. This is how you got into trouble in the first place.*

"Logan," she repeated, her eyes growing concerned.

"I marked you, Wyn. Goddess help me, I did. I know we should have talked about it, but it just kind of happened. You and I… today… it was so intense, so fucking perfect. And before I knew it, my fangs were at your shoulder."

"So am I really your girlfriend?" she asked. A coy smile broke across her face. A small part of Wynter wished Logan had shared this information prior to biting her, but a bigger part, her heart and wolf, rejoiced.

"Yes you are. But Wyn, it's more than that. You do understand, right?" She thought this was funny? Jesus almighty, he'd been full of angst over telling her and she was joking?

"I know it's important to wolves. But you know I'm not all wolf, at least not yet." She stole a quick kiss, catching him off guard. "Guess that means you're my boyfriend."

"Yes I am," Logan agreed, pulling her toward him. "And so much more."

"My Alpha."

"Yes, that too. But, sweetheart, there's no one but you for me. And me for you," he tried to explain.

"You know, when we made love, I felt it. The princess, she loved that kinky wolf thing." She gave him a sexy smile and winked. "So tell me, prince, does this mean that I get to bite you back?"

The thought of her teeth at his neck caused his cock to jerk to attention. The wolf within paced, craving her mark. He howled at Logan, wanting to declare that he was her mate. But Logan reined in his wolf. Wynter had accepted that he'd marked her, but he could tell from their conversation that she didn't understand all the implications. How could he expect her to really know, given that she'd been human? Perhaps it would be better to just let her adjust to the idea that she was his girlfriend. After all, they'd just met. She hadn't even shifted yet, nor had she met his pack. There were many factors that could affect a successful mating, and he knew it.

"There's nothin' I'd like more, sweetheart, but you're going to have to wait until after you shift."

She frowned.

"Hey, I didn't make the rules. I just follow 'em."

"How about we start making some rules of our own?" She pressed her lips to the side of his neck directly underneath his earlobe and speared her fingers through his hair. Sprinkling kisses downward, she began to writhe her hips over his. "Now that I know you like conference tables, tell me, what do you think of bathtubs?"

"Bathtubs?" Logan grinned. "Bathtubs are great. But are you sure you feel well enough? How's your head?"

"I'm feeling so much pain. It's terrible," she purred, rubbing her breasts up and down against his chest. "But I'm afraid rest isn't the medicine I need."

"Ah, I see. Perhaps we need to play doctor. Sounds like you need one…hell, I think I need one. You're clearly not the only one suffering." If he didn't get inside her soon, he thought he'd explode.

"We can't have that, now, can we?" she teased, biting at his lower lip. God, he tasted good. His hard slippery body was all hers and she intended to explore every square inch of him.

The last string of Logan's restraint snapped as her teeth pulled at his mouth.

"Hold onto me. Wrap your legs around me," he demanded as he hoisted them out of the tepid water. Capturing her lips, he kissed her passionately, sweeping his tongue against hers. Within seconds, Logan was out of the tub. He pressed Wynter's back flush to the wall, clutching her by her bottom. She moaned in appreciation; the roughness sent a lightning bolt of desire to her pussy.

"Fuck yes," she cried as he moved his lips from her mouth to the crook of her neck, peppering her with kisses.

"I can't control myself around you. Bedroom," Logan grunted.

He wasn't sure if he was talking to her or himself at that

point. He'd almost taken her against the wall. A shred of sanity reminded him that she'd been hurt earlier no matter her protest that she was fine. The wall could wait for another day. Without watching where he was going with her, he clumsily made his way over to the bed. They fell into it together with Wynter's legs wrapped around his waist.

Logan rolled Wynter onto her back, straddling her hips. Kissing her neck, he began to slowly move downward until his face rested in the valley between her breasts. He sighed in amazement; he'd never get used to how beautiful she was. He cupped each breast, bringing them together so he could easily move from one nipple to the next. Tracing his tongue along the outside of her right areola, he brought the taut peak into his mouth, gently sucking, before repeating the process on her other tip, tenderly making love to them.

Wynter lolled her head backwards, electrified by the sensation of his kisses to her skin. When he took her breast, the aching in her womb threatened orgasm. Not wanting to come so quickly, she raised her head and opened her lids. Logan, lavishing attention on her pink nipples, looked up and caught her eyes. Connected in a gaze, Logan slid downward. Still holding her breasts, he kissed her abdomen, making sure to leave no spot unattended. When he reached her pussy, he gave her a naughty smile.

"Sweetheart," Logan darted his tongue through the seam of her wetness. "I'll never get enough of you. You have the sweetest, most beautiful pussy…and it's mine."

Wynter gasped as Logan pressed two long fingers into her core, stroking the length of her nerves. She contracted against him, the urge to come rushing over her.

"Logan," she panted. She was close, so close. "Oh God."

Parting her labia with his other hand, Logan sought out her sensitive hood. Finding his prize, he lapped at her clit. The second he felt her tighten around his hand, he suckled harder, using his tongue to flick at her nub. Relishing her juices, he moaned, creating a vibration that pushed her over the edge.

Wynter saw stars as her orgasm crashed onto her. Lifting her hips into his mouth, she sought all he had to give. Unrelenting, his rough tongue stroked her until she was thrashing on the bed, splintering into a thousand pieces. Calling out his name was her only relief; the pleasurable assault had left her breathless yet still yearning for him to fill her with his love.

Logan licked his lips, enthralled by the taste of her cream. Slowly ascending his mate, he took in the sight of the pink lips that he'd made so swollen. Divine. Wynter's legs fell open to his body, allowing him to rest between them. Taking his cock in his hands, he stroked himself through her slick folds, drawing out a few more shudders from her.

"Wyn, sweetheart," he uttered. Her eyes flew to his. "Feel me. Feel us."

Logan thrust his rock hard shaft into her hot core. Wynter gasped at the welcome intrusion, bringing her arms around his waist. As he plunged in and out of her, she raked her fingers down his back.

"Ah..." Logan cried. "Fuck yeah."

"You're mine," she whispered into his ear.

The wolf in him roared. Her words ignited his passion to new heights. The controlled rhythm came to a halt when he pulled out.

"Logan," she protested.

He effortlessly flipped her over until she was on her knees. Holding her up by her belly, he guided her into position.

Wynter wanted this, for him to take her, make her his. Blind to him, the waiting drove her insane as she presented herself to him. She felt the cool air at her opening.

"Yes," she screamed as he thrust into her.

"Aw yes, take me, Wyn." Logan sucked a breath, trying not to come. She felt so incredible, fisting him tightly. Seated fully in her, he held still for a minute trying to regain his composure. With one hand wrapped around her waist, he used the other to pet her back, running his fingers down from her shoulders to her ass. As he slowly started to move, he cupped her bottom, letting his thumb brush over her tiny rosebud.

"Please," Wynter heard herself begging. The pad of his finger at her puckered flesh sent sparks flying all over her skin. She wanted to be utterly filled, and sought his touch.

Sensing Wynter's signal, Logan inserted his thumb into her tight hole, slowly but surely penetrating her. He found it incredibly hot to watch his finger disappear into her and sucked a breath at the sensation. It was as if he could feel her walls tighten around his cock in response.

"That's it, sweetheart. Is this what you need?" he crooned, knowing it was.

She moaned in pleasure. "Yes, Logan, don't stop," she pleaded.

"That feels so good to me too, baby. Your ass is so perfect. I'm going to fuck you here soon. Do you want that?" He continued plunging his hard arousal into her in tandem with his hand.

"Hmm," was all she could manage to say. The overwhelming sensation of being filled rocked her world. If she thought she could take his cock in her ass, she'd tell him, but she knew she needed more preparation to do that.

When she didn't respond with words, Logan withdrew his finger. "Tell me, Wyn. Do you want me to stop? Do you want my cock in you…right here?" He traced the pad of his thumb around her puckered skin, waiting on her answer.

"Yes…don't tease me," she cried, pushing backward.

"Oh yeah, someday soon, baby. I think we need to get you a toy," Logan told her. Without missing a beat, his hand found her again, reentering a digit into her anus. Pressing in and out, he added a second finger. Everything constricted as he did so, causing him to shake. Fuck, he was going to come.

The fullness in her bottom and pussy bombarded Wynter. She trembled as the ripples of ecstasy rolled through her body. Screaming Logan's name, she continued to shake as she collapsed into the bed.

Heaving and fighting for air, Logan thrust one last time, acquiescing to his earth-shattering release. Spilling himself into her, he rolled them to their sides so that he could spoon her. His incredible, resplendent mate had taken his heart and soul. He silently celebrated, aware that he was falling for her.

Chapter Nineteen

Wynter woke to the sound of yelling. Immediately recognizing his voice, she jolted out of bed. *Oh my God. Jax is here. Where are my clothes?* She tore across the room, opening Logan's closet doors. He'd neatly placed her bags in the corner and had even hung up a few of her dresses. How long had he been awake? She heard curse words through the shouting. Not good. She yanked a sundress over her head, thankfully managing to put on her bra and panties in her panic. Throwing the bags aside, she slipped her toes into a pair of flip flops. As fast as her feet would carry her, she tore down the hallway and descended the circular stairway.

"She's sleeping. And for the last time, she's fine," Logan shouted at Jax.

"What the hell did you take her for? Goddammit, you should've known this could happen," Jax yelled, pacing Logan's family room. "If you don't go up there and get her right now, I'm doing it myself."

The strikingly handsome New York Alpha's eyes flared

in animosity. He ran his hand over his platinum-blonde hair in frustration. Jax was pissed that Wynter had gotten hurt trying to find a cure for Emma. He was even angrier with himself and felt guilty for every last thing that had happened to her, getting kidnapped and now being taken by the New Orleans' Alpha. It was entirely his fault. He should have never allowed her to go work for ViroSun. He should have more thoroughly investigated them. Jax had promised her mom and dad, his longtime friends, that he'd watch over Wynter. Yet, he'd fucked up royally, gone and sent her into a bloodsucking hellhole.

"You'd better stand down, right now, Chandler. For your information, we had to bring her, because she's the only one who knows about this little virus you kept secret. And for the record, you're the asshole who sent her off with vamps. You are the reason this happened to her, not me. So you'd better just calm the hell down," Logan growled and turned his head to the hallway. He sensed immediately when she came into the room. Logan caught a glimpse of her blond curly hair rounding the corner and swore. "Shit."

"Jax!" Wynter screamed in delight. God, she had missed him.

"Princess!" Jax called out, opening his arms to her.

She jumped into his embrace, and he spun her around. Wynter, oblivious to Logan, hugged Jax tightly. Crying in happiness, she pressed her face to his shirt.

Logan growled at the sight; Dimitri caught sight of his Alpha about to attack and held him back. *What the fuck was she doing? Did they not just have the 'I marked you' discussion?*

How the hell could she touch him so intimately? Logically, Logan knew that Wynter hadn't slept with Jax, that he was merely her guardian. But as he watched her in the arms of another man, he didn't give a damn. Jax was a single wolf. A male. An Alpha male.

All reason was lost as he watched his mate mold her body to Jax. Like a match to kindling, his anger flared in both jealousy and betrayal. But he refused to be reduced to a dog groveling over a bone. He wasn't about to trash his home over a hug. Logan was nothing if not self-disciplined. The challenges had forced him to become the master of restraint. Logan's jaw tightened as he forced his beast into submission.

"Get off me," Logan spat at Dimitri.

"You okay?" Dimitri asked, unsure whether or not to release his Alpha on Jax. An unmated male wrapped around another man's mate could turn a situation ugly pretty quick.

"I'm fine." He shrugged out of his hold, and stormed toward Jax.

"Get away from her," Logan instructed. Barely restraining the urge to punch Jax in the face, he took a deep breath, fisting his hands at his sides.

"What?" Wynter asked, bewildered. Shocked by Logan's dominant tone of voice, she stilled.

"I said. Get off her, Jax. She's mine," he warned.

The words resonated with Wynter. Realizing the implications, she fell out of her embrace with Jax but still held tight to his hand. Was Logan angry? She didn't understand what was happening, but instantly comprehended the fury in Logan's eyes. Slowly releasing

Jax, she wrapped her arms protectively around her waist. Why were they fighting? Jax's fingers on her shoulders alerted her that he, too, was upset. As his hands left her skin, she registered the hurt in his eyes. Or was it guilt?

It took all of two seconds for Jax to understand why the Alpha had gone feral. He grabbed Wynter by her shoulders, brushed her hair away and just as quickly released her.

"You goddamn marked her? Are you fucking kidding me?" Jax exclaimed indignantly. "My Goddess, Wynter, did you agree to this?"

"I…I." Wynter found herself cowering. Digging deep, she mustered the courage to face him. "Yes, I mean, no. But yes, when I found out…Jax, I care about Logan…a lot."

Logan's face visibly relaxed, but she was still too close to Jax. He knew what Jax was going to say next.

"You marked her and didn't talk to her? What the fuck, Alpha?" Jax walked around the sofa, fell back into it and grabbed his head with his hands. "No, don't even tell me anything else. This can be undone. Wyn, you can come back to New York with me. It will take a few months but you'll get through this. It'll fade and you can find a suitable wolf."

Logan looked to Wynter, and they both addressed Jax at the same time. "No."

"Jax, stop it. I'm not going back to New York. I just told you I care about him. He's claimed me and I'm happy. You just need to accept this," Wynter said softly. She didn't want to challenge him but there was no way in hell she was returning to New York. She needed to be firm on that point.

Wynter loved Jax, but she wasn't going to let him steamroll her decision to be with Logan.

"Oh, you'll go back to New York," Jax promised.

"No I won't," she countered.

"You will go. As your Alpha, I order you to go back to New York with me. Do you understand, Wynter Isabelle Ryan? Staying here with him is not an option. You are going to turn into a wolf. You have no choice but to obey me," Jax told her, giving her a hard stare.

Logan watched the interchange, trying his best to let Wynter handle it. Telling Jax she'd made a choice to stay with him warmed his heart. And Jax needed to hear this news from her, not him. But when Jax attempted to give her a direct order, Logan chose to intervene.

"She's my mate," Logan stated confidently. "And as such, you cannot order her to obey you. She's mine. I'm her Alpha."

Wynter's jaw dropped at his words. *Oh my God. What did Logan just say?* She was his mate? Wait, wasn't that something you asked someone first? She couldn't be sure of those nagging wolf rules, but wasn't that like an engagement of sorts? Her mind warred between smacking him or throwing herself at him and tearing off his clothes.

"What?" This was getting better by the minute, Jax thought. He closed his eyes trying to concentrate. How could this have happened? He should have known better. The Alpha wouldn't have marked her otherwise. But still, he had to ask. "Are you sure?"

"I am," Logan insisted, his eyes locked on Wynter's.

This was so not the way he'd imagined himself telling her. Hell, he'd hardly had time to come to terms with it himself. He watched the conflicting emotions play across her face when he'd said the word: mate. Logan swore to himself he'd make this up to her somehow. He shouldn't have done it like this. Even though he'd never been mated before, he damn well knew that it wasn't something you just announced in a room full of people without talking to your mate about it. Granted, mated wolves didn't always come to the realization at the same time, but it was treated with sanctity, with respect. Given the situation, Jax gave him little choice. There'd be no way he'd ever let him take his mate to New York.

"Well, fuck me," he heard Jax say. "I still can't believe I allowed this to happen. You're right about one thing, Logan; I should have never let Wynter go work for that company. I will be forever sorry for that. Wynter should have…"

"I am right here, you two. Oh my God. There's so much testosterone in this building you'd think we were at a bull fight." Wynter was pissed. Not only would she have appreciated the 'will you be my mate?' discussion in private, she was mad at Jax for thinking he could have simply pulled that 'Alpha is ordering you' bullshit. She hadn't seen that side of Jax since she snuck out her bedroom window at sixteen to go to a party with her friends.

"Listen up, both of you." She didn't care at this point whether she challenged them or not. This was her life they were discussing as if she were a child. Having enough, she glared at them and held up her fingers, ticking them off as she spoke. "Number one. This is my life. Not yours, oh great Alpha, Jax. And not yours either, oh great mate of mine. Number two. I am not going to New York. Do you remember why I am even here, Jax? For Emma. Was it the best plan in the world for me to go in there alone? Obviously not. But I'm a scientist, not a cop. And we've still got work to do. And whether you like it or not, I care about Logan a lot. And not like friends. We're lovers. And despite his apparent lack of ability to inform me of these important wolf thingies, like 'hey I want to mark you' or 'hey, I think you are my mate', I want him...He's an incredible person and from what I've seen, a great Alpha. Saved my ass more than once. I think you owe him a little respect."

Wynter blew out a frustrated breath, waiting for the other shoe to drop. She'd been so mad; she hadn't given too much thought as to how the Alphas would react to her heated lecture. Both men glanced away in embarrassment, from time to time, as she pointed out what they'd done. Logan's eyes fixed on her as soon as she'd told Jax they were lovers. Her heart warmed, seeing him smile. She wished she could stay mad at him for at least an hour, but his sexy expression melted away her resolve like sun on ice. She looked away to collect her thoughts, and caught Dimitri sitting on a kitchen stool grinning at her. *Glad he's finding this so amusing.* Unfortunately she wasn't finished giving the two Alphas a piece of her mind.

"And third...third, we all need to work together for Emma's sake. I don't know what they've done, but I was close. So close to finding a treatment. Not a cure, but something that would give her quality of life. Buy me time to work further on it. I need you both to do this. Please. This isn't about me anymore. We've got to get the person who killed Dana. The person that wants to turn my knowledge into a weapon."

Logan bit at his lip. Goddess, she was magnificent. And right. She definitely had a point about Jax. If Logan took Wynter to the country, he could entrust Jax to help cover the city. Aside from Léopold, he needed an ally, someone who understood the enemy and wasn't a vampire. Before he and Jax had gotten into a shouting match, they'd actually had a civilized discussion about Wynter turning wolf and had strategized for an hour about what to do next. But when he told him about what had happened with the explosion, Jax demanded to take Wynter back to New York. Before he knew it, they were arguing over Wynter like two kids fighting over a piece of candy. He rubbed his hand over the back of his neck and sighed.

"I'm sorry. You know I care about you. I'll respect your choices." Jax paused and glanced to Logan. "And your mate. But I still want to talk with you. Alone."

Logan shook his head and rolled his eyes. The guy really didn't give up. He supposed that after everything he'd done for Wynter over the years, he was entitled to have alone time with her. *But take his mate away from the safety of his home? From him?* No fucking way. Logan raised an eyebrow at Wynter in hopes she'd feel his emotion. Since he'd marked her, he'd started to sense her state of mind; confusion, anger and sadness swirled through her consciousness.

"Logan, I want to talk with Jax for a little bit. We need time," she pleaded.

"Fine, you can talk here. I'll go to my office," he countered.

"Alpha, don't take this the wrong way, but I want time alone with her in private. You and I both know there is no such thing as private as long as we're here," Jax argued.

"I'll go," Wynter decided. The truth was that she needed to have a heart to heart with Jax. As loath as she was to leave Logan, she wasn't sure she could do that knowing he was listening to their every word. She wanted privacy.

"Wynter, do you really know what you're asking?" Logan responded angrily. His mate was leaving with another unmated male, one not from his pack. His wolf snarled, wanting him to refuse her.

"Yes I do. You need to remember that I'm not all wolf yet, *mate*." She didn't mean to sound bitter but she couldn't quite forgive him that quickly. "I won't be long, but I am going."

Logan approached her like a stalking panther, his eyes wild and his mouth tight with anger. Placing his hands around her waist, he pulled her against his chest. Ever so softly, he pressed his lips to hers but never deepened the kiss. It was a goodbye kiss, one he hoped she'd regret. But he wasn't going to keep her against her will. She'd come to him willingly or not at all. When he released her from his embrace, Logan's demeanor seethed in dominance.

Wynter, still reeling from the kiss, brought her fingers to

her lips. She hated that Logan was so angry, but he needed to understand that she owed Jax. The least she could do was grant him a few hours of her time.

"Funeral's this evening. If you aren't back, I'm coming for you, sweetheart," Logan vowed fiercely, his gaze fixed on hers. He watched her quietly nod and turned to address Jax. "Take care of her, Chandler. I'll be in touch."

Affronted, Logan supposed that perhaps Wynter did need to talk with Jax, but that didn't mean he had to like it or agree with her. He'd decided to let her go as a penance of sorts, given the way he'd fucked up telling her about how they were mates. But when she returned, they'd have a long discussion about loyalty, because she wasn't showing a whole lot of it by going off with Jax.

"D, make sure they get to Jax's hotel safely. Wait for her," he ordered. Logan shot Wynter an icy glare before he turned to walk away.

Wynter's eyes brimmed in tears as Logan took off down the hallway toward his office. None of this made sense. Torn, she questioned her feelings for both Jax and Logan. Deep in her belly, the connection with Logan grew stronger every minute of the day. She'd called him Alpha and meant it. But with Jax here, a conflicting sense of what was right confused her. Since she'd told Logan she planned to go talk with Jax, she supposed she needed to go and get it over with so she could return on time.

The way Logan had spoken to her left her wolf trembling. It was as if she could literally picture her rolling in submission, exposing her underside. Despite her desire to acquiesce to the commanding Alpha, she wasn't entirely wolf. Her human psyche continued to pay credence to her reasoning by telling her that Jax was her guardian, not Logan.

Dimitri slid the door open with a loud banging sound, and gestured for her and Jax to leave. As quickly as she caught his eyes, she averted them. Damn, Dimitri was angry with her as well. Well wasn't that just great? She swore she'd fix things when she returned. But for now, she'd made her bed and had to lay in it. Exhaling loudly, she walked through the door and out of Logan's home.

They rode in silence back to the hotel. Wynter ignored Jax, staring aimlessly out the window. Ten hours ago, Logan had made love to her. Within the strength of his arms, she'd belonged. As her feelings grew stronger, she could feel herself falling for him. But now, his words played in her mind. *Mate. She was his mate?* It wasn't as if she didn't desire Logan, but the revelation, in front of Dimitri and Jax, no less, had shocked her. She wondered if by going with Jax, Logan had interpreted her actions as disrespectful, as if she'd chosen him over her mate.

Even the ever-jovial Dimitri had been cool, refusing to look at her when she'd entered the car. The minute she'd stepped away from Logan, it'd felt uncomfortable. Her wolf clawed and whined, giving her a raging headache. It was all she could do to keep from crying. As if sensing her anguish,

Jax slowly put a comforting arm around her shoulder. No matter what had happened in her life, he'd supported her. This was why she needed to go talk to him. So why did it feel so awful?

"Come on, Princess," Jax coaxed. "It's not all that bad, is it?"

"Then why do I feel like shit?" Wynter laid her head on his chest and glanced up to catch Dimitri's frosty glare. She quickly closed her eyes, trying to ignore him.

"Because my dear, he's your mate. Your wolf, she won't like being away from him, especially since he's not marked," he explained casually. "Sorry, I reacted poorly. It's just you and I; we've been together for a long time. I'm not ready to let you go."

She smiled.

"And I'm not used to you being a wolf…not at all."

"I don't know what they did to me," she confided. She felt like a little girl again, hoping he'd chase her nightmares away.

"Logan told me all about it. We'll find out, Wyn. I don't understand it either. But what's done is done. I promise you'll make it through this…your shift."

"But you were so angry back there."

"More like surprised. I consider you mine, but you aren't really…well, not at all now. You were almost like a daughter at one time. But over the years, we've grown into a comfortable friendship. I'll miss you. I suppose I always knew this would happen. But it won't change my being protective of you. That's in *my* nature. Can't be helped," he reflected.

"Logan's so angry with me. I feel bad."

"Don't worry, we'll have you back in no time, your wolf will calm down."

"And what about his wolf? I feel like I did something wrong. Not just wrong, but like I hurt him," she told Jax.

"No, Princess, you didn't do anything wrong. But it does rub against the way of wolves. You agreeing to come with me is a very rational, human thing to do. A very Wynter thing to do. Can't fault you there. And me asking you to go…well, I knew Logan wouldn't be happy, but you're my family. I haven't seen you in months. Goddess, Wynter, I'll never forgive myself for letting you go," he confessed. "This is my fault."

"No…" she began to cry.

"Shhh, I won't hear it. You were my charge. My responsibility. Logan was right. When we get back, we can have lunch and talk about how I can help you both with this colossal fail we've created. The one thing that drives me is that Emma's still hangin' on. And if there's something we can do without putting you into harm's way, then I want to do it."

Wynter wanted to argue with him and tell him that she already was in danger, but she assumed he knew that. It was why he'd been freaking out at Logan. Meanwhile, Logan had done nothing to deserve the death they'd brought to New Orleans. Guilt racked her, but still, after everything that had happened, she wasn't sure she would have done anything differently.

By the time they got up to Jax's suite, Wynter was

famished. Opening the door, a warm, familiar face greeted her.

"Hey missy, welcome back. Come on now, give me some sugar," Jax's beta, Nick, told her, giving her a big hug. "Why the sad face? What's wrong?"

"Long story," Jax sighed, taking a seat at the large dining table. Thank Goddess Nick had had lunch delivered. "Sit, let's eat."

"Talk and eat. What gives?"

Jax looked to Wynter. "Do you want to tell him?"

"Abridged version? The vampires who kidnapped me made me work on the virus, but I escaped. Logan Reynaud, the New Orleans' Alpha, rescued me then took me into his home. Apparently the vamps infected me with something during one of their lovely feeding sessions. So, by the way, I'm turning into a wolf." Wynter paused to grab a diet soda. She twisted the cap off, took a drink and snatched a wrap off the tray. "Let's see, what else? Oh yeah, the vamps are still trying to kill me, Logan marked me and I just found out I'm his mate. Yeah, I think that pretty much sums it up."

Both Jax and Nick exchanged a look of surprise. Although she'd been shaken in the car, she appeared to be recovering nicely. She had always been a fighter, Jax knew. But every time she rebounded, it still amazed him that a human so fragile could have the bravery of a lion.

"So, wait, have you mated, have you bonded with Logan?" Nick practically shouted.

"No," she shook her head and pulled her hair aside to

show him. "Marked. As in he marked me. Apparently I have to wait until after I shift. So looking forward to shifting…not."

"It'll be okay, Wyn. The way your Alpha tore into me today, I have every confidence he'll protect you. He's an honorable wolf," Jax assured her.

"You say that as if you like him. Just a while ago, you guys almost ripped each other's heads off. It was a real love fest, Nick," she noted with sarcasm.

"That's what Alphas do. We jostle for territory, establish dominance. What you saw today, that was child's play, nothing more."

She rolled her eyes. Men. Wolves. "Well, Logan was good and pissed at me when I left. Some mate I am."

"Yeah, I bet that went over well. Jesus, Jax. What were you thinking taking her away from him?"

"I'm a selfish prick, okay? What do you expect? I haven't seen her for months. Besides, she'll go back after lunch."

"I'm the one who decided, Jax. He's my mate." She nearly choked on the word, tears threatened. The longer she was away, the worse she felt. A change of subject was in order. "Tell me about Emma. How's Mika?"

"Mika's good, really good," Nick winked.

"No way!" Wynter exclaimed, slapping his arm.

"Way," Jax replied. "Bad wolf, Nick."

"No, Alpha, I'm a very good wolf. Why do you think she likes me so much?" Nick teased.

Wynter couldn't believe her friend had hooked up with Jax's beta. How could she have missed that one? She fought the urge to call Mika right then and there. God, how she missed her.

"As for little Emma, well, she's hanging in there," Nick commented. "Good days, bad days. I don't know, Wyn. She's about the same. But damn, I wish we knew what was wrong."

"I'm close. Although I haven't done anything since I escaped the lab. But we've got a laptop. They got it before the car exploded." She tried not to react to Nick's pained expression as she mentioned what had happened. "Jax can fill you in on what all happened...fun times. Anyway, that laptop could have my data on it. Or not. We'll see. The vamps scrubbed it but Dimitri's going to try to recover it. I would have asked this morning how he was making out with it but well, you know...with all the yelling and whatnot, that didn't happen."

"A cure?" Nick posed the question.

"No. 'Fraid not. But it'd give her quality of life. She could lead a normal life again with medication," Wynter speculated. It wasn't a panacea but it would be a far cry from spending her days bedridden.

"Logan told me he's taking you out of the city. Said he's setting up a lab at his house," Jax mentioned.

Wynter stilled. Seemed her sneaky mate was always two steps ahead of her. No wonder the man was Alpha, she thought. "A lab, really, he said that?"

"Yes, he's very committed to helping you, us. Of course, he doesn't want whoever is doing this to proliferate a virus. But he mentioned Emma. He wants to help her...for you."

Jax smiled. "It didn't make sense why he was going to such a great extent to help us when I first spoke to him. But that was before I knew you were his. And just like that, all the pieces came together."

Wynter's face flushed like a schoolgirl, thinking of Logan. She really could fall in love with him. No matter what had happened this morning, they'd work through it.

"Ah, love is a wonderful thing," Nick declared with a broad smile.

As if caught with her hand in the cookie jar, Wynter looked down and shoved the wrap into her mouth.

"Wyn, in all seriousness, if you aren't in agreement with this mating, you don't have to stay here. I mean, I'd have to be an idiot not to feel the chemistry between you and Logan. But if you're having second thoughts, you, as a wolf, aren't required to mate with him. This isn't the dark ages," Jax explained.

"What?" Wynter looked up and found both of them staring at her.

"Do you love him, Princess?"

"Maybe," Wynter blurted out before she had a chance to take it back. She decided to backpedal but as she considered how she felt, it was hard to deny her feelings. "I mean I think I could fall in love with him. He's just so caring and loving and larger than life. It's unbelievable. I don't know how this happened."

Nick and Jax both laughed.

"What?"

"Nature, baby," Nick remarked.

"You can't control it," Jax said. He leaned back into his chair and sighed. "Love, she will come for all of us, and there isn't a damn thing we can do."

"I wish we'd talked about this before...this wolf stuff." She smiled, at a loss for the correct terminology. "It's just that even though I can feel something in me, what I think is my wolf...but I feel human too. I know why you wanted to protect me from wolves, from the pack, but now, I'm so alone."

"No, never alone. Your Alpha, he's there for you, to guide you, to love you," he corrected her in a serious tone.

"But how do you know? How do you know I'll be fine?"

"Logan may be a new Alpha, but he's been a beta. And he's been a wolf for a very long time. You must trust him." Jax fell short of telling his lovely human friend that she'd need to submit.

All wolves in a pack must submit for order to exist. She'd learn in time, but he suspected she might have a rough go at it. He'd love to help her, but it was something she needed to do on her own. No lecture could teach that life experience.

Wynter continued eating, considering Jax's advice. The more she thought of Logan the more she missed him and sought to smooth over their disagreement. The look in his eyes when she'd gone with Jax tore at her heart. After another thirty minutes of catching up, Wynter told Jax that she needed to go. He assured her that he wasn't leaving New Orleans and was on call should they locate the lab again. Jax walked her down to the lobby where Dimitri was waiting to take her home. Giving Jax a hug and kiss to the cheek, she quickly departed, walking over to the awaiting car.

Dimitri held open the back door as if he was a chauffeur. Ignoring his gesture, she slipped around him and into the front passenger seat, waiting for him to join her. Apparently, Logan wasn't the only one who needed to talk. His cold disposition had not warmed since she was gone. If anything, he'd spent some time in the freezer. Dimitri slammed the back door and strode around to his side. He sat down, buckled up and started the car without looking at her.

"What? Just say it already," she ordered, like the alpha female which she was becoming.

"Why'd you go with him?"

"I told you already, he's like family. And just because I'm Logan's mate, he's still my friend. I haven't seen him in months. Why do you care anyway? It's not like I'm your mate," she snapped.

"Because darlin', when my Alpha's unhappy, and he's very unhappy at the minute, we all feel it. I know Jax is your family, but you've gotta see what this does to Logan," he pleaded.

"I'm sorry, Dimitri. I am. I didn't mean to upset Logan, and I certainly had no idea you'd be affected. You have to remember that I'm new to this," she said softly. Wynter placed a caring hand on Dimitri's shoulder. "And to be fair, Logan has his own explaining to do. This is not all my fault."

"Yeah, sorry about that mating business."

"Sure you are. You looked real broken up about it earlier.

That smile of yours...geez. It really wasn't funny." She gave him a small grin.

He smiled in return, recalling the conversation and laughed out loud.

"I love Logan but man, watching him fall for his mate is kind of funny...very funny actually. You have to give him credit, though. He'd rather risk you being mad at him by telling everyone you were his mate than let another wolf take you away. And he's a new Alpha...going up against Jax like that. Logan is one tough motherfu....well you get the idea."

"I'm glad you were entertained. Because me...I was pretty surprised that he kind of just blurted that out. I mean, it's not like I don't really like Logan. He's incredible. Loving and sexy and..." she said, dreamily, until Dimitri cut her off.

"But the commitment, Wyn. With wolves, it's more, so much more."

"You've marked someone? Mated?"

"Hold on there, cher. No way. Let's just say that like Logan, I've been 'round a long time. Watched my fellow wolves fall deep into their mated bond. Sometimes it goes smoothly. And sometimes," Dimitri paused, concentrating on his driving as it had begun to rain, "well, not so much. But I'll tell ya, it always goes. Because Mother Nature, she gets her way. No use fightin'"

"How mad is he?"

"Logan? Scale of one to ten?" He contemplated. "Ten when you left. Maybe a seven or eight now. And here we are...home."

Wynter cringed. *Would he forgive her? Would he punish her?* Like vampires, wolves had their own interpretation of life's rules. As the gate slid open and they drove into the carport, her stomach flip-flopped. Was he waiting for her? What should she say to him? The car stopped, jolting her back to the present. Dimitri opened the door for her and they both ran into the house, in an effort to escape the downpour. The sliding glass door opened. She hoped Logan would be expecting her, yet she was greeted with silence.

"Upstairs," Dimitri told her, his hand still on the door. He wasn't planning on staying for whatever was about to go down between Logan and Wynter. Even though he loved Logan like a brother, there were things he had to do on his own, and this truly fell in that category.

"Thanks," Wynter whispered. Brushing a kiss to Dimitri's cheek, she fled to her Alpha, disappearing around the corner and up the staircase.

Chapter Twenty

Logan felt her the second they drove onto the property. Silently he breathed a sigh of relief she'd returned, but struggled to understand how she could have left him in the first place. While he fully comprehended her familial relationship with Jax, he'd claimed her. Any true she-wolf would have never gone off with an unmated male wolf under similar circumstances. But Wynter wasn't really a wolf yet. Even if she was about to transform, she hadn't been raised wolf, wasn't even a hybrid. She couldn't possibly appreciate the ramifications of her actions. Logan wanted to forget, forgive, but he simply didn't have that luxury.

Already, he'd spent too much time with Wynter. After nearly killing himself to secure his position as Alpha, he should be leading his pack, not worrying about a human. If she were only a human, it'd be an easy decision. But no, she was his mate. A mate who knew essentially nothing about wolves. What kind of sick joke was the Goddess playing? Logan wondered what would happen if he rejected fate. Maybe he was wrong about her being his? He wished.

Whenever she was within five feet of him, his wolf clawed to mate her. There would be no denying him once Wynter shifted.

In the meantime, he resolved to focus on the pack. Convulsing in rage over Wynter's departure had hurt them. Every wolf would have felt his anger, wondering what had caused his virulent excitation. They'd stress, which was the very last thing the pack needed. After the long months of mourning Marcel and enduring the uncertainty of who'd lead them, he'd finally established peace. Today, though, his temper threatened the sanctity he'd worked so hard to create.

The hot spray of the shower had allowed him time to meditate, bringing a sense of balance and stoicism to his thoughts. The solace of his newfound impassivity clarified his strategy. He and Wynter simply could not continue down a path of misunderstandings. There was no other choice. When they got to the bayou, Wynter would learn to submit, learn the way of the wolves. He'd teach her lessons, not just in acquiescence but the importance of her role within the pack. Whether she liked it or not, he fully anticipated her wolf would emerge at the full moon. He'd prepare her for their new life together. As the Alpha's mate, the pack would look to her for guidance, direction. But in order for her to fulfill her role, she must accept him as Alpha and her own transformation.

Her footsteps at the door excited his wolf, but he refused him access. Now was not the time. Dana's funeral started within the hour, and his calming presence was required.

Logan planned to do nothing less for his pack, even if that meant isolating Wynter. The rumination over the quandary would wait. For at least a few hours, he planned to ignore her, focus all of his attention on Fiona and the pack. It was the least he could do.

Wynter's heart caught in her throat, seeing her magnificent Alpha at the mirror. Incredibly handsome didn't begin to describe how she saw him. Black pinstripes ran the length of his long legs. His trousers hung easily on his tapered waist, hugging over his bottom, a crisp white dress shirt tucked into them. She watched as he knotted his tie, never losing focus from his task.

"Logan," Wynter called tenderly.

"The funeral's at six. Dimitri and Jake will take you. Once you get there, stay with Jake," he explained coldly. He turned, took his suit jacket off a hanger and dressed.

"We need to talk," she pleaded, walking toward him. The need to touch him overwhelmed her.

Logan adjusted his collar, giving himself one last look in the mirror, never seeking eye contact. He ignored her request and sought to leave the room.

"You'll need to pack your things. You can use the bag I left you in the closet. We're leaving immediately after the burial."

As Logan passed by, Wynter grabbed onto his sleeve, pressing her forehead into his chest. God, he smelled so good. She wanted to apologize, ask for forgiveness, but also talk to him about being his mate. There were too many questions. She needed him to quell her fears, confirm he still cared.

"Please, Logan. Don't do this," she whispered.

Logan tugged his arm from her grasp, calmly backing away. Indifference washed over his face. No longer was the lover present, but the leader; the Alpha commanded the room.

"Get dressed. You have forty-five minutes," he said, looking at his watch.

"Jesus, Logan. Come on," she felt her voice escalate. "I need to talk to you."

"Right now, Wynter, this is not about you. Or me. There is a woman, a wolf. My wolf," he stressed in his dominant tone that told her he was all business. "She's dead. My pack needs me. They need me strong, whole and calm. I can't do that when I'm with you. Not now."

Wynter hung her head and closed her eyes. She wished she could hide her face from him entirely. His withdrawal was too much to bear. She bit her lip; the pain was a welcome distraction from the suffocation blanketing her crushed heart.

Logan could sense her pain as clear as if it were his own. He wanted to take her into his arms, tell her they'd work it out, and then make love to her all night long. Gathering every ounce of willpower he had, Logan turned and walked out the door. After the funeral, she'd be his, he promised himself. Until then, the pack held his full attention.

As Logan walked out the door, Wynter allowed the tears to flow. As if swept into a storm, she no longer knew which direction she was traveling. Having lost her only life preserver, she struggled to keep her head above the swelling waves, yet it wasn't enough. She stumbled into the bathroom and turned on the shower, allowing the cold water to pelt her skin. She slid down the wall, until her bottom hit the floor and she crawled into a ball, sobbing, wishing she had never heard of wolves.

"What's up?" Dimitri nodded to Logan, handing him an umbrella.

"Good, here comes Jake," Logan responded, not answering Dimitri directly.

Jake slid open the door and shook the rain off his head.

"Hey," he greeted. "Nothing like a rainy funeral in the dark. Good stuff."

"Yeah, I don't expect many of us to shift if this rain keeps up," Dimitri added.

"Alpha, you okay?" Jake asked with genuine concern. The anger rolling through the pack earlier had rocked them hard.

"Yeah, I'm good," Logan lied. "I should be asking how you're doing. You took a hard one out there last night."

"Good to go. Thanks to you," he nodded. "Hurt like a motherfucker. Stayed wolf all last night, though, just to be sure I was okay."

"I'm gonna walk over to Fiona's and meet the girls there," Logan told them.

Dimitri cocked an eyebrow at Logan. "Hey man, let me preface this by 'I'm not tellin' you what to do'."

"But you're going to anyway? Let's hear it."

"That's what your beta is for." Dimitri clapped his hand on his shoulder. "First, it's raining cats and dogs. You could just take the car with us. Second, you think it's a good idea to be around the girls without Wynter? I mean, this mating thing doesn't seem to be going so smoothly for either one of you and I'd hate to..."

"I'm not going over there to fuck them, D. Fiona's sister died. I'll be careful not to touch them a lot, but let's be clear, okay, tonight is about Dana. Not me. Not Wynter. And it's sure as hell not about my mating," he huffed. "And yeah, this whole mating thing is not exactly what I thought was going to happen, but then again, I never thought in a million years that my mate was going to walk into my life as soon as I became Alpha. I certainly didn't expect her to be human."

"Yeah, not optimal," Dimitri concurred.

"I'll deal with this...with Wynter, when we get out of the city. I'm not looking to hurt her, but I've got to be with the pack. You know this. Fiona. Luci. They are pack and need me too...especially tonight."

Logan slid open the door and righted the umbrella.

"As for a little rain, it never hurt anyone. Might actually do me some good to breathe in the petrichor. Love it."

"Petrichor?" Dimitri asked, shaking his head. Someone had been doing crossword puzzles again. A strange stress reliever for his Alpha, but whatever it took.

"The smell that comes with the rain, my friend, the smell. Nothin' better." Logan laughed and pressed open the black canopy.

Dimitri laughed but then his thoughts turned dark. He hoped his Alpha worked out things with Wynter sooner than later. He'd caught the wince on Logan's face upon hearing the faint sound of crying coming from his little wolf upstairs. They'd both tried to ignore it as if it wasn't happening. He knew Logan was giving his full attention to the pack, trying to concentrate on maintaining a sense of tranquility for them. And it wasn't the time to get involved between him and Wynter. Sometimes it was better just to let the dust settle.

He looked into a mirror that hung in the kitchen and adjusted the knot in his tie. He hated funerals. Luckily he hadn't attended many for wolves, but still, many of his human friends had passed over the years. As he glanced down at his black shoes, ones that seemed uncomfortably tight, he sighed, knowing what the night had in store for them all. The funeral was going to be as much fun as…well, a funeral.

Within minutes, the clicking of heels let him know Wynter was ready. She rounded the corner, dressed in black with a small tote in her hands. Wet ringlets surrounded her reddened face. Wearing no makeup, she still looked beautiful and determined. She made low maintenance look chic, Dimitri thought. Unsure of what to say, Dimitri gave Jake a knowing smile and went to the closet. Logan had bought Wynter some things she'd need for the trip, and he'd asked him to give them to her.

Wynter had pulled it together after a five minute crying jaunt. Angry and confused, she refused to let life or her lack of control over it hold her down. Ever since her parents died, she'd been fighting. She wasn't sure if or when she'd work things out with Logan, but she still had a purpose: get the data, work on a treatment for Emma. Her other goal was to get through the shift. If Logan rejected her because of a human mistake, then she'd leave and go back to New York. As Jax had explained it, she didn't have to mate him if she didn't want to do it or if he decided a human wasn't suitable for an Alpha's mate. She'd be devastated but she'd get through it. Like the loss of her parents, like being held captive and tortured, she'd dig deep and continue with her life. Self-preservation was a strong motivator.

As she glanced down to her black oxford shirt and matching pencil skirt, she wondered if Logan had selected the outfit himself. And what if he didn't? What if he'd asked those women to do it for him? She shoved the nasty green monster to the back of her mind. No, she would not go there. Still, it hadn't been with the clothing Dimitri had originally brought her to wear, nor were the black leather pumps.

She sighed. None of this really belonged to her. It was merely an illusion of reality. Her life had been stolen. Everything she'd had in her purse was gone, taken by her captors. Smoothing down the soft fabric of her sleeves, she made a mental note to contact Jax's secretary to have her forward her mail. She also needed her home laptop in order to report her credit cards stolen. Every last shred of her personal information was digitalized. His secretary could just download the info and send it to her. She could purchase a new laptop online, but she still needed a cell phone. Maybe tomorrow, she'd arrange to go to a local cell phone carrier where she could purchase a new one.

Dimitri's hand on her shoulder startled her out of her daydream.

"Here, Wyn." Dimitri held up a royal blue trench coat. "Go ahead, put it on. It's nasty out there."

Gratefully, she shrugged into the garment, noticing it was from Burberry. As she buttoned it up and buckled the thin black leather belt around her waist, she considered how she'd never splurge on something so extravagant. She looked up to Dimitri who attempted to give her a black patent leather clutch. Was he giving her someone else's purse?

"But this isn't mine…I mean I lost my bag…" she started.

"He knows. Here take it. I'm guessing it's got all the basic lady stuff in it," he surmised, turning off the kitchen light. "A gentleman doesn't go through a lady's purse."

"Since when are you a gentleman?" Jake joked.

"Hey now, go easy, bro. I am so a gentleman." Dimitri laughed and turned back to Wynter. "And before you ask, Logan got these things for you. I swear, that wolf shops more than a woman does. But then again, you can't walk two feet around here without running into a store of some kind."

"Thank you," she replied thoughtfully.

Logan shopped for her? She wasn't sure why the thought of him doing so made her feel a little better, but it did. The man surprised her at every turn. It made her feel that even if he'd been mad, he'd still cared enough to think of her. A flicker of hope sparked. As she headed out, safely between Jake and Dimitri, the sound of thunder clapped in the distance. She'd have to wait until after the funeral, but later tonight, she hoped they'd talk about what had happened.

A police officer ushered the crowd into the cemetery as the sheets of rain sliced through the lights of his emergency vehicle. The crowd of nearly a hundred people carefully shuffled through the narrow stone walkways. Battery operated lanterns illuminated the pathway toward the crypt. Between the cracked pavement and pebbles, Wynter feared she'd take a nosedive into a marbled tomb. She wrapped her hand around Jake's arm in an effort to steady her feet. Unable to see ahead, she wondered how the jazz band managed to continue playing in the deluge. Yet the funeral dirge pounded a sad beat into the night.

By the time they neared the tomb, the music ended. The small space was thick with people and Wynter struggled to find a spot to stand, settling against the cold stone of another's resting place. Creepy, she reasoned, but there was literally no room for all the living who had come to mourn. Through the bodies, she spotted Logan, who stood next to Luci. Her hateful eyes bore into Wynter. Surmising that Luci was engaging her in some kind of sick wolf intimidation, Wynter stared back as if to dare her to touch Logan. Thankfully, their gaze was broken as all heads turned to watch Fiona and an elderly woman, Dana's mother, make their way toward the casket. Logan had explained to her that Fiona was Dana's half-sister; they shared the same father. Yet Fiona appeared close with Dana's human mother as well.

The smell of incense permeated the air as the priest blessed the tomb. The stone tablet had been removed and the rectangular opening had been draped for the service. The older woman sobbed openly, clutching on to Fiona as the final prayers were said. Wynter leaned her head forward, trying to hear the sermon. Upon a final 'Amen', a word passed between Logan and the priest, silencing the crowd. Her heart caught as she realized Logan was about to speak.

"My wolves," Logan began somberly. "Dana. She was our doctor. Our friend. Our sister. She will be missed by our pack. But always remembered. We knew her as hybrid, but she was as much wolf as any of us."

"And that is what got her killed!" Dana's mother screamed, lunging at Logan. Fiona scrambled to hold onto the old woman, but she slipped from her grasp. "Wolves! You killed my husband! My daughter! I hate you!"

Logan easily caught the woman's wrist as she attempted to slap him in the face. "Marguerite, please. I know this pain. I know," Logan cried. "Don't ever think for a moment I don't. Marcel. Dana. We all miss them."

"My baby, Logan, my baby," the woman wailed as she fell into his embrace. "Oh God help me."

Wynter watched intently as Logan cried along with the old woman. It was evident that he knew her well. It was as if Logan's heart had been splayed open for all to see, but he didn't deny the woman's grief. No, he mourned with her, held her until she calmed. Others wept alongside them as the torrent fell from the skies.

Wynter's feet began to move before her brain had a chance to process what she was doing. A sharp tug on her arm reminded her of where she was. Tears stung her cheeks as Jake pulled her toward him. Her wolf sought to comfort her mate, to care for him. But it wasn't just her wolf, it was Wynter. Every part of her being needed to soothe him. As if Logan sensed what was happening, his eyes pierced the crowd and locked on hers. Both unable to speak or move, it seemed as if centuries passed while they locked in a gaze. The roar of a thunderbolt caused her to look up to the heavens, losing eye contact.

Logan felt Wynter's concern, but it was the touch of an unmated male that caught his attention. But soon, he realized Jake was holding her back. She was coming for him. The caring expression on her face told him how much she needed him. The unspoken encouragement from his mate drove him to continue. Releasing the woman back to Fiona, he touched a loving hand to Dana's coffin.

"Dana, my friend. You will never, ever be forgotten. Your death will not go unpunished. I promise you, as I stand here today," Logan's voice cracked as he fought his emotion, "you will be avenged."

As he spoke his last words, Dana's mother nodded in approval. The funeral director gestured for his workers to remove the draping. Logan gave a silent signal to Dimitri that it was time to place Dana into her final resting place. Six men held the casket by its handles, lifting it gently into the tomb's upper vault. As it disappeared into the dark chamber, Fiona, and Dana's mother led the procession of people to the exit while the sounding trumpets played, 'When the Saints Go Marching In'.

Surreal as it was, Wynter watched as the people poured back into the narrow paths, silently thanking God no one had been struck by lightning. As if all the air had left her lungs, she struggled to make her way out of the cemetery. She concentrated, putting one frozen wet foot in front of the other. Small fingers grasped her wrist, and she peered under the umbrella to see Fiona standing in front of her.

"I am so sorry for your loss," Wynter managed genuinely. If anyone knew loss, it was her.

"Thank you for coming. I know it mustn't have been easy," Fiona related with understanding. "I'll see you in a few days."

Unsure of what to say, Wynter dipped her head in acknowledgement and gave her a sympathetic smile. A gust of wind pushed both women onward toward the exit. Wynter gasped for breath and held tight to Jake, stumbling through the icy puddles. Jake pointed to a waiting limo, and she blindly followed. Relief filled her as a car door opened, and she fell, shivering, into its warm confines. Jake quickly pressed his hip to hers, forcing Wynter to move over into the next seat. As the heat hit her feet, she glanced up to find Logan staring at her.

Chapter Twenty-One

Wynter's stomach dropped as the elevator lurched toward the sky. She didn't understand why they were in Logan's high-rise, but kept quiet on their ascent. Fighting the claustrophobia, she closed her eyes after it passed the floor where she'd first met Logan in his office. A resounding jolt forced her to focus on the opening doors. Rain blew into the small chamber, causing her to gasp. What the hell? Instinctively, she covered her ears upon hearing the deafening whirl of the helicopter blades. Wind hit her face, and she stopped, frozen in disbelief. A small push between her shoulder blades put her feet back in motion, propelling her toward the blinking lights.

The pressure from the spinning rotors sprayed air and water onto them as they crossed the helipad. Wynter felt Logan wrap an arm around her waist, guiding her into the dimly lit cabin. Shocked as she was, she was relieved to be out of the weather. The soft tan leather seats felt smooth on her palms. She took in her surroundings, noticing that the luxury helicopter had four seats, complete with plasma TV screen and bar. Peering forward, she spotted a pilot through the small privacy glass.

Logan sat down next to Wynter, closing the door after Dimitri. Having never been in a helicopter, panic rose in Wynter's throat. She looked to Logan and Dimitri who both appeared solemn but altogether calm as if they'd done this a million times. But of course they have, she thought to herself. Meanwhile, all she could think about was crashing in the middle of the night inside the little tin can. A very lush, expensive tin can, but still it was night and it was raining. Both of those factors could not be good, she reasoned.

"Why are we..?" she began to yell over at Logan, her face white with fright.

He reached behind her seat and grabbed a pair of headphones. Ever so gently, he placed them onto her ears, gliding his thumb down the side of her cheek. Wynter gazed into his eyes, wanting desperately to talk with him about what had happened, but as she went to open her mouth, he looked away and put a set on his own ears.

"Why are we taking a helicopter? Are you sure this is safe?" Wynter asked, her voice laced with alarm. "It's raining."

"Not optimal but it's let up some. Besides, the wind has died down and there's no fog. We don't want to take any chances getting ambushed on the roads. Don't worry, it's safe."

"'Bout forty-five minutes to an hour, if the weather cooperates. You've never flown in a whirlybird, cher?" Dimitri inquired with a relaxed smile.

"No I haven't," she replied, gasping as they vaulted up into the night sky. Her fingernails dug into the leather, and she hoped they wouldn't leave scratches. She watched in wonder as tiny lights below flickered in the distance as they buzzed toward their destination.

Logan, unable to take another minute of his self-imposed isolation, reached for Wynter's hand. Slowly peeling her fingers from the seat, he placed her palm on his leg, and caressed her fingers. Goddess, he missed touching her. The small gesture sent loving tendrils throughout his body, reminding him that she really was his mate. When they got home, they'd have to have a long discussion about their relationship, her future as a wolf.

"It's okay, sweetheart," he assured her in a tender voice that he hadn't used since before she'd left to go with Jax. He continued to massage her hand, sliding a thumb into her palm. "Just rest. We'll be there soon."

Wynter relaxed into the small but poignant contact. Her hand burned with warmth radiating from his thigh, and she fought the urge to lean into him, to touch him, to kiss him. As if her body obeyed his directive, she let her forehead rest against the cool window. Within seconds, she'd fallen fast asleep to the soft lullaby of the humming blades.

Creaking metal woke Wynter. The silence that followed told her they had landed. Logan, who'd already begun exiting, extended his hand.

"We're home," he told her.

Home? No, his home, not hers, she thought. But still, that small spark of hope told her to embrace her future with optimistic curiosity. Her heart fluttered in response. With a cautious smile, she clasped her palm in his, accepting his assistance down the steps.

It was only a short ride from the helipad to Logan's house. When they'd exited the car, Wynter eyed the blue tarp which covered the exterior of the huge contemporary house. It appeared unfinished yet lights glimmered through the undraped casement windows. Floodlights illuminated the fresh landscaping, and the smell of newly laid mulch and fragrant roses permeated the night air.

The rain had subsided, and they quickly made their way up the walkway towards the entrance. Logan flipped open a security pad and typed in a code. The lock clicked open and he turned the handle. As they entered, she followed Logan's lead and kicked off her sodden shoes, thankful she'd gone without stockings. In a few minutes, her feet would dry nicely and the smooth hardwood floor felt soothing to her sore toes.

"Adèle," Logan called.

Wynter looked around the foyer that led into a spacious great room. A modern rectangular shaped gas lit fire blazed atop its round white stones. The black pit, outlined in stainless steel, stood out against the cream-colored Kasota stone hearth. Three tall vases filled with ornamental grass sat atop a thin dark wooden mantel.

A soft purring creature rubbed against her legs, startling

Wynter. She knelt down, petting the sweet cat who meowed and pressed its head into her hands.

"Well, hello, kitty," she said softly, touching its ears.

"I see you've met Mojo," Logan acknowledged.

"Hmm? You have a cat?" Wynter replied in surprise, trying to hide her amusement.

"Here kitty, kitty. Come to Daddy," Logan sang in his best baby voice. The small black ball of fur ran toward him, purring voraciously, and he scooped the kitten into his arms, placing kisses on her head. He continued to talk in a soft voice, pretending to talk to the cat while really answering Wynter. "Yes, I have a kitty. And she's such a good girl, aren't you? Who's a good kitty?"

"Mojo," she repeated, smiling.

Wynter watched in amazement as the Alpha tenderly caressed the sweet little creature. Of all things she thought might happen tonight, this certainly was not one of them. As this terrifyingly attractive side of Logan was revealed to her, she fought the urge to run up and kiss him. The wanting, the temptation was so great; she forced herself into the floor, remaining rooted in place.

"She's not very much into Voodoo, but she's lucky," he explained, petting her and rubbing his face into her soft fur. He caught Wynter examining him as if he had four heads. "What?"

"I'm just…I don't know, surprised. I love cats, but a wolf with a cat? Seems counterintuitive." *And sexy.*

"Yeah, that's what Tristan thought too. His mate runs an animal shelter. One day, I spent quite a bit of time in her cat room. And what can I say?" He shrugged, fixing her with his eyes as if he was talking about her and not the cat. "I fell in love. You know, sometimes, Dr. Ryan, we can't control who we fall in love with. Sometimes even when things don't make sense, they actually make the most sense in the world."

Wynter blushed and looked away. Oh God, she wanted to touch him so badly. Heat filled her body. Desire pulsed through her veins. She tried to think of anything but sex. What was wrong with her? Just as she'd mustered enough bravery to respond coherently, a portly woman with a gray bun wandered into the foyer. Logan let the cat jump to the floor, approached and gave her a hug.

"Ah, Adèle. Meet Wynter. Wyn, this is Adèle. She's kept me in one piece since I've moved home."

"Nice to meet you." Wynter noticed how at ease Logan was with his housekeeper.

"Wynter va rester avec moi," he told the woman. Adèle ran her eyes over Wynter before conceding that she was welcome.

"Oui, oui. Bonjour, Wynter," Adèle greeted. She briskly turned on her heels, speaking rapidly in French. She waved an arm, gesturing for them to follow. "Allons, le dîner est prêt."

"Merci, I'm starving," Logan picked up a piece of fluffy white bread out of a bowl and quickly stuffed it into his mouth before she had a chance to protest. "Merci beaucoup pour obtenir la maison prête. Everything looks great."

Adèle pointed to the large glass dining table, and promptly set out another place setting for his guest. Logan sat at the head of the table and gestured for Wynter to sit at his side. Wynter, famished, obeyed, not sure what she should do next. The enticing aroma of a basket of warmed New Orleans-style French bread teased at her nose. Adèle set out two large bowls of what Wynter thought was gumbo, and plates of salad.

"Salade. Gumbo. Pain," Adèle ticked off her creations and then took off her apron. "See you tomorrow, no?"

"Oui, and thanks again, Adèle. The place is really coming together," Logan noted.

She smiled and nodded, but appeared to be in a hurry to leave. "Oui, Monsieur. Soyez le bienvenu." With a wave, she took off toward the back of the home. A door shutting let them know they were alone.

Following Logan's lead, Wynter dug into the delightful gooey mixture with her spoon. They ate in silence. She noticed that like the great room, the kitchen was sparsely decorated. Dark cherry cabinets and hardwood floors were offset by the white granite countertops. The only item on the counter alongside the wall was a coffeemaker. No dishes or glasses sat atop the oversized rectangular island. In fact, there wasn't much décor at all. No pictures on the walls. Not even a clock. Taking a deep breath, she could smell the new drywall and paint and wondered how long Logan had lived here.

As if he read her thoughts, he was the first to speak. "I just built it," he commented without explanation.

"It's beautiful," she replied.

"It's empty," he countered. "But someday soon, it'll be more of a home than a house."

"How long have you lived here?"

"I haven't."

"Hmm?"

"This is the first meal I've eaten here…with you," he stated, meeting her eyes. Had she no idea how important she was to him? How important she had yet to become? It was killing him. The silence. The lack of understanding. And most of all the lack of intimacy. Intimacy which had shattered into a million bits when she left him to go with Jax. It was time to talk, to not just mend their relationship, but set it on a course that would solidify their future.

Wynter stilled at the realization that he'd brought her here, to his home. He'd told her that he'd lived in Marcel's home, but this was a new beginning. It had been something special he'd built on his own and now shared with her. Her chest tightened, and she struggled to come up with the right words.

"Logan, I…I'm sorry," she began. "Today…it's just that everything has moved so quickly. And not just this…this thing between us. It's everything."

"This thing," he said tersely. "This thing is not a thing. It's a bond, Wynter. I've marked you. We're mates. It's not simply a choice we make. It either is or it isn't."

"Yes, but I…" she placed her spoon on the table and wiped her mouth.

"Do you have any idea what I've been through over the past two months?" Logan asked rhetorically, well aware she couldn't possibly comprehend the struggle he'd endured. The low calm of his voice was edged in a controlled indignation. "My friend, Marcel. We grew up together, spent a lifetime as friends. He was Tristan's brother, but they both are my family in every sense of the word. Two months ago, I sat with his blood on my hands. I watched as the life drained from his eyes."

Logan coughed, sucking back his emotions. Enough tears had been shed. "And minutes before that, do you know what I did, Wyn?"

She quietly shook her head.

"I killed a man…with my own hands. Not as wolf. As a man. That death is on my hands." He held his palms upward, staring at them as if they were dripping in blood.

"That night, I vowed to Marcel that I'd lead his pack, to take care of his wolves. Marcel begged me…I didn't want this, to be Alpha. My role as beta was comfortable, respected. I loved Tristan. It isn't something I did lightly," he reflected, placing his palms down on the table. "But it is done. For the last two months, I've fought challenges. Bloody, ripped up fur and bruises, week after week."

"Logan," Wynter gasped quietly. *What had he been through?*

"I may've vowed to be Alpha. But I also earned it. I paid in blood. I paid in sleepless nights. And only this week as I completed my last challenge, I threatened the next wolf who challenges me with death. Do you know what that means, Wyn?"

Wynter could guess but dared not speak it aloud. She remembered the conversation she'd had with Logan about how Fiona's father had died…in a challenge.

"The next wolf who challenges me is dead," he stated emotionlessly. "I cannot tolerate any more instability. For the sake of the pack, the acceptance of my reign must continue. Every time there is a challenge, the pack becomes unsettled. Volatile. It isn't good for them. Or me."

"I'm sorry. Logan, I didn't understand. I don't know what that has to do with us, though."

"It has everything to do with you. Me. Us. Our mating. Today, when you left," he growled, shaking his head in disapproval. "I was so angry. Angry you'd left me to go with Jax. He's unmated. And whoever else you were with was too."

"But how did you know? I didn't..."

"I could smell them on you when you got home. Goddess, Wyn."

"So because you marked me and you've decided we're mates, I can't even go with my family? Are you kidding me?"

"It isn't just that, Wyn. Aside from the fact that you are very much in danger, I had specifically asked you to stay. Granted, I didn't order you as your Alpha. But I came damn close. And you...how could you not see that I needed you to stay so we could talk? I get that you're not wolf, but any she-wolf would have never left her mate...not until she'd claimed him for her own. Not only did you disrespect me by telling me no and going off with Jax, it was as if your wolf rejected mine by leaving."

"I'm sorry, but you've got to understand that I'm..."

"Human," he finished her words. "Yes, yes you are. But not for long, Wyn. The full moon beckons and even if you choose to deny our mating, you'll have to learn to live within your nature."

Frustrated, Logan loosened his tie, took off his jacket and rolled up his sleeves. He stood at the head of the table; his fingers grasped the back of the chair. The animal in him wanted to throw the damn thing, smash it into kindling. But it was not all who he was. He closed his eyes, willing his wolf to calm.

He took a deep breath and blew it out. "I can't do this. Either you need to accept your wolf or I…I don't know. I just know that I've worked too damn hard to become Alpha. Wolves depend on me. And it isn't just the fact that when I get angry or hurt, the pack feels it. If anyone besides Dimitri had seen what you did today, disrespecting me, blatantly denying my request to stay…it'll lead to a challenge. I can't have that happen. Not over us, anyway."

"But I'd never do that on purpose. It's not like I set out to hurt you or the pack today." She ran her fingers through her hair, nervously twisting at it. "God, Logan can't you see what this is doing to me?"

"The bottom line is this. If there's another challenge, I will kill someone. And while I won't hesitate to do it, that wolf is someone's brother, husband, son," he said softly, contemplating what it'd be like to kill again.

Wynter stood and crossed the kitchen, resting her hands onto the countertop. "Please just hear me out. No matter how hard I try, I don't know what it's like. I'm not a wolf." She rubbed her hand over her reddening eyes. "I don't want to cause anyone's death. I don't want to hurt you. I'm so afraid and confused. But there is one thing I know…I want you…like I've never wanted anyone."

Logan approached Wynter, placing his hand on either side of her waist, gripping the cold stone. "And I want you too, sweetheart. But we cannot go on like this. I'm damn sorry someone did this to you, changed you to wolf. You've barely had time to recover from your captivity, let alone adjust to your new…situation. But I can't put my pack in danger. Lots of lives depend on me. I cannot fail them. I get that it is not fair, but you need to decide."

"Decide what, Logan?" She clasped onto the sides of his shirt in desperation. "I'm scared out of my mind. I don't want to hurt anyone but I don't know how to be wolf. I don't know the rules. I can't do this. I don't know how. I'm sorry, I can't…"

Wynter fell to her knees crying, still clawing at his clothing. She'd let her head fall against his shins. Logan wrapped his hands around her arms and brought her up into his embrace, supporting her.

"Wynter, this is not who you are, sweetheart. You can do this. You are strong, not broken. You will learn how to submit within the pack while remaining fiercely independent. You will run as wolf, but maintain your humanity. I promise you to help you shift; support you in everything you do for the rest of your life. But this decision must be yours, not mine." Logan held her tightly. His own tears brimmed; he needed his mate. Please Goddess, do not let her give up.

Struggling to catch her breath, Wynter swore Logan was

doing something to calm her. His scent, his touch, his aura, everything that was of his essence protectively encased her body and heart. Her wolf howled, begging her to run free with her mate. On the verge of collapse, Wynter steeled her resolve. A fighter. Yes, that's who she was. Tonight, however, she was a lover, Logan's mate. Trembling in his arms, she raised her chin to meet his eyes.

"I choose you. Us. This makes no sense to the part of my mind that demands data, evidence and all the other things that I've learned in my years as a scientist," she breathed, placing her hand to his heart. "But my heart. My wolf. I need you."

Logan sighed in relief, pressing a kiss to her head. "You sure, baby? Because I'm ready to start this right now…to teach you what it means to be wolf."

"I'm sure." All her senses on alert, she'd fully committed to doing whatever it took to learn how to be wolf, to be Logan's mate.

Logan leaned in and gently kissed her. His wolf celebrated in anticipation of their union. He tenderly sucked at her lips, licking at her until she opened fully to him. Her sweet taste tempted him, beckoning the urge to make love to her right then. But he knew better of it. He'd patiently demonstrate what it meant for her to submit, to be nothing more than the wild animal that lurked beneath the surface of her skin.

Wynter gave in to his will, tasting, indulging in the warmth of her Alpha. She felt his hands leave her sides, and she pressed up further against the counter's edge. As he ground the hard evidence of his arousal against her belly, she registered his fingertips on her skin. She went to help him, and he grabbed her wrists.

"Hands to your sides, Wynter. Don't move," he growled.

She gasped, complying with his demand. Fingers grazed her belly once again. A tear of the fabric sent her shirt buttons flying. The loud sound of the plastic studs hitting the floor sounded like hail pelting a roof. Cool air brushed her chest as he ripped off her shirt, yanking hard at the sleeves and throwing it across the room. A hand around her back deftly released her bra, leaving her bare to him. Panting with need, she struggled to catch her breath. She never lost eye contact as he tore his lips from hers.

"An Alpha," he began in a tense, sexy tone that wrapped around her soul. Logan trailed his lips down her throat and between her breasts. But he didn't kiss or lick her, he merely hovered, letting her feel the heat of his body, "he's patient. He doesn't act impulsively. Despite the temptation, he waits until the optimal moment to strike."

Wynter resisted the excruciating desire to move. She closed her eyes, relishing the effect of his nearness to her tight nipples. Strong hands on her hips rapidly spun her so she was facing the counter, holding her upright so she wouldn't fall.

"Do you feel it, Wyn? Our bond, it's growing. I'm your Alpha. Your wolf knows. I feel her," he told her seductively. He slid a large strong hand around to her belly. Without touching his lips to her skin, he drifted them close to her shoulder. "And she…she feels me." He pressed his burgeoning erection into her bottom.

Wynter sighed at the welcome feel of him against her. She wished he'd just take her. No, instead, he was teasing her, teaching her. She'd promised to learn. Taking a breath, she tried to relax into his hold. But as she felt his hands at her waist, her heart raced once again.

Logan deftly unzipped her skirt and jerked it down, exposing the creamy skin underneath. He smiled at her hot pink lace thong, the one he'd selected earlier. Slowly, he glided his hands over her hips and hooked his thumbs into the flimsy fabric. He bent at his knees, teasing it off of her legs and feet until she was bare. With a flick, he sent it flying across the floor. *Much better.*

"Do you see how a wolf restrains his own needs, all in an effort to take care of his wolves?"

His hands grazed over the globes of her bottom, barely touching her. The heat between his skin and hers threatened to combust, but he never gave in to the need. Denying her his touch, he reached upward into her hair, wrapping the long strands around his fist. Gently tugging, he pulled her head to the side, revealing her neck. He growled at the sight but still only brought his lips within an inch of the skin and spoke to her.

"I will teach you what it's like to be wolf, to submit. Are you ready for that, sweetheart?"

Wynter moaned, breathing hard. Was she ready? Naked, she felt both emotionally and physically exposed, while he stood fully clothed.

Logan gently tugged again at her hair, until her eyes met his.

"Answer me," he demanded softly.

"Yes," she cried. The torment of him not touching her was nearly unbearable. But before she had time to think about it, he turned her once again so that she was facing him. She watched nervously as he removed his tie.

"Your senses. They are all that a wolf has. As humans, we rely too much on our sight to tell us what we know. We ignore what our heart tells us because our eyes can't see it. Up," he directed, lifting her up onto the large granite island. "Lay back, Wyn."

Wynter struggled to understand what he was doing. He wanted her on this cold countertop? What the hell?

"Don't question. Just do it. Go on now. You're okay, now. I promise you'll enjoy it." He winked, helping her to scoot backwards. He took her head into his hands, tenderly placing it on the hard surface. "You okay?"

She nodded, unsure of where this was going. Despite her apprehension, the ache between her legs throbbed in anticipation. The heat of her skin cooled against the sleek stone. Logan held up his tie, and she almost choked. *What did he plan to do with that?*

"It's all right, sweetheart. Just removing one of your senses. Educational purposes, I assure you," he laughed.

"Yeah right," she giggled in response. Why was she so aroused? At least he wasn't tying her up, but still she'd been laid out naked on a platter for him to do what he wished, and she grew wetter and wetter by the second.

"Seriously, this is not just about trusting me, which you very much need to learn how to do. Nor is it about submission, which you seem to be doing nicely right now," he encouraged.

His dick was so hard he thought his balls would be blue for the rest of his natural life. The sight of his mate splayed out was more than he could take. He wanted so badly to plunge into her, but he reminded himself that there was more at stake besides him getting his rocks off.

Logan wrapped the tie around her eyes until he was certain she couldn't see. "No peeking. You okay?"

"Yes," she breathed. The anticipation of what he'd do to her was maddening. "Please Logan, hold my hand."

"You look beautiful, baby. So gorgeous." Logan briefly kissed her lips and took her hand in his, sending calming waves to her body. The self-control of a saint was all that kept him from taking her right then. "Breathe in and out, Wyn. That's it. I can't hold your hand the whole time but we'll start with something easy. Smell. Wolves, we rely on scent to give us all kinds of information. To hunt prey. To track enemies. To seek out our lovers," He kissed her shoulder. "Scent, it is essential. Tell me what you smell."

Wynter inhaled deeply. Food. Well that made sense, they were in the kitchen. A faint odor of bleach. Maybe another scent, a comforting scent. Logan. "I smell you." She smiled. "Not cologne. It's something else. It smells so good. It's woodsy and fresh and…my wolf, she likes it."

Logan smiled. It was a start. Releasing her hand, he moved to her head and kissed her again. Then he turned and cracked open the window above the sink.

"And now?"

Unable to see, she knew immediately he'd introduced another variable. "Grass? And roses. That could be cheating because I did see them when I came in as well as the mulch. But there's something else…it's musky. Earthy."

"The bayou," he confirmed. "Anything else?"

Wynter's face registered surprise. "It's crazy," she said in disbelief. "We're alone?"

"Are we? You tell me?"

"I think I smell…do I smell Dimitri? Oh God," Wynter exclaimed in embarrassment, wondering how she knew that.

"It's okay, he's not here." Logan smoothed her hair back with his hand. "But he told me that he planned on a run tonight. See how amazing you are?"

"But how do I know..?"

"Instincts. Forget your human self for the moment. Just close your eyes, and look for your wolf. Let her help you. Okay, let's move on," he suggested, brushing his fingertips over her belly. "Hearing. It's the single most acute sense we've got. Rustling of prey. Danger approaching. What do you hear?"

A hot coil built within the pool of her womb as Logan grazed over her stomach. If he'd just move his hand down further. The minute his petting edged her closer to orgasm, he stopped. She squeezed her thighs tightly but no relief came.

"Wyn?" Logan's voice jarred her back to her erotic lesson.

"Yes, um, hearing," she stammered. "Crickets. No, it's louder than that. Cicadas maybe? Frogs…yes, a bullfrog. A splash. Something in the water."

"When you shift, you'll be able to identify all of nature's sounds. To be able to discriminate so discretely you can tell whether a fox is matin' or fightin' a mile away," Logan whispered in her ear.

Wynter sucked air as his warm breath touched her neck. "Please," she begged. Her full heavy breasts tingled in hopes they'd be touched.

"Patience, little wolf. Perhaps the next two should be combined. Touch and taste. No longer having hands, your paws and claws will grip at the dirt, protected by your toughened pads. But as wolf, touch is mostly felt with the tongue." Logan traced the tip of his tongue around one of her areola, until she moaned. Resisting, he retreated and opened a cabinet, extracting his next surprise.

"Open your mouth, Wynter," he ordered, cupping her chin.

"What?" she gasped. Her pulse quickened.

Logan drew his finger across her lower lip, and then dipped it inside. *Fuck yeah, it felt too good.* He'd meant to open her mouth, but she'd latched onto his finger sucking it as if she was giving him a blow job. Her warm tongue swirled around the pad of his finger, and for a few glorious seconds, he indulged. Carefully taking back control, he pulled his digit out enough to skim along her bottom teeth. Her natural reaction was to open. He smiled in response to hers; she'd clearly known what she'd been doing to him.

"You taste so good, Logan. Like you belong to me," she sighed.

"Our taste, our smell…as mates, we're attracted to one another like magnets to iron," Logan said as he positioned the small plastic bear at her lips. "Mouth open. That's it, baby. Now taste."

He squeezed the honey onto her lips, watching as her tongue darted forward to lap up the nectar.

"Honey," she moaned with a smile.

Logan leaned forward and brushed his lips against hers, pressing his tongue into her mouth. They gently sucked and licked at each other until the sticky sweetness was gone. Logan pulled away, leaving Wynter breathless and moaning. With great speed, he walked to her feet. He parted her legs revealing her wet center.

"As wolf, we eat meat and even small berries now and then. But it is the taste of your arousal that drives me mad, sweetheart." Logan paused. He leaned forward and dragged his tongue along the inside of her thigh, but stopped short of her core. He stroked her pussy softly then drove two fingers deep within her. Plunging in and out, he watched as her juices coated his hands, then pulled out of her and brought his fingers to her lips, painting them. With ease, he slipped them into her mouth. "You taste delicious. Better than any meal I've ever had. Better than any wine I've ever known."

Wynter shook with excitement. At his hand she almost came, but he'd withdrawn leaving her empty. She sucked and lapped at his fingers, tasting the evidence of her own arousal on them. Moaning and undulating her hips upward, she sought the friction that never came.

"Please," she managed to say. "I can't take it. Please, Logan."

The sight of Wynter so open and the feel of her sucking him broke his restraint. Logan unbuckled his belt and freed his cock. He retrieved his fingers from her mouth and once again sunk them back into her pussy; his thumb gently applied pressure to her clit. As he continued to bring her toward orgasm, he walked around the island so his hips were near her face.

Wynter cried Logan's name. His fingers stroked the tender strip inside her channel, and she almost flew off the countertop. Writhing her mound up into his hand, she struggled to hold back her climax. Unable to see, she felt the heat of his body radiate close to her, a kiss to her neck.

"Suck me," Logan told her, guiding his pulsing shaft toward her mouth. The silken head of him brushed her lips.

In the darkness, Wynter rolled onto her side, blindly searching for the hardness of his sex. With Logan's assistance, she wrapped her small hand around him. Bringing his swollen flesh to her lips, she licked at his seam, taking in his salty essence. Trembling, Wynter took the length of him all the way into her mouth, allowing the tip of her tongue to play along the underside of his swollen flesh. She rocked her head back and forth, relishing the taste of her mate. Using her hands and lips, she gripped him tightly as she sucked.

Logan dragged in a breath. Her hot mouth suctioned

him, pistoning up and down. Drenched in her wetness, he felt her core tighten around his fingers. Unrelenting, he swept the pad of his thumb across her swollen hood once again. As she began to lose the thread of control that held her together, he withdrew his cock, allowing her to fall over the cliff of ecstasy.

Wynter moaned at the loss of him. She wasn't sure of the exact moment she'd embraced the submission, nor did she understand why her body responded to his touch with terrific exuberance. All thought went, lost with the last graze of his fingers. A wall of energy slammed her, driving her into climax, and leaving her shuddering in release. Wynter's chest heaved, trying to recover from the high.

Logan leaned forward to remove his tie from her eyes. Like Wynter's presuppositions about what she thought was wolf, the silk blindfold fell to the floor. Logan smiled as she moaned and gazed up at him. He cupped her face, admiring his spectacular mate. Captivated by her honesty and reckless abandon, his chest tightened with an overwhelming yet unfamiliar passion. Had he fallen in love? Rationally, he'd always known that he could find his mate, but after a hundred years, he'd happily remained single. Now everything was changed forever. A single chance meeting in an alley had resulted in a life-altering experience he could have never anticipated or understood. Only in this moment was he cognizant of the ramifications. Life would never be the same and he didn't want it to be.

With the ache building again, Wynter wiggled her hips in an effort to reach him. She opened her eyes, drinking in the sight of him. His hair was wild; the look in his eyes wild with desire.

"Logan, please," she cried.

"I'll give you everything you need, baby. Every day, every minute, every second."

Tugging her by her hips, he lifted her bottom until it reached the edge of the counter. Logan lifted her legs up over his shoulders, wrapping his hands around her thighs. He pressed against her entrance, thrusting into her pussy in one smooth stroke. As he penetrated her tight heat, his cock slid back and forth into his mate. Groaning, Logan built a slow rhythm, resisting the urge to pound into her relentlessly.

"More, harder," Logan heard her cry.

The demand sent his wolf into a wicked state. With a low growl, Logan cupped her bottom with one hand and wrapped his other arm around her waist. As he lifted her into the air, Wynter wrapped her legs around his waist. Logan spun, crashing his back into the refrigerator. He bent his knees so that he could lower his hips and pump up into her, all the while capturing her breast with his lips.

Like a raging animal, Wynter raked her hands into his hair, and licked the side of his neck. Entirely filled with all that was Logan, she abandoned her humanity and let her wolf run free. In truth, this was who she was with Logan. Passionate. Unrestrained. And totally, utterly in love.

"Please, Oh God," she screamed against his skin. "Take me, Logan."

"Sofa," he grunted.

Logan struggled to kick off his pants while managing to stay pressed inside Wynter. Forced to release her rosy peak, he looked ahead, stumbling forth until he reached the large soft couch. Roughly, they fell into the cushions, Logan thrusted between her legs.

As her head hit the pillows, Wynter nipped at Logan's chest. He was untamed, and she loved it. Logan smothered her body, penetrating deep into her hot core. In response, she scratched her nails down his back nearly drawing blood, encouraging him to go deeper. Licking and sucking, she tasted and smelled and immersed her senses in him like he'd taught her. Her mate, masculine and muscular, drove into her over and over. She raised her pelvis in response, rocking her clitoris against his hips. Each torturous exquisite brush to her tiny nub sent her body singing. As if he was directing the orchestra, he edged her toward the finale. Her heart thumped against her ribs; she struggled to breathe.

"You are wolf, Wyn. Do you hear me? And you're mine," Logan told her. "Fuck, you're fisting me so tight; I'm goin' to come soon. I feel you baby, come with me."

"Yes!" Wynter screamed and then bit down hard on his shoulder. The hot explosion of her release caused her to shatter underneath him. From head to toe, rippling ecstasy flowed through her body.

Logan saw stars as her pussy tightened around his throbbing cock. Growling in his need to possess her, he pumped into her fiercely. As her teeth met his skin, he soared over the edge in unknown pleasure, pulsing his seed deep into her womb. All the air rushed from his lungs in a loud grunt as the last wave rolled through him.

"This is crazy." He laughed into her neck, aware of how wildly they'd just made love. "You have no idea what you do to me."

Wynter giggled, still trying to catch her breath.

"You bit me." He laughed harder.

"You fucked me on a kitchen counter," she answered. "I'll never look at food the same."

"Nor will I." Logan pressed up onto his forearms. "Are you okay? I'm crushing you."

"I'm fine. Please don't go yet. Just stay like this," she breathed, nuzzling her face into his chest.

"There's no place I'd rather be," he assured her.

Letting his body go limp against hers, reveling, he smiled, realizing that he'd set out to teach her a lesson, but by Goddess, she'd schooled him long and hard in her love. Never again would he be alone.

Chapter Twenty-Two

Wynter felt as if she was floating in heaven. After they'd made love, Logan had arranged a soft bed of lambskin and pillows on the great room's floor, creating a temporary Eden. Nestled against Logan's chest, she stared into the dancing flames of the gas lit fire which flickered behind the glass. She shivered, thankful for the heat that radiated onto their skin.

"You cold?" Logan asked, pulling the cashmere blanket over her shoulders.

"Just a little, thanks."

"You're a million miles away. What are you thinking about?" he asked softly and brushed a hair out of her eyes.

"You. Me. Us. It's unbelievable. I mean we barely know each other, really. But this feeling," she tapped her fingers over his heart. "It's intense. And romantic. And wild."

"Regrets?" Logan wondered if she was having second thoughts.

"No way," she replied decidedly. "It feels like I've been asleep my whole life, and now? It's an awakening of sorts.

I've never in my life known anyone like you, Logan. Tonight…it was incredible."

"And I've never met anyone like you, either." Logan pressed his lips to her hair. "I've never taught a human to be wolf. Even tonight, Wyn, it won't be a sliver of what you'll feel tomorrow."

"Lying there exposed like that…having my eyes covered helped me to concentrate. The only thing missing was how I will see when I'm a wolf. I'm super-excited about getting badass night vision," she laughed.

"You're something, you know that?"

"How so?"

"You're like this little livewire. The secretary thing…I'm still not over that. And waking up to what you did to me the other morning….those things just don't happen to guys every day."

"Not even to Alphas?" she asked coyly.

"Not even to Alphas," he stated truthfully, "even ones as old as me."

"How old are you?"

"Old enough."

"Old enough that you remember the turn of the nineteenth century?" she guessed, knowing both wolves and vampires lived a long time.

"Old enough," he repeated, smiling at her insistence. Another reason why he was falling in love with her. She was tenacious.

"Come on, you have to tell me. I'm going to be your mate. Let's see…old enough to remember President Lincoln?"

"You really want to know? I don't want my young hot mate running for the hills when she finds out," he joked.

"Yes, I do. I love that you've experienced the world. Well, maybe not the women part but I don't mind, really."

"Born 1871. President Ulysses S. Grant was in office. So I missed President Lincoln by a few years."

Wynter silently computed the years in her head. "One hundred and forty-two."

"You got it." He gave her a tight hug. "Yeah, things were different then. Simpler but harder. I wouldn't exactly say, 'good ole days'. I love the technology we've got now."

"Are your parents still alive?" Wynter drew lazy circles on his stomach.

"Yes ma'am. Papá and Maman took to traveling a few years ago."

"Are they from New Orleans too?"

"Yes and no. Maman came over from France in the early 1700s. Papá, he arrived as part of the Spanish rule a few years later. Nowadays, they travel around the world but still stop home from time to time. I traveled a lot as a pup too," he reminisced. "They're going to love you, sweetheart."

"I wish you could have met my Mom and Dad. God, I miss them. When they died, I was so angry."

"How did they pass?"

"I was told it was a carjacking…they'd been downtown. It all happened so suddenly. When you're a kid like that…well, I never got closure. Maybe that's what bothered me most." Wynter really didn't want to talk about it. She'd worked so hard to learn how to accept the loss. She watched the firelight frolic across the cathedral ceiling and stark walls.

"I like your house." She changed the subject.

"Thanks. It still needs work, but I couldn't spend another night in Marcel's place. It's a reminder of his death and my tumultuous birth as Alpha. The good memories outweigh the bad, but I figure it's time I make a few new memories of my own." Logan smiled. "You could help me, you know. I mean, we haven't talked about it, but I want you here with me…in my home. Wait until you see the wildlife. It's beautiful."

He didn't want to freak her out but he'd be lying if he said that he'd accept her living anywhere else but with him. He knew it might not be easy for either of them. But the strength of the mating bond drove their attraction, the need to be physically close. They could fight it and try to live apart, but he knew it would be excruciating. Still, empathizing with her human mores, he trod lightly around the subject. They had time to get to know each other while she stayed with him, at least until they caught the killer.

Did Logan just ask her to live with him? Wynter wasn't sure what exactly he was saying. If they mated, did that mean they were married? She felt as if she'd gone to Las Vegas and got involved in some quickie wedding. And even though once upon a time, her conservative nature wouldn't have entertained the idea, she was too far gone. She'd fallen in love with Logan, the man and the wolf. She couldn't understand how she could feel so intensely so quickly. As much as she wanted to tell him, she couldn't. She hadn't even considered what would happen to their relationship once they mated or even after they were finally out of danger.

"When we mate, does that mean we are married?" It popped out of her mouth before she could take it back or at least ask in a more diplomatic way.

"You're funny," Logan laughed. He'd been worried about sharing his feelings and asking her to stay with him, and now she was asking if they were married, a very human thought.

"Hilarious, I'm sure. Seriously, if we mate does that mean we are...you are my...you know?" She playfully tapped her hand to his chest.

"No, sweetheart. Getting married, it's a human thing. But mating," he traced a finger down her cheek and across her lips, "it's deeper...visceral."

"What do you mean?"

"It's private, a ritual between you and me. Afterwards, we'd announce it to the pack. And only mated wolves can get pregnant, have pups," he explained. "Now marriages, well, they come and go. I know it's a commitment, but it's a human tradition. Is that something you wanted, Wynter?"

She quieted at his question. Did she want to get married? After everything that had happened to her in her short life, she really never considered it. Sure, as a little girl she dressed up and played bride, but once she was an adult, it never seemed that she'd find someone she loved enough to commit to fully, let alone marry...until now.

"Well, I'm not sure of that," she hedged. "I suppose I've

never really loved anyone enough to consider it. When I tell you that there has been no one in my life like you, it's true."

"Hmm." Logan couldn't help but kiss her again. His ego did love to hear that.

"So I guess I'll take a rain check on that question, Alpha," she grinned.

"Tomorrow's a big day." Logan wanted to talk to her about her shift but it wasn't until now that he'd felt she trusted him enough to broach the topic. "Full moon."

"Do you really think I'm going to shift? I know I'm changing but without the blood work, how can I be sure?" Wynter tried to feign courage but it wasn't working. She was scared to death about what would happen to her tomorrow night.

"Yeah, I do think you're going to shift. I don't know what they did to you sweetheart, but I meant it, I can sense your wolf." Logan brushed her hair out of her eyes. "It's part of the reason we needed to have that little lesson tonight. I needed to know where you stood. Would you be able to embrace your senses? Would you trust me without argument? Submit? Could you learn how your actions impact the pack? It's important to know going into this."

"All wolves submit to you?"

"Yeah, it's how it has to be. We need order. With order, there's peace. With peace, the pack is happy, healthy. Everyone can focus on livin' their life and not fightin'."

"Sexually? Like you did to me tonight? Will you take others? Because if you do, I don't think I can..." Her words trailed off.

"Look at me," he told her. Logan waited until their eyes met. "There is no one else for me but you…ever. Do you understand?"

"Yes." Relief flooded over her.

"Now that doesn't mean other she-wolves won't try to undermine you or test you. Don't get me wrong, as a human, you're tough. You survived two long months in that hellhole. That says a lot about a person's will to survive. But even among the females, they fight for rank…to be alpha."

Wynter didn't even want to think about that. The thought of fighting just so she could establish herself within an animal ranking system disgusted her.

"Sorry, I didn't mean to scare you." Logan could tell by the pale look on Wynter's face that he'd said too much. He should have known better than to think she could even conceive of such things happening to her. Logan was certain that his little she-wolf was indeed alpha. But that was something she'd have to learn on her own.

"It's okay, I need to know," she replied. *Not really okay, but what the hell am I supposed to do about it?* "Tell me about tomorrow. The shift."

"You know all those senses we played with?"

"Uh huh."

"You'll feel them heightened as if everything is turned on to overdrive. At first, it's hard to control, but you'll learn quickly how to dial it up or down, depending on the situation. You've already been learning to control it whether you've been conscious of it or not. A human wouldn't have scented D tonight. You did that, because you allowed your wolf to do it. She's there."

"It was incredible," she recalled. "I still have no idea how I knew it was him."

"You've spent time with him, right?"

"Yeah, but still, humans don't do that kind of stuff."

"And there you go. You're wolf. She knows him."

"He's been kind to me," Wynter admitted. "It's strange. That first day, we kind of got off on the wrong foot, but then something changed. It sounds stupid to say this, but it's like he knows what to say to help me when things aren't going so well."

"It's not stupid at all, Wyn. He's my beta. He has a pulse on the pack and helps me lead them when necessary. He can calm wolves. It's hard to explain. I know you can't see it yet, but we're linked, the three of us." Until she actually shifted, there was no way she could possibly understand the extent of the bond he and Dimitri had. "Speaking of D. He's going to stay with us tomorrow, as you shift, run and then afterwards. Jake's going to take the pack for me. We may run with them too, but I want to see how you feel."

"What do you mean?"

"Well, it's kind of like when our young wolves first change. We don't just let them around the older wolves right away. They stay with their mammas and papas for an hour or so, then are told to stay in a certain area with just each other. We can't just have them challenging the older males right away. There'd be trouble."

"Well don't expect that out of me," she said indignantly.

"That's the thing, Wyn. You don't know how you really

are going to feel until after you shift. You may feel territorial, hungry, playful. Probably, very, very horny afterwards."

"Are you kidding me? Stop it." Wynter pushed at his arm.

"No, no I'm not. I mean, I just went through something like this with my Alpha and his mate. It's not a joke."

Wynter pushed out of his arms and sat up, legs crossed. "What do you mean exactly?" *Please don't mean what I think it means.*

"Sex, it's something we've become very good at doing." He winked and pulled her toward him. "You and I are excellent at it actually. I can't imagine what it'll be like after you shift."

"You had sex with Tristan's mate?" She pulled away from him. *How could he think this was funny?*

"Come on back down here, baby," he coaxed.

"Don't baby me." She tried to act angry but was really just astonished at what she was learning. With a flick of her hair, she gave him her best eye roll and then smiled.

"Not all sex means that you are 'in love' with someone. Take Tristan. Do I love him? Yeah, I do. He was my Alpha and still is one of my best friends. And his mate, Kalli, she's wonderful, but I wasn't in love with her. But we are friends, and she needed me. *They* needed me. So yeah, I helped with her shift back into the pack. Not really the same situation though. She'd been wolf already, just not around a whole pack."

"So how do you feel about Dimitri?"

"I love him too. He's been a friend ever since we got caught bootleggin' in the twenties."

"What?"

"The gulf coast was a crazy place then, rumrunners and such. But I digress. That's a story for another day. Your shift…where were we?"

"Dimitri, I think."

"It's the shift. It doesn't just affect your basic senses. Your libido will be flying high like a kite. I want him to be there in case…in case we need him."

"Okay," she said, contemplating what he was telling her. She couldn't comprehend wanting to make love to him more than she already did. Was he implying that he wanted Dimitri to be with them? "So I'll want to be with you. I'll just be more enthusiastic?"

"Yeah, kind of like that." He could tell she was having a hard time wrapping her head around what he was trying to tell her. "But you may need…more."

"Don't take this the wrong way. It's not that I don't find Dimitri attractive. I mean, I'd have to be dead not to, but Logan, I don't think that I'd want to do…well, what you're suggesting."

Logan simply smiled and shrugged. "It's up to you, Wyn. But I think that for at least your first shift, you may want this. I won't lie; it won't be easy for me to share you with him."

"You didn't want me near Jax."

"No, I didn't. My wolf, he doesn't really want you near any unmated male. But he knows Dimitri. And for this shift…I want it to be special for you. If this is what your body needs, we'll do it."

"But I don't think I'll need that." Wynter laid back down into his arms, wishing she could stay human. "I don't get it."

"The best I can explain it is that when the full moon hits, us wolves, we're already sexual creatures. We crave the touch of others. Someone who is a friend by day may be a lover during the full moon. Consensual, of course," he added.

"Have you ever watched someone make love?" she asked with great interest. "Well, besides in that vampire club the other night."

"Yes." He smiled broadly. His little wolf never ceased to amaze him. Was she a voyeur? "Like humans, certain wolves like to watch or be watched. It can be a turn on, without a doubt. Is that something you'd like to do?"

Wynter felt his eyes burn over her body at the question. What was she thinking? Threesomes to voyeurism in the course of two minutes was a little bit too much information to process.

"Maybe yes, maybe no," she replied, satisfied with her noncommittal answer.

He raised an eyebrow at her.

"What? Okay, maybe. I can't say I'm not curious. But not tomorrow, okay? I don't think I could do that."

Logan laughed.

"I'm not a prude you know," she protested. A giggle escaped her lips remembering what they'd just done in the kitchen. "Not sure what could have given you that impression. The conference room should have dispelled that notion…not to mention that I just made a nice dessert for you."

Logan's cock jerked as a vision of her lying naked on the countertop flashed in his head. He slid his hand from her belly to cup her breast. Watching her with his beta would be sexually exhilarating. But it would have to be her decision and hers alone.

"Tomorrow, if we do this, it isn't permanent. It's something we could do to make your shift the most amazing experience of your life. But it's still your choice. As mates, the only bond we have will be to each other. I love D. He's my beta and will always be part of our lives, but he won't fall in love with you."

Wynter closed her eyes trying to picture herself sandwiched between the two incredibly sexy and dominant men. She wanted to hate it, she really did. But the thought of them filling her, consuming her made her pussy throb; wetness teased her thighs. Lost in her dream, she startled as Logan brushed his knuckles lovingly across her cheek.

"Sweetheart, what ya thinkin' about?"

"Everything," she admitted softly without saying the word. *Ménage.* She decided right then to wait and see what happened after her shift. If she trusted her wolf, like Logan had been telling her to do, she'd make the right decision tomorrow night. "I want you to know that whatever happens tomorrow, the only person I want is you…just you."

Logan gently kissed her and spoke softly, his lips still

touching hers. "You are the only one for me, too. Only." Kiss. "You." Kiss. "Ever." Kiss.

Wynter sighed. She almost told him that she loved him but thought better of it. What would he say? Yes, he was committed to her, that much he'd said.

"I got you a gift," he said with a devious grin.

She kissed his chest. "Hmm, Dimitri said you like shopping."

"He does know me well."

"I'm kind of surprised you got me anything, considering how mad you were."

"Just because I was upset, don't think that for one minute I wasn't thinking of making love to you. In fact, at this point, I might not think of anything else for the rest of my life," he teased. "Okay, let me up. I'll go get it."

"It?"

"You'll see."

The devilish smile on his face made Wynter wonder exactly what he'd gotten her. She fell onto her back, closed her eyes and relaxed. Like he'd taught her to do, she listened intently to see if she could catch a clue to where he'd gone. She heard a door opening and shutting then the patter of his feet coming toward her. She glanced upward to find her gloriously naked mate standing over her, his erect cock jutting outward. Oh yes.

Logan dangled a red and black bag in front of her, blocking her view of his arousal. The fancy packaging sprouted tissue paper and ribbons, making it appear as if it had come from an expensive store. He wagged his eyebrows with a big grin, and she knew she was either in big trouble or in for the best time of her life. Maybe both.

"What's in the bag, darlin'?" she drawled in her best southern accent.

"Well, you know, sweetheart. I've got plans for that sweet lil' ass of yours." Logan knelt down, straddling her legs, hovering an inch over her pelvis so as not to crush her with his weight. He set the bag aside so that he could get comfortable. His aroused flesh pressed into her belly as he leaned in to quickly suck an exposed nipple.

"Well, sir, I do think I might enjoy that," she teased. Why bother with coyness when all she wanted was to be filled with Logan morning, noon and night. She continued in her role as a belle. "It's all the rage, I hear."

"You're a naughty girl, you know that?" Logan laughed. She wanted to play again?

She nodded and licked her lips. After the talk about a threesome, she was more than ready to make love again. Her eyes darted back and forth between his purchase and the mischievous expression on his face.

Logan grabbed the blanket and tossed it aside so he could get a full view of her luscious body. Sliding his palm down her belly, he reached for the bag and pulled a small glass object out. He held it up so she could see it. The bulbous end caught the light; it curved slightly tapering into a ringed handle.

"Toys?" This is what he'd been shopping for? She laughed, excited at the prospect of trying something new with Logan.

"Why yes, Dr. Ryan. I've got a couple of fun toys, in fact. But I thought maybe we'd start with this one. Then, move up to something larger."

"Something larger, like this?" Wynter captured his cock in her hand and gave it a smooth stroke. Logan hissed in delight.

"Oh, don't you worry, baby. You'll have plenty of that tonight, but first let's start small," he suggested. He retrieved a small bottle of lube and flipped it open. "But first, my little tease, open those legs and let me taste how hot you are."

Wynter released Logan as he rose above her. She let her knees fall aside, like he'd asked, allowing him to see all of her. Giving him a playful smile, she licked her fingers and then slowly glided her hand down onto her mound. Captivated by what she was doing, Logan watched intently as she slid a moist digit into her slick crease, parting herself for him. She moaned in response, all the while taking in his reaction.

"Goddammit, Wyn, that is so fucking hot." Logan lay on his stomach, his head between her legs, gaining better access to the heart of her.

His hands clutched her inner thighs as he speared the tip of his tongue into her channel. He felt her startle and then push down onto him in rhythm as he fucked her with his mouth. Once, twice, three times. Withdrawing, he licked over her fingers, groaning in delight.

"Ah baby, no more. Rest your hands on your belly," he instructed. She'd come if they kept going and he wanted her first orgasm to coincide with their new toy.

"Please," she begged. His tongue inside of her nearly sent her into release. The emptiness was killing her.

"Here we go," he told her, spreading the cool gel onto the smooth crystal. Letting his fingers tease her anus, he circled it and slowly pressed one, then two thick digits inside.

"Oh my God, yeah," she moaned. With ease, she began to writhe her hips as he pumped in and out of her. She cried as she felt Logan swipe his tongue through her folds, teasing her further.

"Ah, don't stop," she whined when he withdrew both his mouth and hand. "Logan."

"We're just getting started," he grinned. Smoothing the cool object through her folds, he let it graze over her nub until it found its destination. The tapered tip prodded her puckered skin. Logan pushed and twisted slowly.

"Ah, yes. It feels so...good." Wynter sighed as she relaxed into the sweet pressure. Similar to Logan's fingers, the glass knob wasn't too large yet created a sense of delectable fullness.

"Look at that...all the way in. How does it feel?"

"Full, but not too full. No pain...just pressure. But I need..."

Logan knew exactly what she needed. Plunging his finger into her hot sheath he began to explore her nether lips with his thumb. She'd want him to bring her all the way to orgasm by touching her clit, but he'd save that pleasure for later.

"So wet and pink, sweetheart. I love your pussy," he told

her and licked at her inner thigh. As he did so, he pulled out the glass instrument and pushed it back in, causing her to gasp.

"Ah, Logan, I'm so close..."

"Touch your breasts, Wyn. Oh yeah, just like that." His cock was so hard, he could barely move. He watched her take her perfectly shaped mounds and knead them. "Now, play with your nipples."

Through heavy-lidded eyes, Wynter caught his gaze and did what he told her. The sensations were overwhelming. His hands on her labia, the fullness in her bottom and now the pleasurable ache in her tight peaks...it was too much, but not enough.

"You are so hot, baby. My dick is like fucking steel. You are gonna make me come just watching you," Logan groaned. He took his hand away from her heat so that he could take out the next toy. "We need to speed this up because I can't take much more of just watching."

The pressure eased as Logan slid out the glass plug. Wynter looked up to see him preparing a much larger, pink silicone object. Before she had a chance to ask, the cold lubrication pressed at her back hole.

"This one's a little larger, okay? I'll go slowly." Logan inserted it an inch and noticed a grimace on her face. "You're okay, sweetheart. Push into it. That's it. Almost in."

As the plug breached the first ring of muscle, pain flared and then quickly subsided as she bore down. Within seconds, a wonderful pleasure filled her completely. Logan's tongue lapped at her clit, while his fingers added voluminous bonus. Wynter cried Logan's name, bucking her hips into his face. Relentlessly his tongue grazed at her nub. She dug her fingernails into his scalp.

Logan wrapped his lips around her clitoris and suckled her. Wynter screamed so loud she thought she'd wake the dead. Her ass and pussy rippled in orgasm while Logan continued to drink of her essence. Granted little reprieve, she heard Logan growl right before he flipped her over on her stomach.

"Ah yeah, that's it, Wyn. Goddess, you're so beautiful," Logan praised as she knelt on her hands and knees. Holding the plug in place, he waited until she was in position. Scrambling with one hand, he scooped up a control, a surprise he'd kept for Wynter. He positioned the head of his straining cock at her entrance. With a grunt, he plunged into her, sheathing himself completely. Her quivering walls pulsated around him, nearly making him explode.

"Don't move," Logan bit out, digging his fingers into her hips. Fuck, he really was going to come. He breathed in and out, slowly gaining control. Withdrawing, he pumped into her slowly. Logan could feel the probe caressing his shaft through the thin barrier.

Resting her weight on her forearms, Wynter's head fell forward. She'd never been so satiated in her life. Even though she'd just come, she could feel the ache building once again as if someone was turning a crank, winding her up....soon she would spring loose.

"Oh God. I can't even describe. Logan, I never knew." So many thoughts raced through her mind while she endured the marvelous penetration. Again and again, his velvety steel sex stroked her channel of nerves. At the precipice, she moved in his rhythm as her release threatened. "I'm going to come again. Please."

Logan felt the contractions around his cock and prayed what he was about to do wouldn't make him come before she did. Depressing the button, he clicked on the remote, causing it to vibrate. Logan tugged at the vibrating plug, withdrew it and pressed it in again. At the same time, he imbedded himself into her tight pussy. He'd decidedly gone from the frying pan into the fire. Between the vibrations and her walls milking him, Logan fought the urge to climax.

"Yes, please. Oh God, what is that? It feels…it feels amazing. Don't stop," she encouraged. So full, she gasped as the vibrations spread from her bottom to her pussy. Welcoming the dark intrusion, she pushed back on him, allowing him to guide it in and out of her. Wynter knew she was going to come again but wanted to fly at the same time as Logan. Pleading for more, she lost the ability to speak coherently. "Fuck me, fuck me now. I'm…going to…again."

Breathing heavily, he looked down to see his rigid flesh disappearing into his sweet mate. She gripped him like a vise, the plug tantalizing the length of his shaft. At her words, Logan began to surge in and out of her and with a final thrust, he slammed into her, stiffening in release.

As Logan took her one last time, Wynter came with him. The deep shuddering orgasm reached every cell in her body. Shaking with ecstasy, she fell to the floor, bringing him on top of her. He quickly brought them safely onto their sides and removed himself and the toy. She moaned as Logan stood, covering her tingling skin with a blanket.

A warm cloth between her legs silenced her calls for him. Logan tenderly cleaned both Wynter and himself, discarding the towel and the toys into the bag. Cradling his mate into his strong arms, he lifted her. Euphoria rushed over Logan as he trod up the steps to his room. He'd never experienced such contentment. His heart felt as if it would burst; he loved Wynter with all of his being.

Wynter cuddled against Logan, kissing at his chest as he took her upstairs. He smelled of sex and masculinity, and she resolutely immersed herself in his scent. Within minutes, Logan had snuggled them into his feather-soft bed, and she lay wrapped in his arms. Abounding with happiness, Wynter reveled in the drugging sensation. As she drifted off to sleep, the words she'd been holding back slipped from her lips, *I love you.*

Chapter Twenty-Three

With the room bathed in sunlight, Wynter nuzzled against the pillow. The fog of sleep hung thick in her mind. Reaching blindly for Logan, she stretched a long arm across the bed and found it empty. A groan escaped her lips. Sweeping her arm back to her body, she caught the thin edge of a paper. A note? She squinted as the beams of light accosted her vision. Adjusting to the brightness, she read it: *Good Morning Sweetheart, Breakfast is downstairs. Had an appointment I couldn't miss. Love you, Logan.* Love? Oh God…she'd told him she loved him. Maybe he didn't hear it. Or maybe he did? She wasn't sure how she imagined telling him she loved him, but she had hoped she wouldn't fall asleep afterward.

After she'd used the bathroom, she showered and got dressed. Deciding on simplicity, she'd thrown on a sports bra, pink tank top and black yoga pants. She finger combed her wild mane, pulling it into a messy bun. Taking a glance at herself in the mirror, she looked and felt relaxed despite the fact that someone was out to kidnap her. She shoved the negative thoughts away, but reminded herself to ask Logan about getting the lab equipment. Unsure of what had happened to her blood samples, she wanted to test herself as soon as possible.

Giving her wolf senses a tryout, Wynter closed her eyes. From what she could tell, coffee was on but she couldn't smell anything else. Some wolf she was. Laughing inwardly, she went in search of Logan.

As promised, bagels and croissants sat in a linen-covered tray on the kitchen table. She bit into a crescent-shaped flaky goodness, releasing a sigh. Worth every calorie, she thought. As she looked for the coffee, she caught a glimpse of the granite-covered island, and her cheeks blushed. Never again would she look at that counter the same way or forget the most incredible sensual experience of her life.

Spotting a carafe, she poured herself a large mug. The chicory tasted every bit as good as it smelled. A blur of movement outside caught her attention. She crept over to the window cautiously, unsure of her safety. Upon a closer look, she saw Logan, Dimitri and a child. Logan was pitching to the young boy, who looked as if he was hanging on the Alpha's every word. Dimitri crouched behind him pounding his glove into a catcher's mitt.

This was Logan's appointment? Wynter smiled. She opened the slider, waved at him and then shut the door behind her. Logan winked and then quickly focused back on their game. The patio stones warmed her bare feet but she managed to make it over to a comfortably worn Adirondack chair. Sitting under a large southern oak tree, she admired the trailing sprigs of resurrection fern that carpeted its trunk and sprawling branches. Nearly two hundred feet from the house, the slow moving bayou teemed with wildlife.

A crack of the bat drew her focus. The boy hit a far one that went sailing over Logan's head. Logan took off in a sprint to get the ball while the hitter ran invisible bases. Dimitri waited at home base ready with a high five. Logan gave the kid a thumbs up in response.

Captivated, Wynter watched the Alpha and his beta instruct the boy. Fluctuating between serious discussion and excitement, the trio played baseball. She watched in both curiosity and admiration. A warmth settled in her chest as she witnessed yet another side of Logan. She'd seen him as a fighter, the first night she'd met him. Later as rescuer. Then at his office, the commanding businessman. She'd seen the Alpha, the leader giving the eulogy. The lover, who was adventurous, dominant and caring. And before she could stop the thought, she pictured him as a father. Father to her own children.

Wynter's words resounded in Logan's mind. *I love you.* Maybe she hadn't meant to say it…but she had. All he knew was that he loved her too and couldn't wait for her to shift. Because once she shifted, she'd be able to mark him. Then after they caught the killer, they'd formally mate. It would be fucking torture waiting; his wolf would protest.

He hated leaving her in the morning, wanting nothing more than to sink himself back into her sweetness. But he'd promised René a game of ball. Practice really. Little league was coming up in the spring. Soon all the pups would be over at his house, wanting to play with him. Logan prided himself on his pitching skills, but always made sure he let the boys get a hit off the Alpha. He taught skills and tried to boost their confidence.

Before René came over, he'd talked with Dimitri about helping with Wynter's shift. Logan wanted Wynter's first transformation to be peaceful and erotic, not traumatic. Not only could Wynter's libido go off the charts, he worried that the she-wolves would attempt a challenge. Two months had gone by and he'd already watched them fighting for their place in his life. And there was no denying the fact that Luci had shared his home. He thanked the Goddess he'd never given in and had sex with her. Regardless, she'd aggressively defend what she perceived as hers. Logan told Dimitri how he planned on letting Jake take the pack while they kept pace with Wynter. Slowly they'd merge, when she was ready, not a second before that. He'd keep her safely tucked between them until the time was right. Fiercely protective, he swore no one would harm a hair on her head.

Logan watched as Dimitri approached Wynter. He'd asked him to talk with her before tonight. Even though it wouldn't be the first time he'd ever shared a woman with Dimitri, he made it clear to him; Wynter was his and his alone. As such, his beta would have to pay close attention to his directions. While his beast possessively insisted on keeping her to himself, he suspected her shift would be rough. They'd let Wynter decide how much or how little sexual relief she needed afterwards. He expected that by the afternoon, her senses would flip into high alert, causing her to become extraordinarily aroused. Hunger. Thirst. Smell. Lust. Her body would prepare for the metamorphosis.

Anticipating a spectacular experience, Logan struggled to contain his excitement. He could not wait to see her as wolf. Keyed up, he needed an outlet. Challenging René to a race, he took off in a sprint across the property.

"Hey cher," Dimitri said with a smile. He pulled off his shirt revealing the prominent ridges of his stomach. "Damn, it's hot."

"Yes it is." Wynter smiled. She couldn't stop her eyes from roaming over his expansive chest. As tall as Logan, he looked as if he was a body builder, not too bulky, but broad and hard. *Shit, what the hell was wrong with her?* "Game over?"

"Yeah, René's a great kid. Logan's runnin' him back to his mamma's."

"Looks like fun."

"So, uh, made up with the Alpha, I see," he commented.

"Yes." Her cheeks turned pink. Just what had Logan told him? *Bad wolf.*

"How're you feelin' today?"

"Um, okay."

"Logan and I talked this morning. About your shift."

"Did Logan tell you everything?" she asked with a small smile, trying not to look at his chest.

"Let's just say that we have few secrets. Kinda comes with the territory." Dimitri took the seat next to hers, laying his head back on the wooden surface. "We trust each other.

He knows that no matter what, I have his back. And yours."

"Like tonight?" Damn straight she was going to bring it up. Embarrassed or not, this was her life.

"Like tonight," Dimitri concurred, trying to discuss the topic without making her uncomfortable. "But don't worry. Logan will do whatever he has to do to make everything go smoothly."

"And you?" She noticed Logan walking toward them. He, too, had taken off his shirt. Holy hell, the man was hot. She coughed, trying to focus on what she'd been saying.

"Yeah, me too." Dimitri smiled at Logan, guessing he could hear at least part of their conversation. "Won't lie, cher, I'm looking forward to watching you shift, to helping you."

"I'm scared. But I guess this is going to happen whether I like it or not." Wynter glanced over to the bayou and then bowed her head. "I want you to know that I really appreciate everything you've done for me...your talks, the encouragement the past couple of days. I know this hasn't been easy on you either. Whatever happens tonight...I trust you both."

"Logan and I won't let anything happen to you. It's going to be one of the greatest days of your life." Dimitri smiled at Wynter, reached over and took her hand in his. He wanted so badly to be able to explain the rush she'd feel, but he reasoned it was of no use. Tonight, she'd run with them and learn the way of the wolves. He was confident she'd do well once she shifted.

Wynter squeezed his hand. She'd meant what she'd said.

She trusted them, both Logan and Dimitri. Together they'd get through the night.

"Well hello, Logan, have I told you what a beautiful mate you have?" Dimitri said as Logan approached.

"Yes, you have. *My* mate is beautiful, isn't she?" Logan gave him a sardonic smile. He'd told him to talk, not drool.

"Very." Dimitri laughed, enjoying their easy banter.

Logan leaned down and gave Wynter a kiss. *His mate.* So perfect for him.

She reached up to him, pushing her hands into his sweaty hair. Her tongue swept into his mouth. A long drugging kiss ensued and before she knew it, she'd jumped into his arms, her legs wrapped around his waist.

Logan could tell she was starting to feel her increased arousal already. He shuddered to think what would happen later. Thank the Goddess he and his beta had a plan to get through the shift. But until then, he'd have to get her to rest. He smiled into her kiss, breaking away with a sigh. His forehead to hers, they both struggled to catch their breath.

"Hey Wyn, baby, you okay?" he asked gently.

"I...I'm sorry. I'm just so...so..." Oh God, what was happening? She'd woken feeling so happy, so refreshed. Now, she was hot and hungry, for both food and sex.

"I know. Come on, let's get you inside. Your wolf, she's rising. How about we go get something to eat? It'll help." Logan continued to hold Wynter and walked over to the back door.

"But I ate already," she protested, but her stomach rumbled.

"Your wolf's preparing. Eating'll help take the edge off. Being around D probably isn't helping either."

"What?"

"She knows my beta's scent. She'll want to be around him, to touch him."

"But Logan, this makes no sense. I only want you." Humiliation doused her arousal. She buried her head in his shoulder.

"It's okay, Wyn. This is just your body doing this," he reassured her, hugging her to his chest.

Logan yearned to tell her that he loved her, but the timing was off. With her impending change, he only sought to soothe her symptoms. Soon, he'd tell her, but with Dimitri watching and her on the edge, now was not that time.

Wynter retreated into herself. Her emotions, lusting after Dimitri upset her sense of what she knew was right. The night before she'd confessed her love. Unexpectedly, but still, those words fell through her lips. And today? Today, she nearly creamed her shorts over a hot, shirtless beta. What kind of a horrible human being did that? She shook her head, realizing she was no longer human. Yet she wasn't convinced she was one hundred percent wolf. She was made unnaturally, not born a shifter. Sanity would elude her until she ran her own blood tests; she needed to know who and what she really was

The day wore on and Wynter became increasingly restless. Her skin crawled. Her ears rang. Her stomach growled in hunger, despite eating as Logan had told her to do. Wringing her hands up into her hair, she pulled at the blonde springy tendrils, causing a twinge of pain. Sickening as it was, it salved the unending need to scratch and bite. Holed up in the bedroom, she tried to sleep it off, but had only managed a small nap. Logan advised her not to wear constricting clothing, so she'd thrown on a sundress sans underwear. It was far too suffocating; her skin felt raw and chafed against the soft cotton.

She hated that she was changing. None of what had happened had been in her control. Unfair and hurtful. Her parents dying. Being forced to live with Jax. Held captive for months. And now forced against her will to shift into an animal. She despised it. She'd have to make the only choice she had which was to carry on and endure it. Headstrong and determined, she pounded down the stairs, ready to face her Alpha.

Logan had planned a surprise, but things weren't going well. By late afternoon, Wynter had grown more and more uncomfortable and cranky. Unsure what they'd done to her to turn her wolf, he couldn't be certain how smoothly she'd shift. In only a few short hours, they'd know. He hated seeing her in such pain and abhorred the fact that he couldn't control it. That was what he did well: control, dominate. Yet hour after hour, it became more apparent that they'd have to let nature take her course.

By the time Wynter came downstairs, Logan noticed

that she looked wild with agitation. Sexy as ever, her unruly curls sprang in all directions. Despite her discomposure, he knew her wolf would be amazing, but he thought better of telling her. For now, he'd orchestrate a diversion of sorts, a lesson on the bayou. He smiled as he led her outside to the waiting airboat. Nothing was more fun, and he suspected it would give her a rush, interrupting the cycle of negative thoughts playing in her mind.

"What is this?" she asked, not sure what they were doing on the docks.

"It's a boat," Logan answered with a wink.

"Yeah, I see that. Is it safe? I don't want to get eaten by alligators. Really, I've had enough fanged creatures sinking their teeth into me lately."

"Nothin' safer. This is our home, chérie and we're goin' to show it to you," he drawled, doing his best imitation of his beta. "We promise to keep you away from the snakes…even though we might eat them later. Maybe go crawfishin'."

"Don't let him fool you, cher. Logan may be a city boy, but he knows his way 'round the swamp…almost as well as I do. Wait 'til you see him pet the gators. He likes to kiss those pretty lips," Dimitri joked.

"Hey now, I may have been up north for the past fifty years, but it's like ridin' a bike. And hell, I've well made up for it these past couple of months," Logan told them. "And he's wrong about the lips…it's their nice white teeth that I like to see."

Wynter rolled her eyes. "As long as those pearly whites

stay far away from me, we'll be good to go. Remember, I'm a city girl."

"Ah well, we'll see about that after you shift, baby." Logan gave her shoulder a comforting squeeze. "First, we're gonna go out into the lake a bit, and then we'll take you back in the swamp so you can see it in the daylight. And then, we'll boat on over to our running grounds."

Wynter eyed them both suspiciously. *See it in the daylight?* What was that supposed to mean? He did not think she'd be going into a swamp at night? Not happening.

"Here ya go." Logan handed her a pair of yellow earmuffs as Dimitri fired up the engine. With a small smile, she promptly put them on, cautiously looking forward to her boating adventure.

By the time they'd sped through the lake and hit the swamp, Wynter's body thrummed in exhilaration. The rush of the wind and intermittent spray of water combined with the speed sent her heart racing. She was having fun. It had been so long, she barely recognized the sensation. Smiling from ear to ear, she glanced over to Logan who was pointing to blooming bushes of swamp-rose mallow. The hibiscus petals, in white and pink, brought a splash of color to the otherwise green and brown landscape.

Dimitri cut the engine, and they all took off their earmuffs. Wynter scanned the horizon, astonished at the beauty all around her. Insects sang in the twilight. Blue sky and clouds reflected in the water as the sun went down. Ancient cypress trees stood proud, their knees poking up toward the heavens. Logan tapped her shoulder and held his fingers to his lips to quiet any potential conversation. He pointed to a great white egret poised immobile, hunting for his next meal. The majestic bird took notice of them drifting toward the bank, and took off in flight toward another fishing ground.

"It's unbelievable," she said, swiveling her head.

"Hey Ace," Dimitri called. He dug out a small bucket. A prehistoric swish of a tail followed and eyes rose above the water. "Come on over here."

Wynter reached for Logan's hand and turned so she could watch.

"D likes to feed his boy," Logan commented.

"Ace? How does he know that's the same one?"

"They're territorial. And live a long time too. This is his spot. There's a few of his girls…see there on the bank." Logan called attention to a couple of alligators who were basking in the final rays of the sun.

Wynter watched in great delight as Dimitri held up the raw chicken. The reptile lurched out of the water and snapped it up.

"Amazing," Wynter gasped, grinning at the same time.

"They're just a small part of the ecosystem. This place…it's special."

"Do you all come here a lot?"

"Not enough. As much as I love this place, I'm in the city a lot of the time. Even when I lived in Philly, we split our time between the city and mountains. It's the same here. Poor D is goin' to have to get used to livin' in the French Quarter. But you can't really run wolf in town, so if we want to go for a run, this is the place."

"You run in the swamp?"

"Yes and no, cher. We've got lots of open land that's easier to run on but if need be, we know how to walk in the swamp," Dimitri explained.

"But we'll save that lesson for another day," Logan finished.

"We'd better head out. It's just about time to hit the preserve. Who's up for a sunset?" Dimitri asked. He wiped his hands on a towel and readied to start up the engine.

"Thanks for bringing me here. I love it…it's breathtaking." Wynter tried to hide the emotion rushing up into her throat but a traitorous tear fell. She swiped her finger at her eye, capturing it. With a small smile, she sighed.

"It's going to be okay. Just stick with your wolves, baby." Logan kissed her cheek.

A subtle sense of relief showered his conscience, knowing she liked the swamp. Even though he'd grown up in the French Quarter, his parents had made sure he'd spent plenty of time running in what at that time was considered the 'far country'. Good thing, too, because over the centuries, the city had grown, sprawled over its open spaces and now this land belonged to his wolves. It represented his culture. The bayou. The swamp. Home to his wolf.

Her words of admiration soothed his need for her acceptance. He supposed he hadn't realized just how important it was that she'd approved of his home, the way he lived. A house he could change, but everything else? No, she'd either welcome or reject his world. A final test, the pack, awaited not just her, but him as well.

As the motor roared, Logan wrapped his hand over hers. His gut told him that she could do it. It might not be easy, but fuck easy. Nothing lately in their lives had been easy but that didn't equate to impossible. Like his challenges, he'd won them all right but not without difficulty. Nonetheless, victory had been all the more sweet. He'd kill to make this work, but knew she'd have to fight on her own. And then she'd face the pack. No, not easy. But sometimes the best things in life were hard and well worth the fight.

Chapter Twenty-Four

Dimitri stayed back to tie off the boat. He watched his Alpha and mate through the trees, sensing the struggle. In all his years, he'd never known a human to shift. They were born wolves, not made. Yet defying nature, this was going down. He hadn't told Logan, but he was seriously worried about the pack's reaction to Wynter. Not only was she from New York, she was human. Sure, the pack would welcome a mate for their Alpha, but they'd expected her to be one of their own, and without a doubt, wholly wolf.

The she-wolves had been chasing around Logan since he'd replaced Marcel. Luci, especially, had staked her unofficial claim by continuing to live with Logan. Up until several days ago, she'd made it her daily ritual to knock on Logan's bedroom door. And while he knew Logan had only comforted her, Luci wasn't going to take his impending mating well.

Cognizant that Logan had been busy with Wynter and also Dana's death, Dimitri had hesitated to broach the subject with him. But tonight, he was prepared to step in and assist. And that didn't just include helping Wynter sexually. Yes, he'd grown fond of the little wolf. But at the moment, he was more concerned about her safety. Dimitri had already decided that he'd step in and stop a fight, if necessary. Sure, he'd take a hard hit for intervening but so be it. A direct challenge to Wynter wouldn't negate her status as Logan's mate, but still, it was within a she-wolf's right to attack and kill if necessary. If someone challenged Wynter and she lost, it would further distract Logan from leading the pack. Within days if not hours, another challenge for Alpha might be issued. Logan had promised to kill the next wolf who challenged him, and Dimitri was confident he'd make good on his word

No matter how sexually adventurous she'd felt, Wynter's human notions clashed with her emerging wolf. She watched as Logan stood naked before her, cajoling her to shuck the dress. Wynter reluctantly undressed and immediately covered her breasts with her hands. Realizing that the rest of her body was already exposed, she forced her arms to her sides.

"Come here, Wyn," he told her. Magnanimously nude, she was a spectacular sight, Logan thought. "You trust me?"

"Yes," she responded quietly, looking at her feet. She could feel Logan and Dimitri's eyes on her skin. She was frightened out of her wits. No matter how much she'd told herself this was going to happen, she still wasn't prepared.

A surge of nausea rolled her stomach. Reacting, she bent over, her hands on her knees, willing her stomach to hold the food. She coughed and gagged, managing to push the bile back down her esophagus. *Please God. I will not throw up…no throwing up…especially in front of Logan. Be brave. I can do this. No, I will do this.* She closed her eyes and took a deep cleansing breath. With a whoosh, she blew it out through her mouth. *Logan is with me.* Logan. Oh shit. She'd almost forgotten he was watching her ridiculous panic attack. She stood up and gave him an apologetic smile.

"Are you okay? As gross as it is, if you need to throw up, go ahead. Believe me, you wouldn't be the first."

"You're being nice."

Logan smiled. "Well, it's the pups who usually hurl their first time, but you're kind of like a pup."

She shot him an annoyed look, her hands on her hips.

"Okay, more like a super-hot, naked human lady wolf," he laughed. "Seriously, baby. Nothing and I mean nothing bad is going to happen tonight. We'll shift. We'll run. We'll make love." His voice was low and dominant, guiding her wolf.

She simply nodded, allowing him to take her hand in his.

"Look at me, sweetheart," Logan instructed. When her eyes met his, he continued. "I'm sorry this happened to you…I really am. No matter how much I want you as my mate, I'd never force a shift on you. It sucks. It's not fair, even. But there's no stopping nature. This is like skiing, baby. Sure, it's a little dangerous. You will most definitely fall. Probably will be sore afterwards. And a little dirty. But most certainly, you will have fun. And before you go hatin' my analogy, you've never been skiing with me…and you will love it."

"I like skiing," she disclosed with a small smile. "I'm from New York."

"And someday, we'll do that together too. But today, you'll shift. So let's do this thing, okay?"

"Okay." As soon as she'd agreed, her skin tingled as if she'd stuck her finger in an electrical socket. She looked up at the full moon. As if it reached out with a firm hand striking into her heart, she seized, unable to speak.

Logan saw Wynter freeze and knew immediately it had begun. Damn, this was not how a pup or anyone was supposed to shift. It shouldn't be done under duress. Transformation was a celebratory milestone. Logan focused within, drawing on his inherent Alpha power, attempting to soothe her mind. But her immobility continued and within seconds, she began to shake uncontrollably, saliva dripping from her mouth as if she'd gone into a full grand mal seizure.

Logan put his hands onto her cheeks, forcing her to look at him, but her vacant stare told him she was lost within her own mind. Dimitri sensed trouble and ran to his assistance, but Logan waved him off with a hand. He and he alone would coax her out of the paralysis that had taken over her body.

"Wynter, concentrate on my voice. Listen to me. No matter what's going on inside of you, I know you can hear me. I'm your Alpha. And as such, you will do as I say. Your wolf. She knows this. And you do too. You need to let go. Let me in." Goddess, it shouldn't be this way. He hated to be harsh with her but he needed to force her wolf to the surface. "Close your eyes."

Unresponsive, Wynter continued to quiver.

"Close. Your. Eyes. This is an order from your Alpha. Do it now," he growled.

Recognition registered in her pupils. Her lids flickered but still didn't shut. Her wolf rolled submissively onto her back, yelping in response. At his voice, she struggled, clawing to get out, to run with her mate.

Small though it was, Logan knew she'd heard him. He'd have to be more forceful. A dominant, almost foreign voice emerged. "Wynter, I'm commanding you to shift. Now close. Your. Eyes."

Logan's authoritative directive speared through the palpable numbness that had arrested Wynter's muscles. As if someone had smashed a rock through a pane of glass, her humanity shattered into pieces. Her eyes snapped shut, and the wolf emerged. Utter agony ensued as the metamorphosis completed. Gagged by the shift, her scream pinged within her own consciousness, and she thought she'd died. Mouth opened, no tortured cry would save her. But within seconds, she heard a howl pierce the night air. Blinking her eyes, she realized the animalistic noise had come from her. For it was she, the wolf, acknowledging her shift, calling to her mate. As Logan came into focus, she caught sight of his proud smile.

Logan held his breath as she changed before his eyes. Her silent screams tore open his gut. With great restraint, he held back, allowing her to transform independently. There could be no other way. And within seconds, the red-haired, blue-eyed, she-wolf lay on the dirt.

"Look at you, sweetheart," he whispered and crouched down to the ground.

Goddess, she was every bit as resplendent in her wolf as in her person. His heart constricted seeing that she'd gone into submission. With her ears backward and tail curved under her backside, she whimpered and quivered in fear. Slowly reaching forward, he held his hand out to her.

Distressed and disoriented, Wynter sniffed and licked Logan's hand. She knew her mate. His scent, his taste. Thank God, he was still here with her. He didn't leave. She focused on his voice and touch. Everything about him seemed to calm her and felt peaceful.

"That's right, it's me. I won't hurt you, baby," he assured her, rubbing her ears. He nodded to Dimitri, who'd stripped in preparation for his own shift. But as his friend drew closer, Wynter growled and bared her teeth. "Come on now, it's okay. It's just D. You know he won't hurt you either."

Wynter saw movement, a human. Defensively, she snarled at the incoming danger. An innate desire to protect surfaced.

Logan eyed Dimitri. "Slowly, D. She looks like she wants to bite. And considering you're nekkid....well, go easy. You've got a low hanging target there," he joked.

"Ya got that right. Geez, she may have just shifted but she's a feisty one." Dimitri carefully sidled up to Logan. He slid his hand down Logan's arm, picking up some of his scent, and then presented a palm to Wynter. He knew that she'd eventually know it was him. But at the moment, the overload on her senses made it difficult for her to process.

Another hand came toward her. Cautiously, she nosed his skin. Logan. Dimitri. Yes, she knew Dimitri, cared for him. A lick of his skin cemented her acceptance. While she'd not tasted Dimitri, both his scent and touch happily appeased her wolf.

"That's it, baby. See, told ya, it's just D," Logan coaxed, continuing to caress her fur.

He smiled over to Dimitri, who also had begun to pet her neck. A pivotal moment for them all, he supposed. His mate, a human, had shifted. And he and his beta had just borne witness to the extraordinary phenomenon. Both men, without jealousy or expectation, nurtured the new little wolf. As she relaxed into their calming strokes, Logan smiled at Dimitri before addressing her.

"Okay little wolf, we've gotta shift too. I'm gonna go first, then D. Don't be afraid now. We won't be able to talk to you like this when we're shifted. But you'll know what to do, I promise. The only thing I ask is that you stay close. Even though the ground here is firm, there's plenty of trouble to get into, so stick with us," he told her as he broke contact. He stood up while Dimitri continued to rub her. "This'll just take a second."

Logan's tall form morphed into a large gray wolf. Towering over Wynter, he pressed his muzzle into her neck, licking her snout.

Wynter snuggled into Logan's long and soft tongue. She relished his wolf, desiring his scent on her fur. In return, she licked up under his chin. In a blink, a second dark gray wolf nudged her alongside of her mate. *Dimitri.* Surreal as it was, she licked both wolves, her Alpha, his beta. Caring and loving, as beasts and men, they'd protected her.

Logan and Dimitri backed away from Wynter, waiting for her to stand. They both knew she'd be unsteady at first. It was expected of all new pups. Standing on four legs, instead of two, naturally would throw her for a loop. But like riding a bike, she'd never forget how to do it once she learned. It was almost painful to watch. Logan thanked the Goddess he was in wolf form so he didn't need to hide a smile. She pushed up onto all fours only to wobble and fall. But never being one to give up, she immediately rebounded. A few steps, then within seconds, she ran joyous circles around him and his beta.

Wynter couldn't believe how easy it was to run around like this. Sure, she'd stumbled a bit, but now she took off like the wind. It was freeing. And fun. She wondered if she'd wake up any minute to find this had all been a dream. But as she followed Logan and Dimitri and the night wore on, she became more comfortable in her newfound reality and a vigorous wave of curiosity overtook her. In a surge of confidence, she raced ahead of her boys, weaving in and out of the trees. A sound caught her attention; she stilled. Both Logan and Dimitri froze, having heard it too, a grunt echoing throughout the woods.

Instinctively Wynter crept toward the noise, but Logan quickly blocked her, contemplating whether or not they should try to attack it. A wild boar would make an excellent meal, but they weren't the easiest prey to catch. With few natural predators, the razorbacks had become an invasive species, disrupting the natural balance of the environment. Nasty, they'd been known to attack animals and humans alike. Despite the known difficulties and dangers associated with hunting one, Dimitri and Logan loved a challenge and had eaten them many a time. A harmless bunny rabbit would have been a better choice to teach Wynter how to hunt. But on the other hand, showing her how the pack worked together to kill big prey was an important lesson that she had to learn eventually. And who better to teach her than him?

Without warning, the feral pig charged at Logan and Wynter, trying to ram them with its head and tusks. Dispersing, the trio confused the prey. Logan growled at the animal while Dimitri rounded from behind. Wynter, having never hunted, hungered for it but also innately sensed the danger. She watched as the dominant males circled the beast. In synchronicity, the Alpha and his beta assaulted the animal. Logan took it on head first, biting into its snout. Dimitri bit into the flank. Even though the boar wasn't fast, its tough skin made it exceptionally difficult to kill. The coordinated attack continued for several minutes, until the squealing pig faltered. As it did so, Wynter cautiously approached. Logan tore off fresh meat, and made room for Wynter to participate in the hunt.

After killing and eating a good portion of the boar, the threesome padded under a tree and lay down. His little wolf had done well, Logan thought. She'd known not to interrupt when he and Dimitri made their first lunge at the wild game. Smart and cunning, she'd waited until it was on the ground to assist. Some wolves weren't always so clever, ending up with a gouging, courtesy of the pig.

A rustle of leaves alerted Logan that the pack was approaching. His ears perked and he barked to Dimitri. In anticipation, they stood protectively flanking her. The integration into the pack was another critical task in her transformation. And for Logan, it'd been the first time he'd run with pack since he'd issued his ultimatum. If anyone challenged him, death lingered as the outcome.

Hunting had sated Wynter's wolf. Alongside her men, she awaited the pack members. She shoved any nervous emotions aside, and assumed a dominant positioning. She may not have had much pack experience, but she knew enough that she planned on being an alpha female. And now especially, with Logan as her mate, she wouldn't let another female, wolf or woman, touch him. Keeping her head held up and tail outward, she dared another to approach.

A black wolf padded forward. *Jake.* Strange, somehow she knew it was him. She sniffed. Yes, his familiar scent pleased her wolf. He'd been her protector. An ally. A gray wolf trailed behind him. *Zeke.* Yes, she was getting good at this. An angry presence invaded her peaceful thought. Smaller white and brown wolves padded toward them. Fiona, the brown. Luci, the white. Around them, others filtered toward them through the trees.

Wynter attempted to read them. Instinctively, she became aware of her given ability to assess the state of the pack. Concentrating, she allowed the lines of communication to spring to life. Logan was feeling protective. Dimitri felt guarded. The pack? The pack resonated with a mixture of both inquisitiveness and jubilation. They loved their Alpha. His contentment reflected their own emotions. The need to please him was paramount in their lives.

She allowed each wolf to approach her, but Logan bared his teeth preventing anyone from getting too close. Dimitri, too, remained next to her, unwilling to leave her side. Optimism rode high within her spirit until a rush of fur crashed into her, sending her flying onto her side. Searing pain shot through her flank, but stumbling, she managed to right herself.

Confusion racked her senses, and as she looked around, she quickly surmised that Luci had blindsided her. The white wolf rushed and snarled at her, and Wynter growled in response. Only seconds passed before Wynter's wolf interpreted Luci's action for what it was: a challenge. Grateful that her human mind didn't have time to contemplate the complexities of the situation, her wolf raised her head, and snapped. Luci charged her and they both rolled on the ground. Wynter yipped as a white hot streak tore at her ear. Panting and staggering, the pair of fighting wolves briefly separated at the sound of their Alpha's bark.

Wynter, surprised at her own voracity and aggression, snarled at Logan when he attempted to intervene. Rage and possessiveness drove her to continue the fight. From the very first time she'd seen Luci, she'd known that she was a threat. *Threat to me. Threat to my mate.* Wynter snapped; her lips pulled high, exposing her canines. Despite her position, Luci continued to approach, staring at Wynter, snarling. Exploding from a crouched position, Wynter rushed Luci and tore at her fur. The first drop of blood to her tongue incited her to continue her offensive strike. By the time her assault ceased, Luci laid belly up. Her wolf insisted on nothing less than death, but Logan's voice stopped her from tearing out the white wolf's throat. With her teeth buried deep into the flesh of Luci's neck, she heard human words, Logan screaming, commanding her to stop.

Stunned, Logan watched as Wynter launched herself at Luci. He knew all too well the need to establish dominance. After Luci initiated the challenge and Wynter successfully managed to avert the attack, he'd grown confident that she truly was alpha. He wanted nothing more than to protect her from the darkness. But being in pack meant establishing rank, something she had to do on her own. And since she'd snarled at him, indicating her wish to proceed, he wouldn't deny her what she sought. But what he had not expected was that she'd attack Luci until she'd pinned her to the ground, intending to slaughter her. While he held no sympathy for Luci, he couldn't allow Wynter to kill the she-wolf. Unfortunately Wynter was too far engrossed in her beast to listen to his wolf's warnings. Shifting to human, he yelled at her to release.

"Wynter, let her go! Do not kill her!" He watched as she disengaged her jaw from the fur, but still held a firm paw to the other wolf's belly. Logan blew out a breath. *Holy fuck, she'd almost killed Luci.*

A slow burn racked the side of Wynter's head, but she shook it off, refusing to show weakness. With a snort, she accepted Luci's submission, removing her paw. Raising her hackles and tail, she padded over to Logan's human form, awaiting his order. His hand on her head, his approval warmed her heart. She scanned the pack once again, registering their state. Anger? No, respect. More so, every single one of them understood her position and who Logan was to her. It was crystal clear. *Mine. He's mine.*

Chapter Twenty-Five

Logan, still unclothed, held Wynter in his arms, wrapped in a blanket. By the time they'd run back to the boat and shifted back, she'd collapsed in exhaustion. Goddess almighty, he hadn't witnessed a fight like that between two she-wolves in a long time. And never had the challenge been about him. While he hated that she'd been injured, she'd done what she needed to do, securing her place as alpha female. No one would mess with her.

Dimitri pulled the boat alongside the swamp cabin, and Logan disembarked. While the modest structure didn't have running water, Dimitri had set up a portable shower. Tossing the soiled blanket to the floor, Logan turned on the solar-powered contraption and stepped under the spray. He scrubbed the dirt and blood off of Wynter first and then handed her over to Dimitri who waited with an oversized towel. Allowing his beta to take her still sleeping form inside, Logan quickly finished his own shower. By the time he entered the cabin, Dimitri had already tucked Wynter into the king-sized futon and was lighting the oil lamps.

"Thanks, man." Logan strode across the room to his mate and sat down next to her. He smoothed his hand over her hair. "She's incredible."

"Can you fucking believe she almost killed Luci?" Dimitri asked, still shocked at how they'd fought. He made his way back over to the door.

"No I can't. But I have to tell you, there's part of me that feels a little better knowing that she can protect herself. I hate to even think about it, but we both know it's not over," Logan affirmed thoughtfully. A day in the country wasn't nearly enough to make him forget that Dana lay bricked into her tomb. Nor did he forget the car bomb that had almost killed Jake and Wynter.

"I made some progress with the laptop. Got some data for your girl. Let's hope she can work her magic until this asshole pops up again or Devereoux finds his demon seed."

"I had a lab set up in the garage today. She doesn't know yet. I'm going to show it to her tomorrow. It's important she can test herself, her blood. She's worried."

"She may be worried but she looked all wolf to me. Tonight, she didn't seem any different than the rest of us."

Logan cocked an eyebrow at Dimitri. "Yeah, except that she almost killed another wolf on her first run with the pack. You ever seen a pup do that? No fucking way. She's strong…unusually so for a new wolf."

"Can't say I've ever seen it but damn glad she took down Luci. Don't get me wrong, Luci can be a great girl, but she's been eyeing you ever since Marcel died. You knew that wouldn't sit right with Wyn."

"She doesn't want to share her mate," Logan reasoned.

"And you do?"

"I love you, D, but not really." Logan shook his head; his face grew tense with concern. "Listen, I don't know how she's going to feel when she wakes up. I mean her shift didn't go so well. I've never seen a wolf shake like that. And then she wouldn't shift. You saw what happened…I had to command her to do it. And what just went down with Luci? I guess we'll just have to see what happens next. But I need you here."

"Whatever you want. I won't lie; I'm looking forward to being with both of you. Must be the moon…or it could be that I remember how sweet she felt in my arms the other night…yeah, that's it," he teased.

"Yeah, I'm pretty sure this'll be a one-time gig for you, so don't get too attached."

"Got it." Dimitri smiled and grabbed a towel.

"Hey D."

"Yeah." He stopped before going out the door and turned to his Alpha.

"Thanks." Logan's eyes met his beta's. His voice took on a gentle but serious tone. "I mean it. Thanks for being there. Not just tonight…but the past couple of months. I know Marcel wanted this for me, but if you hadn't been there…things might have been way different."

"No problem, man. We all loved him. But he was right about you." He glanced to Wynter and back to Logan. "And about her shift…you're right, it was rough. But she'll be okay. Sometimes things don't turn out how we think they should be. Just how they're supposed to be. However the hell it happened, she's wolf now."

Logan silently regarded his beta. Words couldn't be truer. He hadn't set out to be Alpha nor did he choose a human for a mate. Life, destiny; it chose him, not the other way around. This new chapter in his life may not have been a walk in the park, but he'd come to terms with it.

"Hey, tonight's a celebration," Dimitri offered.

Logan gave him a small smile. "Ah, yes. Well, it seems my mate has taken to sleeping. Unusual reaction to shifting but nothing about her is mundane, that's for sure. Go get a shower and then come join us, okay?"

"I'm gonna check the boat one more time and clean up." Dimitri gave a final wave and left.

Logan threw back the covers, got in bed and pulled Wynter against his torso. He pillowed her head on his chest and ran his hand over her arm, taking her hand in his. His ferocious little mate had torn up out there tonight. The sight of her forcing Luci into submission was fucking unreal. And a huge turn on to his wolf.

Wynter snuggled into Logan's warmth. As her senses awakened, so too, did her desire for him. Her eyes fluttered open and she pushed her leg over his so that the length of him rested on her thigh.

"Logan," she purred.

"Hey baby, how do you feel?"

"Hmm....horny," she laughed. Too tired to sit up, she took in her surroundings from the safety of Logan's arms. Bare wooden walls and a tin roof gave no clue to where they'd taken her. "Where are we?"

"Our cabin."

"You have a cabin?"

"D and I always had one…even before I moved to Philly. So when I got back, we ripped the old one down and put this up. Can you smell that cedar-like scent?"

"Hmm." She nodded.

"That's the cypress."

"Cypress?" Wynter's voice took on a higher octave as she realized exactly where she was. "Are we in the middle of the swamp? At night? With alligators? Bugs?"

Logan laughed. After hunting a wild boar and nearly killing Luci, his delicate little human was back.

"Yes, sweetheart and you're safe. Nothin's going to get you out here besides D and me. This place is sealed up tight. We've got everything we need to survive the night…food, water, a bed. It's peaceful." He kissed her again. "Secluded."

"Secluded, huh? I like the sound of that," she replied huskily. She ran her hand over the ridges of his abs and then traced her fingertip around his flat nipple.

Logan reached for her wrist. "You were gorgeous tonight. A red wolf." He circled the pad of his thumb into her palm. "So wild. And fierce."

"It felt freeing. It was like my wolf…she knew what to do. Some part of her, she knows already how to act." Wynter blushed then shook her head. It still seemed unbelievable that she'd shifted. "It's crazy, right?"

"No, not crazy. That's what it's like. And we're going to be doing a lot of it while we're here."

A memory flashed in her mind, her teeth in a wolf's fur. She looked up at Logan for assurance. "Oh God, is Luci okay? I remember…I bit…"

"She'll be fine. You listened to me, that's the important thing," Logan confirmed.

"I just remember feeling so mad. Did you see how she freakin' rammed into me?"

"Yeah and I'm thinking the fight kind of needed to happen, but I wasn't expecting it tonight, that's for damn sure. But after you growled at me…well, I let the fur fly."

"Sorry." Wynter cringed at the thought.

"Don't be." Logan shrugged.

"What are you saying?" Wynter pushed up on her elbow so she could better see his face.

"Luci, she wants to be the alpha female. If you hadn't made her submit, she wouldn't have stopped coming after me."

"But she's not your mate."

"No, but that wouldn't stop her. I wouldn't ever choose her but as you can imagine, it wouldn't be good for us if every time you weren't around she tried to touch me. Just imagine me coming home with her scent. How do you think that would make you feel?"

"I'd fucking kill her," Wynter stated emotionlessly.

"Yeah. You almost did," Logan replied. "But now, rank's been established. It'll all fall in place. And it happened in front of the pack which is good."

"When did I get so bloodthirsty?" Wynter laid her head back down on his chest. She'd meant the words, 'I'd fucking kill her.' *Was this who she was now?*

"Just stop the train, Dr. Ryan. I know what you're thinking. And you're not a monster. You are, however, wolf. You put her in her place and for that, I'm thankful. Now speaking of being hurt; how's that ear?"

"I'm fine."

"Let me see." Logan pulled her up, so that she was facing him. Pushing her hair to the side, he inspected her ear closely and sucked on her lobe. "Good as new."

As his warm breath caressed her neck, the ache between her legs thrummed with need. When she'd told him she'd felt horny, that didn't begin to describe what was happening to her. Heat rushed to her face, and she pushed the covers aside, trying to cool her body.

"Logan, I…I…" Embarrassed by her state, she tried to hide her face in her hands.

"It's okay, baby. I'll take care of you. I promise by morning, things will be better." He trailed kisses down her neck.

"Touch me," she begged.

Logan caressed her breast, pinching a diamond tip. She moaned, wriggling into him.

"Logan, I think there's something wrong. I'm so…so…" Wynter gasped, pressing her forehead to his chest. She struggled to find the words to describe the sensations afflicting her body. The aching, painful desire was unbearable.

Logan slid his hand around the nape of her neck and brought his lips to hers. Deepening the kiss, he reveled in her taste as their tongues intertwined. They both fought for breath as passion overtook them. His cock thickened in response. Wrapping his hand into her hair, he lost himself in her. He found her sex, and he plunged a finger deep into her tight heat. Straining to hold her, his pecs bulged as she bucked against his tantalizing assault.

Wynter's whimpers were silenced by his mouth. She fervidly kissed him, biting at his lips and sweeping her tongue with his. The delightful suffering plagued every cell of her body from the inside out. Wynter released an animalistic cry as her claws extended from her fingertips and she quickly withdrew them. As the pressure built inside her, she arched her back like a cat. Logan's fingers stroked her bundle of nerves, but it wasn't nearly enough to assuage the tension. The pulse of her orgasm teetered at the brink, eluding her until the pad of his thumb massaged her clit. Screaming Logan's name, her release shattered. She wished it had been enough, but within seconds, her body reignited.

"Logan, please make love to me. I need more," she cried, climbing on top of him, savage with arousal.

"Come here, baby." Logan wished her transition hadn't been so difficult. As much as he loved her adventurous sexuality, he knew she'd be in pain if they didn't appease her wolf. The sound of the door shutting, alerted him to Dimitri's presence.

Wynter looked up to see Dimitri standing at the bottom of the bed. His tanned muscles flexed underneath the beads of water that still clung to his chest. *No, it was wrong.* Her conscience warred, struggling to rationalize her desire for him. Although not her mate, Dimitri represented safety and protection, Logan's friend and confidant.

"Logan, I'll be fine. I just need..." *How could she want to be with two men? Someone other than her mate?*

"Wyn, it's okay. We're here for you." Logan pressed a quick kiss to her lips. Holding her face in his palms, he gazed into her eyes. "What you feel...us...this isn't wrong or dirty. It's what you need. It's a part of your change. And you're beautiful. You're the most beautiful woman I've ever known. This...tonight, the three of us, even if it never happens again, it's special."

"But..." *What if he hated her afterwards? Rejected her?*

"You're mine, baby. D knows that. He's the only person on this Earth who I'd ever trust with you...with us. No matter what we do, you belong to me. Always." Logan growled and then kissed her passionately.

"Yours," she breathed into his mouth. Oh God, she was going to do this. *Her men*...at least for tonight. She trusted Logan on this journey. Most of all, she loved him.

Logan briefly pulled his lips away from hers. Looking into Wynter's eyes, he spoke to her slowly and lovingly. "Listen to me Wynter, you're in control tonight. Now let us take care of you."

Wynter's eyes teared and she nodded. She felt too much. *Too much emotion. Too much desire.* But she'd made her decision.

Dimitri approached slowly. Naked, he sprawled onto the bed. His Alpha's mate's scent enticed him, but he patiently waited. Logan was right. This was special. Over a hundred years on the Earth, and never had he experienced the shift of a human. The enormous respect he held for Logan only heightened the importance of the evening.

Logan wanted to give Wynter the world and then some. Gently, he picked her up by her waist and laid her onto Dimitri so that she was cradled between his legs, her back to his stomach. He looked over to Wynter, who smiled, then above to Dimitri. Reaching for his beta's wrist, Logan placed his hand onto her breast. Dimitri responded, caressing her soft peaks.

"That's it, D. Feel our little wolf," Logan instructed. "Isn't she amazing?"

"Oh Goddess, yes," Dimitri bit out as he touched her, his cock swelled against her ass. He pushed her hair aside and licked at her neck behind her ear. "Cher, you smell so good."

"Dimitri," she breathed.

Logan settled between their legs, his belly pressed to Wynter's. He rested on his forearms so that he could feast on her breasts. Wynter threw her head back, baring her neck to both Logan and Dimitri. Submitting to them both, she allowed the erotic experience to envelop her.

"That's a girl. Feel us," Logan coaxed before taking her nipple into his mouth. He swirled his tongue around its tip. A small bite elicited a gasp from his mate. Logan pressed his hand down between her legs, startling her as he swiped his fingers through her glistening folds. He withdrew his hand and extended it to Dimitri, who met his eyes.

"Taste," he ordered.

Dimitri complied, opening his lips as Logan's finger pressed into his mouth. He moaned, savoring the unique sweetness. So intimate, Dimitri had never tasted from another man but couldn't refuse. And shit, if it didn't make his cock throb.

Wynter watched in fascination as Logan fed Dimitri. *So fucking hot.* It surprised her that he'd touch him so gently. Their closeness had always existed but this was more. Her body flared in response. She rocked her bottom against Dimitri's growing arousal.

"Delicious," Dimitri groaned.

"Relax, sweetheart." Logan slid his body downward until he reached the apex of her legs and held her thighs apart. "Open, that's it."

Wynter caught his eyes, aware that she was fully exposed to them. She shivered as Logan softly grazed his finger through her labia and over her clit.

"Logan, please," she pleaded.

"She's so beautiful, isn't she, D?" Logan kissed the top of her mound, teasing her.

"Oh yeah," Dimitri agreed, taking Wynter's breasts back into his hands while kissing her shoulders.

Logan smiled up at Dimitri and then to Wynter a split second before he swiped his tongue through her swollen lips. His balls tightened as he drank in her creamy essence. She grunted in pleasure as he speared his tongue into her core, and he could tell that she was going to come within seconds.

Dimitri, wanting to taste more of Wynter, slipped out

from underneath her, kissing along her collarbone until he reached her breasts. He took a nipple into his mouth, sucking and teasing it with his teeth. She stabbed her fingers into Logan's hair and then Dimitri's, holding them to her skin. She was so close to release. Logan at her pussy. Dimitri's lips on her breasts. And as she felt a tongue trail down her stomach, the energy of her arousal slammed into her.

"Logan, I'm going to..." She tried holding it back, but it was of no use. As the orgasm rolled through her, she was vaguely cognizant of them switching positions.

Unspoken signals passed between Logan and Dimitri as they moved seamlessly so that Dimitri took over for Logan; his mouth suckling Wynter's clit. Logan pressed up onto his knees, positioning himself at her entrance. He watched Wynter's head loll back into the pillow as he plunged his cock into her wet pussy. Unrelenting, Dimitri continued to suck her swollen nub while Logan pumped in and out of her hotness.

Wynter fought for breath as a second climax claimed her. Her eyes flew open and she saw Logan holding her legs, pressing into her, Dimitri's head now in between her legs.

"Yes, fuck, Wyn. So goddamned tight." Logan almost forgot where he was, lost in the heat of his mate. He saw her blindly reaching, grabbing Dimitri's hair. "D, Wynter needs you."

Dimitri licked his lips and knelt up so he could go to her. He hissed as Wynter's hand quickly wrapped around his stiff shaft.

"Take him, Wyn. That's it," Logan directed, still thrusting in and out of her.

"Dimitri, come. Come to me," she ordered, never letting go of him. She moaned in protest. He was too far away for what she had in mind.

Dimitri made his way up to Wynter and leaned up against the headboard next to her. Whatever she wanted, he'd do, but he wouldn't initiate. Dimitri sucked a deep breath as she drew him to her, lapping her tongue at his plump head. He closed his eyes tight, bracing himself as she began to lick his cock.

As Wynter took Dimitri's hardness into her mouth, her eyes locked on Logan's. A hard thrust forced her to gasp.

"That's so fucking hot, sweetheart. Suck him," Logan told her.

He couldn't freaking believe how erotic it was to see her like this with his beta. He watched as Dimitri fought the pleasure, his eyes locked on Logan's. Unexpectedly, no possessiveness or jealousy registered. Love for both of them pulled at his heart. He allowed the rise of his own release to build, knowing they both were so close to coming.

Wynter moved in rhythm with Logan, meeting his thrusts with her own. No longer able to keep her eyes open, she sucked Dimitri hard. Relaxing into the taste of him, she allowed him to fuck her mouth while Logan fucked her pussy. The rush of it all drove her further into her untamed passion. She moaned and released Dimitri, realizing she was going to come again.

"So close, Logan. Please," she begged.

Logan circled his fingers over her clitoris. In response, her quivering channel fisted more tightly around him. He breathed deeply, fighting his own need to come.

Wynter cried out loud as another climax smashed into her, leaving her shaking and rebounding to meet Logan's pelvis. She fought to breathe as the tremors continued to roll throughout her body.

Logan rocked in and out of her slowly, his forehead pressed to hers and he kissed her deeply. He knew Wynter's hand was still on Dimitri's cock, gently stroking him. It felt surreal, joined like this with them. It was one night. It might never happen again. But for tonight, he'd have his mate and beta the way he'd envisioned, sharing them both and they with each other.

"Logan, it feels so good," she panted. "Oh God."

"Do you want us, Wyn?" Logan asked, his eyes pinned on her. "Both of us?"

"Yes," she whispered, nodding. Even though they shared this moment with Dimitri, she felt closer than ever to Logan.

Logan's heated breaths morphed into a shallow sigh as he slowed his pace. With his mate at his chest, he noticed that Dimitri had closed his eyes, presumably trying not to come. Reaching for his beta, Logan pulled at his arm, rolling him onto his side so that his stomach was flush against their sides.

"Come, D. We need you," Logan told him.

Dimitri acceded. He allowed Logan to rest his hand on her belly between both Logan and Wynter. The contact sizzled, solidifying their relationship. His erection pressed against her hip. Kissing along the side of her breast, Dimitri's gaze settled on Logan.

"You sure about this? Logan? Wynter?" Dimitri needed to be certain this was what they both wanted.

Logan nodded. "Sweetheart, there's no going back."

"Please, it's so…so…I need this," she cried into Logan's shoulder.

Every square inch of her body tingled with desire. Unhinged, she nipped at Logan's chest. Her pussy ached, her body craved more. She moaned, aware that her canines were extending. Her wolf wanted to mark her mate, she wouldn't be denied.

"Now," she demanded.

Logan smiled at a wide-eyed Dimitri. It struck him as funny that he, the Alpha, and his beta were being commanded by his feisty little mate in bed. Damn, she'd gone wild.

"You heard her," Logan managed right before he kissed Wynter so she'd stop biting so hard at his chest.

She needed to claim him, he knew. Her wolf demanded it. And his wolf, traitor that he was, rolled in submission, awaiting her bite. The furry beast could have cared less if his beta was here or not. Logan sat up and flipped Wynter onto her stomach. Dimitri helped, taking her into his arms so that her head rested on his chest. With her stomach pressed against his beta's, Logan shoved up her lush mane, laving his mark with his tongue. *Mine.* Gliding his hands down her back and sides, Logan reached for a tiny bottle next to the bed.

Wynter felt the cool gel on her bottom and wiggled up into Logan's caress. As he pushed a slippery finger and then another, into her anus, her breath caught. She moaned into Dimitri's chest, relishing the pleasurable fullness. Undulating her hips, she encouraged him to pump in and out, stretching her.

"Yes, don't stop. More, I need more. Please, I can't wait." She rubbed her mound against Dimitri's belly, seeking pressure. She sighed as Dimitri met her need, slipping his fingers through her folds, easing her ache.

Dimitri thought he'd come just from having her atop him. He couldn't wait to be inside her, but Logan had to go first.

"That's it, just relax into D. Feel his fingers on your pussy." Logan heard her sigh as he saw Dimitri's fingers flicker down through her pink lips.

Withdrawing his own hand from her, Logan lubricated his cock, making sure it was well covered. Gently, he spread her cheeks and guided the head of him into her tight hole. Slowly, he pressed an inch into her ass. Like a vise, she squeezed him. He heard her moan in response.

"You okay, baby?" So goddamn tight, she was, Logan wasn't sure if he could keep going.

Wynter sucked a breath as he pushed into the first tight ring of muscle. Without warning, air rushed out of her lungs as Dimitri simultaneously plunged a finger up into her core. As the burn set in, she dug her fingernails into his shoulders. She swore she'd pass out from the incredible feeling of being taken by both men.

"Don't stop. It's so good."

Holding her waist, Logan slowly eased inward until he was completely sheathed. Dimitri's fingers inadvertently glided along Logan's shaft through the thin membrane, causing him to pause. *For the love of the Goddess.* It took all of his restraint to keep from coming. He bit his lip, hoping a little pain would distract him.

"Now D," Logan directed. He could barely speak, afraid he'd orgasm before they got started. Holding his hips still, he waited for Dimitri to slip into Wynter.

Wynter groaned as she felt Dimitri press into her. Holy shit, it felt incredible. Altogether full and sated, she'd never forget this experience for the rest of her natural life, immortal as it was. In tandem, the men began to move within her, igniting a magical pandemonium held only in check by the power of her Alpha. Tendrils of excitement traveled clear from the top of her head to her toes.

Soaring through the motions, she craned her neck to look up into Logan's eyes. Her ragged gasps broke the silence of the room as she held his gaze. Logan bent his head forward, offering what her wolf sought. The pulse in his neck called to her and before she knew what she was doing, she'd sunk her teeth deep into his skin. As she did so, Wynter flew apart, hurled off the edge of reason. Shuddering, she exploded, her orgasm flowing through her veins with uncontrollable abandon.

"I'm coming…Ah yeah," Logan groaned. Wynter pulsated around his shaft at the same instant Dimitri's cock slid against him through the thin tissue that separated them.

Fuck, she wouldn't release him, Logan thought. Sweet agony claimed him as she marked his skin. Stiffening, he spilled himself deep within his mate.

In a haze, Wynter heard Dimitri tell her he was about to come. As he tried to pull out of her, she fought him. No, she wouldn't leave him to skulk off on his own. They'd consensually decided to make love. And that meant, they'd come together. "No, Dimitri."

Dimitri relented to his Alpha's mate. Sweet Jesus, the she-wolf was persistent. And with his cock so far in her pussy, he found it hard to argue with her. With a labored breath, he gave in to her, to them both. Riding the wild wave, he came long and hard, pressing his head into both Logan's and Wynter's shoulders.

Wynter let go of Dimitri, allowing Logan to bring her back with him into bed. She snuggled into his embrace. Her mind had a hard time believing what she'd just experienced yet not a shred of regret shadowed her thoughts.

"That was amazing," Wynter declared happily into Logan's chest. *I love you.* She wanted to tell Logan how she felt about him but with Dimitri there, it didn't seem right.

"Yeah it was. Goddess, baby, you're going to kill me." Logan laughed, still trying to catch his breath.

"And me too," Dimitri concurred, panting. "It's a good thing this is a one-off. I don't think my mere immortal self could handle you two on a regular basis. Wynter has a lot of energy."

"Me?" Wynter giggled.

"Yeah, you." Both Logan and Dimitri responded, laughing along with her.

"Well, this isn't my fault. I blame that little red wolf you all said you were so fond of. She's a bit excited to be out and about. How am I supposed to contain her?"

"Ah, Logan. I fear your mate's learning already."

"Oldest trick in the book, baby. Blame it on the wolf," he joked.

Wynter felt light and tired, but sated. "Thank you, both of you. I can't imagine doing any of this on my own."

Dimitri pulled away and went to get a towel.

"Where do you think you're going, beta?" Logan didn't want him to leave just yet.

"Be back in a minute," he called, going outside.

"Why don't I feel strange about this?" Wynter asked Logan. "And why don't you feel jealous?"

"I love him, Wyn. He's been there for me when no one was. And you?" *I love you…more than words can say.* "You're my mate."

"It really was special. But it's you…you changed my life." Tears brimmed in her eyes. "You saved me. If you hadn't been there…I just don't know…"

"Sweetheart, come on now. No tears. You were spectacular." He stroked her hair.

The tears that followed broke his heart. It wasn't that he didn't understand why. She'd just shifted. Her life was forever revolutionized. Gone was her human self that she'd always known. There was no going back.

Dimitri unerringly let the door slam and looked over to see Wynter sniffling. Considering the situation, he went with humor. "I leave for five minutes. Five freakin' minutes and this's what happens? No, no, no. Not having it."

He handed Logan warm washcloths and was relieved to hear a small laugh spill out of Wynter.

"Sorry, I'm just feeling....a little overwhelmed." She wiped the tears away with her fingers, and gave them a small smile. "See, all better, really."

"You okay now?" Logan asked with a brush of his lips to the back of her hand.

"I'm good. Promise," she replied softly.

It had been a long day for all of them and he knew exactly why Wynter had cried. He loved her so much, and like a dam bursting, the emotions of the night had escalated them all to a new high. As he proceeded to gently clean her, he wondered if his tiny mate had any idea that she held his heart in her hands.

Wynter cuddled into Logan's embrace, wishing the night would never end. She couldn't stop thinking about how much she loved Logan. As if she had been crashed over by the waves of a tsunami, her heart had been swept up by the Alpha.

Chapter Twenty-Six

Interesting, the Mistress thought. She watched through the tall grass as the red wolf pinned the white one. Absurdly strong and alpha, Wynter might be more difficult to kill than she'd anticipated. The Mistress knew her intellectual acuity far exceeded her physical capabilities. This was exactly why she needed the virus to bring the Acadian Wolves to their knees.

She snickered, amused by their show of dominance. It was a farce. The Mistress, through her loving command, would teach them all what true domination looked like. No more challenges would exist under her sovereignty. Her fanged beasts would cower as would the bloodsucking paranormals who sought dominion over wolves. The Directeur had met her needs nicely, doing her bidding as she saw fit. But even he would become obsolete once the Mistress snared control of the pack. For now though, she'd indulge his fantasies.

Fascinated by Wynter's shift, the Mistress drooled in anticipation of the day she'd kill the abomination they'd created. Wynter's blood was ready, thoroughly metamorphosed by her transformation. It belonged to the Mistress. Like a ripened grape, it was time to pluck it off its vine, crush its flesh and strain the juice. Yes, it was time to reap what she'd sown. She smiled in delight. *Enjoy your victory, little Red Riding Hood, the cold embrace of death will be coming for you soon.*

Logan swore out loud when he read the tattered note: *I'm coming for her soon. Enjoy your last days. The Scientifique is mine.* Who the hell could have walked onto his land and shoved it under his front door? He snapped a picture with his phone and messaged it to both Chandler and Devereoux. Afterward, he immediately called Dimitri and insisted they run a background check on the owner of the known lab locations. Frustrated, he couldn't sit back and wait for Devereoux to figure out who had taken Wynter. They'd find the killer on their own, without the vampire.

He asked Dimitri to scrub the laptop again before turning it over to Wynter. They'd analyze every last email, every last byte of data to see if there was a pattern to the flow of information. The hardest decision Logan had to make was not telling Wynter about the ominous message that'd been left for them. She'd been through so much distress over the past few months; he didn't have the heart to worry her. There wasn't a thing she could do about it anyway.

As expected, Wynter had been exhilarated when he'd

shown her the newly created lab. It was the least he could do, considering the circumstances. Immediately, she started taking blood samples, not only from herself but from both him and Dimitri. At his request, Chandler donated his blood as well, and Emma's samples had been sent by FedEx from New York. Obsessed and determined, Wynter worked day and night.

Selfishly, Logan wanted more time with her, but the lab provided her with a welcome distraction, keeping her safely in his home. Even though the killer had found out where she was staying, Logan had increased security, ensuring no one could get into the house without his permission. The place had been sealed tight, preventing further attacks. It'd be a cold day in hell before they took her from here, he thought.

The most difficult task for Logan had become resisting his growing need to mate. Each time they made love, he fumbled to tell her how he felt. Goddess, he loved her. But he wanted the memories of their love to be untainted, and right now, they both were obsessed with the killer. Their mating should be extraordinary and peaceful, not laced with the flashbacks of hatred and death.

For the past two days, Wynter had done nothing but work and make love. As wonderful as it was, she still hadn't told Logan she loved him again. Always on the tip of her tongue, she felt as if she was waiting for the right moment. She kept thinking it would be when they mated but he'd delayed it. She wasn't sure of the technicalities of mating, but her wolf was not at all happy. Logan told her that he wanted to wait until they caught the killer. But a small part of her questioned his decision. Why didn't he want to mate with her now? Her wolf didn't understand and neither did she. Why hadn't he told her he loved her? Admittedly, she felt his love every time he smiled at her or caressed her hair, but something about those three little words…she needed to hear it, to tell him. Hell, she needed to tell the whole damn world.

As she looked at the data, she held her excitement with bated breath. While her own blood had showed abnormalities compared to typical wolf samples, unusual gene markers indicated significant anti-viral capabilities. She'd extracted the genes, inserting them into Emma's samples. As impossible as it seemed, her blood had irrevocably irradiated the virus. Given that random mutations could occur within human populations, she considered that perhaps somehow Emma's immune system had been weakened. As she'd known, Emma's blood, as hybrid, didn't register as pure wolf. Her human genes adulterated the wolf genes which provided immunity. A miniscule variation existed within the genetic code. Her initial assumption that Emma had been deliberately infected appeared to be a less plausible theory than random mutation.

But who had genetically modified her own blood? How did they do it? All the time she'd lived in captivity, had they been working on the genetic alteration suspecting it would cure Emma's affliction? If that was true, Wynter's blood had been cultivating for weeks as if she were a human petri dish.

No wonder they wanted her so badly. But how would they know if their experiment had worked? They couldn't have known she'd shifted for sure, could they? If they knew she'd successfully shifted, they'd want her back…her blood. Like a possession to be owned, they'd seek out their experiment and wouldn't stop until they had her back. With the virus and the antidote, they'd be able to blackmail, extort and torture others at will.

Startled by her discovery, Wynter inserted the needle into her vein. As she collected the vials, Logan knocked on the door. It was time to tell him. She wanted Jax to personally take her blood to Emma. She'd send the instructions for delivering her plasma in the right dose.

"Hey sweetheart…whoa, what ya doin' there?" Logan asked.

"It's my blood. I'm doing my final tests. I was right," she confirmed with a tight smile.

Logan kissed her cheek and quickly backed away, giving her space to finish. He took a seat at her desk next to where she was standing, grabbing a container of bandages off of a tray.

"I need to get this blood to Emma."

"Okay." Logan's brow creased with worry. Her heartbeat raced, and he could tell she'd come to some kind of conclusion he wasn't going to want to hear.

"They won't stop looking for me, Logan. They'll need my blood. They created me…my wolf," she began.

"I won't let them have you. They can't get you here," Logan interrupted. "Listen to me; that bastard may have done something to you, but that doesn't change who you are inside."

"Don't you see? My genetic structure's been altered. I'm not like you. I'm not human. I'm a monster."

"No, you're not. Stop with this. You're perfect the way you are. Don't ever think otherwise."

Wynter shook her head. Her small smile never reached her eyes, because she knew the truth about what they'd done to her. She loved him so much. She loved that he didn't care what she was or that her genetics weren't quite wolf or human. But she knew her next suggestion wasn't going to go over well. With a small tug, she withdrew the needle from her arm, applying pressure with cotton to the pinhole in her flesh. Later, she planned on extracting more blood, increasing the quantity to pints. If something happened to her, she wanted to make sure there was enough of her blood for future research…for a cure. She steeled her resolve and wiped the bead of sweat from her forehead.

Without asking, Logan readied a Band-Aid. He gently took her arm and applied the dressing.

Wynter blew out a breath, and looked up into his concerned eyes.

"I think we need to use me as bait." There, she'd said it.

"No," Logan told her firmly, without missing a beat. What the hell had she been thinking? So not happening, he thought.

"Please, Logan, just hear me out. He's coming for me. *They're* coming for me. It could be more than one person. Léopold said he made other vampires. Anyway, it doesn't matter. I don't want to just wait here like a sitting duck. We could use me to draw him out, then you and Léopold could catch him. It's the only way..."

"No," Logan repeated. He released her arm and took note of at least fifty vials of blood, Wynter's blood.

"But why won't you listen? I'm telling you that I'm what they want. I'm their antidote. They won't give up. I don't know how they figured out that my blood would cure Emma. They could already have samples of my pre-shift blood. I didn't test it, but it's possible that even then my cells could have cured the virus. If we set up a trap...you could be there. I wouldn't be in any real danger."

"I said no." Logan slammed his palm onto the desk a little harder than he intended. He wasn't so much angry with Wynter as he was with the entire situation. But she needed to understand how serious he was. He didn't want her wandering off and doing something foolish that could put her and the whole pack in danger.

"And for the record, I am listening. But as Alpha, I've made the decision. You will not be used as 'bait' as you so casually put it. I've asked Dimitri to track down the IP address locations of every incoming and outgoing email on that laptop. Within the day, we should have the information we need to look at patterns, possibly identifying where they went next. We cannot risk having something happen to you. No, let me rephrase that, I will not risk having something happen to you."

He glanced again at all the blood-filled tubes. "I'm already concerned something's happening to you. What the hell is with all the blood, Wyn?"

"I'm fine," she dismissed him. Standing too quickly caused her to wobble. He rushed to her side and placed her back in the chair.

"Sweetheart, what are you doing?" Logan knelt before her and exposed her inner arm sporting the bandage.

"I said I'm fine." She pushed at his hand and looked away. Admittedly, she'd taken too much blood, but with her preternatural healing, her sense of balance would quickly return.

"Talk to me, Wyn. What's going on?" Logan shook his head. Damn stubborn little wolf.

A tear threatened to fall from her left eye and she deftly captured it with a finger.

"I just…I know that they aren't going to give up. I don't know about Emma's illness. If it's a random genetic abnormality, then it could happen to another hybrid. The chances are small but I just thought if I stored enough of my blood…I didn't have any bags here or an IV, so I started with the vials…" Stupid, stupid idea, she thought. A cloud of desperation rained overhead.

"Baby, look at me." Logan waited until her red-rimmed eyes met his. "This virus, we only know of one wolf, one hybrid who's been affected. You told me yourself that you don't believe it's mutated yet. Jax will get your blood to Emma. He can be there within the day. As for all this blood…" Logan paused and glanced to the vials.

"It's admirable that you want to store it for future use in case we need it. I get that. But you can't beat yourself up about this. Nor should you turn yourself into a pincushion. If you want to store some bags, we'll order the IV supplies and make it happen and do it later. Right now, though, you need to take care of yourself. You've been working nonstop, barely eating or sleeping. I need you," he told her lovingly.

"I'm just so worried. Something's going to happen. Something bad. I can feel it. I need to make sure there're enough samples of my blood in case..." She knew Logan only wanted to protect her, but the overwhelming sense of foreboding shadowed her thoughts.

Logan refused to admit his visions. It was a dark part of him that he'd openly share with her once she was safe. Last night, the nightmare had surfaced once again. This time, it was clearer; Wynter's face, her neck splayed open. He screamed while the life drained from her body. Refocusing, Logan rubbed her knee and placed his forehead on her thigh.

"I know you're worried. But you have to trust me." He raised his head and took her hands into his. "I'm not going to use you as a lure. I love you too goddamn much. You're not just my mate, you're everything to me."

Wynter's heart caught in her chest. *He loved her.* As the words fell from his lips, she took his face into her hands, and he kissed her palm. "I love you too. My Alpha, I love you so much."

Logan pulled her down into his embrace, kissing her forehead, her cheeks and finally claimed her soft trembling lips. Gently, he coaxed her mouth open, his tongue found hers and they lost themselves in their love, reaffirming their future. Hearts bursting with passion, they took their time exploring and tasting each other.

Logan tore his lips away, pressing his forehead to hers. Chest to chest, their lips were mere inches away from one another.

"I want you to know how badly I want to mate with you. I love you more than life itself. But when we complete the ritual, it'll be without fear, without death. Our day, Wyn; it will belong to no one else but us, do you understand?"

"Logan, I've never felt like this in my life. I wondered why…why we hadn't. I don't understand it all but my wolf…she's there. I want to be your mate in every sense of the word."

"And you will be…forever." Logan captured her lips again, pouring reassurance and love into their kiss. Visions be damned, no one would take her from him…not ever.

The next day Fiona called the house asking if Wynter could go into town to shop. As much as Wynter wanted to get out, she and Logan decided that it wasn't safe for her to leave. At Fiona's suggestion, Logan reluctantly agreed to a short boat ride, allowing the girls to do some crabbing. He figured they all could use an hour or two relaxing. After being cooped up in the house, their wolves were going stir crazy. He hadn't told Wynter yet, but he and Dimitri had narrowed down a few locations where they suspected the killers might have been. Tonight, they planned, along with

Devereoux, to do reconnaissance.

When Fiona contacted Wynter, she felt relieved that a member of the pack showed interest in getting to know her. Before they left, she and Fiona ate a light brunch, discussing Dana's passing and also Luci's challenge. Wynter had been worried that other females would read her aggression as being unfriendly, but Fiona showed no animosity. Rather, she explained that even though she and Luci were friends, it was the way of wolves. She did, however, thank her for showing mercy and not killing the she-wolf.

By the time she'd made it down to the dock, Wynter's optimism had returned. The winter sun beat down, warming her exposed skin. Logan brushed a kiss to her cheek, helping Wynter onto the boat. She spied the red and white race vessel, wondering how fast it would go. As she made her way onto its deck, she settled into a comfortable leather seat. Fiona followed her, bringing a bushel of branches she'd secured into a tarp. Wynter knew it had something to do with the crabs but wasn't sure for what. Drinking in the sight of Logan preparing for launch, she couldn't help but notice his well-defined pecs that strained against his white t-shirt. As he pushed on his sunglasses and went to work, Wynter smiled at how totally unaware he was of his uber-sexy presence.

The sleek Cigarette purred as Logan fired up the engine. Guarding Wynter was his priority. There was no way he'd let her go out on the lake by herself with Fi. She'd been right about them coming for her. Despite not seeing the threatening letter they'd delivered to his home, she knew. If he didn't discover the lab's location with the new intel, it'd just be a matter of time before they attacked. A strike in broad daylight was unlikely, but the hum of the six hundred horsepower engine put his mind at ease. Another boat would be hard pressed to outrun his speedboat if they tried.

Unbeknownst to Wynter, Logan had assigned Jake to take up the north shore where Fiona planned on laying her crab trap. A trained sniper, he'd scan the area for trouble. Zeke took his post, fishing at the old Hanover dock, a mile off from where they'd set out to make their stop. It seemed like a lot of work for one run out to the lake. But Wynter was wound tight, and he felt his wolf pacing in response. Their self-imposed seclusion was taking its toll on both of them. He wasn't built to stay indoors for days at a time. Even in the city, he'd get out, running as a human. His dream home felt like it had turned into a prison. The fresh air would do them all some good, and later in the evening, he and Dimitri would resume the search for the killer.

By the time they reached the open lake, Wynter felt as if a weight had lifted. The high speed boat ride had been exhilarating. It was as if the wind against her face had blown away her cobwebs of worry. It wasn't lost on Wynter how much trouble Logan had gone to so they could get out of the house. Part of her knew he just wanted to get her out of the lab so she'd stop obsessing about the virus. Her work would never be done, she thought. Regardless, it warmed her heart that he'd protect her and go to such great lengths so they could all have a few fun hours in the sun.

Soon, they'd reached their destination, and Logan cut

the engine. The long, thin dance boat bobbed in the open water. Logan gave the go ahead to the girls. He took Wynter's hand and helped her up the steps so she could lay out on the bow. She shook off her shoes, preferring to go barefoot. Even though it was February, the weather was expected to go into the eighties, so she'd thrown on a bathing suit underneath her clothes. Carefully, she trod onto the smooth fiberglass, laid out an oversized beach towel and sat down. Fiona trailed behind her, carrying the large bound bundle of sprigs.

"Hey, girl, can you hold this rope for me?" Fiona asked, letting the blue tarp fall open onto the bow.

"What are you doing?"

"Oh this? It's Wax Myrtle. I'm goin' bunch it up and throw it into the lake."

Wynter gave her a confused look and glanced back to Dimitri and Logan who didn't look at all surprised. She thought it funny that with such an expensive shiny toy, he could have cared less that Fiona had just laid out a huge canvas on it. She loved that no matter his means, at the end of the day, Logan was down to earth. No pretenses, what you saw was what you got.

Fiona began to tie up the branches and continued. "Yeah, the pre-molt crabs love this stuff. They crawl in and then we'll come back later, pull it out and shake 'em out. Normally, I'd haul this mess in my little skiff, but since that's not an option today, Logan said I could bring it here. Anyway, about the crabs, we catch 'em before their shells return, then we'll eat soft shell crabs."

"Oh," Wynter said, amazed. "So...uh...how did you learn to do this?'

"My daddy. Some folks sell 'em. I just eat 'em. Tasty little critters," she commented as she worked to bale up the plants. Plucking off a leaf, she crushed it and handed it over to Wynter. "Smell."

Wynter took the gooey green mixture and sniffed. She thought better of commenting about Fiona's father, remembering what Logan had told her. "Mmm...nice."

"Yeah, isn't it? They've been using it for hundreds of years. It's our way." Fiona eyed Wynter as she continued to handle the aromatic plant. "You really are a city girl, aren't ya?"

"Born and bred. I may not know how to catch crabs but I can get you from Midtown to Soho faster than anyone else...even at rush hour," she joked. "Have you ever been to the Big Apple?"

Fiona tightened the knots. "Um, yeah. Was there a few years ago. Art show...a charity event. I'm very interested in new artists. I have a little gallery in the quarter. Well, it's more of a natural herb and art gallery combo. I'm technically the pack healer, but that doesn't pay the bills," she quipped.

"I'd love to see it sometime, the art. I haven't spent much time in New Orleans, but it really is very unique. You can feel the history speaking to you, if you know what I mean."

"So Wyn, how are you doing? What I mean is, how do you like being a wolf?" Fiona changed the subject, hurling the bundle overboard. A red bullet-shaped crab float tugged at the surface. She folded up the tarp.

"I've only shifted once, but yes. Logan, he's..." She gave him a backwards glance. She couldn't see his eyes behind the sunglasses but suspected he was watching her. Wynter searched for the right words to describe her situation, unsure how much to share with the young she-wolf. Fiona seemed friendly but she also was friends with Luci. "He's been very supportive."

"Ah, is that what you humans call it? Supportive? I bet he's been very supportive...all day and all night long, huh? Just look at that mark on your neck." Fiona rolled her eyes and relaxed against the side of the boat.

Wynter laughed and absentmindedly traced her fingers over her shoulder. She looked over again at Logan who smiled at her. Deciding on honesty, she turned back to Fiona.

"He's my mate." There, she'd said it. She'd told one person, a friend, about Logan. And it felt freeing and girly. She wished Mika was the first friend she'd told. But Fiona had been kind enough to bring her out on the water, care about how she was doing.

"And?" Fiona drawled with a wicked smile.

"And what?" Wynter asked coyly.

"Do you love him?" Fiona whispered as if she was getting ready to hear a national secret.

Wynter knew Logan could hear every word of their conversation but still, Fiona insisted on whispering. It struck Wynter as funny and she began to giggle, as did Fiona. Just as she was going to respond, something caught her attention. To the east, a medium-sized, black sailboat drifted toward them.

"Hey, that boat over there. He's coming toward us," Wynter observed with a growing panic. As far as she was concerned, any stranger was a potential threat.

Logan pulled out the binoculars. A man in white shorts and a pink polo shirt struggled with the sail control lines while a woman lay on the blood-tinged deck. He suspected she was down with a boom injury. Even experienced sailors were susceptible to accidents, but by the look of things, the man on deck appeared confused, lines strewn every which direction. *Damn fools.* Too many times an overconfident wannabe rented too much of a boat and ended up needing rescue.

"A tourist," Dimitri offered, after taking a look for himself.

"Yeah, probably," Logan hedged. He opened a storage hatch and pulled out his Beretta. The Alpha and his beta exchanged an unspoken conversation at the sight of the weapon. "Just in case."

"Here she comes. About fifty feet off. She's gonna hit starboard," Dimitri warned. He pulled open the back storage compartment and pulled out a couple of boat fenders. He handed one off to Logan and they tied them to the cleats to prevent damage.

"Hold on there. Girls, sit tight," Logan told them as the boat approached. He fired up the engine and then unlocked the safety on the gun. The sailboat slowed as it approached, lightly bumping their speedboat.

The stranger looked to be in his early twenties. His preppy shirt was dotted in crimson stains. The woman on deck laid still, her face away from them.

"Oh my God, I'm so sorry, mister. The boom, it just snapped. Now my girlfriend's hurt. I swear I've had a few lessons, but I can't seem to figure out this radio," he blabbered.

It was a good show, Logan thought. Still, something seemed off. He could hear the hum of the other boat's engine. He sniffed. More than two scents filtered through the air, both vampire and human. Logan knew that although vampires could be extraordinarily dangerous at night, they were rendered virtually human during the daytime.

"We'd be happy to call it in. Anyone else on board?" Logan inquired.

"No sir, just me and my girl. Listen, she took a bad hit to the head. You wouldn't happen to have a first aid kit? This boat's a rental. I can't find anything," he said, rubbing his eyes.

Liar. Logan tightened his grip on the gun.

"D, get on the radio and call it in," he directed.

Never taking his eyes off the man, Logan looked at the woman splayed on the deck, using his peripheral vision. Dammit, she lay unmoving. He hated to leave someone in peril, especially in the middle of the lake, but he'd send another boat to investigate. His immediate concern was getting Wynter away from the stranger. The sailboats glided side by side so that the bows were even, and Logan wrapped his hand around the throttle. But before he had a chance to gun the boat, Fiona quickly stood up and jumped over to the other boat.

"Fiona," Wynter cried, grasping into the air as she tried to pull her back. Wynter rushed to the side of the boat nearest to Fiona, extending her hand to her, hoping she'd jump back. "What are you doing? Get back here."

Too late, Fiona had already gone to the woman. "What does it look like I'm doing? I'm going to help her."

Logan had been so focused on the man, he hadn't had a chance to stop Fiona. What the hell did she think she was doing? Pack healer or not, she'd better get back on the damn boat. Both he and Dimitri tensed at the sight.

"Fi, back on the boat now," Logan demanded, never taking his eyes off the stranger.

"But I can help her. She's still breathing. It may just be a concussion."

"Not a question. It's an order. Get your ass back here now," Logan growled.

Wynter observed the interaction, scrutinizing the slain woman. She swore that she wasn't breathing. Her hands looked too pale...gray. What kind of healing did Fiona think she was doing? That woman was dead.

"Logan," Wynter croaked into a gust of wind. Could he, too, see the woman was not alive? Confusion swept over her.

Logan could not understand why Fiona, a naturally submissive she-wolf, was defying his direct order. There was no time to contemplate her punishment. No, the only decision was to leave Fiona on the sailboat. He knew

Dimitri wouldn't be happy, but he needed to get Wynter to safety. Something wasn't right.

Fiona busily fussed with the woman, flipping her over onto her back, blocking their view. It appeared she was attempting some kind of resuscitation.

"I need help," Fiona said, ignoring Logan.

The stranger knelt next to Fiona as if to provide assistance, then yanked her upward toward him. He pulled a gun, aiming it at her head. Using her as a human shield, he kept her in between him and Logan.

"Let her go," Logan demanded. He pointed his gun at him, but couldn't get a clear shot off.

"No, I don't think I will," he laughed. "Do you know what a silver bullet can do to a wolf's brain? Messy, messy. She may survive. Maybe not though."

"It's two against one, asshole, put the gun down," Logan insisted. He sensed Dimitri behind him, who'd also aimed a gun.

The stranger continued to laugh. "You kill me, I kill the girl." He pulled Fiona's hair, making her scream. "Tell you what; I'll make a trade. This girl for that one." His eyes fell onto Wynter.

"Not happening," Logan snarled.

Wynter began to crouch backwards. She'd gone too close to the other boat when she'd gone to retrieve Fiona.

"Don't move, Wynter," the stranger called out to her.

Wynter froze. *How did he know her name? Oh God no, they really are here for me.*

"I have sharpshooters on land," Logan explained coolly. "You'll never get away."

As if Logan and Dimitri weren't in the boat, the man continued to speak to Wynter. "You want to save your friend, doctor?"

"What?" Wynter gasped.

"I said; do you want to save your friend here? You know these wolves aren't as tough as you'd think. Not so hard to kill them, really. With silver in her brain, it'll take her months to recover. No, a shift won't fix this so easily, I'm afraid."

"Don't listen to him, Wyn," Logan yelled.

Wynter looked up at Fiona, whose cheeks and neck were streaked with tears. She couldn't quite see her eyes because her head had been wrenched backward.

"What do you want from me?" Wynter screamed at him. It felt as if a black tunnel was closing in, she couldn't escape. She couldn't live with the blood of another wolf on her hands. It was her fault they'd come to Logan's pack. Her responsibility. She should be the one to die, not Fiona.

"But you already know the answer to that, don't you, Dr. Ryan? Shame to kill this she-wolf, but we will. In fact, we'll take out this whole damn pack if we have to, but I guarantee you this, it will not end. You belong to him. He will not stop. I know he'll take special pleasure in killing your Alpha. Don't think we can't get to him. We left him a note the other day…right at his door."

Shocked, Wynter looked over to Logan. No, it couldn't be true. Logan would have told her.

"Wynter, don't listen to him," Logan cautioned. Wynter's face had gone white. "Get away from the side of the boat."

The stranger laughed maniacally. "I see the great Alpha is keeping secrets from his mate. It's true. The very night you shifted, we were at his house."

"Logan?" Wynter questioned. When he didn't answer right away, she knew it was true. They'd been at his home? Dear God, if they could get to her there, there'd be nowhere they couldn't find her.

"Wynter, listen to me, now. It was just a note. No one was in the house. Fiona, she'll be fine. She's a strong wolf."

"You lie, Alpha. Do you really think I'd bring a knife to a gunfight? These hollow-cavity bullets will mushroom her brain apart with one shot. She's not going to make it back, not like she used to be anyway. And that's if she manages to shift afterwards. No, this little girl's goin' to pop like fireworks."

Wynter tried to drown out his words but it was no use. Her own guilt tore at her heart. Was she really going to sit and do nothing while this monster put a bullet in Fiona's head? God, she loved Logan…so much. Reverting to her training, she considered the known facts, the data. True, Logan would be angry if she sacrificed herself for Fiona. But his boat was powerful, much more so than the small sailboat. Logan would follow, save her and Fiona, too, would be safe. The most important fact was that if she didn't go, another Acadian wolf would die…at her hands.

"Your choice. What's it going to be? You or the wolf?" He dug the muzzle into Fiona's temple and she screamed.

Logan could see that Wynter was lost in her thoughts. Goddammit all, she was considering it. As much as he cared for Fiona, he couldn't lose his mate. His breath caught and he lunged to restrain Wynter to keep her from going. Dimitri broke for the throttle.

"I'm sorry," Wynter cried softly as she leapt over to the sailboat. She skidded onto the deck and fell to her knees.

"No!" Logan screamed. "No, he's going to kill you. Get back here now."

Wynter's body collapsed into the rough landing. She scrambled to stand upright but the man kicked her in the stomach. Her face hit the side of the boom, tearing her lip open.

"Let her go," Wynter pleaded. Her face throbbed but she breathed through it. "You don't need Fiona…just take my blood. No more…no more…I'll do whatever you want. Let her go now."

The stranger cackled wildly and threw Fiona to the floor. With a jerk, the engine roared to life and the boat sped forward. Wynter attempted to push Fiona into the water. If they could get off the boat they'd have a chance.

"Jump," she told her, but Fiona held tight to a cleat.

Logan tore to the helm and jammed the throttle forward. They hadn't gotten far. In his speedboat, they could easily catch up and he'd jump over to get Wynter. But his boat lurched only a few feet before the motor died.

"What the fuck? This is a brand new boat," Logan cursed, banging the dashboard. "Take the wheel." He jumped in the back to check the inboard. Within seconds, he'd located the source of the issue. "Shit. There's a nick in the fuel tank fill hose."

Logan spun and aimed his gun at the tall dark figure that had Wynter by the arm. He knew he could hit him but the man slyly pulled Wynter against him as a shield. Targeting the engine, Logan fired off six shots to the stern. The bullets ricocheted off the screeching motor. As the man instinctively moved to the right to look at the damage, Logan pulled the trigger again, clipping him in the shoulder. He watched the pink-shirted form hit the deck but no longer could he see Wynter, as she too, had fallen.

Pain shot through Wynter's body as fingers grabbed her hair, pulling her to her feet. The man slammed her up against him, holding the gun to her head. With her back to his chest, she faced Logan whose boat grew smaller as the distance between them widened. A loud gunshot jolted Wynter, and she tried to wretch her body out of his grip. Blood sprayed as more shots rang out. As she felt his grip loosen, Wynter tumbled onto the deck. She clawed at the slippery surface, intending to jump, when the chill of a second voice blanketed her consciousness. As she caught a glimpse of the familiar face, her heart stopped. *The Directeur?*

A blur of revolting confusion and hopelessness overtook her body. No, this couldn't be happening. Wynter glanced at Fiona who now sat comfortably, almost peacefully staring toward the horizon. Deception. Betrayal. The Directeur grabbed Wynter, pulling her off her feet into his deadly embrace. She prayed for strength as she let the anger roll through her mind. Anger was good, she thought. It might be the only thing that would save them all.

The sailboat careened away while Dimitri and Logan helplessly watched in disbelief. One fucking hour on the lake. Four men on guard, and within seconds, they'd taken her and Fiona. As they sped off into the distance, the miles-wide freshwater sanctuary hid their path of escape. Logan screamed out to the heavens in agony. His mate was gone.

"Search every goddamned house," Logan growled.

"I'm sorry," Dimitri offered.

"No, D. No words. Action. You," Logan pointed to Zeke and Jake, "every boat. Every pack member needs to be accounted for. I want every wolf up at Marcel's old place now. I don't give a shit who's in the city. Every damn wolf is to get their ass back here immediately," he ordered. "Someone came into the marina today and cut that hose. I want to see the video now."

Enraged, Logan paced as he barked out orders. Someone had betrayed him, he was certain of it. First the car bomb. Now this. No, it wasn't happenstance that the hose was cut. It had been deliberately done in such a way to allow them enough gas to go out to the lake, but not enough to get back. Whoever had done it knew exactly where they were going and how long they'd be on the lake. It may have been a vampire who'd killed Dana, but it was a wolf who had helped coordinate Wynter's abduction. No one but one of his own wolves would have had access to his boat.

"The pack will be at Marcel's soon. You want to ride

with?" Dimitri asked, trying to block the emotion he felt emanating from Logan. His Alpha's caustic rage seethed through his own brain as if they were his own thoughts.

Logan shook him off. As much as he loved D, he couldn't bear to be near him. He was scarcely containing his beast as his unbridled wrath escalated. It wouldn't be good for Dimitri to be so close to him.

"I'm taking my bike. You take the SUV." Logan stopped and rubbed his eyes. "Seriously, D. This ends tonight. I'm going to tear up this entire swamp looking for her. She's got to be here. Every single marina's been secured. No one could land a chopper except at the helipad. Jake's sent men to check the outposts along the lake. No, whoever's done this is still here."

"Hey, I'm with ya, but we're talking about literally thousands of square acres of swamp. In the dark. They could pull off anywhere, skip into a car and be gone."

"No," Logan growled. "Wynter's here. I can feel her."

"But why would they stay here…it doesn't make sense. Logan, I think…"

"Because they're goin' to kill her. They don't need her anymore. My guess is now that she's turned, all they want is her blood." Logan took a deep breath and blew it out, trying to think clearly. "Text Devereoux. I want him here now. And before you ask, I don't care how he gets here. Send the bird if you need to. His line is responsible for this fucking mess. I'll kill him myself if he doesn't comply and you can quote me on that."

Dimitri pulled out his phone and started making calls.

Logan went to his gun safe that was located in the laundry room. He extracted several guns, ammo, and strapped on a harness. He preferred to go wolf, but he wasn't taking any chances. In the bayou, his wolf may not be able to get to shore fast enough. A bullet, however, would.

By the time they'd reached Marcel's home, Logan was convinced he knew who had sabotaged his boat. Ferocious, his wolf sought revenge. Nothing but having his mate back safely in his arms would assuage his rage. He killed the engine and jumped off his motorcycle.

"Hold up, Alpha," Jake called over to him.

"What'd you find out?"

"I don't know…it doesn't make sense," Jake hedged, incredulous as to what he'd seen on the video.

Luci rushed over to Logan, eyes down. "Alpha," she greeted.

At the sight of her, Logan lost it. If anyone had reason to attack him and Wynter, it had been Luci. He should have recognized her aggressive behavior. How she'd connected with the vampires, he didn't know, but he was about to damn well find out why.

"Just where the hell do you think you're going?" As Luci turned to walk away, Logan grabbed her arm.

Jake stepped between them.

"Jake, get out of my way. This is between Luci and me," he snarled.

"But Alpha," Jake began.

"I told you, Luci and I have business." Logan turned his gaze back to her. "I should have known better than to let you stay in the pack. You've been so hot to get in my bed ever since he died. Seriously, did you even care about Marcel? Now listen good, I'm only going to ask you this once. What did you do with Wynter?"

"I didn't…I swear. It wasn't me," she cried.

"Where. Is. She?"

"I didn't…"

Jake put his hand over Logan's, risking a fight. He couldn't let Logan continue after Luci, even though she deserved at least a little bit of his ire.

"Alpha, please. You need to see this," he pleaded.

"What?" Logan asked. His eyes flared.

"The video. Your boat. Luci didn't do it. But someone else from the pack is on there…I'm sorry," Jake said, shaking his head.

"Who? Who did this?" Logan demanded.

"See for yourself." Jake pulled out his mini iPad, and pressed the play button.

Logan couldn't believe it. Of all the people in his pack, it made no sense. The person hadn't even tried to hide from the camera. Instead after they'd cut the line, the perpetrator purposefully stared into the lens and smiled.

Chapter Twenty-Seven

Wynter's wolf whined in agonizing pain, begging to shift. Instinctively, she knew a transformation could heal her injuries, but as she called on her wolf, nothing happened. Her head lolled back against a rough surface and she licked her cracked lips. An iron-tinged crust stuck to her tongue. She felt heavy, drained. Wynter slid her fingertips down her sides and felt metal on her midsection. She shook her head, willing her eyes to open. As she looked to her torso, she was shocked to see the silver chainmail corset that had been fastened to her body. Tugging at the seams, she couldn't get it to budge.

The lethargy didn't stop her from scanning the room for a clue to where they'd taken her. *A dilapidated cabin? Was it the cabin they'd been in the night she shifted?* The lack of screened windows and rotted wood told her no. Listening as Logan had taught her, she could hear the cicadas but other than that, she was met with silence. She knew, though, that she had to be somewhere in the swamp.

Her plan had failed miserably. She wondered what had

happened to Logan. There was no way that boat could have outrun him. Why hadn't he come for her? Did they shoot him like they'd threatened to do to Fiona? Wynter stifled the small sob bubbling in her chest. She needed to conserve her energy. She needed to escape.

"You okay?" Wynter heard the question and glanced over to see Fiona sitting in a chair.

It appeared her hands had been fastened behind her back. But there was something odd about her demeanor and posture. On the boat, after Wynter had tried to get her to jump, she'd held on. Then within minutes, she'd rested on the boat, almost as if she were relaxed, content. But now, Fiona had been bound. Had Wynter imagined what she'd seen? No, there had definitely been something strange about Fiona's behavior and even now, her face was bright. Unlike Wynter, whose face was bruised and puffy from crying, Fiona's complexion was clear. But why would Fiona help the vampire? And why was she playing a victim unless she weren't one?

"I'm fine. I can't shift. What is this thing?" Wynter asked, trying to act unsuspecting.

"Silver," Fiona responded without even looking.

"Our kryptonite."

"What?"

"A human throwback. Superman."

"It won't kill you," Fiona told her with an icy stare. "The vampire. He wants to know what you know about the virus."

Wynter gave her a sardonic smile and laughed bitterly.

"I just bet he fucking does. Well I wish him good luck with that."

"You have to tell him. He promised to let you go."

"No, he promised to let *you* go. And he didn't. You're still here, Fiona. He's a liar."

Fiona rolled her eyes. "The man on the boat? He's not in charge. No, I speak of the Directeur."

"What? How do you know that name?" Wynter demanded, attempting to stand. She bent her knees and pushed upward, bracing herself against the rickety wall.

"The Directeur told me himself. He wants to know if you managed to cure Emma's virus," Fiona said emotionlessly.

"How do you know about Emma?" Wynter found herself yelling.

"He told me. He said she's sick but that your blood, it'll cure her."

Wynter closed her eyes and took a deep breath. He knew about her blood as she'd suspected. A rush of nausea poured over her and she struggled not to vomit.

"He saw the New York Alpha in New Orleans. He knows that you sent blood to Emma…your blood. He watches you…always. So tell me, did it work?"

"Yes…yes it worked. Why do you care, Fiona? He's got you tied up. Why are you asking me these questions?"

"So it's true then. Have you figured a way to modify the virus? To make it portable?"

A chill crept up Wynter's spine. Fiona was privy to details…details no one but she and Logan knew. And she hadn't jumped from the boat. Was this all for show? Even if Wynter had been close at one time to isolating the virus, allowing others to inject it, she'd never tell a soul. She'd die first.

"No," she lied. "I haven't been working on it. Emma is cured; that's all that matters."

"He knows how to do it. He found a way while you were gone. Did you know he also is a scientist? Perhaps that is why he reveres you so?"

"What?" Wynter couldn't believe Fiona's words.

"It's been him all along. His company. His research."

"Why are you telling me this? How do you know so much about him? They were going to kill you out there on the lake. Why didn't you just jump when I told you to?" Wynter's voice strained. She eyed the door. So weak, but if she could make it outside maybe she could find something to remove the silver.

"I think it's time," Fiona said. She pushed out of the chair, placing her hands on her hips. Uninjured and altogether healthy, she gave Wynter an evil smile before clapping her hands. "Come."

The door flew open and a tall, good-looking vampire entered the room. She knew him...Yes, the man from the boat. Her mind swam with possibilities. No, she'd met him before...at the club...with Léopold. Shocked, Wynter tried to run but Fiona easily stepped in front of her and shoved her to the ground.

"You...you...how could you? And Fiona...Logan's going to kill you." Wynter heaved in a deep breath. On all fours, she looked up to the vampire.

"She really is naïve, isn't she?" Fiona merely laughed.

"You and Phillip shouldn't have hurt her. Just look at what you've done, Mistress. You cannot treat her this way if she's going to work for me." The vampire shot Fiona a nasty look, clearly not pleased.

"Work for you? Are you kidding me? Why would ViroSun be involved with something like this? Who are you?" Wynter laughed and cried at the same time. She rolled onto her bottom, unable to stand.

"Dear scientifique, one question at a time. May I?" He retrieved a crisp handkerchief from his suit pocket and attempted to give it to Wynter. She brushed him away.

"Very well then," he sniffed. "Let's start at the beginning, shall we? My name's Étienne. Étienne St. Claire, son of Kade Issacson sired by Léopold Devereoux. And as my Mistress has introduced, I am the Directeur."

He paced, letting his hands speak flamboyantly into the air.

"However, there is one small discrepancy you should know…you see, we are not ViroSun nor have we ever been. True, though they exist, we forged the necessary documentation to make you believe you were working for them."

"No, I went to the interview. The building, the stationery…I interviewed with them. I met with people. This isn't possible." Wynter shook her head in confusion.

"Ah well, all fake I'm afraid. A necessary expense to make you believe you were going to work for them. You were so eager to find a cure for your friend."

"But how did you know?"

"I travel to New York quite often. And lucky for me, I'd attended one of your speaking engagements. I found it quite captivating…the notion that someone, a supernatural, could be infected with a feline virus. She's a lovely speaker," he told Fiona, who rolled her eyes and pretended to look at her nails. "It didn't take long to find your 'Jane Doe'. Emma's medical records and her blood were easy enough to get at the hospital. I can be very convincing."

"But I'd been working…the lab. There were others with me," Wynter countered.

"Were there? We kept you isolated. Do you recall ever meeting anyone after you insisted on leaving?"

Speechless, Wynter closed her eyes. Like a great illusion, the curtain was revealed and she, the fool, was left the victim of a great hoax. How could this happen? She'd researched the company. The high pressure interview had been held in one of the most conspicuous midtown skyscrapers. They'd done intensive background checks, interviewed her friends, Jax.

"My scientifique, are you listening?"

"Stop calling me that!" Wynter cried.

"But you are so special," he insisted, trailing a long finger over her hair. "Really, darling, did you think you'd stay away from me so long? The Mistress, she's powerful, but I admit, I've crushed on you like a school boy."

"True," Fiona spat out in disgust. Her forehead furrowed. "He's quite obsessed. Too much so."

"But I digress. You see, Fiona and I, we knew each other from New Orleans. She's quite the devious little witch, but not so strong. Power doesn't come easily in the wolf pack...brawn over brains and such. And for me, let's say it's tedious being at Kade's beck and call. But this virus, if it could be used on wolves, well, one can easily extrapolate...vampires could be next."

Wynter shook uncontrollably and rubbed at her eyes. She felt her limbs grow cold. Was he insane? There was no way an animal virus could be transferred to vampires.

"I know what you're thinking. Little Emma's illness is a random mutation...it couldn't possible affect vampires. But the mutation is just a spark we need to turn our discovery into a blazing success. We need to think big...research new ways of modifying the genetic structure of those who are invincible. And as we've proven, even a human can be changed."

"What did you do...my cells? I have to know," Wynter pleaded, her voice barely audible. She stared into his cold black orbs. "You're sick, you know that?"

"Now, now. No need to be nasty. You should be grateful for what I've done to you. I've given you a gift." He smiled proudly.

"Grateful, are you fucking kidding?" Wynter coughed, nervously pulling at her own hair. She felt as if she was the one going insane. How could this be happening?

"I told you, darling. I'm a scientist. I've been playing with genetic material for many years. It's not exactly new technology. The humans have been tampering with their food supply for a while now, developing genetically modified crops and such. They're resistant to weeds, insects and so forth. They've even successfully developed animal organs for potential transplants. What I did to you was slightly more complicated, but in the same vein. The micro-injection of the recombinant DNA was quite easy once my vampires had you subdued. Really, no pain involved. Of course, unlike humans, ethics don't impede my experiments. No, my dear, this…your genetic transformation was my creation and mine alone…although I must thank Fiona for her genetic contribution. She's quite the sport. In the end, you've turned into a fabulously strong transgenic being, don't you agree?"

Unable to keep the bile down, Wynter turned her head to the side. The contents of her stomach spewed onto the floor and she coughed, wiping her mouth. Hearing the horrific details of what he'd done confirmed her suspicions. Forever altered, her genetic structure had been modified to wolf. She'd been an experiment, nothing more, nothing less.

"And I must say that my theory proved correct. Your blood cures the very virus that afflicts the hybrid. But I still do have one small problem. I've been working on it, of course, and am so very close, but I need to be able to transfer the virus to a pure wolf. For whatever reason, the random mutation isn't strong enough to transfer. And that my darling is why I need you."

"Me? My blood?" Wynter whispered.

"Well, of course we need your blood. And lots of it. But I need your mind, darling. With you at my side, doing research, we can make history together," he explained, taking a seat.

"Are you crazy? I told you I don't know anything. And even if I did, I wouldn't tell you," she snapped.

Étienne growled. Snagging Wynter by the arms, he hoisted her so far off the floor her toes scraped the boards. He held her at eye level, mere inches from his face. "You will do this. Or have you forgotten what used to happen when you refused? Perhaps you need a refresher," he sneered, baring his fangs. "I can't tell you how long I've waited. I won't be denied."

Without another word, Étienne pulled Wynter against his body and sliced his teeth into her neck.

Blinding, searing white hot pain speared down into Wynter's body. Not only had he taken her blood, it felt as if he'd stolen the very essence of her vitality. Optimism. Hope. Love. It had all been siphoned away by the monster draining her life force. Her pale lips parted in a silent scream yet the sound was lost in her chest. Wynter squeezed her eyes tight, her fingers digging into his arms in a futile effort to dislodge him. Like a rag doll hung on a hook, she could not shake free. The noose tightened around her neck, and she fought for air. Cloaked in evil, she prayed to God to take her soul.

Fiona whacked a chair over Étienne's back, causing him to release Wynter. As he raised a hand to strike Fiona, she held a sharp shard of wood to his back.

"You fool," she accused. "We need her blood for testing, for the antidote, and you can't control yourself for five fucking minutes. This is why you need me. You've got no discipline."

As if scolded by his mother, Étienne stepped away from them both and lowered his head. "But of course, Mistress. My apologies. She tempts me so."

"Touch her again and I'll stake you and that monstrosity you've created. Do you think I need you? This…all of this," she continued, looking around the room as if talking about a magical place, "is my doing. I found you, not the other way around. I came up with this plan, not you. And you are not going to fuck it up, do you hear me? Now stop screwing around with her, get her to the computer. We've got maybe three hours before Logan tracks us down, and I want to get out of here."

"Your blood, Dr. Ryan. So wild and pungent." Étienne glanced to Wynter who lay sobbing on the floor. "I do think that genetic modification upped your platelet count, because I feel energized."

"Would you stop pontificating and get her working?" Fiona implored.

"Get up," Étienne coerced, yanking Wynter by her arm. He dragged her across the floor to a small table, picked her up and righted her in the chair. Noticing her neck was still bleeding, he stole a glance at Fiona before dragging his tongue over the wound. He licked his lips. "See, I'm quite in control now."

"If you drink from her while I'm gone, you're dead," Fiona warned. "Keep it up and I'll leave you out here by yourself. Logan and the pack will tear you apart, do you understand? I'm the only one who knows how to get out of here. Get the data and then we're leaving."

"Yes, Mistress." Étienne capitulated. He gave Wynter a slap to her face and flipped open a laptop. "Wake up, scientifique. Time to work. Whatever you've worked on this past week, I want the information recorded now. Blood to virus ratios for the cure, viral portability, everything. The Mistress won't allow me another taste of your delectable blood but she didn't say anything about torture."

"That's better. You're a good boy," Fiona praised. She reached up to smooth over Étienne's hair. "Now, I have to go outside to check the boat. And Phillip too. I'll untie him now."

Satisfied with his obedience, Fiona smiled to herself. As the door to the cabin slammed behind her, she eyed Phillip, Étienne's child, who sat tied to a cypress tree, the silver cord bound around his neck so tightly that he could no longer speak. The acrid odor of burnt flesh lingered in the air. She smiled, picking a few splinters from the fragmented stake she'd created from the broken chair. Phillip's wide-eyed stare bled red streaks down his face. Fiona knelt before him, careful not to soil her skirt.

Phillip had served his purpose on the boat. Pity that he had to die, considering his spectacular performance. As Fiona had suspected, Wynter had bought their orchestrated farce hook, line and sinker. Of course the woman on the deck had been dead. Thankfully, Phillip had left enough blood dripping to make it look believable. Like a well-honed speaker, he'd given his oration and convinced Wynter to give herself up to save Fiona. Bleeding-hearted humans. Fiona had seen the look of guilt plastered across Wynter's face at the funeral. Logan, on the other hand, was about to leave her. As suspected, he'd choose his mate over her, a purebred wolf; all the more reason why he shouldn't be Alpha.

But she'd never be Alpha of Acadian Wolves as long as the ancient ways ruled pack law. She wasn't strong enough to challenge most females, let alone a male. Even her father, a virile male, hadn't been able to subjugate Marcel. Death had been his sentence for the challenge. Her plan had merely started out as revenge for her father's death. Convincing Calvin, Marcel's beta, that he was deserving of Alpha took little effort. Stroking his ego, planting the seed of his dream to rule the Acadian pack was ridiculously easy. She could have easily played alpha female to Calvin. But no, no, no. Unexpectedly, Logan had intervened, killing Calvin, and her only chance of ruling the pack.

Despite the mishap, her alternate plan, dominating the vampire, turned out to be quite ingenious. She'd met Étienne years before, allowing him to fuck and feed from her. When he'd told her of the story of the sick wolf, her idea struck like lightning. If she could control the virus and the antidote, she'd control the pack. Étienne, tired of being Kade's lackey, sought the same goal: power. He fancied himself a scientist of great aptitude and aspired to be known throughout history. She played up his fantasy, all the while directing his actions.

Her only mistake had been relying on Étienne to isolate

the virus, to turn it into a weapon. Even Wynter had failed to produce the virus in a way it could be injected, swallowed or otherwise used to infect another wolf. But this minor setback didn't deter Fiona. As she'd pored through the volumes of genetic and viral research, she believed it was just a matter of time before a researcher made the discovery. No longer convinced that person was Wynter, she planned to kill her after they got the information she'd gleaned about the antidote. They'd drain Wynter, taking her blood for future research.

Étienne's fascination with the girl had grown dangerous. There was no way Fiona could leave the wolf alive. Logan would never stop searching for his mate. Even if he didn't go after them, dragging Wynter through the swamp wasn't an option. A timely escape was paramount. Afterwards, they'd bide their time, review the data, acquire a new scientist and weaponize the virus. Once she had it ready, she'd attack Logan. Then she'd return to take over the pack.

Lost in her thoughts, she eyed Phillip with faux sympathy. Deep in her chest, she tried to conjure empathy but it didn't come. She knew she should care about his fate, but she simply didn't. Apathy had been the beauty of her strategic plan. All of the killing, and she felt no regret. She supposed the closest she'd felt to guilt was when she'd ordered Dana's death. At the funeral, she'd been a terrific actress, all the while unable to feel anything at all. It had been necessary to kill her. She couldn't have allowed her hybrid half-sister to reveal the results from Wynter's blood tests.

Over the past week, she'd made Étienne kill every single one of the vampires he'd created. She scoffed as the bound bloodsucker whimpered at her feet. Poor Étienne, the fool that he was, believed that he could bring the pink-shirted vampire with them. Of all the children he'd recklessly created, she supposed Phillip had been the most useful one of the bunch. Thankfully, Étienne had believed her lie that he could keep his treasured creature. He would have fought her on the decision to kill him. But they needed to move like the wind. It would be hard enough to escape with the two of them. Fiona thought that she almost felt a tiny shred of compassion as she drove the stake deep into Phillip's black heart. But as he turned to ash, she shrugged. She clapped the dust off her hands and smiled, glad to have felt nothing at all.

"Fiona. What the hell?" Logan couldn't believe what he saw on the video.

"Today on the lake," Dimitri began.

"She jumped to the other boat. I thought she was crazy. But she did it deliberately, luring Wynter. She knew Wynter felt guilty about Dana dying. She used it. I just can't fucking believe this. Why?"

"Your guess is as good as mine, but she's got to be working with a vamp. Dana was bitten up good."

"She may be working with a vampire, but look at her. She's smiling. Baiting us. And the letter. She must have planted it. She's been watching us this whole time," Logan spat out furiously.

"Shit," Dimitri began. "You know with the pack, there's not too many secrets. The guys who worked to build the lab, they may have told her."

"Fiona's here," Logan breathed.

"Fi knows this place just as well as we do. She knows we'll find her."

"She's going to kill Wynter for her blood, then take off."

"We'll have to break the search into sections. The whole pack will help," Jake suggested.

"No, let me think. If she's got Wynter, she's going to want to drain her blood. It's what she's after. But she won't use a vamp, though. She's going to need privacy, supplies…to collect it properly. The swamp's too messy. And she wouldn't keep a boat out in the open. She's going to need shelter. A cabin maybe."

"Ours?"

"I think…I think she may have built one," Luci interjected quietly.

"What exactly do you know, Luci?" Logan snarled.

"Nothing, I swear. Fiona's been the same person she's always been. Sweet, gentle Fi. This isn't her…she wouldn't hurt anyone. I know she's on that video," she shook her head and gestured to the tablet, "but I'm telling you we've been friends for a long time. I just don't see how she could be capable."

"How long have you known her really? Marcel, he brought you here. You haven't been with the pack that long,

Luci. Sometimes, we don't know people," Dimitri told her. "I've known her for the past fifty years and there she is…right there. She did this."

"Where's her cabin? We know every single blade of grass out here. I've never seen it. Where's it at?" Logan demanded.

"We do know what's out there, but maybe she's been busy over the past couple of months. We've been preoccupied with the challenges." Even to Dimitri, it didn't make sense, but there was no denying that he and Logan and the entire pack had been distracted by Marcel's death and the fights that followed.

"She took me there once," Luci said solemnly. "Made me promise not to tell anyone. But last month when I asked, she told me that a storm took it out. I believed her. I had no reason to doubt her. It happens all the time, you know. I guess she could have rebuilt something."

"Let's go." Logan glanced at Dimitri and Jake. "Fiona is not leaving this swamp. And bring stakes. She isn't alone out there."

"But what if Wynter isn't…" *Alive.* Dimitri hesitated to suggest it but the reality of the situation was bleak.

"She's alive." The vision of Wynter dying before him played in his mind like a horror movie. He'd be damned if he let it happen. "She will not die, do you hear me? The next person who suggests it can find another pack. She's mine and I can feel her. Now, let's stop wasting time and go."

Wynter pretended to type out information about the virus. She made up data, dates, measurements and ratios. She'd never help to create a viral weapon. They could kill her; drain her of all her blood, but she'd never ever give them what they needed. Wynter had spent the time gathering her strength, deciding she'd try to escape. But first, she had to shift. If she pretended to comply, she might be able to get him to take off the silver. Then, she'd fight with her last dying breath to get away.

"There's nothing more." Wynter pushed the save button as if she were truly cooperating. A reiteration of what they already knew would help to confirm her story, play to his arrogance. "You were right. My wolf blood, it'll cure Emma. Her immunity will show in her viral titers but the symptoms will disappear. It isn't contagious either."

"See how nice it is when we collaborate, Dr. Ryan? Professionals discussing our research," he lectured as if he was a professor.

"Your genetic modification was spot on. My shift was difficult, but it was enough to manipulate the blood. I need to continue the research to learn more about why my blood is counteracting the virus," she continued.

"That's the spirit. We'll set up a new lab in Wyoming. I've grown quite tired of this heat. And the Mistress, well she'll want to return here eventually. Perhaps the mountain air will entice her to stay."

"Out West? Really? I've always wanted to see

Yellowstone." As a camper, not a captive. "When do we leave? I'm a mess."

"Always beautiful in my eyes, darling. Your intellect is captivating," he purred into her ear.

"I'm still weak though. I don't think I'd be able to keep up with you. If I could just shift, I think I'd be okay to go," she suggested innocently.

"We'd need to discuss that with the Mistress. I can't allow…"

"You don't have the power to do it? What I meant to say is that it was your brilliance that researched the genetics, created a wolf from a human. It's the first time it's been done in history. Your name should be published in the New England Journal of Medicine. This is a historic medical breakthrough. It'll have far-reaching implications across the world. I imagine all the Ivy League schools will be clamoring to have you teach," she boasted. She knew she was laying it on thick but she watched in pleasure as his eyes glossed over in dreams of grandeur.

"Sir," Wynter pleaded demurely. Batting her eyelashes, she seductively glided her fingers from her mouth down to the valley between her breasts. "I really am a mess. My lips…my neck. Of course, I'd need to take my clothes off in order to shift."

Étienne's cock jerked in response. How he'd missed watching her in her underwear while he held her in his lab. Viewing her nude was a gift he'd earned, deserved. The Mistress would not approve but she wasn't here, was she? Just a small peek wouldn't hurt. She'd be well enough to travel and he'd fuck her later.

"I suppose it wouldn't hurt, but you must promise to be a good girl." He leaned forward and pressed a kiss to her forehead.

Wynter breathed calmly as his cool lips touched her skin, resisting the urge to flinch. She just needed to shift and then she'd have a chance to escape. In her current condition, she couldn't stand, let alone run or fight. For a second, she thought he'd changed his mind as he stood to retrieve a pair of gloves from his pocket.

"Gloves, darling. The silver," he noted. He knelt before her like Logan had done to her in the lab. "This'll take just a minute."

She squeezed her eyes shut, hoping he'd hurry. Luckily he couldn't get too close to the silver as he wrapped his arms around her, unfastening the corset. Her lungs wheezed as the poisonous metal fell to the floor. A fresh rush of energy circulated throughout her body.

"I think I'm okay," she told him. He'd braced her sides with his hands, his thumbs resting under her breasts. "I need to do this alone. You can watch, of course."

"Of course," he hissed. She was so lovely. And his. With the Mistress gone, he could take her quickly but then thought better of it. He stood and backed away but not before adjusting his erection that strained against his zipper.

Wynter slowly opened her lids and took a cleansing breath. Finally, he'd stopped smothering her. Freed, she could shift. She licked her lips nervously, considering how it would be the first time she'd attempted to do it by herself.

"Go on then," he urged.

"Sorry, I just need a minute to make this work. I'm not as good at it as the others," she told him truthfully.

"Aren't you going to disrobe? I thought you said..."

"I will," she cut him off. The pervert just wanted to see her naked. "I need to concentrate a minute first. The silver, my energy is low."

Wynter closed her eyes again. Breathing in and out, she meditated, searching for her wolf. *Come on, girl, let's go.* In her mind's eye, she saw her wolf crouching, yelping in distress. Another wolf flashed as if she'd seen a vision: *Logan.* She could sense him and was certain he was coming for her.

As Étienne watched, she quickly tore off her shirt, shorts and bikini. The vampire's eyes on her skin repulsed her, but she had no choice. Calling her wolf to the surface, the metamorphosis claimed her. But as quickly as it came her wolf disappeared, leaving her in a naked heap on the floor. She tried to shove off the silver corset that lay across her legs but once again she'd been impaired by the insidious metal. Unable to stand, she scrambled to pull on her shirt and shorts.

"What are you doing?" Fiona screamed at Étienne.

"She needs to shift if she's going to go with us. Also, as you know, the shift enabled her blood count to rise," he explained dryly.

Wynter gave him a look of confusion. Allowing her to shift had been a ruse to get her blood to regenerate? They were going to drain her.

"Idiot," Fiona countered. "You do realize they're coming? Get her blood now. We'll take it with us." She threw a bag at him.

"Sorry darling, this'll only take a minute." Étienne, still gloved, pushed Wynter to the floor, dragging the corset over her torso. He sorted out the needles, tubes, plastic bags now strewn about the wooden planks. "You are a quick dresser, aren't you? Pity."

"No, please," Wynter begged, struggling under the weight of him. She needed to stall. "I promise I'll help."

"Certainly, now just a small prick," he told her, jabbing the hypodermic needle into the crook of her arm. Smiling, he laughed as he did so. "I'm quite good at finding a vein."

Like a quick-moving stream, her blood gushed through the thin plastic tubing, slowly filling the first bag. Wynter turned her face away from him, praying Logan was close. She knew from experience it would take at least ten minutes for him to collect the first pint. A woman of her size probably had only eight pints of blood in her whole body. Even though she hadn't fully recovered her blood volume after his bite, she figured that with her preternatural wolf healing, she might survive after losing four or five pints, which equated to fifty minutes, tops.

"Hurry up with her," Fiona yelled. She took the first bag and then a second from Étienne. "The boat's ready to go. We'll kill her, leave her body. Logan will stay here with his mate for at least a while. We'll have plenty of time to get to shore. It's only a short drive to Mississippi."

"I hate to disappoint you Mistress, but we need to take care in collecting the samples. I don't want to damage the red blood cells. Careful," he instructed. "Put equal bags in the cryo-storage unit and the cooler. Some of these need to be frozen for long-term usage."

"Whatever, just hurry," Fiona said dismissively. "I can feel the pack. They're getting closer."

"I thought you said no one knew where this hellhole was?" he said accusingly.

"No one does," she lied. "Just come on."

She took the third bag and sealed it into the freezer and snapped it shut.

"Just one more bag and then we'll go. She's almost done," he insisted.

"Fine, I'm taking this out to the boat. I'll be right back." *No I won't,* she thought to herself.

Fiona opened and shut the door, careful not to make any noise. With the pack on her heels, time was up. She scurried over to the small skiff, got in and settled the cooling box between her legs. Frozen samples were better than fresh ones, she reasoned. She still had samples of Emma's blood stored safely in another state. All she needed to do was get to dry land. She'd fly under the radar for a month or so and find a new scientist.

As the small outboard purred into the night, she caught the sight of lights in the distance. She smiled coldly knowing her Alpha would find his mate dead. And Étienne would fight to the death, wondering where she'd gone.

"So sorry, I'm afraid this is going to be the last bag, darling. Feeling weak, are you?" Étienne asked, placing it into the cooler.

Wynter's eyelashes fluttered. Unable to speak or move, she lay face up, staring up at the rusted metal ceiling. So this was how she was going to die? A tear ran down her face as she thought of how her life might have been with Logan. They would have mated. Wynter realized she wanted a wedding, with Jax giving her away. She wanted Logan's children. Together forever. But, sadly, it was all a dream. She was dying. Peacefully accepting the inevitable, she closed her eyes and prayed that Logan would survive without her.

Logan's clothes were off as the airboat hit the bank. Man to wolf, he'd morphed to his beast. Wynter. He smelled her blood and couldn't contain the rage. Tearing through the brush, he rammed into the flimsy door. Vampire. His mate. He growled, saliva dripping from his lips, and lunged.

At first, Étienne thought he'd heard Fiona returning, but quickly surmised it was an animal. As the menacing wolf crashed through the door, he clutched Wynter's shoulders and wrapped a muscular arm around her neck. He glared at Logan, daring him to come closer. Grateful that Fiona had taken the frozen blood, he'd have to abandon the rest of the bags. His bargaining chip for his escape was thankfully still breathing, albeit on her way to death. Still, he dangled her in front of the Alpha.

"Good dog," he jeered. "That's right. Look what I've got here."

Logan hit the floor frozen as he watched the vampire lift Wynter into the air by her throat. *His vision. Oh Goddess, no.* He heard and smelled Dimitri and Jake approaching and barked, warning them not to proceed.

"Amazing how responsive animals are when given the

proper motivation? Look at your mate. Like a docile puppy," he whispered in Wynter's ear.

Wynter's eyes flew open. She recognized the three wolves before her but was unable to speak. As the life drained from her body, she wished she could tell Logan one more time that she loved him, but she couldn't utter even a hushed word. Struggling, she mouthed, 'I love you'. Tears fell from her eyes. She hoped he'd find another mate someday, be happy. There was nothing he could do. Even if the vampire released her, she was dying.

Logan transformed to man. His eyes bored into the demon that held his mate.

"Give her to me now," he demanded. Logan recognized the vampire as the one from the club with Devereoux, yet he let no hint of recollection show on his face. A shadow of doubt crept into his head. Just how far was Devereoux involved in this mess?

"What makes you think that's going to happen, wolf? I've got Dr. Ryan. I plan to walk out of here, get on that boat..."

"And what boat might that be? My boat?"

"Fiona...she's waiting," he stammered.

"She's gone." The chinks in the vampire's arrogant armor became apparent. Fiona must have betrayed him as well.

"Liar!" Étienne screamed.

"Jake, take Zeke, go after her. She can't have gone far," Logan commanded.

The walls closed in around the vampire. Choices

dwindling, he'd have to fight his way out of the cabin and take the Alpha's boat to shore. How hard could it be to get out of this godforsaken swamp, anyway? Fiona would surely be waiting for him. Without his brilliant mind, she'd never get what she wanted from the virus.

"My mate. Give her to me now, and I'll grant you mercy." Logan's cold voice resonated throughout the cabin. Dimitri lowered his head.

"I'll give her to you," he smiled. The lilt of his voice wavered in preparation for what he was about to do.

Étienne was a great fighter, he thought. A mere wolf could not challenge him. Wynter's blood had charged his system. He'd created her, and her special blood now ran through him, making him stronger than any supernatural. As soon as he tasted the Alpha's blood, the lupine vitality would flow into his veins making him nearly invincible.

Logan tensed in preparation, waiting on the vampire to drop Wynter. He'd show mercy all right. He'd stake him quickly as opposed to tearing him apart limb by limb and then decapitating him.

"Mine," he growled.

"Not anymore." Before Logan could charge, Étienne extended a large claw. As if slitting the throat of a farm animal, he slashed it across Wynter's throat. Her eyes bulged right before he tossed her to the floor.

"No!" Logan screamed. As he leapt into the air, he transformed into wolf. Flying directly at the vampire, he lodged his teeth into the vampire's neck.

Étienne flailed at the wolf, digging his claws up into

Logan's gut. Eviscerating the Alpha, he tore open the fur. Blood sprayed onto the floor. An enormous burn flared inside Logan yet he refused to release the vampire. He'd killed his mate. No death or torture would appease the revenge he sought. No matter what pain he felt, he'd kill him.

Dimitri transformed to human, scooping Wynter into his arms.

"Wynter, please, oh Goddess," he cried at the sight.

Her pale skin was split open laterally, exposing her trachea's cartilage. He frantically pinched the skin together. Tearing a swathe of cloth from her shirt, he applied pressure to the wound. A sob escaped his lips as he realized it was too late. Logan would never recover from her death, nor would he. Helplessly, he continued to try to stop the bleeding as her heartbeat slowed.

Logan saw Dimitri out of the corner of his eye with his mate. The vision of Wynter dying played out before him. As the vampire shoved his hand up further into his abdomen, he summoned every power he'd been given as Alpha. Strength. Perseverance. Domination. Logan concentrated, focusing his powerful jaw muscles and forced them downward. The crushing pressure sliced through the tendons and muscled tissue, tearing at the vampire's carotid. Wrenching backward, his beast broke away taking the dark flesh with him.

Blood spewed wildly as the vampire stumbled forward, still attempting to leave the cabin. Logan, gravely injured, shifted back to human. Enraged beyond reason, Logan lunged onto Étienne's back wrapping his arm around his already wounded neck. With every ounce of energy he had left, he pressed his knee into Étienne's back, forcing him onto the floor. With a final twist of his arms, he snapped the vampire's neck. Fighting for breath, Logan's beast was unsatisfied. He'd show no mercy. As the vampire's remains twitched on the ground, his eyes searched the room. Stretching to reach the broken chair, he tore off a shard and drove it into Étienne's heart.

Logan roared in agony, turning to Dimitri. While the shift had healed the gaping hole in his abdomen, his heart felt as if it had been decimated. The grief on Dimitri's face confirmed what he'd already known. Wynter was dead. He dropped to the floor on his hands and knees, sobbing. Taking her into his arms, Logan gently cradled his mate.

Fiona leapt from the boat. A few more feet and she'd drive to safety. She knew they were hot on her trail, but she also knew that she was still a few steps ahead of them, as always. Stupid wolves. They always assumed that mere muscle would allow them to lead. Maybe she'd never win a physical challenge, but it was just a matter of time before she had every last wolf begging at her feet. Revenge would be sweet. She'd infect them all with the virus. Then she'd be their savior, whether they liked it or not.

Fiona grabbed the laptop bag and hoisted the small cryo-freezer onto the dirt. Heavy as it was, she only had about a hundred feet to travel through the brush before she reached the small clearing. Shoving the boat adrift with her foot, she set out on her journey. Her eyes darted from side to side. It was quiet. Too quiet, she noted. Not even a cricket could be heard. But she kept on her path, only fifty more feet and she'd be at the car.

With a whoosh, branches split before her eyes. It was dark but she could make out a figure in the moonlight. She sniffed. Vampire. Adrenaline rushed as her mind raced. Had Étienne created more vampires and not told her? He'd been privy to the car's location. She fought to calm her nerves. Why should she fear a vampire? She'd killed many of them while Étienne watched. This was just one more. She crouched in the brush, tore off a stiff branch and began to whittle it into a sharp stake with her claws.

The tall masculine shadow deliberately and confidently tramped toward her until the light of his eyes became apparent. She gasped at the sight of the ancient one. Léopold Devereoux. No, not him. How could he have found her? Like a frightened rabbit, she froze in the darkness, awaiting his approach, hoping he wouldn't see her.

"Ah, I found you," his smooth voice called into the crisp night air. Nearly at her feet, the dark angel loomed. His beautiful but deadly presence resounded in the forest like a drum roll before an execution.

"Petite louve, I smell it. The putrid stink of your evil permeates the air. So familiar am I with the scent," he told her. "You like a chase, no? I assure you this is one you'll not win."

With preternatural speed, he flew to Fiona, snatching her up by her throat. He allowed her feet to remain on the ground as he shook her like a dog with its toy.

"You like to play with vampires? My vampires," he growled. With a flick, he threw her onto the damp earth.

Fiona rebounded, crab-walking backwards, dragging her bottom along the dirt.

"No, Étienne, he came to me freely," she claimed.

"He cannot come to you freely, because he belongs to me," Léopold explained coldly, brushing a weed from his coat sleeve. "And for this you shall die. The only decision to be made is if I should kill you myself? Or perhaps I should let your own tear you to shreds? Such choices."

Léopold smiled casually as the two large male wolves, Jake and Zeke, padded forward. He carefully considered his decision as Fiona sat before him awaiting her fate. His lovely little Dr. Ryan had been tortured by her and Étienne. That alone would have been enough to warrant her death. But the little bitch had gone and killed a wolf using his vampires to do it.

With a glance to the mud, he'd chosen. Oh how he hated to get his new leather shoes soiled.

"The research, the samples. You'll never get them," she stalled, pushing onto her feet.

"You are a devilish schemer aren't you?" he laughed. "A shame you have no discipline. But don't worry your pretty little head. I plan to rectify that right now."

Léopold rushed forward, yanking her upward. He tore open her collar, exposing her long neck. The moonlight glinted off his white fangs right before they pierced her flesh. Her legs flailed, kicking into the night. Neither Jake nor Zeke moved one inch to intervene. Throwing his head backwards, he spat her blood into the grass and tossed her to the wolves.

Her body flinched as she stole looks between the wolves right before they attacked. Barely a scream could be heard as they ripped her flesh until she was no more.

Léopold retrieved a crisp white handkerchief and dabbed at his chin. How he hated messy killings. But responsibility and duty drove his actions. Meting out punishment was never easy, but he watched in pleasure as the wolves executed their own. She'd been a blight who'd caused quite enough trouble. Like the virus she sought to propagate, she'd been eradicated.

As Jake transformed in front of him, he gave Léopold a nod in acknowledgement. Not sure what to make of the vampire, he and Zeke got to work, disposing of Fiona's remains. After they'd fed the alligators, Jake snatched up the laptop so he could give it to Logan.

Léopold strode over to the cooler and flipping it open, saw bags of blood. He tore them open and quickly surmised that it belonged to the Alpha's mate. As he emptied the last of the crimson fluid into the swamp, a hint of dread registered. He sniffed out into the bayou. So much fresher than the samples, it permeated his olfactory senses, exciting unadulterated rage. Wynter's blood. The call of death sang into the night.

Chapter Twenty-Eight

"I can save her," Léopold uttered softly. He watched as the grieving Alpha rocked his mate. Like an animal that had lost one of his own, the wolf refused to release the body.

Dimitri leaned against the wall, his head in his hands. Unlike the Alpha, who was utterly despondent, he peered over to the imposing vampire.

"Devereoux, you need to get outta here. Wyn, she's..." Dimitri couldn't bring himself to say the words.

Although wolves were generally immortal, lethal wounds to the neck effectively killed them. While Wynter's heartbeat was faint, she'd be dead within minutes and shifting was no longer an option. Nothing could be done. As the minutes ticked by, Dimitri had watched his Alpha care for his mate, tell her he loved her. Last words. Last caresses.

"But I can save her, wolf," Léopold persisted.

Logan slowly lifted his head and caught sight of the vampire standing in the doorway. "What?" he choked.

"Alpha, you know my blood can heal wolves." Léopold

proceeded cautiously. The Alpha, immersed in his bereavement, could attack.

"She's too far gone; you and I both know that. I can barely hear her heartbeat. The rattle in her lungs has stopped. Please," Logan begged, tears streaming from his eyes. His voice broke into a cry. "I need to say goodbye. She's going to leave me. My mate…he killed her."

"Please listen," Léopold pleaded. "Think about how vampires are created. In the final moments of our deaths, when the soul teeters between the planes of both the living and the dead, one can be snatched from death's grip, born anew. Wynter, she rests in the thin veil that separates us from the other side. You must let me try."

Logan considered Devereoux's explanation. He'd never in his long life heard of a vampire giving their gift to a wolf. He knew that when they created their own, the child belonged to the sire. Wynter would never want to belong to any other man but him. After the scene in the club, Léopold was far from her favorite person. How would she feel about accepting his blood into her body, taking him on as her sire? Yet, selfishly, Logan carefully weighed the offer. He loved Wynter so much; needed his mate alive. How far would he go to save her?

"Will she be vampire?" Logan asked.

"I cannot say. I won't lie to you, this is generally the outcome, but like I said, I'm not certain. Is she truly wolf? Is she still at all human? Complicated questions, no?"

"She belongs to me."

"As her potential sire, I fully and altogether release her

to your care, Alpha. I do not wish to command her mind. I swear it."

Unable to resist the possibility of her salvation, Logan conceded. "Do it," he whispered.

What choice did he have? If she returned as vampire, he'd love her as much as when she'd been wolf. It was her soul that he loved, no matter her being.

Léopold breathed a sigh of relief as the Alpha capitulated to his suggestion. In truth, in all his years, he'd never converted a wolf. He was unsure about how his blood would affect her, but they had to try. He stripped off his jacket and rolled his sleeve. Positioning himself next to Logan, he bit into his wrist, and offered it to the Alpha. Logan took Léopold's wrist and pressed it to Wynter's mouth.

The blood trickled over Wynter's face. Listless, she wasn't swallowing.

"Command her," Léopold told him urgently.

"I can't feel her...she's gone," Logan insisted.

"It's the only way. I cannot do it."

Logan meditated, searching his mind for his mate. The tendrils of his power discharged, seeking Wynter. He laughed as a jolt of recognition hit him. She was there, here or on the other side, he couldn't tell. Her spirit danced in the wind.

"Wyn, sweetheart," he spoke lovingly. "I need you to listen to me. Please, please come back to me. Hear me and drink."

In her mind, Wynter floated somewhere lovely and peaceful. But she was alone. The familiar voice sang to her heart, willing her like a lure. *Logan? Where was he?* The mist caressed her skin as she glided along her journey. But the voice called to her again. *Drink? Drink what?* No, this place was warm and comforting. Like a mother's womb, she contentedly existed. *Now, Wynter.* Logan. Logan, her mate. Memories of his scent and love flooded her mind. Back to Logan, she needed to find him. *Drink.*

The taste of power slid down her throat, setting off a firing of synapses. Life. Love. Her mate. So far but so close, just within reach. A wisp of hope flickered and she extended her hand to capture it. A little more and she'd awake to him. A river of sanguine vitality permeated her cells, arousing her soul back to Earth.

Astonished, Logan felt his heart squeeze in relief as he watched his mate flare to life, her pale lips suctioning at the wrist he held. The strained look on Devereoux's face told him that he suffered silently. But Logan wondered if the vampire struggled to conceal pain or lust. Léopold Devereoux, her dark savior, was lethal yet benevolent. As their eyes met, a respectful understanding passed between the two men. He'd forever owe the vampire; a debt he'd gladly repay.

"Enough," Léopold grunted.

Logan slid a finger in between her mouth and Léopold's wrist, breaking the seal. Wynter gasped for air, and then choked, blood spilling from her lips. Her eyes flew open; she was shaking as if she were a newborn babe. She cried, a mixture of fear and happiness spinning through her mind as she glanced from Léopold to Logan. The realization that she'd almost died slammed into her.

"Logan," she whispered.

"Sweetheart." Logan cradled her into his arms so that her head rested against his shoulder. "I love you. I love you so much."

"I love you too. I'm not dead?" she asked with a small smile.

"No, you're not. You're very much alive, thanks to Devereoux."

"Léopold," the vampire corrected. "I do believe we all should be on a first name basis, no?"

"Léopold," Logan agreed with a smile. He'd never been so grateful to another person in his life, vampire or not.

Wynter tried to process what Logan had just told her. Léopold had saved her life. She struggled to comprehend it. She had died. His blood. *Drink.* Logan had told her to drink. She drank Léopold's blood? Connecting the proverbial dots, Wynter sat up, pushing out of Logan's arms.

"Am I a…? No, I couldn't be a…?" She glanced from Logan to Léopold then to Dimitri.

Logan cupped her cheek bringing her gaze to his again. He sniffed. "You still scent wolf, so that's a good sign. We don't know how it could affect you, but you're alive and that's all that matters to me."

"Oh God, Logan. I love you so much." Wynter gently pressed her lips to his. Her forehead fell against his as she spoke to him. "I was so scared. I'm sorry for going on that boat."

Logan stopped her from going any further. "No, Wyn, don't blame yourself. We knew they'd come for you. I should never have agreed to take you out there."

"I can't believe Fiona betrayed the pack like that. Oh God, where is she?" Wynter asked in a panic.

"Dead," Léopold confirmed.

"You're sure?" Logan asked. If she wasn't dead, she would be.

"These swamps are quite messy, wolf. All that mud. Just look at my shoes." Léopold rocked back, brushed his slacks and attempted to right his sleeves. "Good thing your wolves showed up to assist me or I may have ruined my suit. Those gators, they do enjoy an impromptu meal."

Logan shook his head with a small laugh. He'd never mistake the vampire's humor for weakness. Léopold was deadly, but he appeared to do the right thing every now and then. Logan couldn't say he fully trusted him, but he'd gained an ally without a doubt.

"Léopold, thank you." Wynter shifted from Logan's arms and extended her hand to him. She could have sworn she saw him blush.

Léopold took Wynter's wrist, gently holding her fingers. He caught Logan's gaze as if to ask for approval. Logan nodded and with a brush of a kiss, he pressed his lips to the back of her hand.

"Anytime, my fine doctor. That lecture. You made quite the impression on me," he winked. "The world needs your beautiful mind. I'm honored to have helped. And should you spring fangs, please call on me anytime for assistance.

But as I've assured your Alpha, you are released from any bond with me, as you and Logan are mates."

Léopold released her hand and stood. He adjusted his pants and scanned the room for his jacket. The black suit looked nearly impeccable as he smoothed out the small wrinkles.

"Dimitri," Wynter said solemnly.

"Wyn." Dimitri scooted next to Wynter and carefully gave her a hug. She'd almost died. The whole pack had come so close to destruction. His eyes rimmed in moisture, the emotion he'd held back burst forth. Logan clamped a hand on his shoulder in an effort to comfort him.

"It's okay, D. She's alive." *Maybe a vampire, though?*

"Look at me. I'm cryin' like a baby over here. How sad is that?" Dimitri laughed in embarrassment and pushed up onto his feet. "I gotta get out of here and relax. Do something manly like go sit in the hot tub with a beer and a cigar."

"As much as I usually love the swamp, I'm with you. It's time to get the hell out of here." In one smooth motion, Logan stood, carrying Wynter.

Jake and Zeke approached the cabin and together ripped away what remained of the door. Logan strode through the doorway, carrying Wynter toward the boat. Dimitri, Léopold and the others followed him.

Léopold glanced at the naked wolves surrounding him and shook his head. *Wolves and their nudity.*

"Seriously, do you wolves ever wear clothes?" he quipped with a raised eyebrow.

"You should try it, vamp. You might like it," Logan replied. He stepped into the boat and cuddled Wynter. "Free like the wind."

"A cold day in hell, mon ami." Léopold shrugged his nose in disgust.

"You gotta loosen up," Dimitri told him.

"Ah, says the man who weeps," Léopold teased with a smile.

"Tears of joy, man. And for the record, I've got plenty of game," Dimitri jibed in return.

"Léopold, maybe you need to start small. A skinny dip, perhaps?" Logan suggested blithely.

"I highly recommend it," Wynter added. Naughty thoughts played in her mind, remembering her time in the pool with Logan.

"A recommendation from the lady? Well, that may be advice I'll take." Léopold appeared lost in a sensual thought. "A beach, no? Oui, that I could do."

"Just add a hot woman into the mix, and he's all in," Dimitri laughed.

"I knew we could convert him." Logan kissed Wynter's hair and reflected on the night's events.

Ironic how one day he'd been single and fighting to be Alpha and today he'd fought for his mate's life, assuring his pack still had a leader. With Wynter back in the safety of his arms, he looked forward to solidifying the bond they'd started. Even if she did turn vampire, he didn't care. As long as Wynter stood at his side, nothing would come between them.

He stole a glance at the debonair vampire who'd saved his mate. On the surface, Léopold wore his years like his designer clothes; tightly reined without a blemish to be found. But Logan's intuition told him that the centuries had taken a toll on Devereoux. He had recognized the familiar loneliness which danced in Léopold's eyes. Had he been a romantic at some point in his life? A courageous fighter, waging war for the greater good? Logan reasoned that he might never truly know Léopold's motives. One thing was certain; the vampire had revealed a side of him rarely seen by others; one that even Logan hadn't known to exist. Léopold, even if just for a moment in time, had cared, not just about Wynter but about the good of the Acadian pack.

Chapter Twenty-Nine

Wynter artfully tied the bows on her pink negligee as if she were wrapping a gift. As she played with the ribbons, she thought about the past few days and how Logan had sweetly cared for her. It hadn't taken long for her blood volume to regenerate after her near death experience. And so far, she hadn't felt any vampiric tendencies. She'd even successfully shifted a few times in the house just to test it out. She laughed to herself thinking about how Logan had enjoyed waking up to find his red little wolf jumping on the bed.

Her brush with death forced her to contemplate the next steps in her derailed career. The choice to go into virology had been born out of her desire to help Emma. And now that she'd done that, she needed to figure out a new future, one that included Logan, pack and hopefully children. But since she'd been injured, they hadn't made love. Logan worried like a mother hen. She knew it was killing him not to press forward with their mating, but since it involved a blood exchange, he'd been reluctant, not wanting to accidentally hurt her.

But her wolf paced impatiently, in anticipation of completing the bond. Wynter looked in the mirror and glossed her lips. She was determined to tempt Logan into their mating. He needn't worry, she was no porcelain doll. She was a red-blooded wolf who couldn't wait to mate with her Alpha. As she brushed out her tight curls, she hoped he would enjoy her plan and be unable to resist her. She laughed to herself, knowing he'd loved to play. Smoothing the see-through fabric, Wynter took a cleansing breath. Yes, this would be fun.

Logan's cock was harder than a cement post. While he'd been more than grateful that Wynter had rebounded, his self-imposed celibacy wasn't going so well. It wasn't that he didn't want to bend her over and sink into her hotness every single time he saw her. At dinner, she'd teased him mercilessly with the grilled kielbasa, and he'd nearly lost his mind. His wolf growled and bit, encouraging him to mate. But he wasn't going to do anything to put her recovery in jeopardy. Unwavering, he'd put her health first and stifled every animalistic thought that had crossed his mind.

As he lay in bed reading, he glanced up, noticing the sound of the bathroom door opening. Logan watched intently as a glimmer of pink teased his eyes. Holy Fuck. What was she wearing? He dropped his iPad, fascinated by the scene. Wynter bent over the dresser, wiggling her bottom. Her creamy globes peeked out at him from underneath the nightie. He swore; damn, his cock could get harder. When she turned around, a broad smile broke across his face. The large map blocked his view and he knew right then and there, she was up to something, a tad more than the average seduction.

Wynter unfolded the New Orleans brochure, smiling coyly. Her horn-rimmed glasses and camera on her wrist added to the character.

"Sir, I've been walking around the city all the day, and I can't seem to find my destination," she told him. She held the paper so that it hid her entire body except for her eyes.

Logan laughed. Was she seriously role playing again? If she didn't show him what was behind that map, he'd leap off the bed. Okay, he was game.

"I know New Orleans well. I'd be happy to show you around. Just where exactly are you going?"

She lowered the map slightly, giving him a view of her ample cleavage. "I'm supposed to meet my friends. I don't know if I should go off with a stranger."

"No stranger here, cher," he said, falling into his best Cajun accent. "I promise to keep you safe."

"Oh dear, now how did I get so lost? Maybe you could help me find my way. I have this map here but I can't seem to make heads or tails of it."

"I'd love to help you out, show you around. Perhaps you'd like to hear music?"

She shook her head. "No, I don't think so."

"A ride on a riverboat, then? Very relaxing," he suggested.

"No." She lowered the map so he could see her dusky nipples. They strained to escape their sexy sheer confines. "I'm looking for something." She pretended to glance at the map.

Logan pushed the blanket off his fully nude form, allowing her a view of his enormous erection. He lazily put his hand behind his head.

Her eyes met his and then took a long peruse of his muscular body. Her pussy clenched at the sight of him. She knew she couldn't keep the dialogue going for much longer. Incredibly hot, he was laid out for her like a delicious dessert; one she'd like to lick from head to toe.

"There's much to see in our fine city," he drawled with a smile, smelling her arousal. His little vixen was getting herself as hot and bothered as she intended to do to him.

"Yes, yes there is. Like the art for example." She smiled and looked down to watch him stroke his shaft. "It's spectacular. I especially enjoy viewing the marbled statue."

Wynter dropped the map further so he could see the crisscrossed pattern of ribbons that begged to be untied. She licked her lips and approached the bed.

"This map, it doesn't seem to help me at all. I'm so glad I found you. I mean, what would I do without such a knowledgeable guide?" She opened her fingers and let the paper drop to the floor.

"I'm looking forward to showing you all the sights and sounds..." Logan began.

"And tastes? I'm so hungry." Wynter's eyes devoured him. She placed her palms on the edge of the bed, bending so that he could get a good view of her breasts.

"Sweetheart, we've got some of the best culinary delights in the country. I'd be more than happy to feed you...all night long." Logan pushed up onto his knees and made short work of meeting her. He wrapped his hands around her waist and pressed his lips to the hollow of her neck.

"I'm starving," she breathed, pushing her fingers into his hair.

"I'll always be here for you Wynter," Logan promised, kissing up her neck. "Always and forever. I missed you so much."

Wynter let herself go limp against him. Back in his arms was exactly what she needed. She tore off her glasses and let the camera slip from her wrist.

"I missed you too, so, so much." She licked and bit at his shoulder.

Logan rolled her onto the bed and slid down her body. Wynter rested her head against the pillows, wiggling against him. Logan smiled and crouched at her feet. Taking one foot, he touched his lips to the inside of her calf. She hissed in delight, pressing her hips upward.

"Logan."

"Yes, mate. Just helping you find your way," he teased, resuming his role. He dragged his tongue up her leg until he reached her inner thigh.

Wynter thought she'd explode in need. It felt incredible.

"You're wicked," she laughed.

"Just helping a tourist in need. I told you; I'm a very good guide. I know all the best spots." He pushed her knees open wider, his face settled into the center of her legs. Pleasantly surprised, he was happy to find she'd worn no panties.

"But I need…" she panted as his warm breath brushed

over her mound. If he'd just touch her, she could breathe.

Logan darted his tongue through her moist nether lips and smiled. "We are about to reach one of my favorite destinations. My sweet little tourist, are you ready?"

Without waiting for an answer, he lapped at her clit.

"Oh God yes," she cried. His rough tongue sent shivers through her body. Her sex ached for him. He was everything she'd ever need.

Logan pulled away for just a second to press two long fingers inside of her. "I do believe we are arriving nicely." He curled them upward into her sensitive channel.

"Yes, right there," she screamed.

Logan brought his lips to her clitoris, sucking and flicking it with his tongue. Her sweet cream coated his face, and he couldn't get enough of her.

"I'm coming, I'm coming," Wynter screamed over and over.

Her pelvis rocked into his mouth and hand. She flailed as her orgasm burst, leaving her shaking and gasping for breath. The tendrils of energy rode through her skin.

Logan gave her a final lick before he crawled up to meet her face to face. The hard tip of him rested at the entrance. Goddess, he loved her spontaneity and how receptive she was.

"Wynter Ryan."

Wynter slowly opened her eyes, still lost in the haze of passion. She smiled at the way he'd addressed her and gazed into his eyes.

"Yes, my Alpha."

"Tonight, I take you as my mate." Logan tugged at the satiny ribbons. Her bodice fell open exposing both her neck and breasts.

His expression denoted a seriousness that told Wynter that this was the time. Their mating. Their bond, forged in love and trust; they'd be together till the end of time.

"You, Wynter. You are mine. Our wolves, our souls, we're mates."

"I love you, Logan. I'm yours." She licked along his collarbone. Slight pain alerted her that her canines had descended.

He smiled with a slight shake of his head.

"What?"

"Ah baby, they're sexy." Now was not the time to tell her, but her normally sharp canines looked slightly sharper. Fangs.

"What is it?"

"Nothing, you're perfect. Now where were we?" He captured her lips with his. Their tongues swept along each other's. Reluctantly, he stopped the kiss and spoke into her mouth.

"Tonight, we mate. Forever you are mine, Wynter."

He rocked his straining cock into her slick channel. She gasped, nodding. As he filled her to the hilt, he reared back and bit into her shoulder. Blood trickled into his throat.

The pleasured pain drove Wynter's need to claim him in return. Her fangs sliced into his skin like a knife through hot butter. Thirsting for more, she took a long draw of her Alpha's blood. Powerful and spicy, her mate's spirit danced within her body. The wave of pleasure hurled her into release, and she convulsed against Logan.

The taste of Wynter's blood caused his wolf to howl in pride. With his beast satisfied, he'd laved at her shoulder. But it was Wynter's erotic bite that sent him into orgasm. Claiming him as her mate, she'd sent him into the hardest, hottest climax he'd ever had in his life. As he erupted inside her, he shuddered as he felt her lick over the wound.

Loving filaments weaved through their hearts and minds. Their bond complete, their wolves nuzzled together celebrating. Logan rolled backwards, bringing Wynter with him. Arms and legs intertwined, her cheek rested on his chest.

"I love you," Wynter smiled.

"Love you too, baby," Logan replied, still trying to catch his breath.

"Everything that's happened," she began thoughtfully.

"Shhh, it's over now." He tangled his fingers into her ringlets.

"I would have never met you."

"True."

"Does the pack know?"

"Yes, but I want a formal introduction. You deserve nothing less. We deserve this. And someday, I hope you'll agree to a human mating of sorts...if that's what you want. Marry me?"

"I'd love that." she kissed his chest. "I hear spring in New Orleans is lovely. As is New York."

"A honeymoon. That's what I'm looking forward to," he

teased. "Somewhere on a beach. A private beach."

"A beach, huh? Sounds good to me. Make sure you bring your whistle," she told him with a naughty grin.

"A whistle?"

"Well, I may need a lifeguard to save me," she suggested.

"I'm all for a little slippery wet play in the ocean," Logan encouraged. "Or maybe we can go as an Alpha and his mate."

"Yes, that sounds perfect," she agreed.

As they fell asleep for the first time as bonded mates, Wynter and Logan embraced the new chapter in their lives. Dark memories would be washed over by love-filled days and sensual nights. The Acadian Wolves found strength in their Alpha. Peace and contentment rippled throughout the pack. A new chapter in their history had begun.

Epilogue

Léopold cursed as he dug into the frozen tundra. Damn bitch really had thought she was clever. Yet it had been fairly easy for the investigator to locate the safety deposit box where Fiona had left the instructions and thumb drive. Léopold suspected that someone local had helped her stash the blood. Samples from Emma, Wynter and others, had been buried deep within the snow in the heart of Yellowstone.

He and Dimitri had traveled together to retrieve the contents of the box. The wolf, with his humor, continued to insist that Léopold needed to loosen up, clearly not having a clue how difficult a task that would be. Regardless, he had succumbed to Dimitri's unrelenting insistence that he take a hot tub. After several cognacs, he'd given in to the persistent wolf's request. Naked in the woods hadn't been half bad, he supposed. However he was certain that it would have been much more tolerable with a suitable female.

As Léopold recovered the vials, wind and ice blew at his face. Dammit all to hell, he should have made Dimitri come with him to dig out the blood. Even with his extraordinary strength, Yellowstone was exceedingly brutal in the winter. But Léopold had encouraged his newfound friend to visit with Hunter Livingston. Brother to Tristan and friend of Logan and Dimitri, Hunter led the Wyoming wolf pack. While it was customary for an outside wolf to announce his presence within another's territory, Dimitri and Hunter were friends. They were aware of his arrival. It was Léopold who wished to be alone, insisting he could dispose of the vials on his own.

With the temperature at nearly fifteen below zero, Léopold snorted in displeasure. Breathtaking as it was, this weather was not conducive to a vampire's metabolism. The deafening silence was indeed thought provoking but he could not wait to be back in the city. Whether it be New York or New Orleans, the crowds made it easy for him to feed whenever he wished. Anything he wanted was a mere phone call away. Luxury beckoned on his arrival. He had a standing reservation at private clubs from jazz to blood. In an instant, his needs were met.

True, it had been a lonely existence. But the darkness of his past wouldn't allow him to feel. Yet he couldn't deny his reaction to watching the interaction between the Alpha and his mate. It had warmed a layer of ice that he'd allowed to thicken around his heart. That kind of love didn't exist very often. Long ago, as a foolish boy, he'd thought himself worthy of love. But it didn't take long for the harsh realities of life to decimate the naïve, human ideals of love and family. It was through intellect and dominance that he'd survived and ruled. Power and prosperity had been rightly earned via battles and business.

As much as he enjoyed the freedom, he wasn't without compassion. In truth, he'd been strangely bothered since leaving New Orleans. He could not shake the touch of Logan's hand on his wrist and Wynter's lips on his skin. Like a lightning bolt, their bond had penetrated deep into his own energy. Their thoughts, pain and passion funneled through his mind. It was as if the brief connection had jarred his memory, the lingering desire for love.

Léopold cursed his weakness and shoved the thought as far away as he could. Like a well-worn shoe, his cool demeanor had been comfortable. As such, he refused to give up his bachelor ways. A stop at Tristan's club in Philadelphia and a quick romp with the twins would refresh his attitude, he thought. Imprudent, sophomoric thoughts of romance and companionship were for others, not him.

Another gust lashed at Léopold. He shoved the vials into the small backpack, zipped it up and threw it over his shoulder. A wail in the distance caught his attention. Damn humans. Damn wolves. They expected another foot of snow tonight, and he couldn't imagine anything but animals traipsing through the forest. Who the hell would be caught dead in the middle of the night in Yellowstone?

Merde. Léopold grunted and pushed himself up onto the tamped down path. West Thumb Geyser Basin, visited often by tourists in winter, should have been desolate at night. With bubbling hot springs and gurgling mud on either side of the trail, he trod carefully toward the noise, and sniffed. Aside from the sulphuric odor, he could make out the faint smell of a human.

"I should have sent the wolf," he grumbled. Unsure of what lay ahead, he knew it wasn't going to be good.

As he approached a small clearing, he caught a glimpse of the outline of a person in the snow. He took a deep breath, vacillating between materializing and actually helping. It was none of his business. He could disappear like he hadn't seen a thing. The scene between the Alpha and his mate played like a movie through his head and he sighed. It must've made him soft because he was leaning toward helping. Damn, fucking wolves. He growled, realizing that his conscience and curiosity would not let him leave. Resigned, he'd check on the situation and then get the hell out of there.

Léopold's feet crunched through the snow, approaching the noise. He caught sight of the body which wasn't moving except for an isolated twitch. The familiar scents of both humans and wolf hit his nostrils…and blood.

"Identify yourself," he demanded. A strange gurgle responded. The small body was wrapped in a blanket, and he grew concerned as he barely heard a heartbeat. There was no way he was siring another human or wolf. Perhaps he'd take them to safety, but no more would he do.

"Do you hear me? Are you hybrid? What are you doing out here?" Léopold really didn't want to touch the blanket. He stared up into the constellations and blew out a breath, contemplating his next move. Whatever was underneath the blanket was barely breathing. It was dying. Perhaps he should just leave?

Another gurgle caught his attention. In all his centuries, he'd nearly forgotten the sound. Unsuccessfully, he tried to shake off the painful memories that flared to life. *Gurgle.* No, it didn't make sense. He fell to his knees and feverishly began pulling at the fabric, revealing the head. The cold dead eyes of a woman bored into him. Why would she bring a…? *Gurgle.* He continued to unwrap the blanket until he saw the source of the sound. A small face peered up at him. Horrified, his suspicion was correct. A baby.

"What the hell?" Léopold heard the sound of barking wolves in the distance and hurried to collect the small child in his arms. "Mon bébé. Who would do this to you?"

He made the sign of the cross over the dead body, tugging the blanket out from under it. Quickly, he swaddled the infant. As the danger grew closer, Léopold cursed. Decision made, he cradled the baby into his jacket, and disappeared into the night.

Romance by Kym Grosso

The Immortals of New Orleans

Kade's Dark Embrace
(Immortals of New Orleans, Book 1)

Luca's Magic Embrace
(Immortals of New Orleans, Book 2)

Tristan's Lyceum Wolves
(Immortals of New Orleans, Book 3)

Logan's Acadian Wolves
(Immortals of New Orleans, Book 4)

Léopold's Wicked Embrace
(Immortals of New Orleans, Book 5)

Dimitri
(Immortals of New Orleans, Book 6)

Lost Embrace
(Immortals of New Orleans, Book 6.5)

Jax
(Immortals of New Orleans, Book 7)

Club Altura Romance

Solstice Burn

(A Club Altura Romance Novella, Prequel)

Carnal Risk

(A Club Altura Romance Novel, Book 1)

Wicked Rush

(A Club Altura Romance Novel, Book 2) Coming 2016

About the Author

Kym Grosso is the New York Times and USA Today bestselling and award-winning author of the erotic romance series, *The Immortals of New Orleans* and *Club Altura*. In addition to romance, Kym has written and published several articles about autism, and is a contributing essay author in *Chicken Soup for the Soul: Raising Kids on the Spectrum.*

Kym lives with her family in Pennsylvania, and her hobbies include reading, tennis, zumba, and spending time with her husband and children. She loves traveling just about anywhere that has a beach or snow-covered mountains. New Orleans, with its rich culture, history and unique cuisine, is one of her favorite places to visit.

• • • •

Social Media/Links:

Website: http://www.KymGrosso.com
Facebook: http://www.facebook.com/KymGrossoBooks
Twitter: https://twitter.com/KymGrosso
Pinterest: http://www.pinterest.com/kymgrosso/

Sign up for Kym's Newsletter to get Updates and Information about New Releases:
http://www.kymgrosso.com/members-only

Printed in Great Britain
by Amazon

23186785R10264